To the women of my family.
Your courage is the reason I am here.
~ Marjorie

Revolution happens in silence with a voice
of authentic people being hidden. I wish to be
the one who can feel like them.
~ Sana

For my sister-in-law, Jennifer Grajales Smith
(1987-2017), who fought the monster inside of
her body for as long and as hard as she could.
~ Jennifer

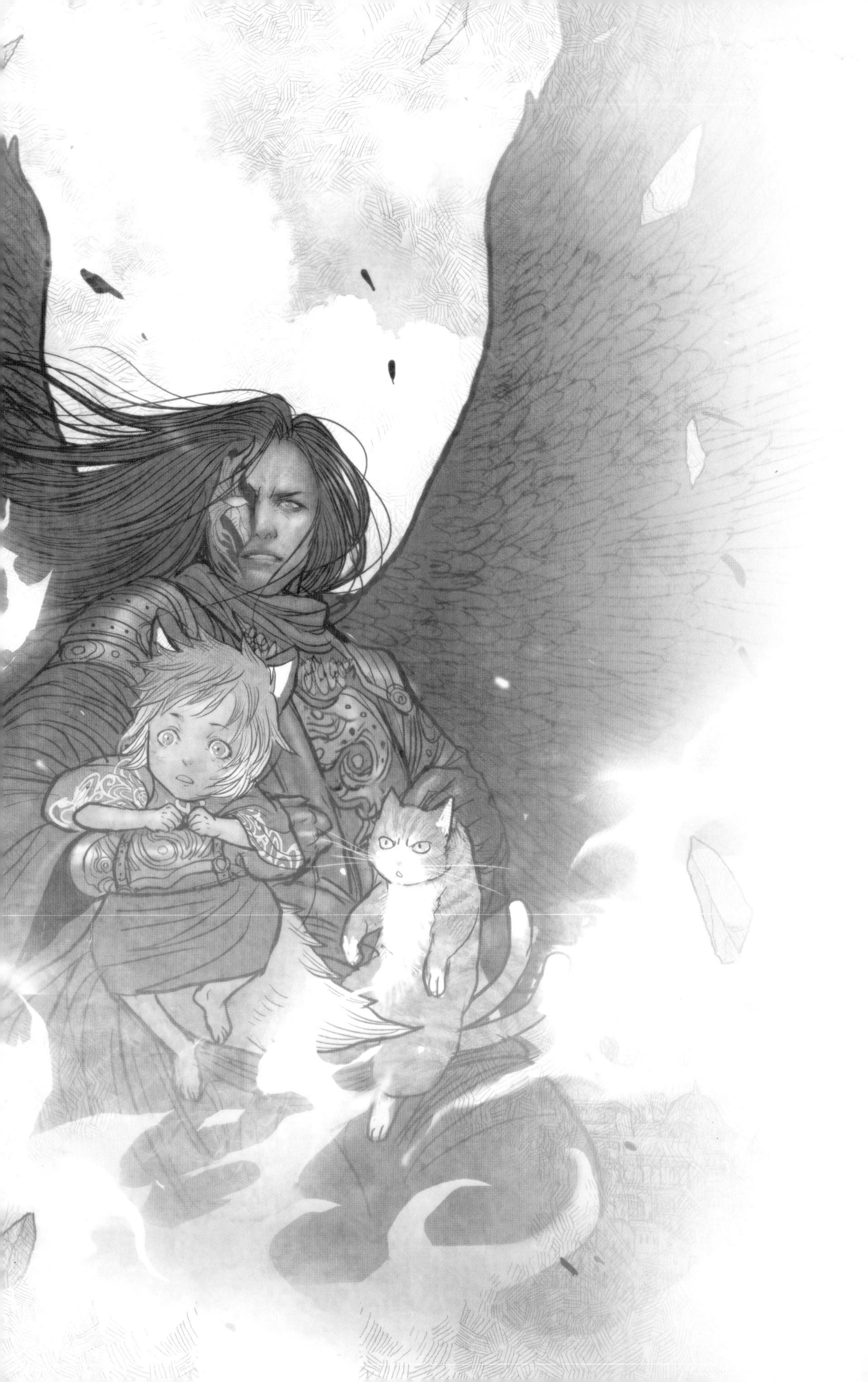

MONSTRESS

VOLUME THREE
HAVEN

Collecting
MONSTRESS
Issues 13-18

MARJORIE LIU
WRITER

SANA TAKEDA
ARTIST

RUS WOOTON
LETTERING & DESIGN

JENNIFER M. SMITH
EDITOR

CERI RILEY
EDITORIAL ASSISTANT

MONSTRESS
created by
MARJORIE LIU &
SANA TAKEDA

GN
MONSTRESS
v. 3

CHAPTER THIRTEEN

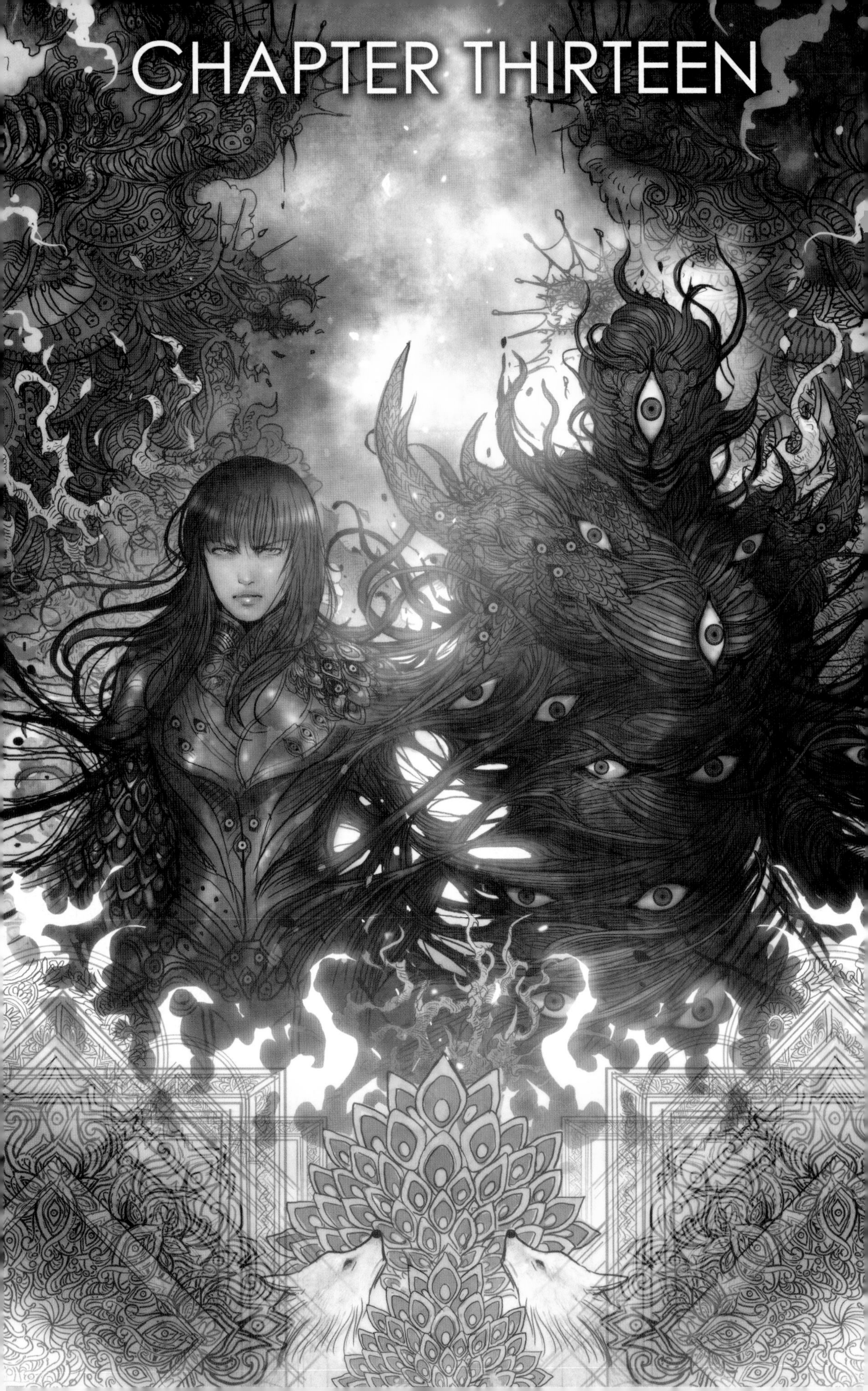

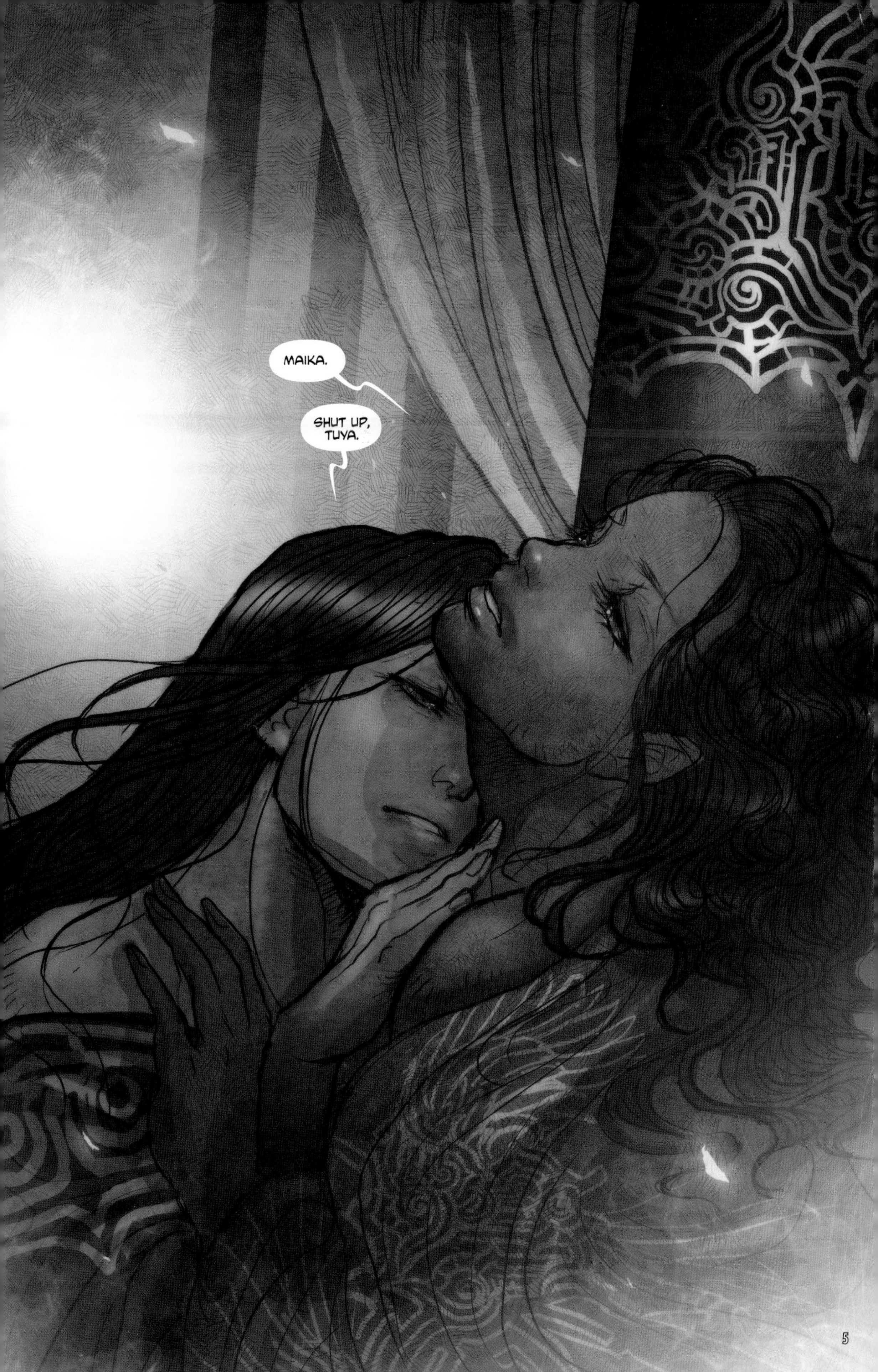
MAIKA.
SHUT UP, TUYA.

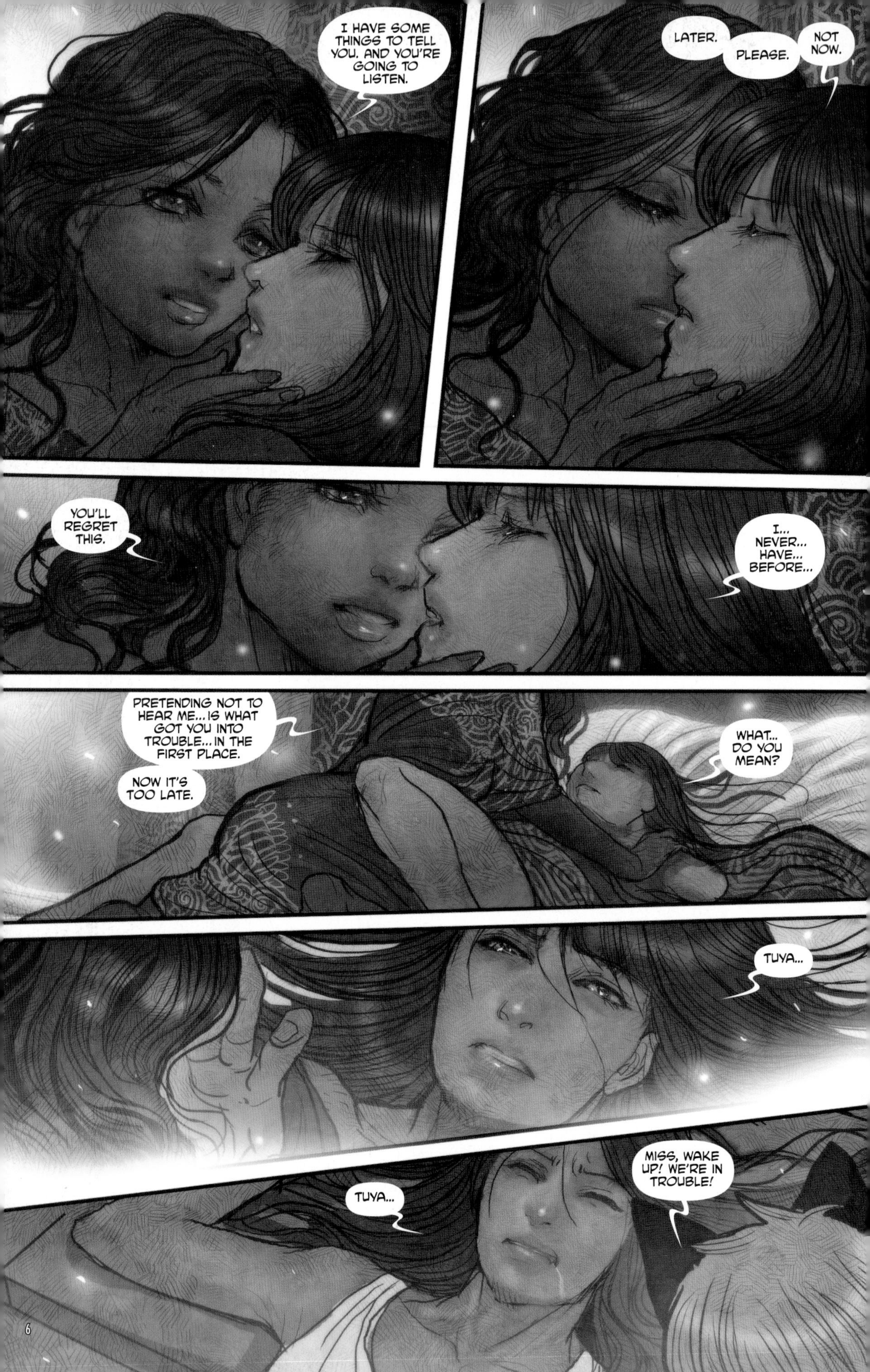
I HAVE SOME THINGS TO TELL YOU, AND YOU'RE GOING TO LISTEN.
LATER.
PLEASE.
NOT NOW.
YOU'LL REGRET THIS.
I... NEVER... HAVE... BEFORE...
PRETENDING NOT TO HEAR ME... IS WHAT GOT YOU INTO TROUBLE... IN THE FIRST PLACE.
NOW IT'S TOO LATE.
WHAT... DO YOU MEAN?
TUYA...
TUYA...
MISS, WAKE UP! WE'RE IN TROUBLE!

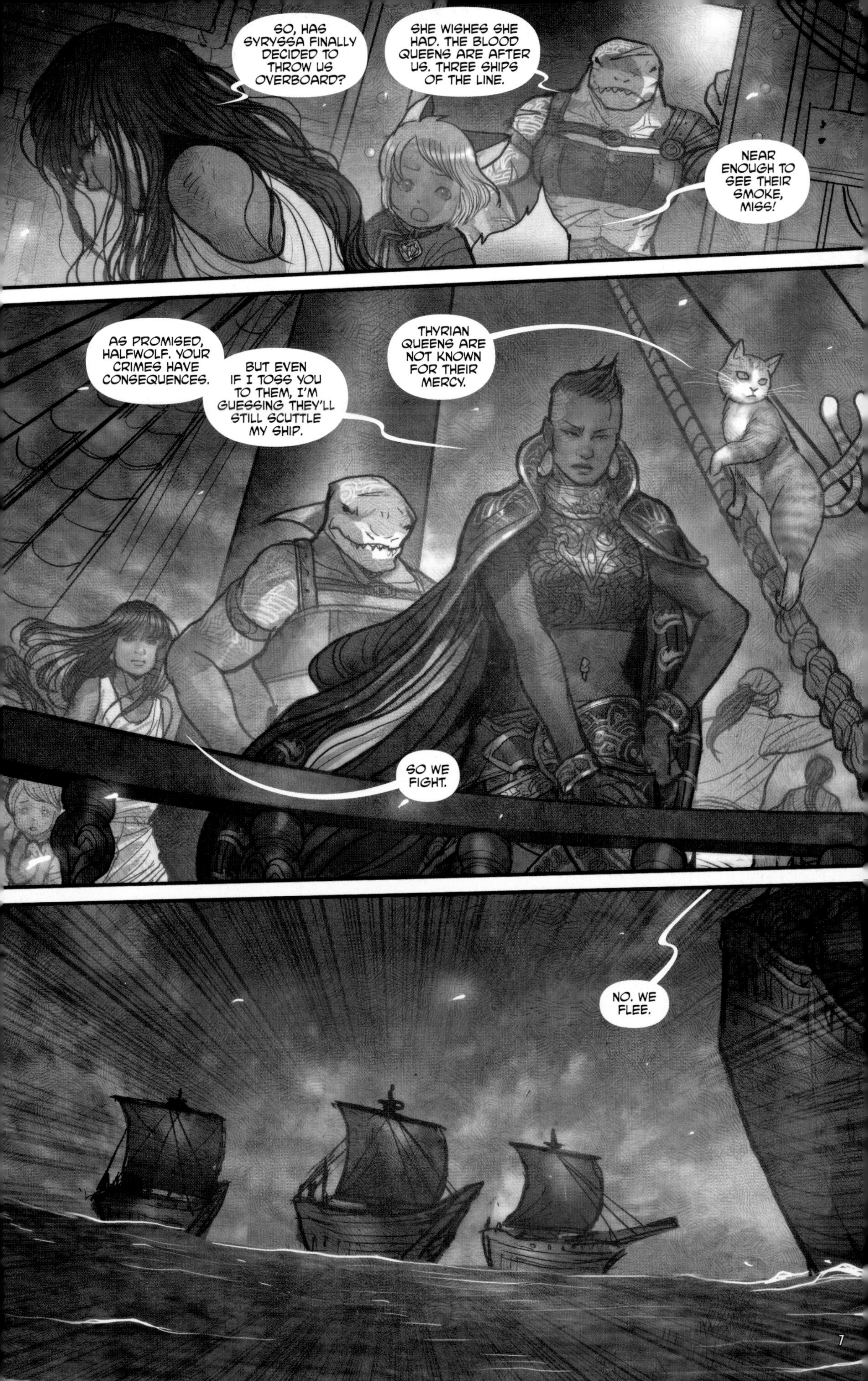
SO, HAS SYRYSSA FINALLY DECIDED TO THROW US OVERBOARD?
SHE WISHES SHE HAD. THE BLOOD QUEENS ARE AFTER US. THREE SHIPS OF THE LINE.
NEAR ENOUGH TO SEE THEIR SMOKE, MISS!
AS PROMISED, HALFWOLF. YOUR CRIMES HAVE CONSEQUENCES.
BUT EVEN IF I TOSS YOU TO THEM, I'M GUESSING THEY'LL STILL SCUTTLE MY SHIP.
THYRIAN QUEENS ARE NOT KNOWN FOR THEIR MERCY.
SO WE FIGHT.
NO. WE FLEE.

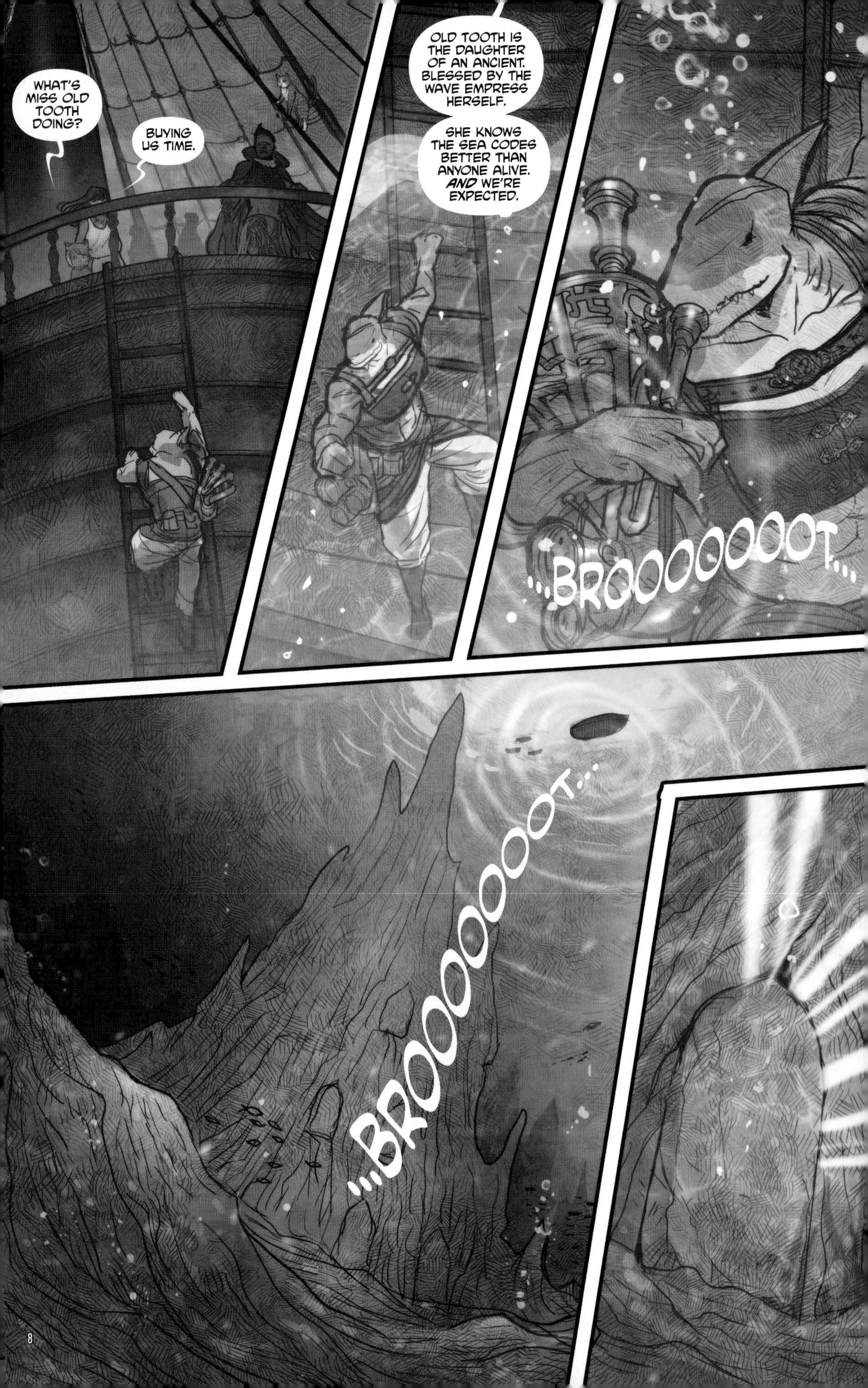
WHAT'S MISS OLD TOOTH DOING?
BUYING US TIME.
OLD TOOTH IS THE DAUGHTER OF AN ANCIENT. BLESSED BY THE WAVE EMPRESS HERSELF.
SHE KNOWS THE SEA CODES BETTER THAN ANYONE ALIVE. AND WE'RE EXPECTED.
...BROOOOOOOT...
...BROOOOOOOT...

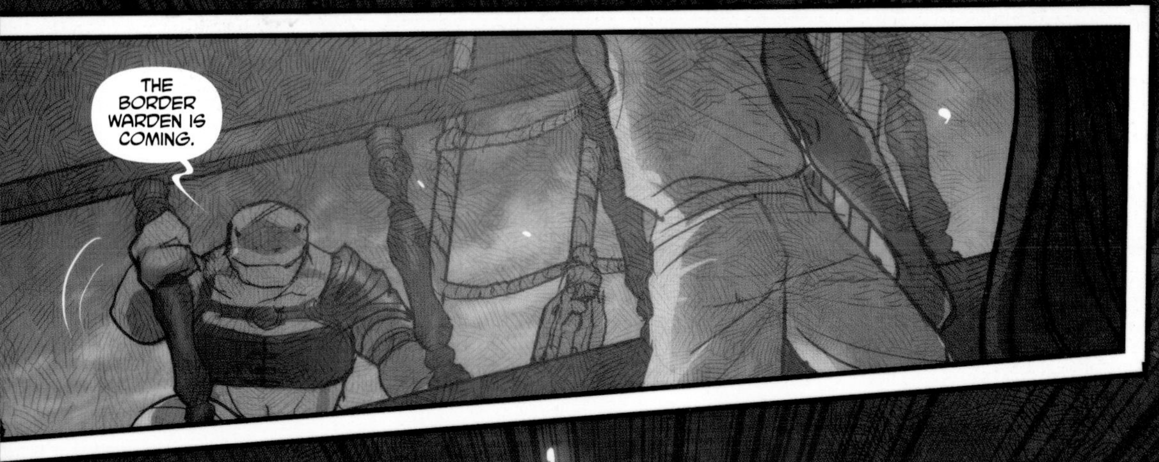
THE BORDER WARDEN IS COMING.

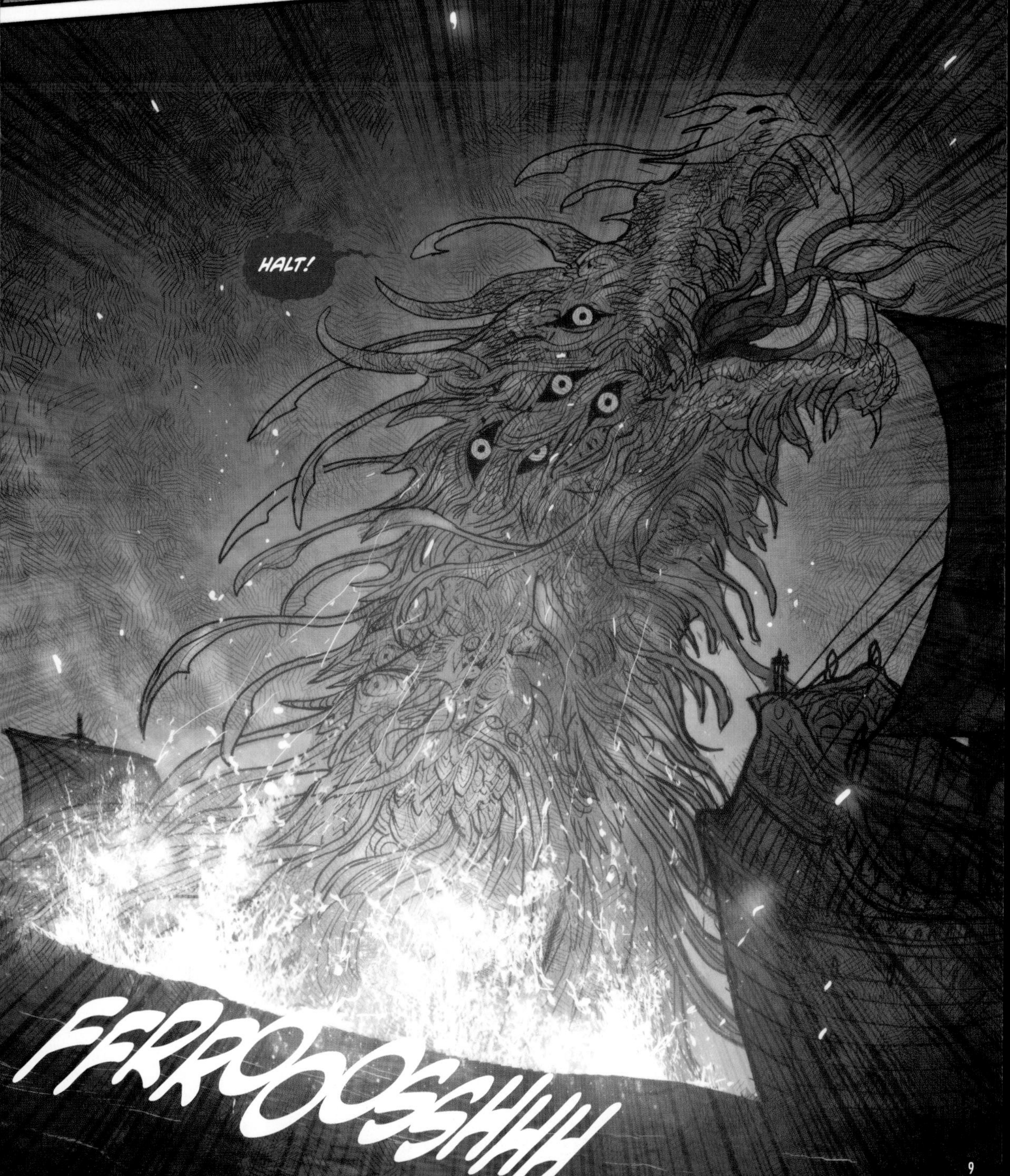
HALT!
FFRROOSSHHH

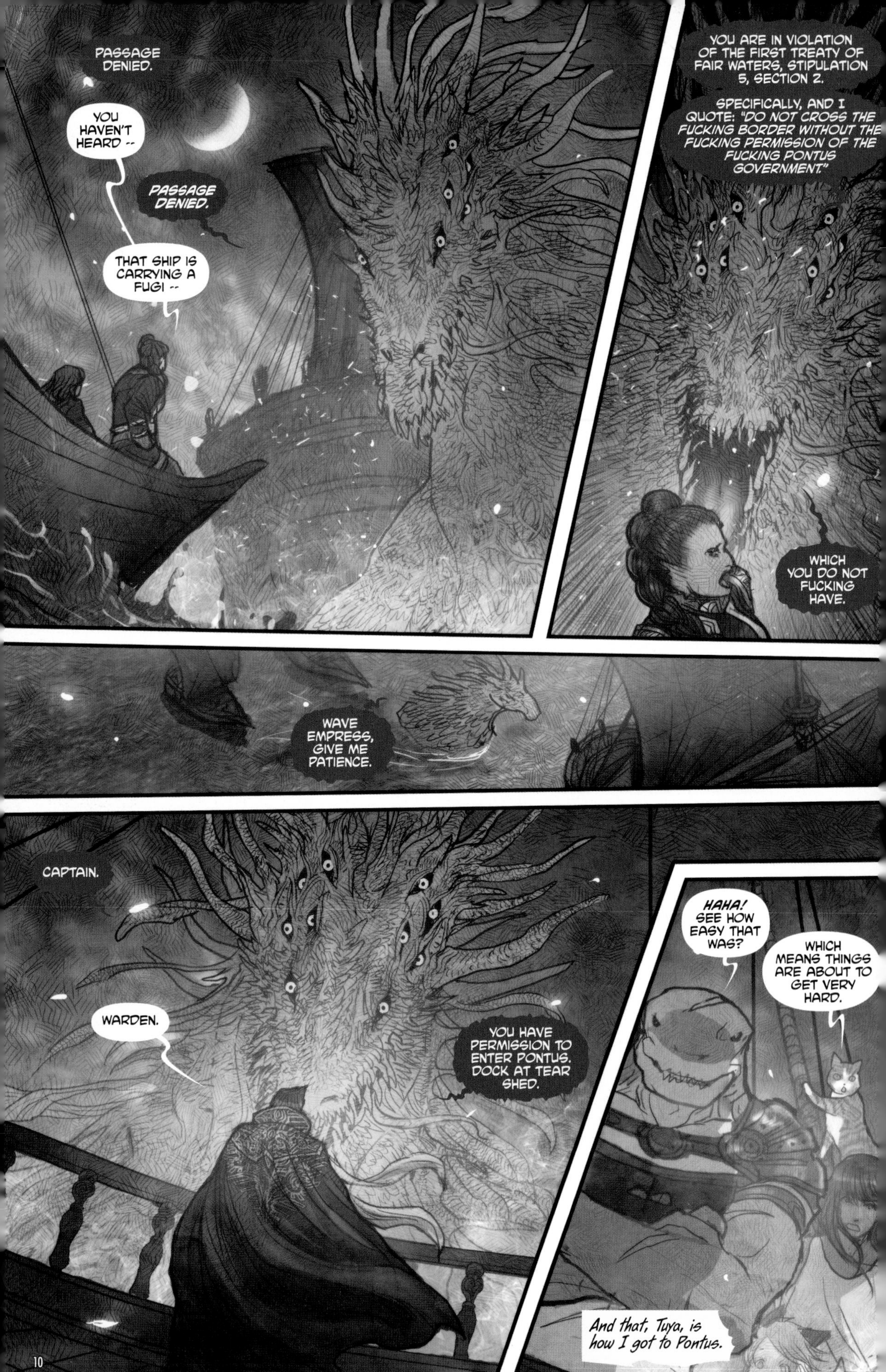
PASSAGE DENIED.
YOU HAVEN'T HEARD --
PASSAGE DENIED.
THAT SHIP IS CARRYING A FUGI --
YOU ARE IN VIOLATION OF THE FIRST TREATY OF FAIR WATERS, STIPULATION 5, SECTION 2.
SPECIFICALLY, AND I QUOTE: *"DO NOT CROSS THE FUCKING BORDER WITHOUT THE FUCKING PERMISSION OF THE FUCKING PONTUS GOVERNMENT."*
WHICH YOU DO NOT FUCKING HAVE.
WAVE EMPRESS, GIVE ME PATIENCE.
CAPTAIN.
WARDEN.
YOU HAVE PERMISSION TO ENTER PONTUS. DOCK AT TEAR SHED.
HAHA! SEE HOW EASY THAT WAS?
WHICH MEANS THINGS ARE ABOUT TO GET VERY HARD.
And that, Tuya, is how I got to Pontus.

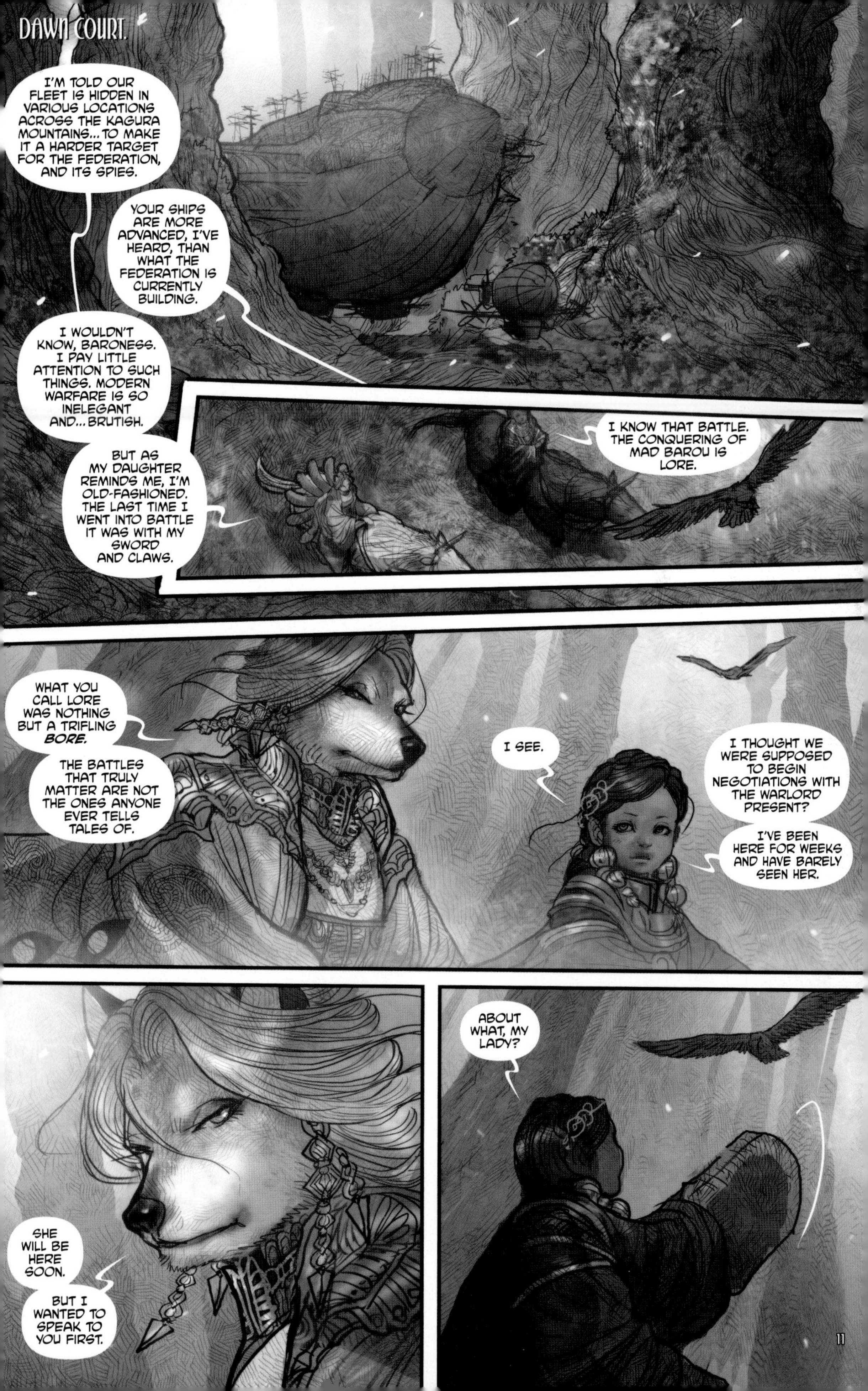
DAWN COURT.
I'M TOLD OUR FLEET IS HIDDEN IN VARIOUS LOCATIONS ACROSS THE KAGURA MOUNTAINS... TO MAKE IT A HARDER TARGET FOR THE FEDERATION, AND ITS SPIES.
YOUR SHIPS ARE MORE ADVANCED, I'VE HEARD, THAN WHAT THE FEDERATION IS CURRENTLY BUILDING.
I WOULDN'T KNOW, BARONESS. I PAY LITTLE ATTENTION TO SUCH THINGS. MODERN WARFARE IS SO INELEGANT AND... BRUTISH.
BUT AS MY DAUGHTER REMINDS ME, I'M OLD-FASHIONED. THE LAST TIME I WENT INTO BATTLE IT WAS WITH MY SWORD AND CLAWS.
I KNOW THAT BATTLE. THE CONQUERING OF MAD BAROU IS LORE.
WHAT YOU CALL LORE WAS NOTHING BUT A TRIFLING *BORE.*
THE BATTLES THAT TRULY MATTER ARE NOT THE ONES ANYONE EVER TELLS TALES OF.
I SEE.
I THOUGHT WE WERE SUPPOSED TO BEGIN NEGOTIATIONS WITH THE WARLORD PRESENT?
I'VE BEEN HERE FOR WEEKS AND HAVE BARELY SEEN HER.
SHE WILL BE HERE SOON.
BUT I WANTED TO SPEAK TO YOU FIRST.
ABOUT WHAT, MY LADY?

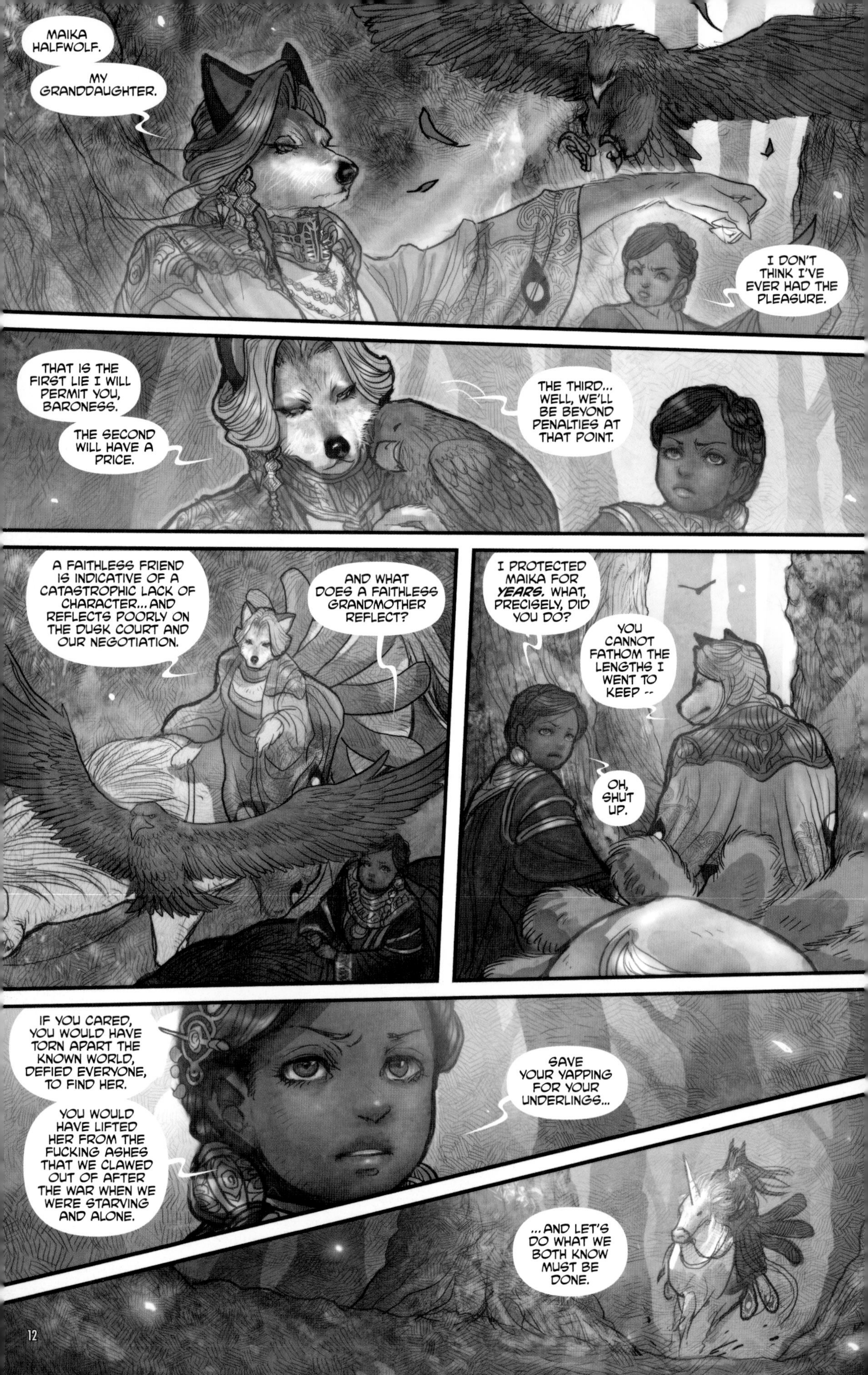
MAIKA HALFWOLF.
MY GRANDDAUGHTER.
I DON'T THINK I'VE EVER HAD THE PLEASURE.
THAT IS THE FIRST LIE I WILL PERMIT YOU, BARONESS.
THE SECOND WILL HAVE A PRICE.
THE THIRD... WELL, WE'LL BE BEYOND PENALTIES AT THAT POINT.
A FAITHLESS FRIEND IS INDICATIVE OF A CATASTROPHIC LACK OF CHARACTER... AND REFLECTS POORLY ON THE DUSK COURT AND OUR NEGOTIATION.
AND WHAT DOES A FAITHLESS GRANDMOTHER REFLECT?
I PROTECTED MAIKA FOR *YEARS*. WHAT, PRECISELY, DID YOU DO?
YOU CANNOT FATHOM THE LENGTHS I WENT TO KEEP --
OH, SHUT UP.
IF YOU CARED, YOU WOULD HAVE TORN APART THE KNOWN WORLD, DEFIED EVERYONE, TO FIND HER.
YOU WOULD HAVE LIFTED HER FROM THE FUCKING ASHES THAT WE CLAWED OUT OF AFTER THE WAR WHEN WE WERE STARVING AND ALONE.
SAVE YOUR YAPPING FOR YOUR UNDERLINGS...
...AND LET'S DO WHAT WE BOTH KNOW MUST BE DONE.

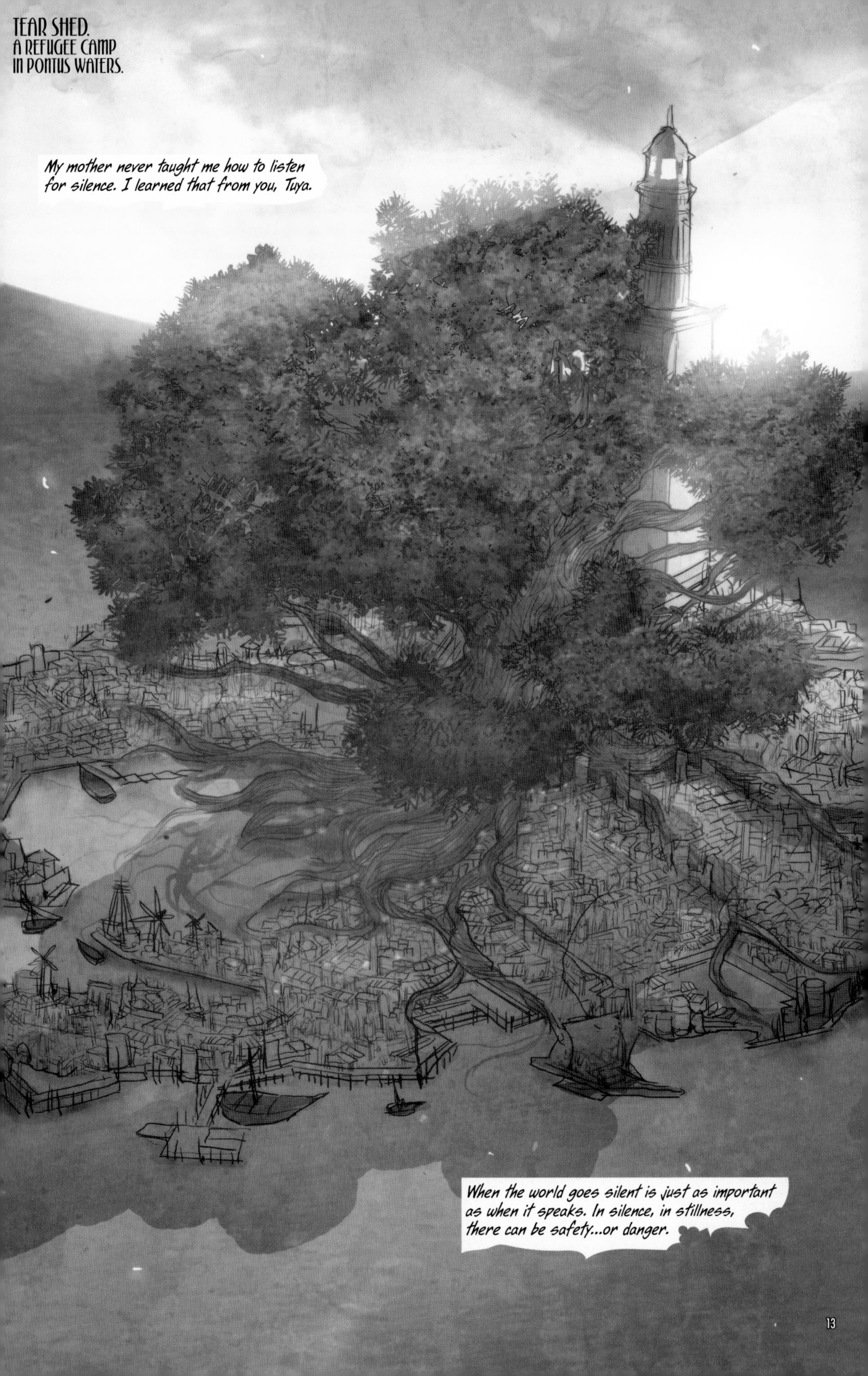
TEAR SHED.
A REFUGEE CAMP
IN PONTUS WATERS.
My mother never taught me how to listen for silence. I learned that from you, Tuya.
When the world goes silent is just as important as when it speaks. In silence, in stillness, there can be safety...or danger.

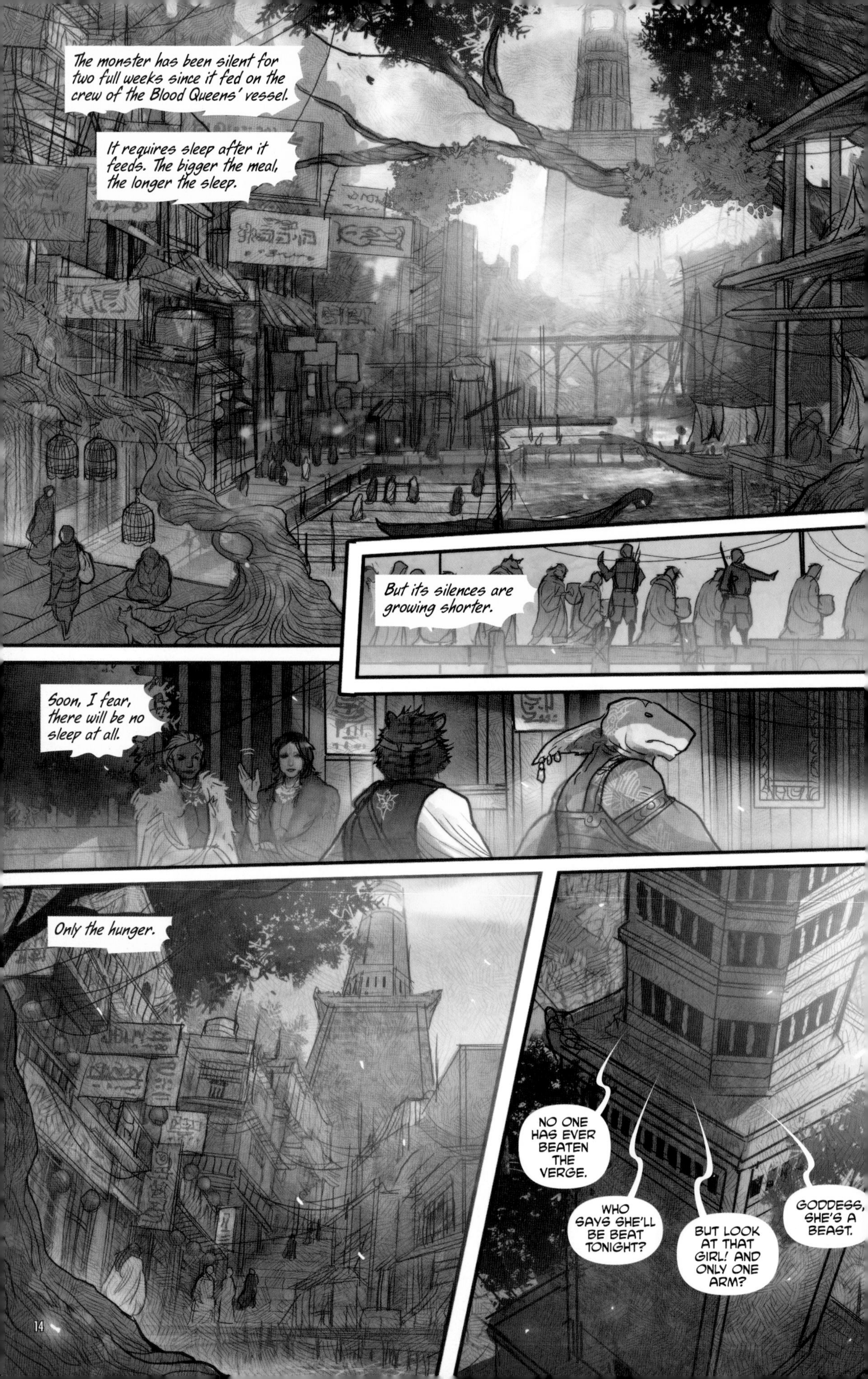

The monster has been silent for two full weeks since it fed on the crew of the Blood Queens' vessel.
It requires sleep after it feeds. The bigger the meal, the longer the sleep.
But its silences are growing shorter.
Soon, I fear, there will be no sleep at all.
Only the hunger.
NO ONE HAS EVER BEATEN THE VERGE.
WHO SAYS SHE'LL BE BEAT TONIGHT?
BUT LOOK AT THAT GIRL! AND ONLY ONE ARM?
GODDESS, SHE'S A BEAST.

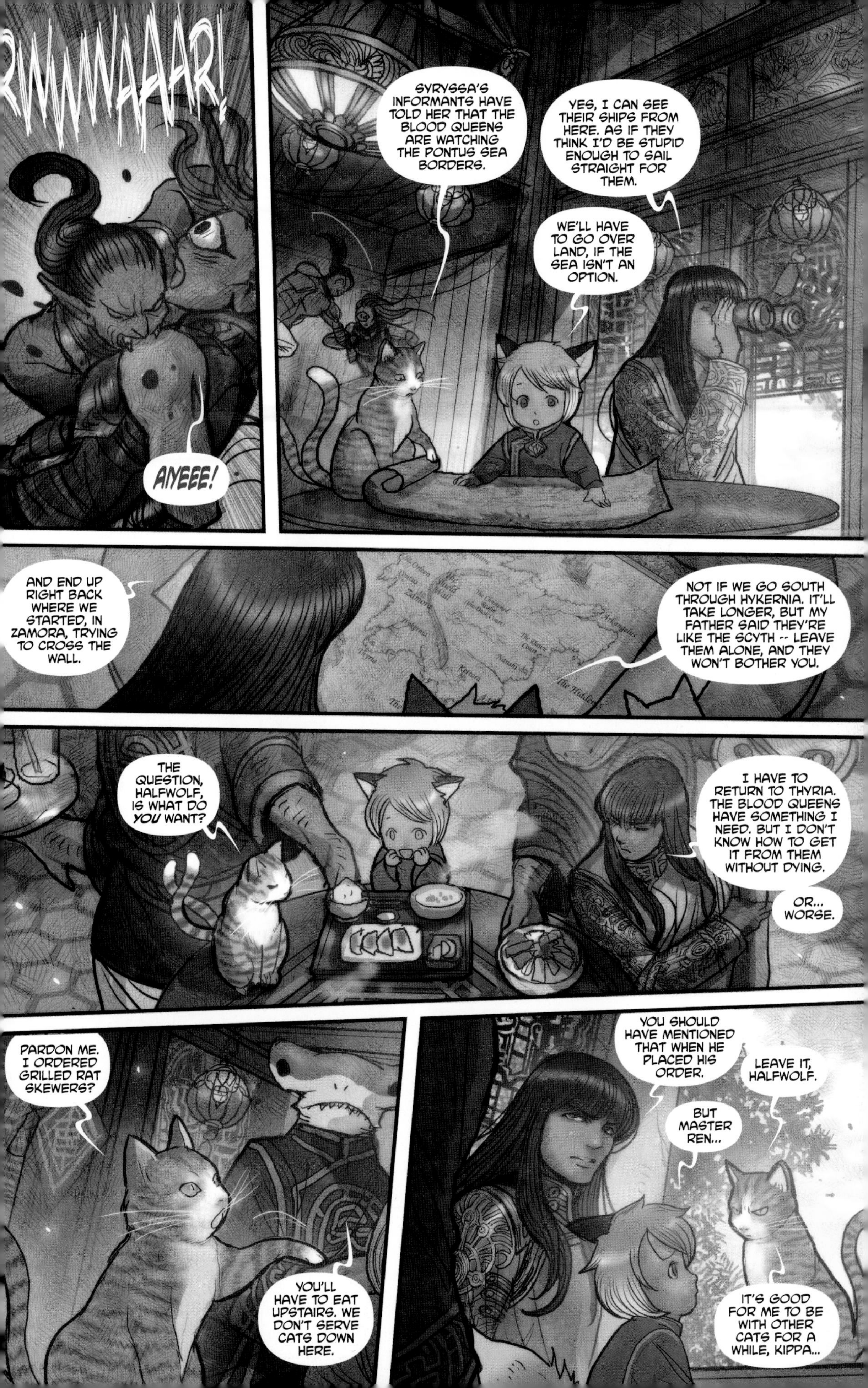
RWWAAAR!
AIYEEE!
SYRYSSA'S INFORMANTS HAVE TOLD HER THAT THE BLOOD QUEENS ARE WATCHING THE PONTUS SEA BORDERS.
YES, I CAN SEE THEIR SHIPS FROM HERE. AS IF THEY THINK I'D BE STUPID ENOUGH TO SAIL STRAIGHT FOR THEM.
WE'LL HAVE TO GO OVER LAND, IF THE SEA ISN'T AN OPTION.
AND END UP RIGHT BACK WHERE WE STARTED, IN ZAMORA, TRYING TO CROSS THE WALL.
NOT IF WE GO SOUTH THROUGH HYKERNIA. IT'LL TAKE LONGER, BUT MY FATHER SAID THEY'RE LIKE THE SCYTH -- LEAVE THEM ALONE, AND THEY WON'T BOTHER YOU.
THE QUESTION, HALFWOLF, IS WHAT DO *YOU* WANT?
I HAVE TO RETURN TO THYRIA. THE BLOOD QUEENS HAVE SOMETHING I NEED. BUT I DON'T KNOW HOW TO GET IT FROM THEM WITHOUT DYING.
OR... WORSE.
PARDON ME. I ORDERED GRILLED RAT SKEWERS?
YOU'LL HAVE TO EAT UPSTAIRS. WE DON'T SERVE CATS DOWN HERE.
YOU SHOULD HAVE MENTIONED THAT WHEN HE PLACED HIS ORDER.
LEAVE IT, HALFWOLF.
BUT MASTER REN...
IT'S GOOD FOR ME TO BE WITH OTHER CATS FOR A WHILE, KIPPA...

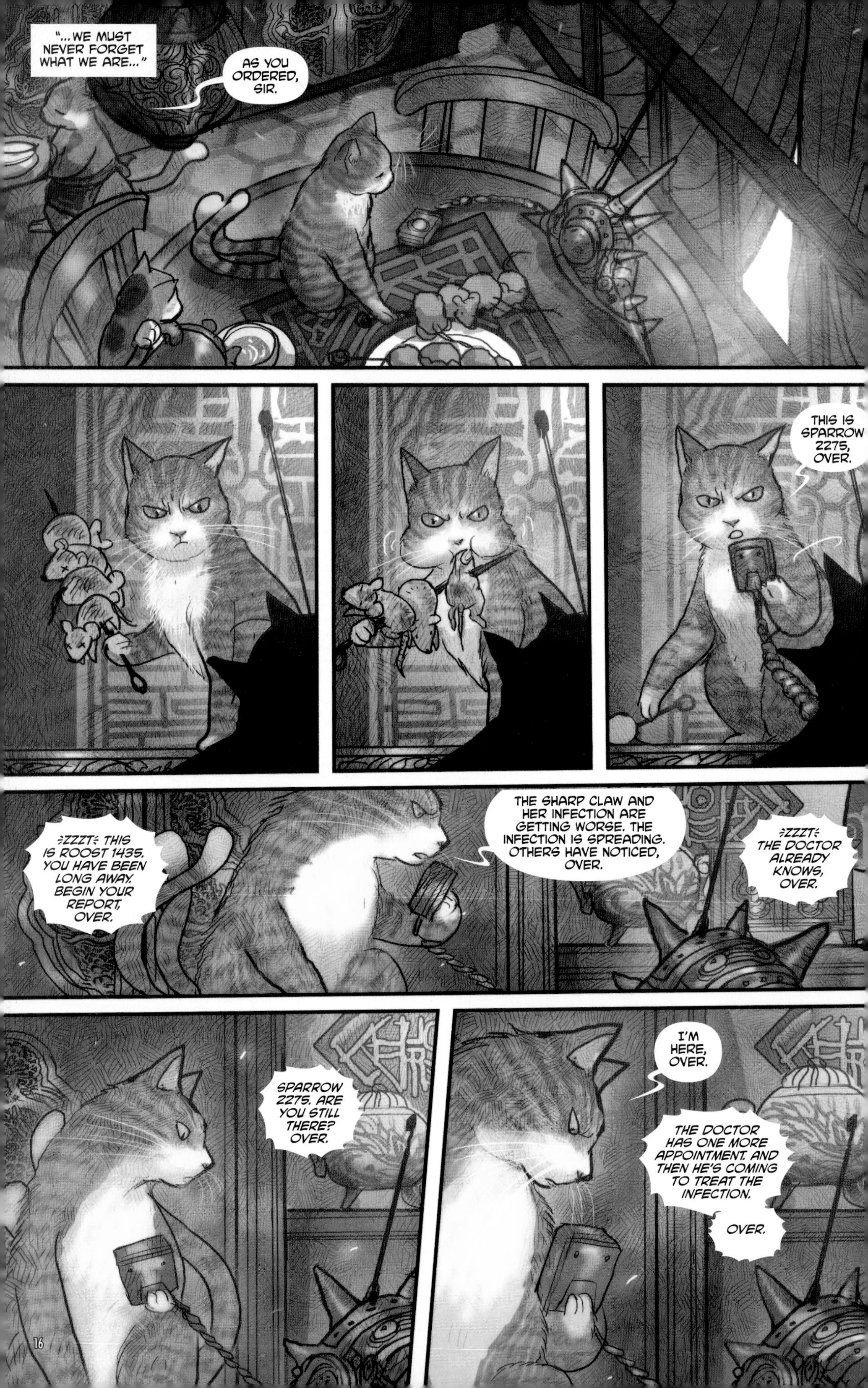
"...WE MUST NEVER FORGET WHAT WE ARE..."
AS YOU ORDERED, SIR.
THIS IS SPARROW 2275, OVER.
ZZZT THIS IS ROOST 1435. YOU HAVE BEEN LONG AWAY. BEGIN YOUR REPORT, OVER.
THE SHARP CLAW AND HER INFECTION ARE GETTING WORSE. THE INFECTION IS SPREADING. OTHERS HAVE NOTICED, OVER.
ZZZT THE DOCTOR ALREADY KNOWS, OVER.
SPARROW 2275. ARE YOU STILL THERE? OVER.
I'M HERE, OVER.
THE DOCTOR HAS ONE MORE APPOINTMENT. AND THEN HE'S COMING TO TREAT THE INFECTION.
OVER.

OLD TOOTH SAID THE JOLLY RAVAGER WILL STAY IN PONTUS WATERS UNTIL MISTER SEIZI TELLS THEM IT'S SAFE TO COME HOME. SHE SAID IT MIGHT BE NEVER.

YOU SHOULD TALK TO CAPTAIN SYRYSSA, MISS. THANK HER FOR EVERYTHING SHE DID TO HELP US.

THANK HER FOR FOLLOWING ORDERS?

I'D RATHER SPEND MY TIME FINDING A WAY FOR US TO GET OUT OF THIS REFUGEE CAMP. IT FEELS TOO MUCH LIKE...

...PLACES I'VE BEEN BEFORE.

MISS! THAT'S MINE!

NO!

IF YOU'RE GOING TO FIGHT ME, LITTLE FOX, WE SHOULD WORK ON YOUR STRENGTH.

A MESSAGE FROM A FRIEND. HE'S WAITING AT THE POETS' CAFÉ FOR YOU. DOWN AT SEA LEVEL, OFF LIGHTHOUSE ROAD.

I DON'T HAVE ANY --

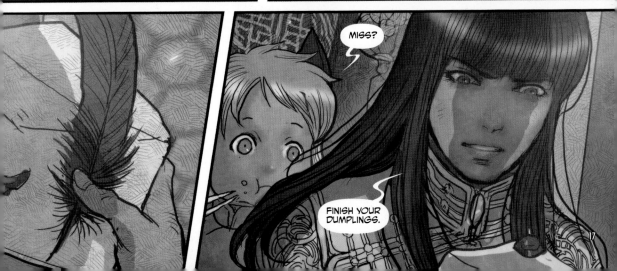

MISS?

FINISH YOUR DUMPLINGS.

17

I WAS BORN IN A REFUGEE CAMP, UP NORTH. I DON'T REMEMBER IT, THOUGH.

COUNT YOURSELF LUCKY. THE NORTHERN CAMPS WERE HELLISH DURING AND AFTER THE WAR.

HOW IS THE... MONSTER-THING?

SLEEPING FOREVER. I HOPE.

IT IS?

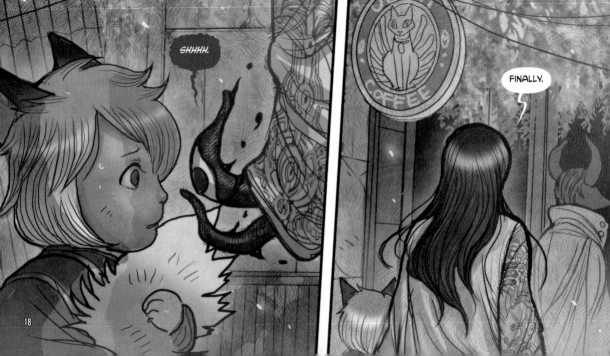

SHHHH.

FINALLY.

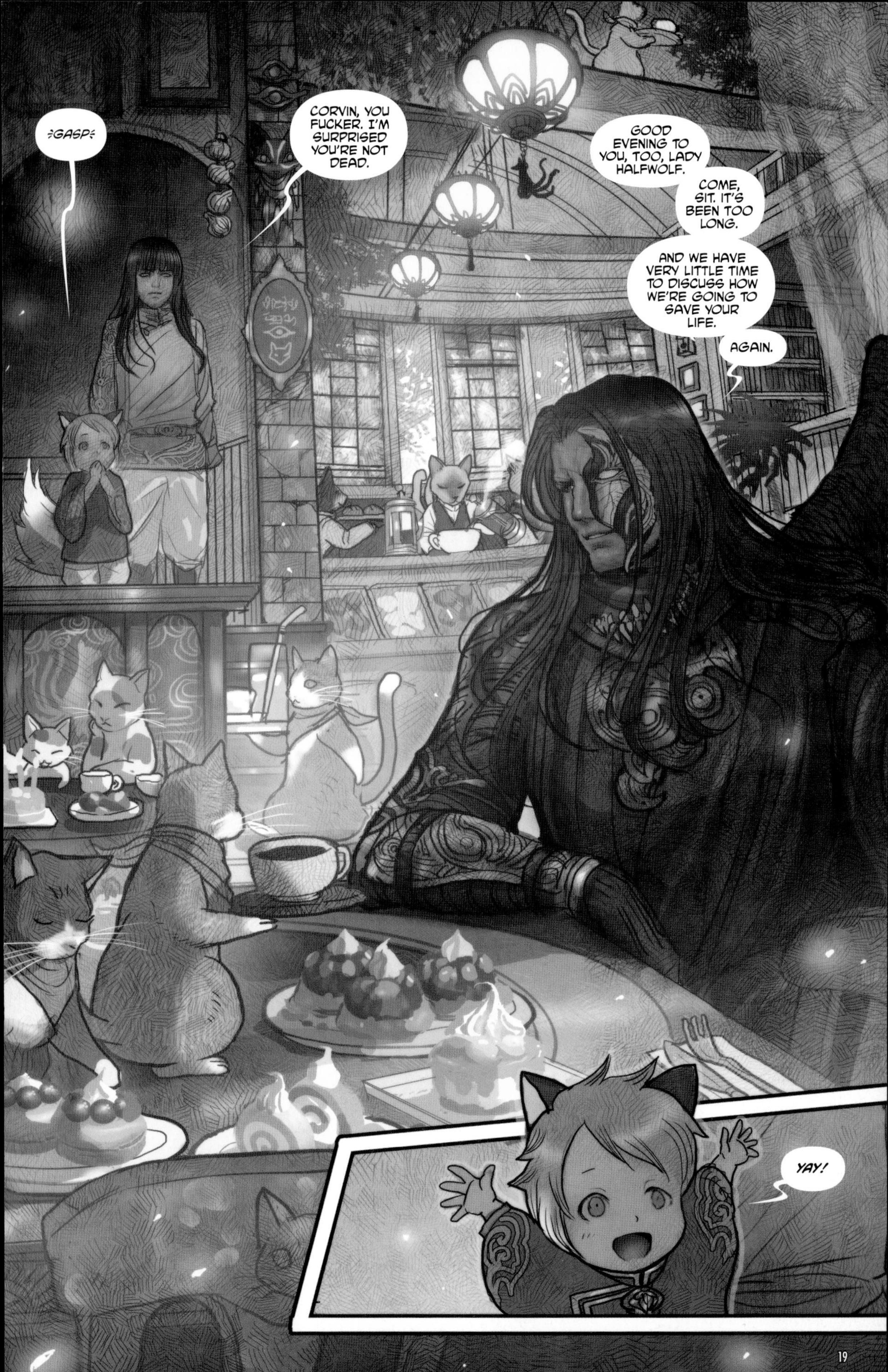

GASP
CORVIN, YOU FUCKER. I'M SURPRISED YOU'RE NOT DEAD.
GOOD EVENING TO YOU, TOO, LADY HALFWOLF.
COME, SIT. IT'S BEEN TOO LONG.
AND WE HAVE VERY LITTLE TIME TO DISCUSS HOW WE'RE GOING TO SAVE YOUR LIFE.
AGAIN.
YAY!

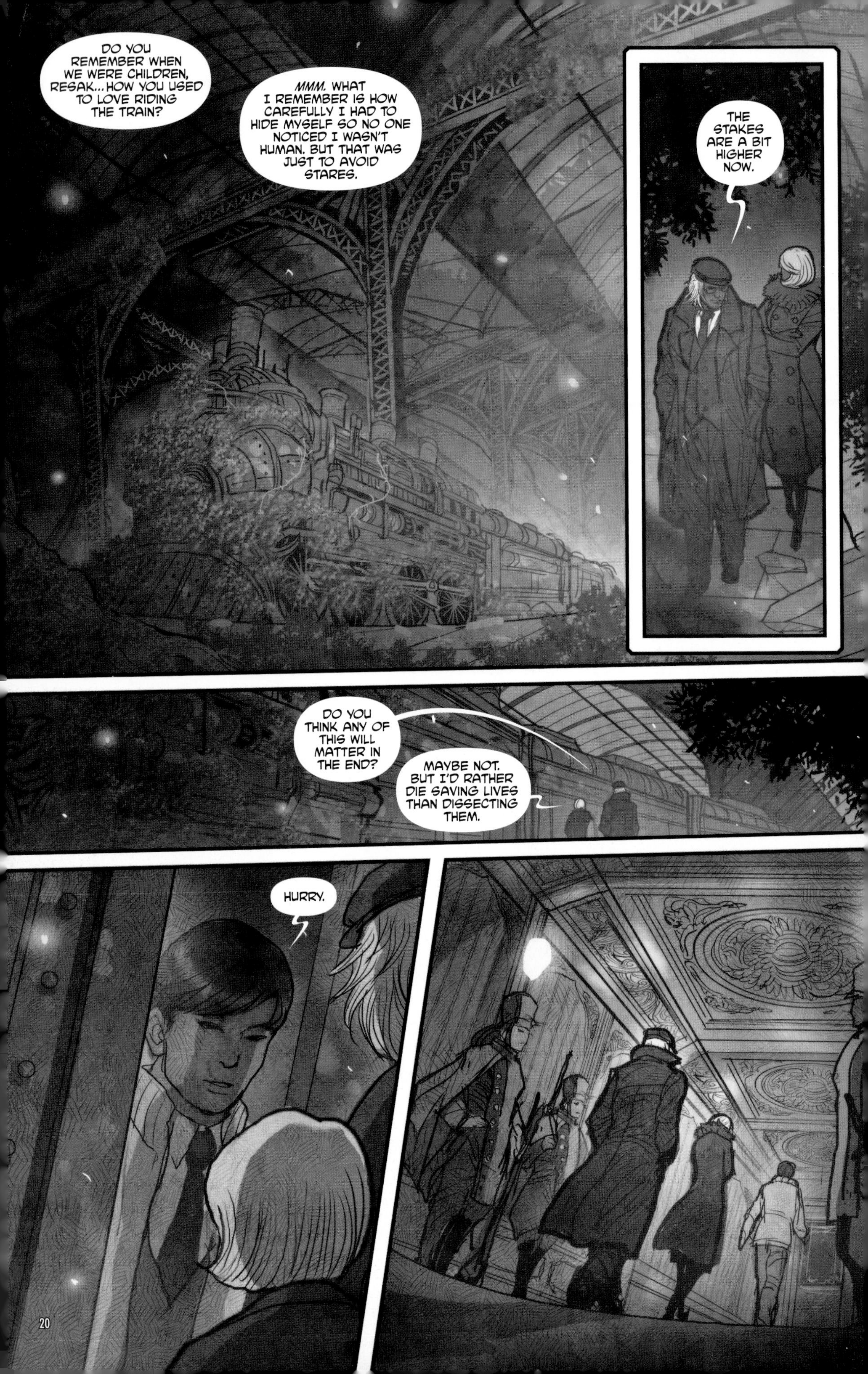
DO YOU REMEMBER WHEN WE WERE CHILDREN, RESAK...HOW YOU USED TO LOVE RIDING THE TRAIN?
MMM. WHAT I REMEMBER IS HOW CAREFULLY I HAD TO HIDE MYSELF SO NO ONE NOTICED I WASN'T HUMAN. BUT THAT WAS JUST TO AVOID STARES.
THE STAKES ARE A BIT HIGHER NOW.
DO YOU THINK ANY OF THIS WILL MATTER IN THE END?
MAYBE NOT. BUT I'D RATHER DIE SAVING LIVES THAN DISSECTING THEM.
HURRY.

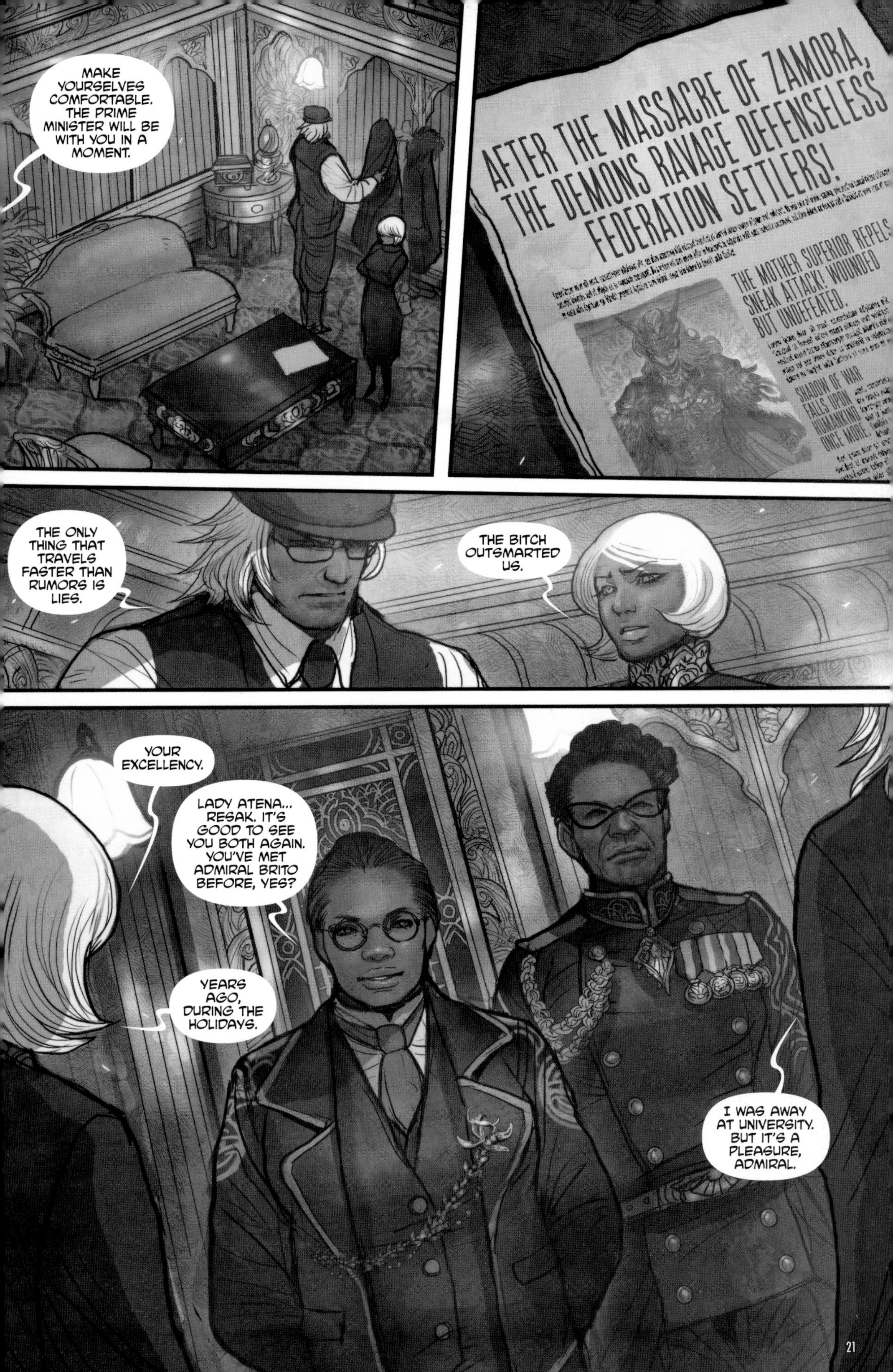
MAKE YOURSELVES COMFORTABLE. THE PRIME MINISTER WILL BE WITH YOU IN A MOMENT.
AFTER THE MASSACRE OF ZAMORA, THE DEMONS RAVAGE DEFENSELESS FEDERATION SETTLERS!
THE MOTHER SUPERIOR REPELS SNEAK ATTACK! WOUNDED BUT UNDEFEATED.
SHADOW OF WAR FALLS UPON HUMANKIND ONCE MORE.
THE ONLY THING THAT TRAVELS FASTER THAN RUMORS IS LIES.
THE BITCH OUTSMARTED US.
YOUR EXCELLENCY.
LADY ATENA... RESAK. IT'S GOOD TO SEE YOU BOTH AGAIN. YOU'VE MET ADMIRAL BRITO BEFORE, YES?
YEARS AGO, DURING THE HOLIDAYS.
I WAS AWAY AT UNIVERSITY. BUT IT'S A PLEASURE, ADMIRAL.

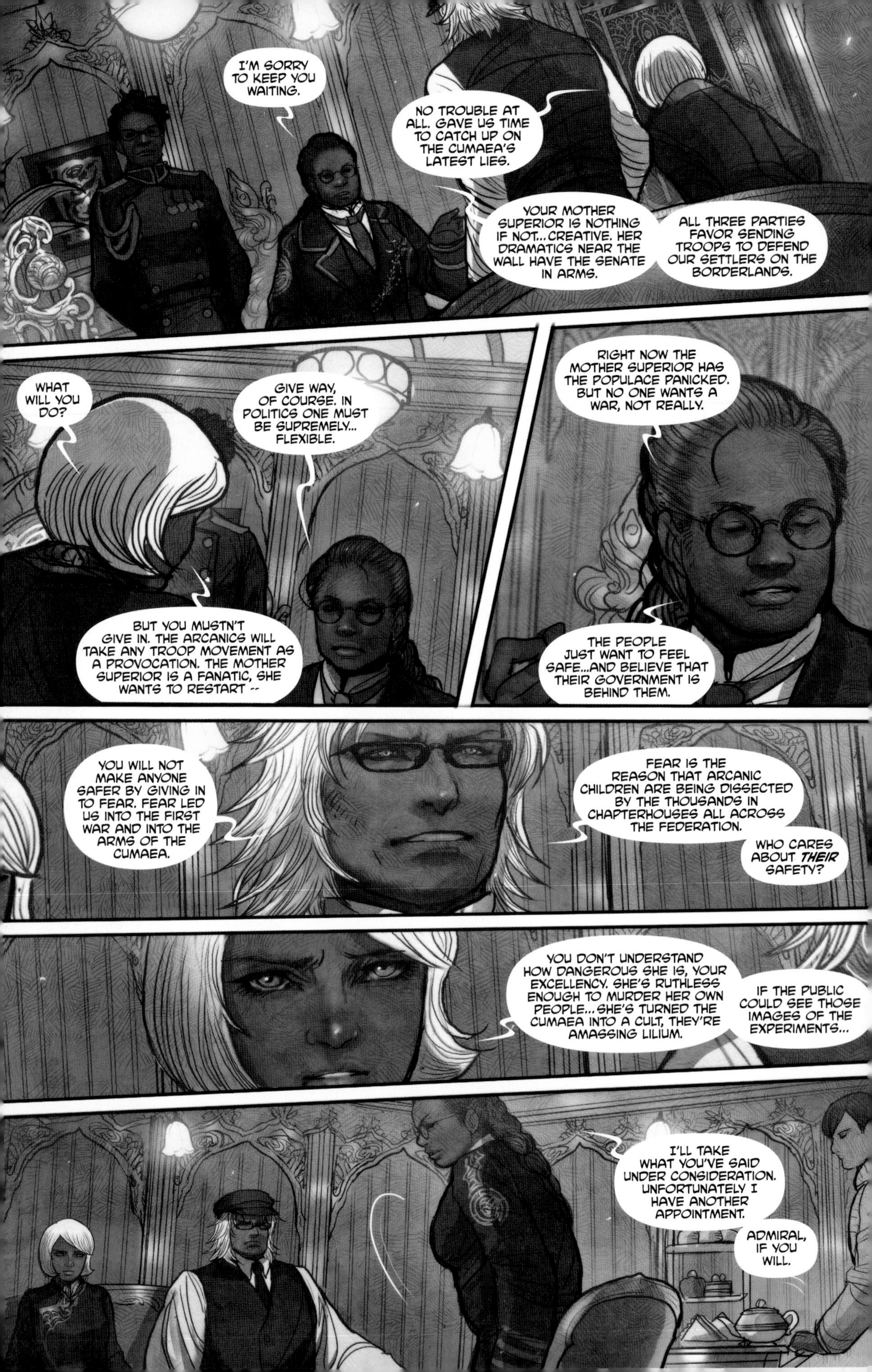
I'M SORRY TO KEEP YOU WAITING.
NO TROUBLE AT ALL. GAVE US TIME TO CATCH UP ON THE CUMAEA'S LATEST LIES.
YOUR MOTHER SUPERIOR IS NOTHING IF NOT... CREATIVE. HER DRAMATICS NEAR THE WALL HAVE THE SENATE IN ARMS.
ALL THREE PARTIES FAVOR SENDING TROOPS TO DEFEND OUR SETTLERS ON THE BORDERLANDS.
WHAT WILL YOU DO?
GIVE WAY, OF COURSE. IN POLITICS ONE MUST BE SUPREMELY... FLEXIBLE.
BUT YOU MUSTN'T GIVE IN. THE ARCANICS WILL TAKE ANY TROOP MOVEMENT AS A PROVOCATION. THE MOTHER SUPERIOR IS A FANATIC, SHE WANTS TO RESTART --
RIGHT NOW THE MOTHER SUPERIOR HAS THE POPULACE PANICKED. BUT NO ONE WANTS A WAR, NOT REALLY.
THE PEOPLE JUST WANT TO FEEL SAFE...AND BELIEVE THAT THEIR GOVERNMENT IS BEHIND THEM.
YOU WILL NOT MAKE ANYONE SAFER BY GIVING IN TO FEAR. FEAR LED US INTO THE FIRST WAR AND INTO THE ARMS OF THE CUMAEA.
FEAR IS THE REASON THAT ARCANIC CHILDREN ARE BEING DISSECTED BY THE THOUSANDS IN CHAPTERHOUSES ALL ACROSS THE FEDERATION.
WHO CARES ABOUT *THEIR* SAFETY?
YOU DON'T UNDERSTAND HOW DANGEROUS SHE IS, YOUR EXCELLENCY. SHE'S RUTHLESS ENOUGH TO MURDER HER OWN PEOPLE... SHE'S TURNED THE CUMAEA INTO A CULT, THEY'RE AMASSING LILIUM.
IF THE PUBLIC COULD SEE THOSE IMAGES OF THE EXPERIMENTS...
I'LL TAKE WHAT YOU'VE SAID UNDER CONSIDERATION. UNFORTUNATELY I HAVE ANOTHER APPOINTMENT.
ADMIRAL, IF YOU WILL.

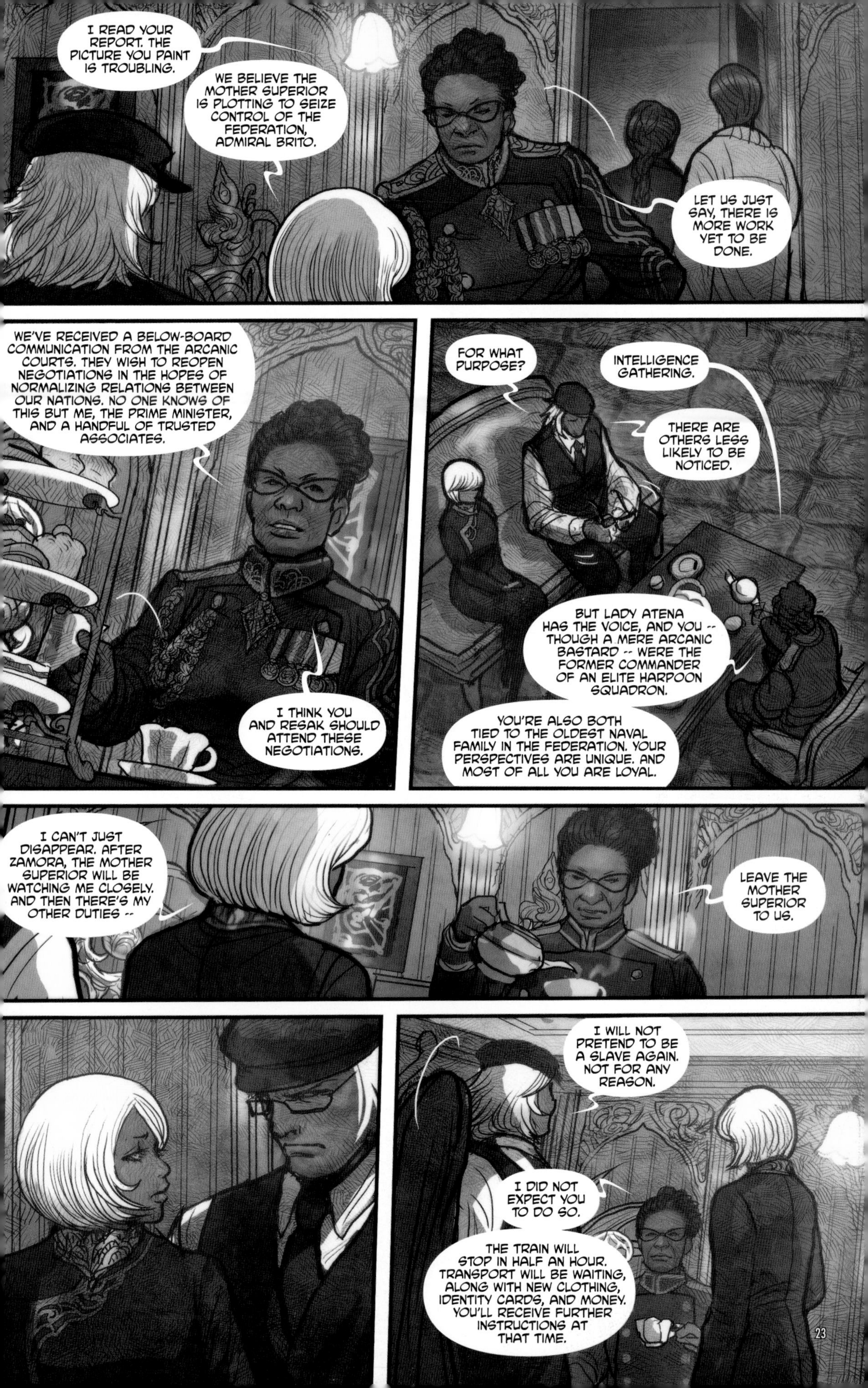
I READ YOUR REPORT. THE PICTURE YOU PAINT IS TROUBLING.
WE BELIEVE THE MOTHER SUPERIOR IS PLOTTING TO SEIZE CONTROL OF THE FEDERATION, ADMIRAL BRITO.
LET US JUST SAY, THERE IS MORE WORK YET TO BE DONE.
WE'VE RECEIVED A BELOW-BOARD COMMUNICATION FROM THE ARCANIC COURTS. THEY WISH TO REOPEN NEGOTIATIONS IN THE HOPES OF NORMALIZING RELATIONS BETWEEN OUR NATIONS. NO ONE KNOWS OF THIS BUT ME, THE PRIME MINISTER, AND A HANDFUL OF TRUSTED ASSOCIATES.
I THINK YOU AND RESAK SHOULD ATTEND THESE NEGOTIATIONS.
FOR WHAT PURPOSE?
INTELLIGENCE GATHERING.
THERE ARE OTHERS LESS LIKELY TO BE NOTICED.
BUT LADY ATENA HAS THE VOICE, AND YOU -- THOUGH A MERE ARCANIC BASTARD -- WERE THE FORMER COMMANDER OF AN ELITE HARPOON SQUADRON.
YOU'RE ALSO BOTH TIED TO THE OLDEST NAVAL FAMILY IN THE FEDERATION. YOUR PERSPECTIVES ARE UNIQUE. AND MOST OF ALL YOU ARE LOYAL.
I CAN'T JUST DISAPPEAR. AFTER ZAMORA, THE MOTHER SUPERIOR WILL BE WATCHING ME CLOSELY. AND THEN THERE'S MY OTHER DUTIES --
LEAVE THE MOTHER SUPERIOR TO US.
I WILL NOT PRETEND TO BE A SLAVE AGAIN. NOT FOR ANY REASON.
I DID NOT EXPECT YOU TO DO SO.
THE TRAIN WILL STOP IN HALF AN HOUR. TRANSPORT WILL BE WAITING, ALONG WITH NEW CLOTHING, IDENTITY CARDS, AND MONEY. YOU'LL RECEIVE FURTHER INSTRUCTIONS AT THAT TIME.

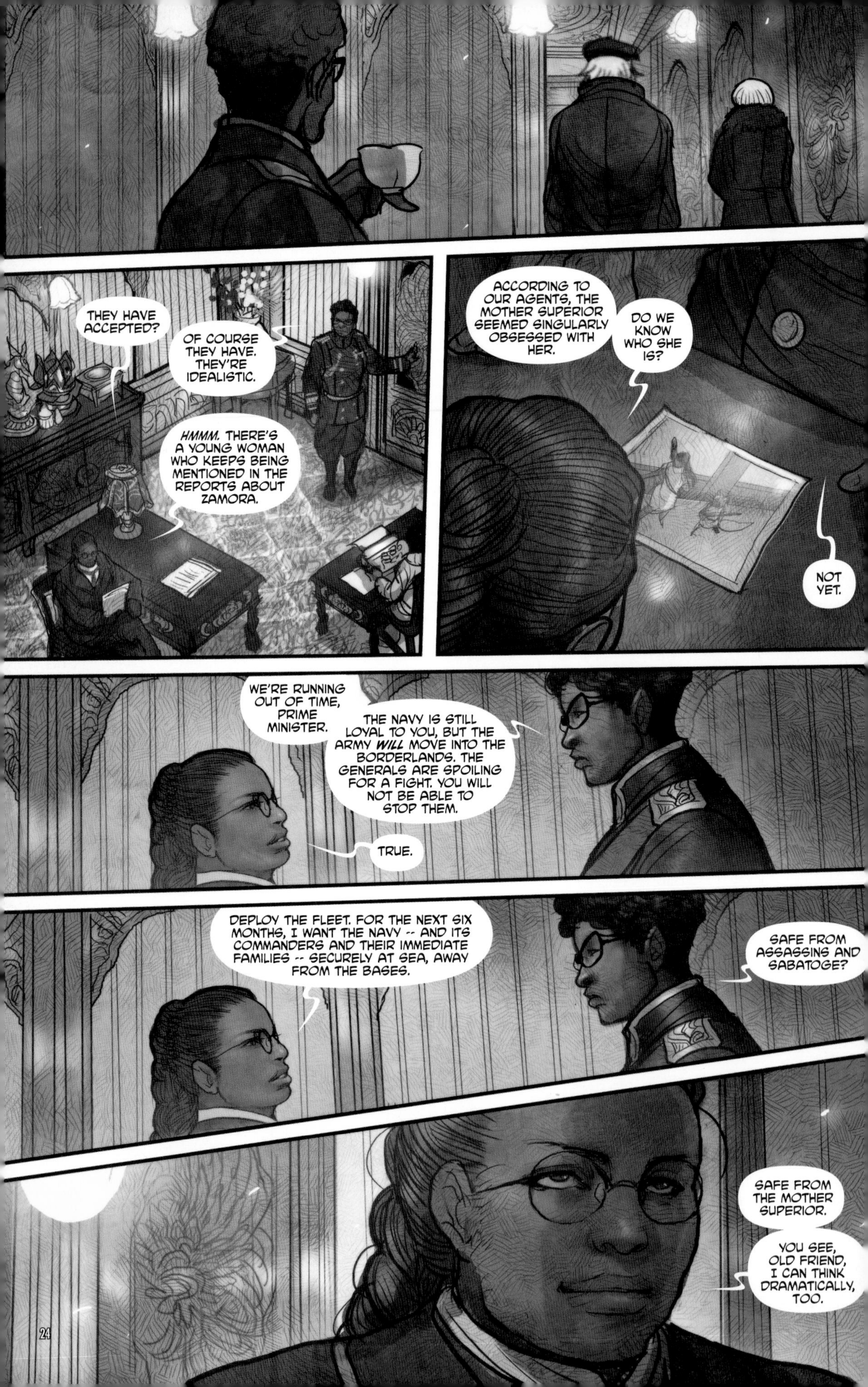
THEY HAVE ACCEPTED?
OF COURSE THEY HAVE. THEY'RE IDEALISTIC.
HMMM. THERE'S A YOUNG WOMAN WHO KEEPS BEING MENTIONED IN THE REPORTS ABOUT ZAMORA.
ACCORDING TO OUR AGENTS, THE MOTHER SUPERIOR SEEMED SINGULARLY OBSESSED WITH HER.
DO WE KNOW WHO SHE IS?
NOT YET.
WE'RE RUNNING OUT OF TIME, PRIME MINISTER.
THE NAVY IS STILL LOYAL TO YOU, BUT THE ARMY WILL MOVE INTO THE BORDERLANDS. THE GENERALS ARE SPOILING FOR A FIGHT. YOU WILL NOT BE ABLE TO STOP THEM.
TRUE.
DEPLOY THE FLEET. FOR THE NEXT SIX MONTHS, I WANT THE NAVY -- AND ITS COMMANDERS AND THEIR IMMEDIATE FAMILIES -- SECURELY AT SEA, AWAY FROM THE BASES.
SAFE FROM ASSASSINS AND SABATOGE?
SAFE FROM THE MOTHER SUPERIOR.
YOU SEE, OLD FRIEND, I CAN THINK DRAMATICALLY, TOO.

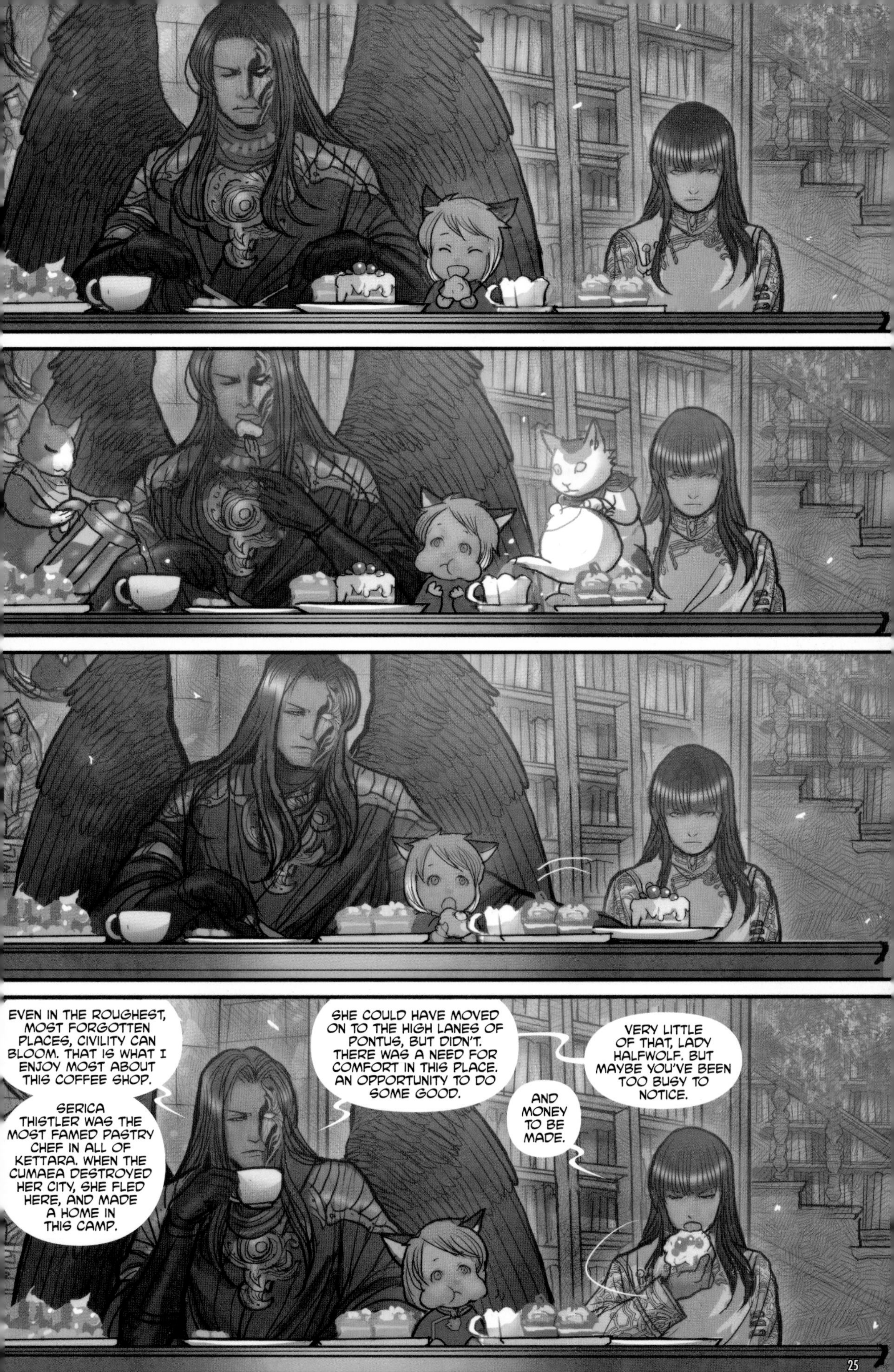
EVEN IN THE ROUGHEST, MOST FORGOTTEN PLACES, CIVILITY CAN BLOOM. THAT IS WHAT I ENJOY MOST ABOUT THIS COFFEE SHOP.
SERICA THISTLER WAS THE MOST FAMED PASTRY CHEF IN ALL OF KETTARA. WHEN THE CUMAEA DESTROYED HER CITY, SHE FLED HERE, AND MADE A HOME IN THIS CAMP.
SHE COULD HAVE MOVED ON TO THE HIGH LANES OF PONTUS, BUT DIDN'T. THERE WAS A NEED FOR COMFORT IN THIS PLACE. AN OPPORTUNITY TO DO SOME GOOD.
AND MONEY TO BE MADE.
VERY LITTLE OF THAT, LADY HALFWOLF. BUT MAYBE YOU'VE BEEN TOO BUSY TO NOTICE.

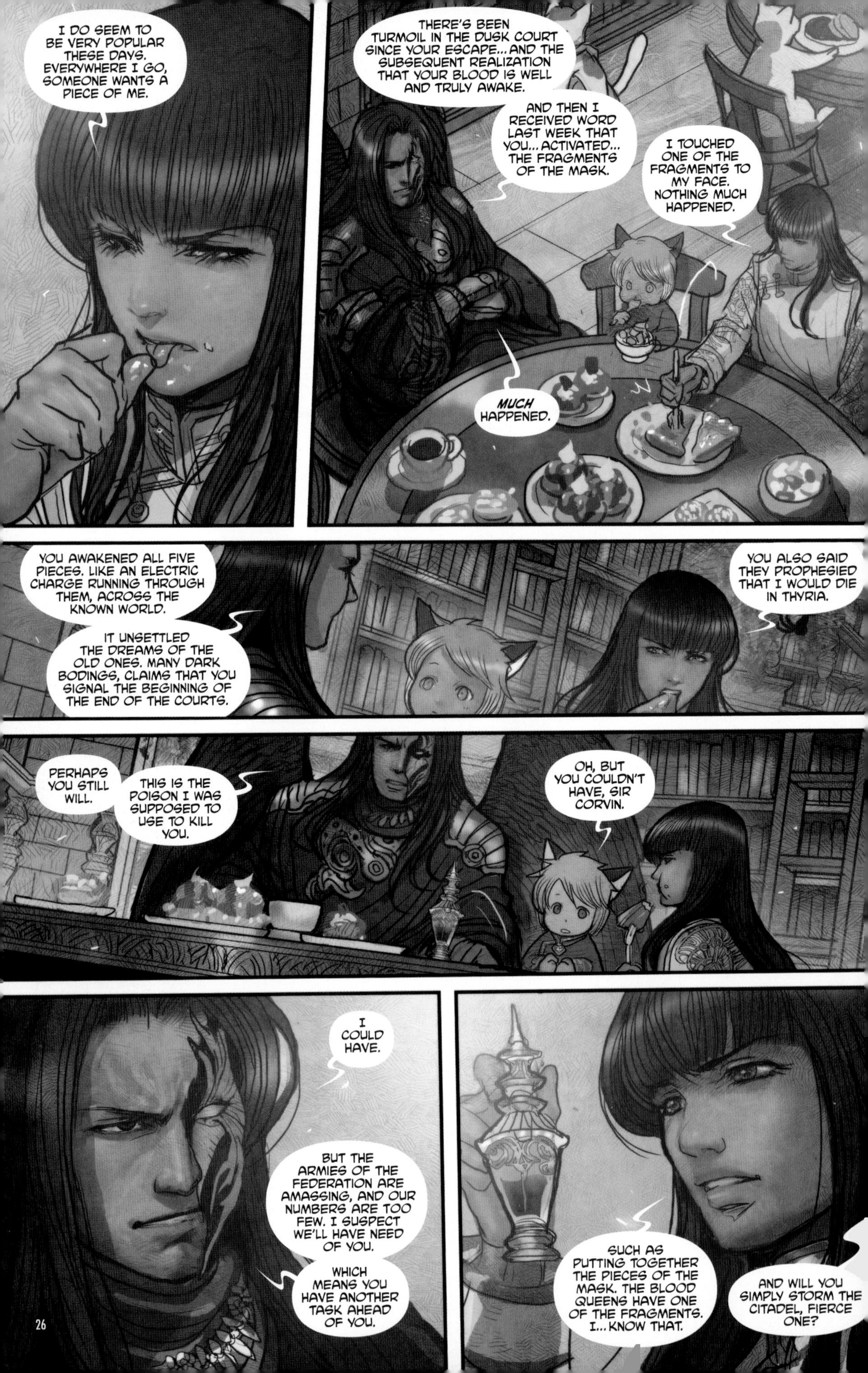

I DO SEEM TO BE VERY POPULAR THESE DAYS. EVERYWHERE I GO, SOMEONE WANTS A PIECE OF ME.
THERE'S BEEN TURMOIL IN THE DUSK COURT SINCE YOUR ESCAPE... AND THE SUBSEQUENT REALIZATION THAT YOUR BLOOD IS WELL AND TRULY AWAKE.
AND THEN I RECEIVED WORD LAST WEEK THAT YOU... ACTIVATED... THE FRAGMENTS OF THE MASK.
I TOUCHED ONE OF THE FRAGMENTS TO MY FACE. NOTHING MUCH HAPPENED.
MUCH HAPPENED.
YOU AWAKENED ALL FIVE PIECES. LIKE AN ELECTRIC CHARGE RUNNING THROUGH THEM, ACROSS THE KNOWN WORLD.
IT UNSETTLED THE DREAMS OF THE OLD ONES. MANY DARK BODINGS, CLAIMS THAT YOU SIGNAL THE BEGINNING OF THE END OF THE COURTS.
YOU ALSO SAID THEY PROPHESIED THAT I WOULD DIE IN THYRIA.
PERHAPS YOU STILL WILL.
THIS IS THE POISON I WAS SUPPOSED TO USE TO KILL YOU.
OH, BUT YOU COULDN'T HAVE, SIR CORVIN.
I COULD HAVE.
BUT THE ARMIES OF THE FEDERATION ARE AMASSING, AND OUR NUMBERS ARE TOO FEW. I SUSPECT WE'LL HAVE NEED OF YOU.
WHICH MEANS YOU HAVE ANOTHER TASK AHEAD OF YOU.
SUCH AS PUTTING TOGETHER THE PIECES OF THE MASK. THE BLOOD QUEENS HAVE ONE OF THE FRAGMENTS. I... KNOW THAT.
AND WILL YOU SIMPLY STORM THE CITADEL, FIERCE ONE?

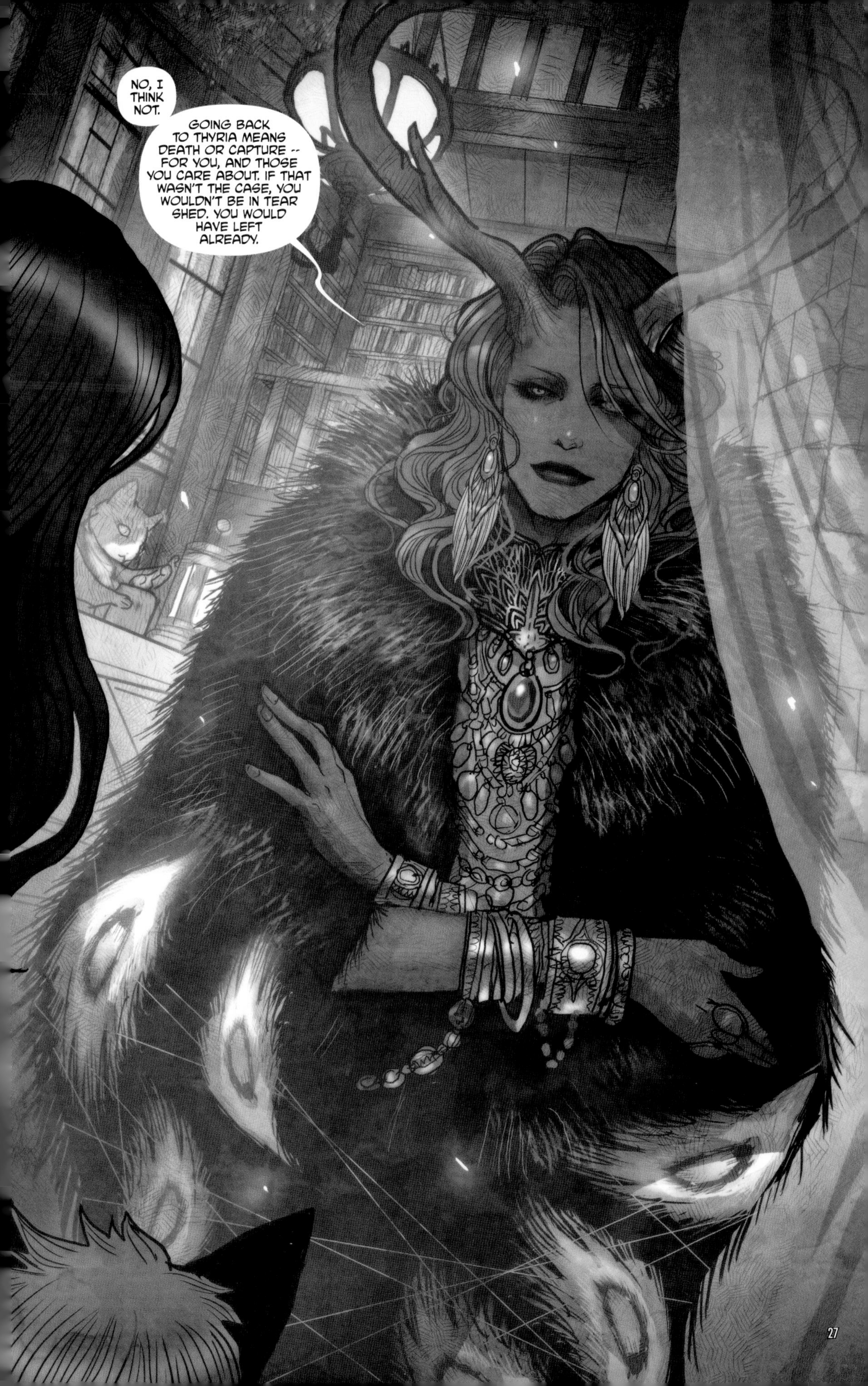
NO, I THINK NOT.
GOING BACK TO THYRIA MEANS DEATH OR CAPTURE -- FOR YOU, AND THOSE YOU CARE ABOUT. IF THAT WASN'T THE CASE, YOU WOULDN'T BE IN TEAR SHED. YOU WOULD HAVE LEFT ALREADY.

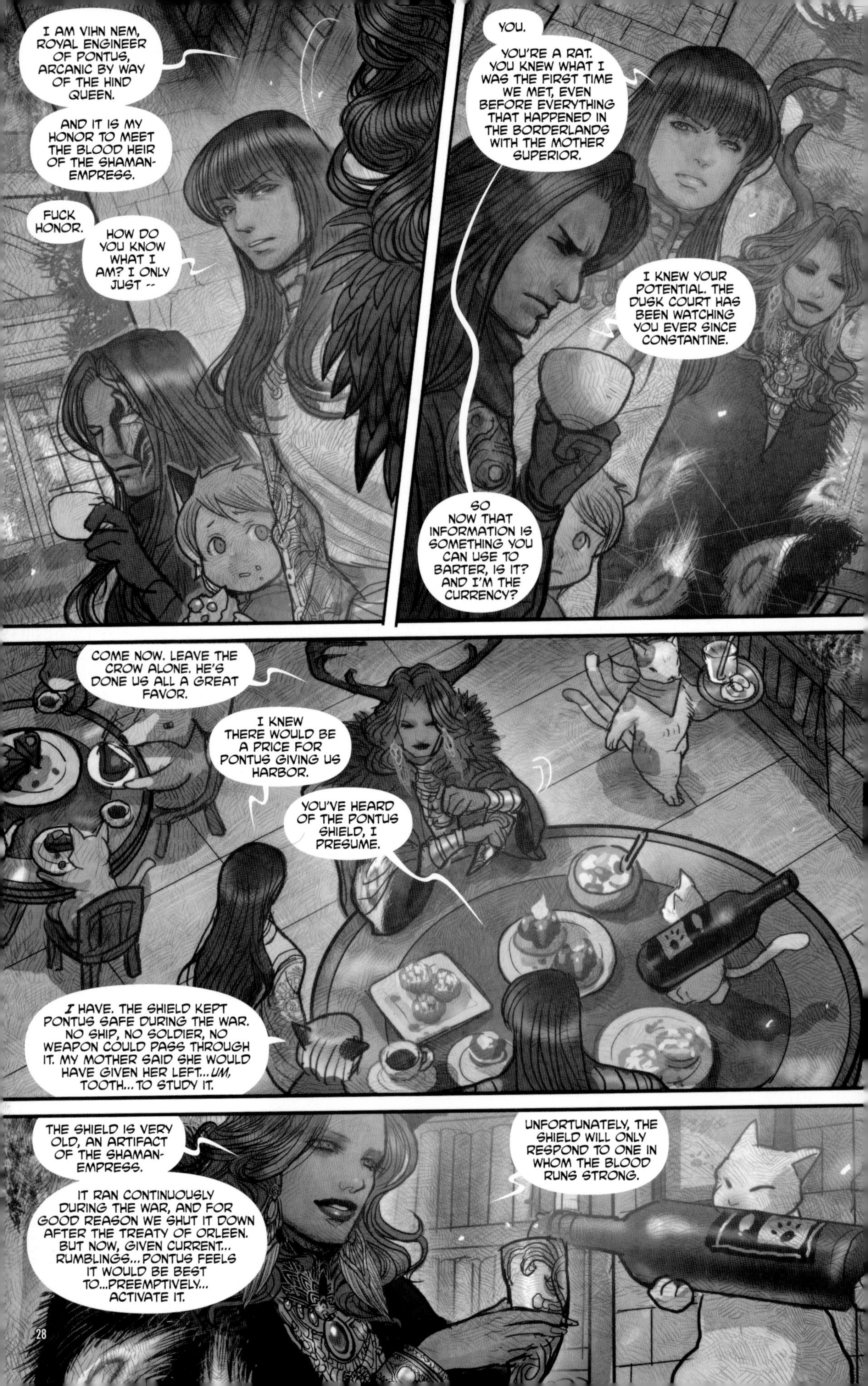

I AM VIHN NEM, ROYAL ENGINEER OF PONTUS, ARCANIC BY WAY OF THE HIND QUEEN.
AND IT IS MY HONOR TO MEET THE BLOOD HEIR OF THE SHAMAN-EMPRESS.
FUCK HONOR.
HOW DO YOU KNOW WHAT I AM? I ONLY JUST --
YOU.
YOU'RE A RAT. YOU KNEW WHAT I WAS THE FIRST TIME WE MET, EVEN BEFORE EVERYTHING THAT HAPPENED IN THE BORDERLANDS WITH THE MOTHER SUPERIOR.
I KNEW YOUR POTENTIAL. THE DUSK COURT HAS BEEN WATCHING YOU EVER SINCE CONSTANTINE.
SO NOW THAT INFORMATION IS SOMETHING YOU CAN USE TO BARTER, IS IT? AND I'M THE CURRENCY?
COME NOW. LEAVE THE CROW ALONE. HE'S DONE US ALL A GREAT FAVOR.
I KNEW THERE WOULD BE A PRICE FOR PONTUS GIVING US HARBOR.
YOU'VE HEARD OF THE PONTUS SHIELD, I PRESUME.
I HAVE. THE SHIELD KEPT PONTUS SAFE DURING THE WAR. NO SHIP, NO SOLDIER, NO WEAPON COULD PASS THROUGH IT. MY MOTHER SAID SHE WOULD HAVE GIVEN HER LEFT...*UM*, TOOTH...TO STUDY IT.
THE SHIELD IS VERY OLD, AN ARTIFACT OF THE SHAMAN-EMPRESS.
IT RAN CONTINUOUSLY DURING THE WAR, AND FOR GOOD REASON WE SHUT IT DOWN AFTER THE TREATY OF ORLEEN. BUT NOW, GIVEN CURRENT... RUMBLINGS...PONTUS FEELS IT WOULD BE BEST TO...PREEMPTIVELY... ACTIVATE IT.
UNFORTUNATELY, THE SHIELD WILL ONLY RESPOND TO ONE IN WHOM THE BLOOD RUNS STRONG.

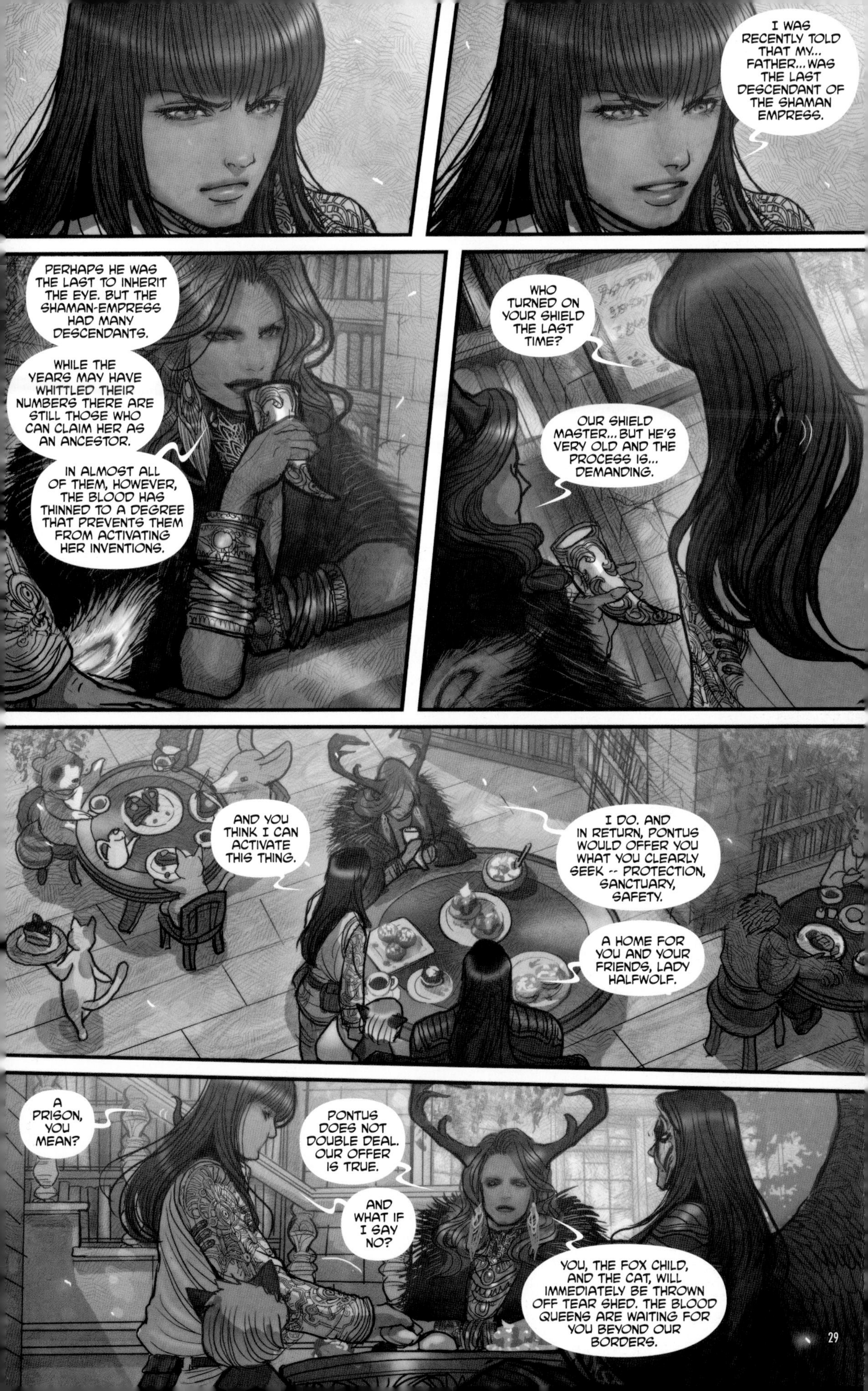
I WAS RECENTLY TOLD THAT MY... FATHER...WAS THE LAST DESCENDANT OF THE SHAMAN EMPRESS.
PERHAPS HE WAS THE LAST TO INHERIT THE EYE. BUT THE SHAMAN-EMPRESS HAD MANY DESCENDANTS.
WHILE THE YEARS MAY HAVE WHITTLED THEIR NUMBERS THERE ARE STILL THOSE WHO CAN CLAIM HER AS AN ANCESTOR.
IN ALMOST ALL OF THEM, HOWEVER, THE BLOOD HAS THINNED TO A DEGREE THAT PREVENTS THEM FROM ACTIVATING HER INVENTIONS.
WHO TURNED ON YOUR SHIELD THE LAST TIME?
OUR SHIELD MASTER... BUT HE'S VERY OLD AND THE PROCESS IS... DEMANDING.
AND YOU THINK I CAN ACTIVATE THIS THING.
I DO. AND IN RETURN, PONTUS WOULD OFFER YOU WHAT YOU CLEARLY SEEK -- PROTECTION, SANCTUARY, SAFETY.
A HOME FOR YOU AND YOUR FRIENDS, LADY HALFWOLF.
A PRISON, YOU MEAN?
PONTUS DOES NOT DOUBLE DEAL. OUR OFFER IS TRUE.
AND WHAT IF I SAY NO?
YOU, THE FOX CHILD, AND THE CAT, WILL IMMEDIATELY BE THROWN OFF TEAR SHED. THE BLOOD QUEENS ARE WAITING FOR YOU BEYOND OUR BORDERS.

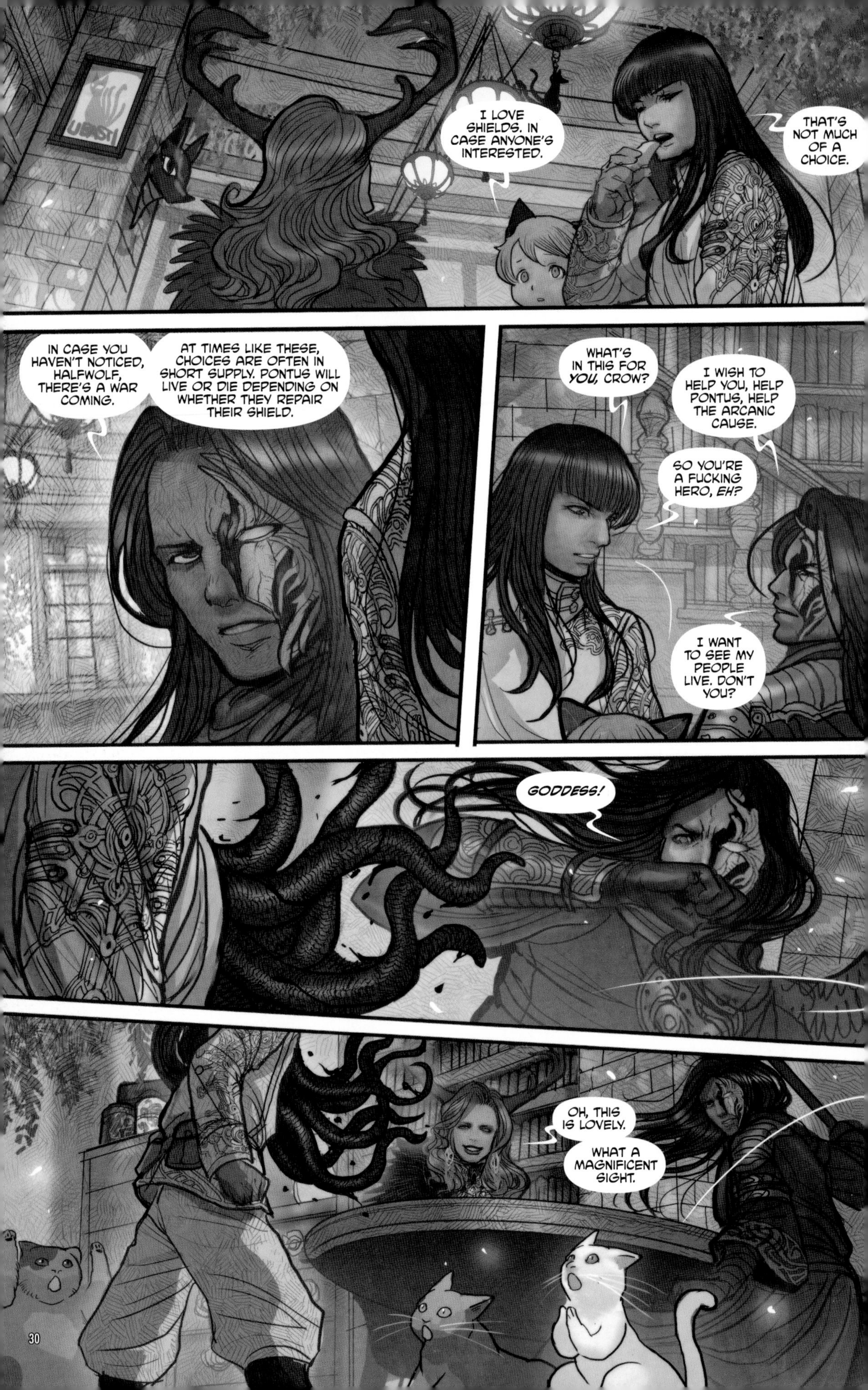
UBASTI
I LOVE SHIELDS. IN CASE ANYONE'S INTERESTED.
THAT'S NOT MUCH OF A CHOICE.
IN CASE YOU HAVEN'T NOTICED, HALFWOLF, THERE'S A WAR COMING.
AT TIMES LIKE THESE, CHOICES ARE OFTEN IN SHORT SUPPLY. PONTUS WILL LIVE OR DIE DEPENDING ON WHETHER THEY REPAIR THEIR SHIELD.
WHAT'S IN THIS FOR *YOU,* CROW?
I WISH TO HELP YOU, HELP PONTUS, HELP THE ARCANIC CAUSE.
SO YOU'RE A FUCKING HERO, *EH?*
I WANT TO SEE MY PEOPLE LIVE. DON'T YOU?
GODDESS!
OH, THIS IS LOVELY.
WHAT A MAGNIFICENT SIGHT.

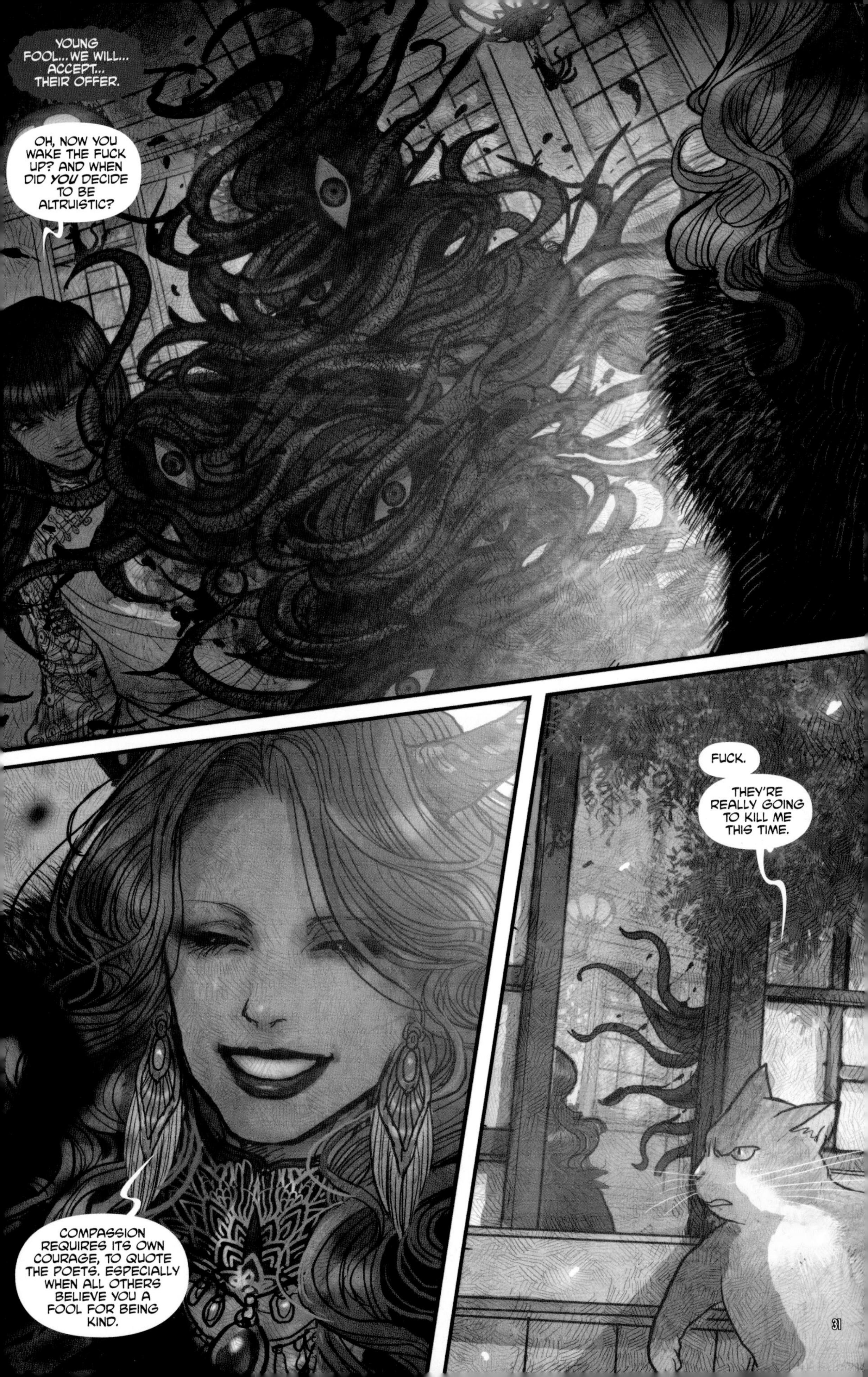
YOUNG FOOL...WE WILL... ACCEPT... THEIR OFFER.
OH, NOW YOU WAKE THE FUCK UP? AND WHEN DID *YOU* DECIDE TO BE ALTRUISTIC?
COMPASSION REQUIRES ITS OWN COURAGE, TO QUOTE THE POETS. ESPECIALLY WHEN ALL OTHERS BELIEVE YOU A FOOL FOR BEING KIND.
FUCK.
THEY'RE REALLY GOING TO KILL ME THIS TIME.

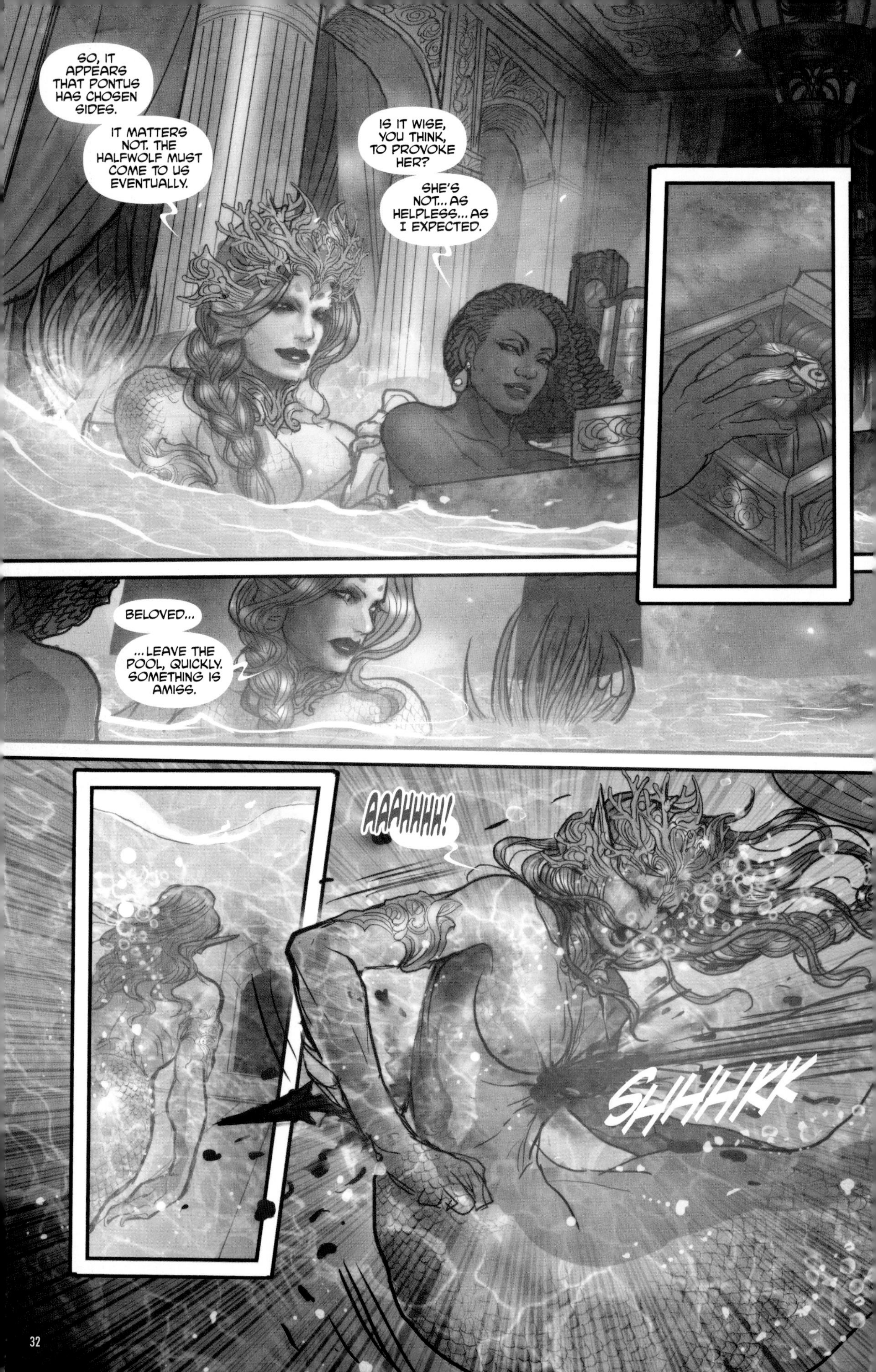
SO, IT APPEARS THAT PONTUS HAS CHOSEN SIDES.
IT MATTERS NOT. THE HALFWOLF MUST COME TO US EVENTUALLY.
IS IT WISE, YOU THINK, TO PROVOKE HER?
SHE'S NOT... AS HELPLESS... AS I EXPECTED.
BELOVED...
...LEAVE THE POOL, QUICKLY. SOMETHING IS AMISS.
AAAHHHH!
SHHHKK

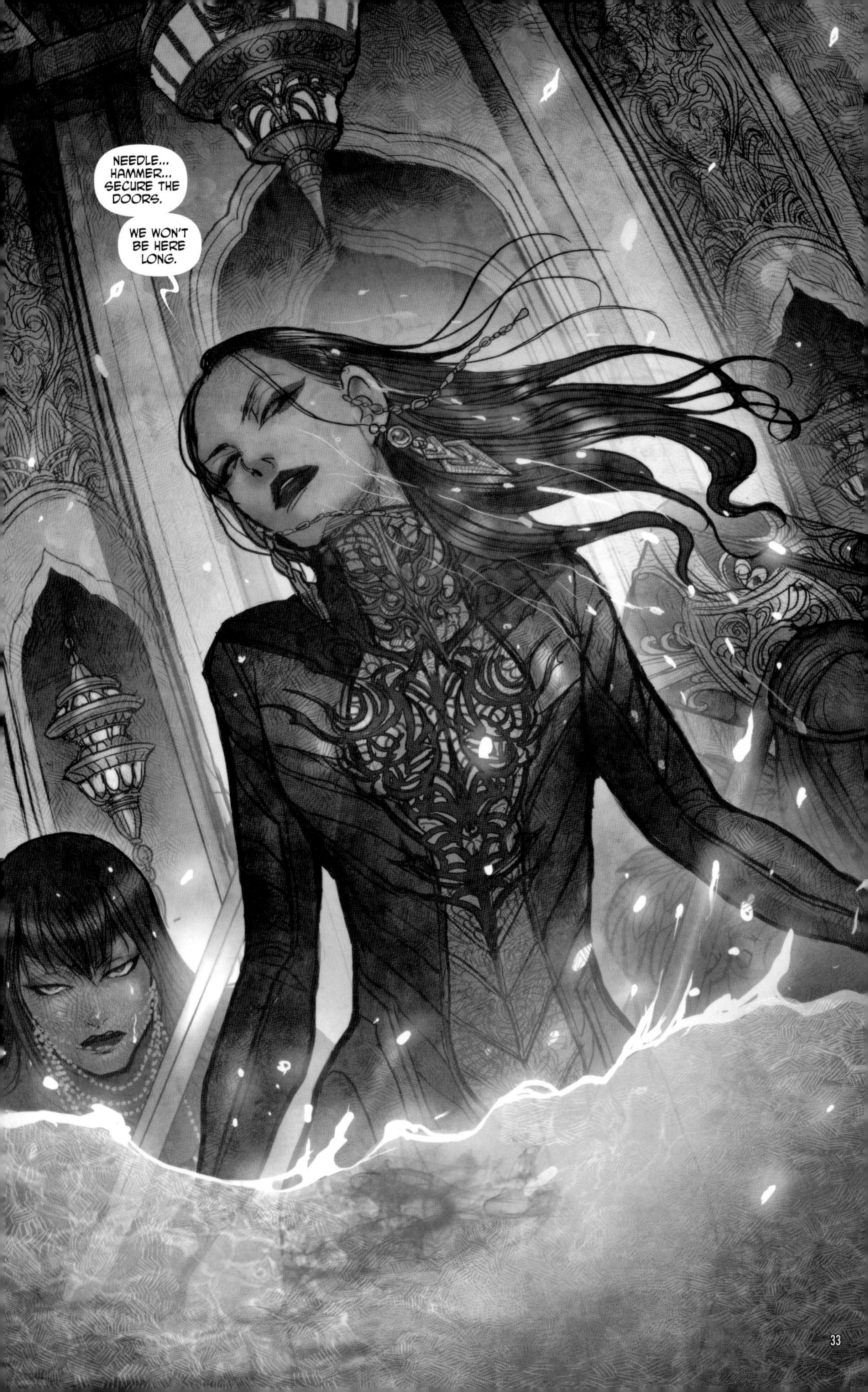
NEEDLE... HAMMER... SECURE THE DOORS.
WE WON'T BE HERE LONG.

An excerpt of a lecture from the esteemed **Professor Tam Tam,** former First Record-Keeper of the Is'hami Temple, and learned contemporary of Namron Black Claw...

It would be a lie to say that the Poets are impartial witnesses to history, though they strive to be exact and sincere, unbiased by resentment and faithful to the truth.

Poets, for all their training and blessings from Ubasti, are still, after all, cats. And cats have been known to tell pleasant lies about ourselves, particularly to outsiders.

Humans and Arcanics, however, are far less willing to record uncomfortable truths, to sit even for a moment with that which is difficult. And so, much is erased – and forgotten.

Consider the fact that the Warlord, Sword of the East, had a twin sister: Moriko Halfwolf, the Blade of Dawn, and the favorite of her mother, the Queen of Wolves.

Another missing fact from the Arcanic histories: both twins were blessed by the Ancestrals, both chosen to command the Arcanic armies as Warlords.

As the eldest, Moriko was the first blessed – and would have made a superior Warlord. She was powerful of mind, impossible to fool, and a ruthless strategist. More vitally, Moriko was favored by their mother.

The younger sister, however, was not without her merits; she was a great warrior, supremely confident, and her hatred of the humans was legendary. She had one other advantage: she looked Arcanic, and tellingly, her older sister did not.

It would be simplistic to argue that the younger sister's appearance alone made her more popular with the people of the Dawn Court. But it would be downright foolish to say it played no part. Moriko might have had the Queen's heart, but her younger sister had their people's.

The Poet assigned to the court, Arkus Furfar, predicted a dire future in which civil war might break out between the sisters and their supporters. But something else happened instead, something strange and unexpected, the sort of contingency for which a Poet must always be prepared.

Moriko, ever the scholar, discovered something in one of the Dawn Court's hidden archives. The Poets never located the precise document, but it changed the trajectory of Moriko's life.

She not only resigned her commission, she abandoned the Dawn Court altogether and began to obsessively search the old ruins of the Shaman-Empress.

The Queen of Wolves held out hope that Moriko might soon return, but her eldest daughter never again set foot in the Dawn Court.

Two years after she absconded, her sister was named Warlord, Sword of the East.

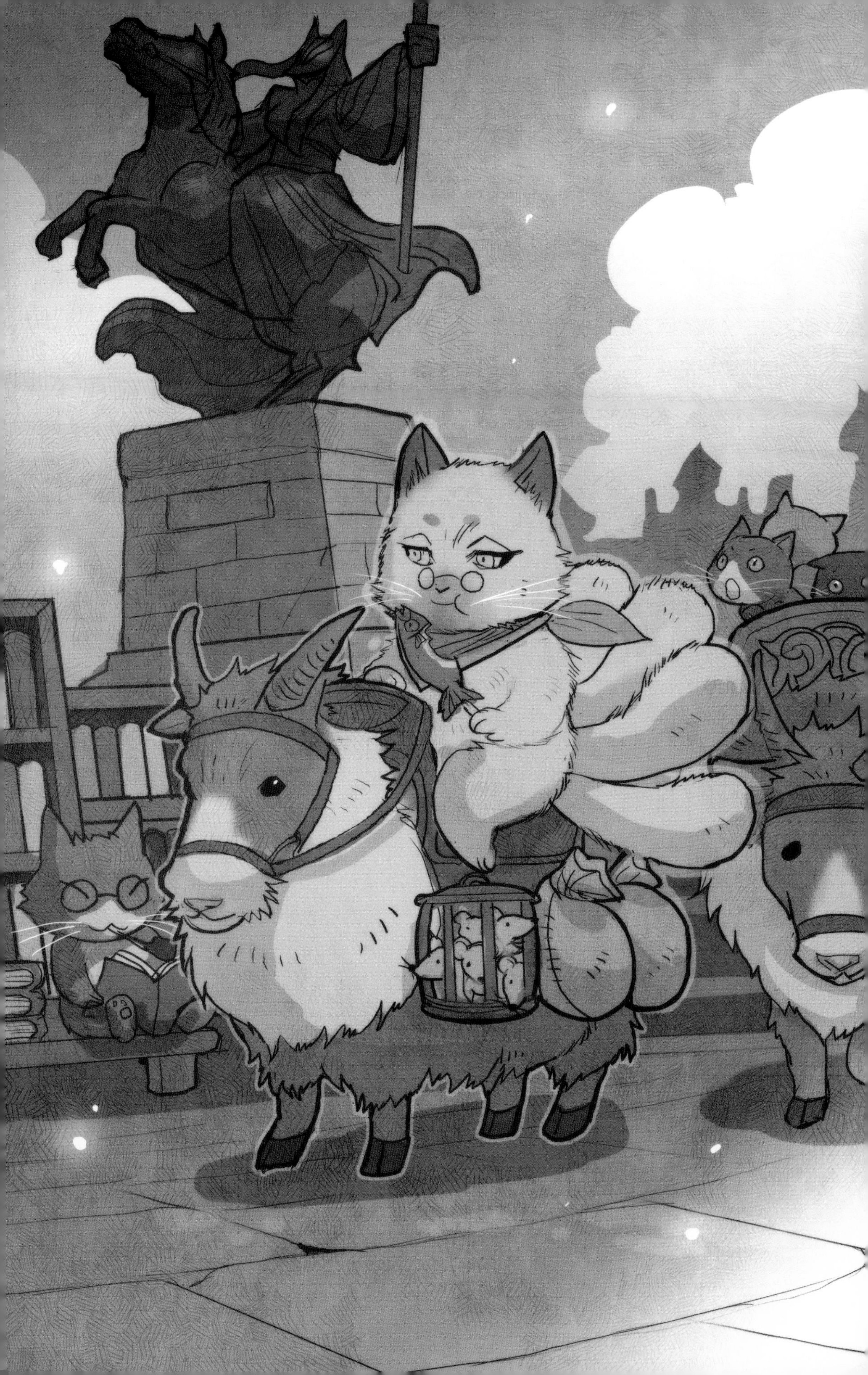

CHAPTER FOURTEEN

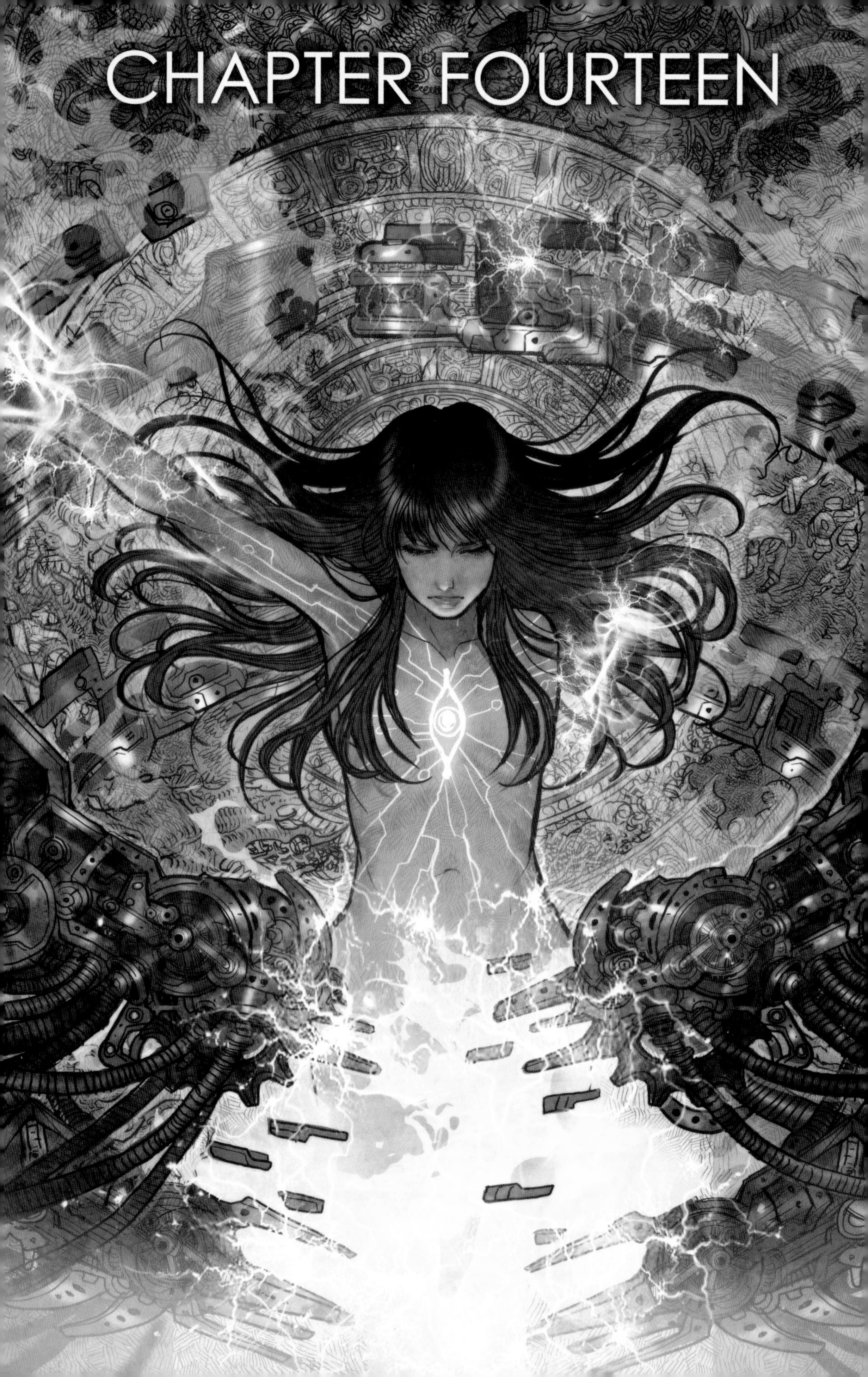

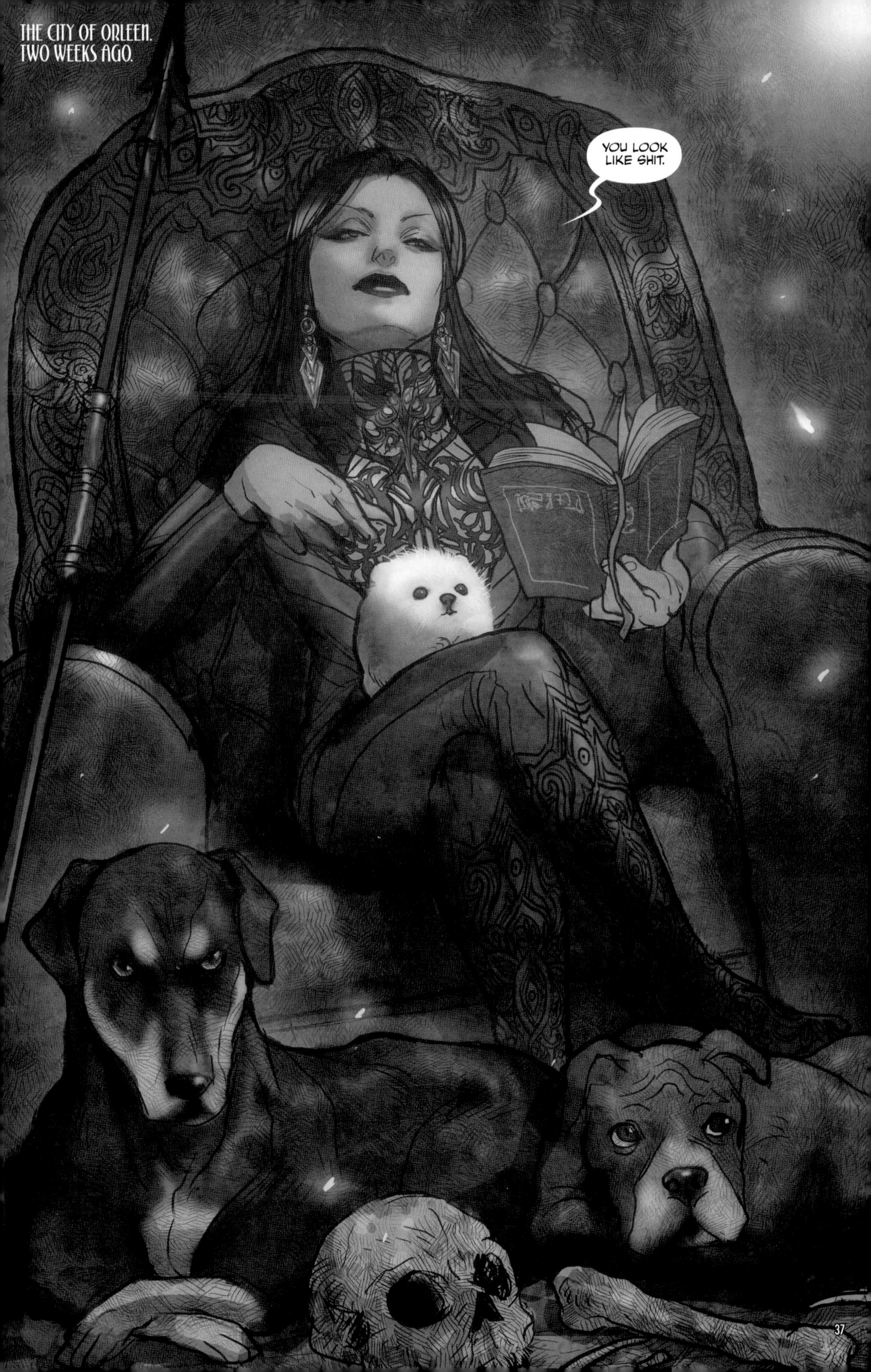
THE CITY OF ORLEEN.
TWO WEEKS AGO.
YOU LOOK LIKE SHIT.

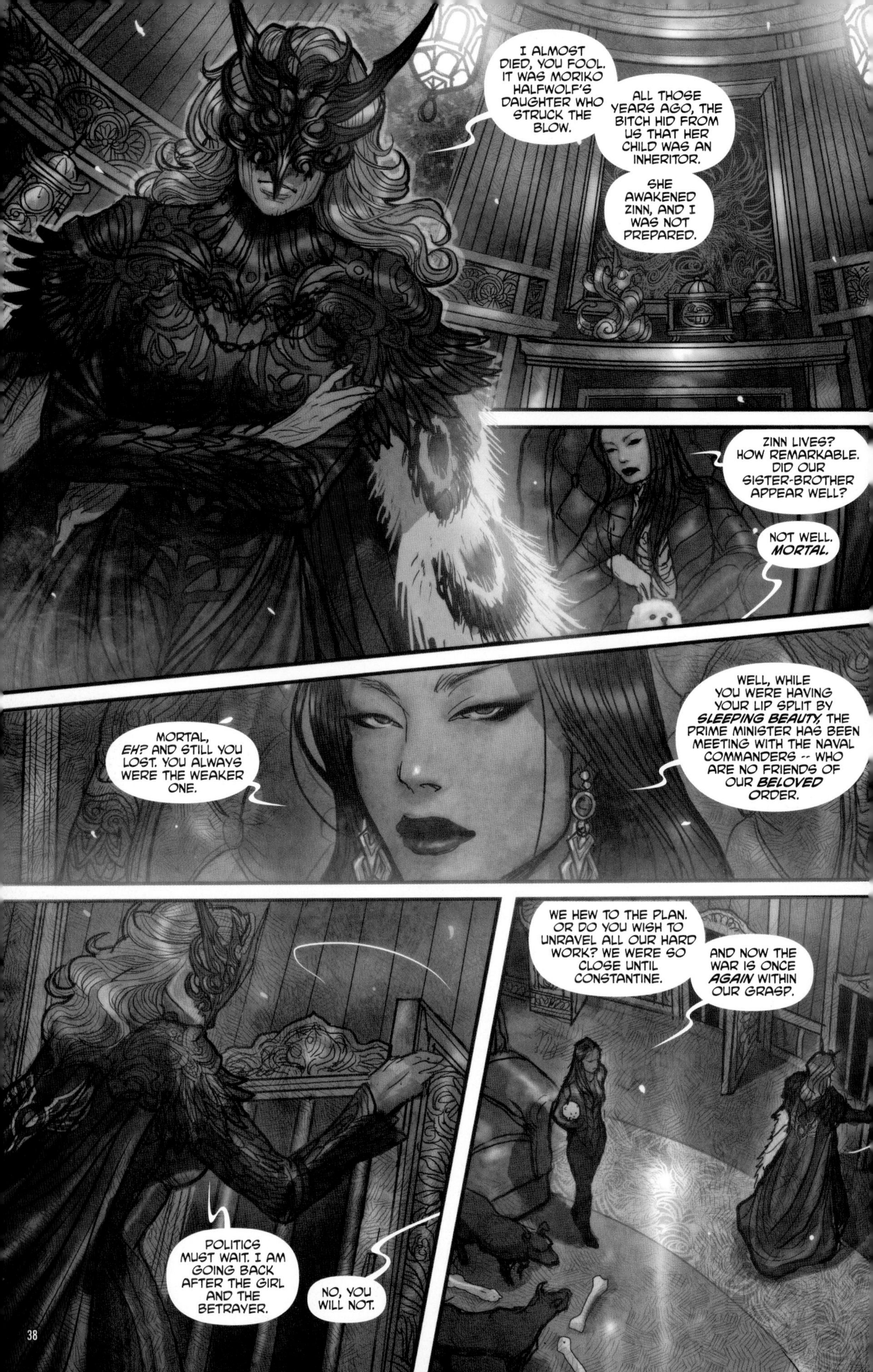
I ALMOST DIED, YOU FOOL. IT WAS MORIKO HALFWOLF'S DAUGHTER WHO STRUCK THE BLOW.
ALL THOSE YEARS AGO, THE BITCH HID FROM US THAT HER CHILD WAS AN INHERITOR.
SHE AWAKENED ZINN, AND I WAS NOT PREPARED.
ZINN LIVES? HOW REMARKABLE. DID OUR SISTER-BROTHER APPEAR WELL?
NOT WELL. *MORTAL.*
MORTAL, *EH?* AND STILL YOU LOST. YOU ALWAYS WERE THE WEAKER ONE.
WELL, WHILE YOU WERE HAVING YOUR LIP SPLIT BY *SLEEPING BEAUTY,* THE PRIME MINISTER HAS BEEN MEETING WITH THE NAVAL COMMANDERS -- WHO ARE NO FRIENDS OF OUR *BELOVED* ORDER.
POLITICS MUST WAIT. I AM GOING BACK AFTER THE GIRL AND THE BETRAYER.
NO, YOU WILL NOT.
WE HEW TO THE PLAN. OR DO YOU WISH TO UNRAVEL ALL OUR HARD WORK? WE WERE SO CLOSE UNTIL CONSTANTINE.
AND NOW THE WAR IS ONCE *AGAIN* WITHIN OUR GRASP.

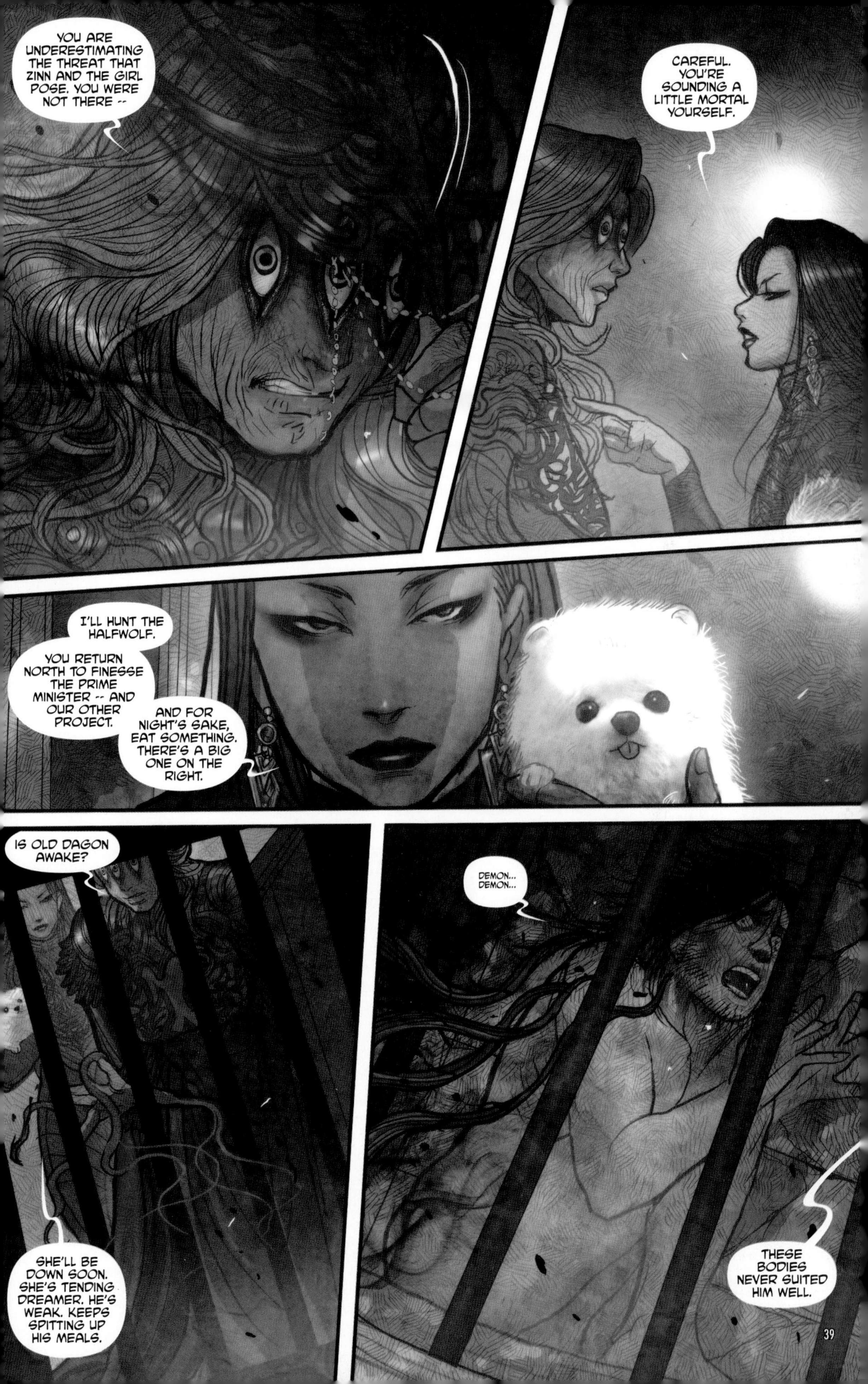
YOU ARE UNDERESTIMATING THE THREAT THAT ZINN AND THE GIRL POSE. YOU WERE NOT THERE --
CAREFUL. YOU'RE SOUNDING A LITTLE MORTAL YOURSELF.
I'LL HUNT THE HALFWOLF.
YOU RETURN NORTH TO FINESSE THE PRIME MINISTER -- AND OUR OTHER PROJECT.
AND FOR NIGHT'S SAKE, EAT SOMETHING. THERE'S A BIG ONE ON THE RIGHT.
IS OLD DAGON AWAKE?
SHE'LL BE DOWN SOON. SHE'S TENDING DREAMER. HE'S WEAK. KEEPS SPITTING UP HIS MEALS.
DEMON... DEMON...
THESE BODIES NEVER SUITED HIM WELL.

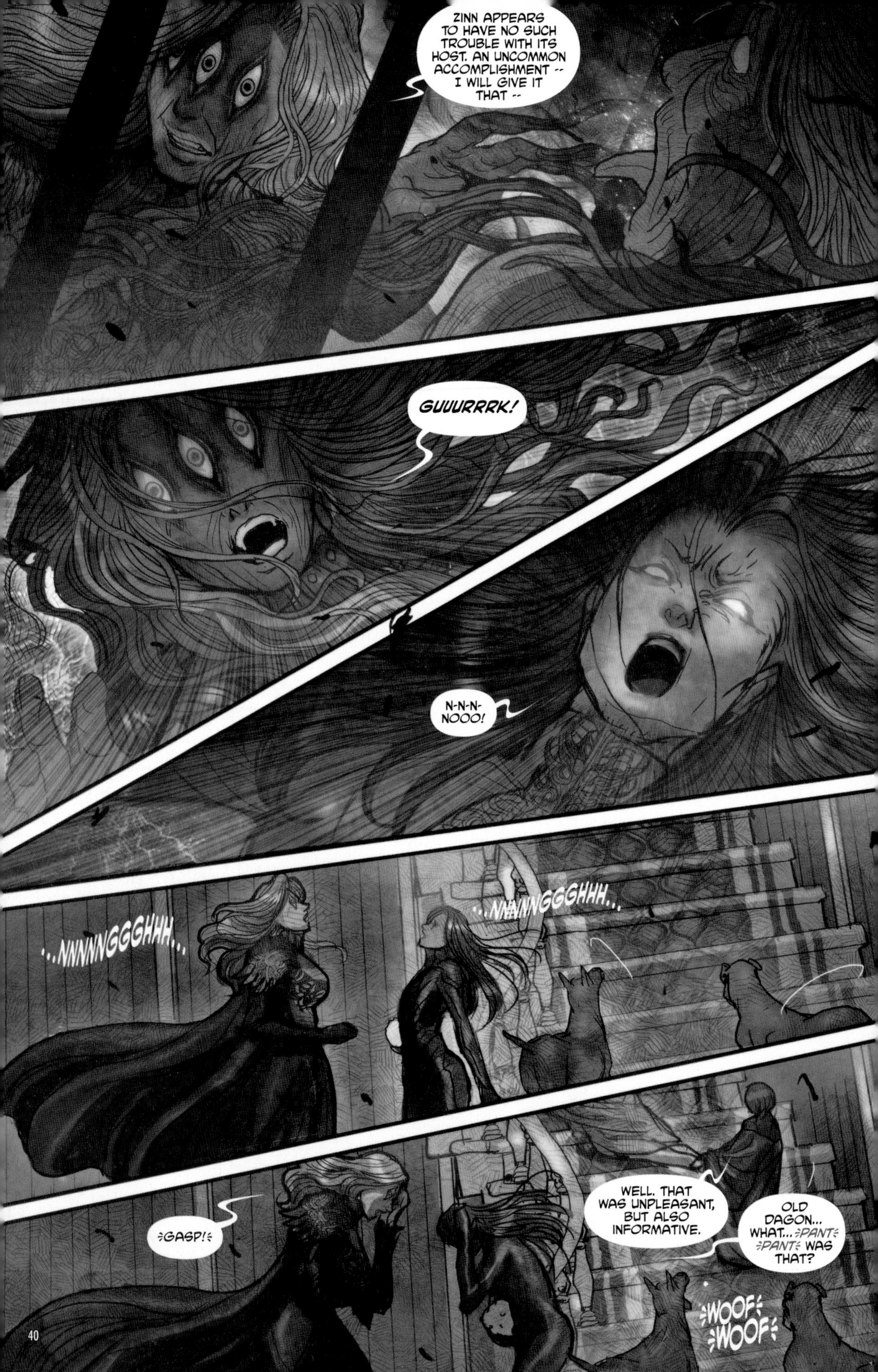
ZINN APPEARS TO HAVE NO SUCH TROUBLE WITH ITS HOST. AN UNCOMMON ACCOMPLISHMENT -- I WILL GIVE IT THAT --
GUUURRRK!
N-N-N-NOOO!
...NNNNNGGGHHH...
...NNNNNGGGHHH...
GASP!
WELL. THAT WAS UNPLEASANT, BUT ALSO INFORMATIVE.
OLD DAGON... WHAT... PANT PANT WAS THAT?
WOOF WOOF

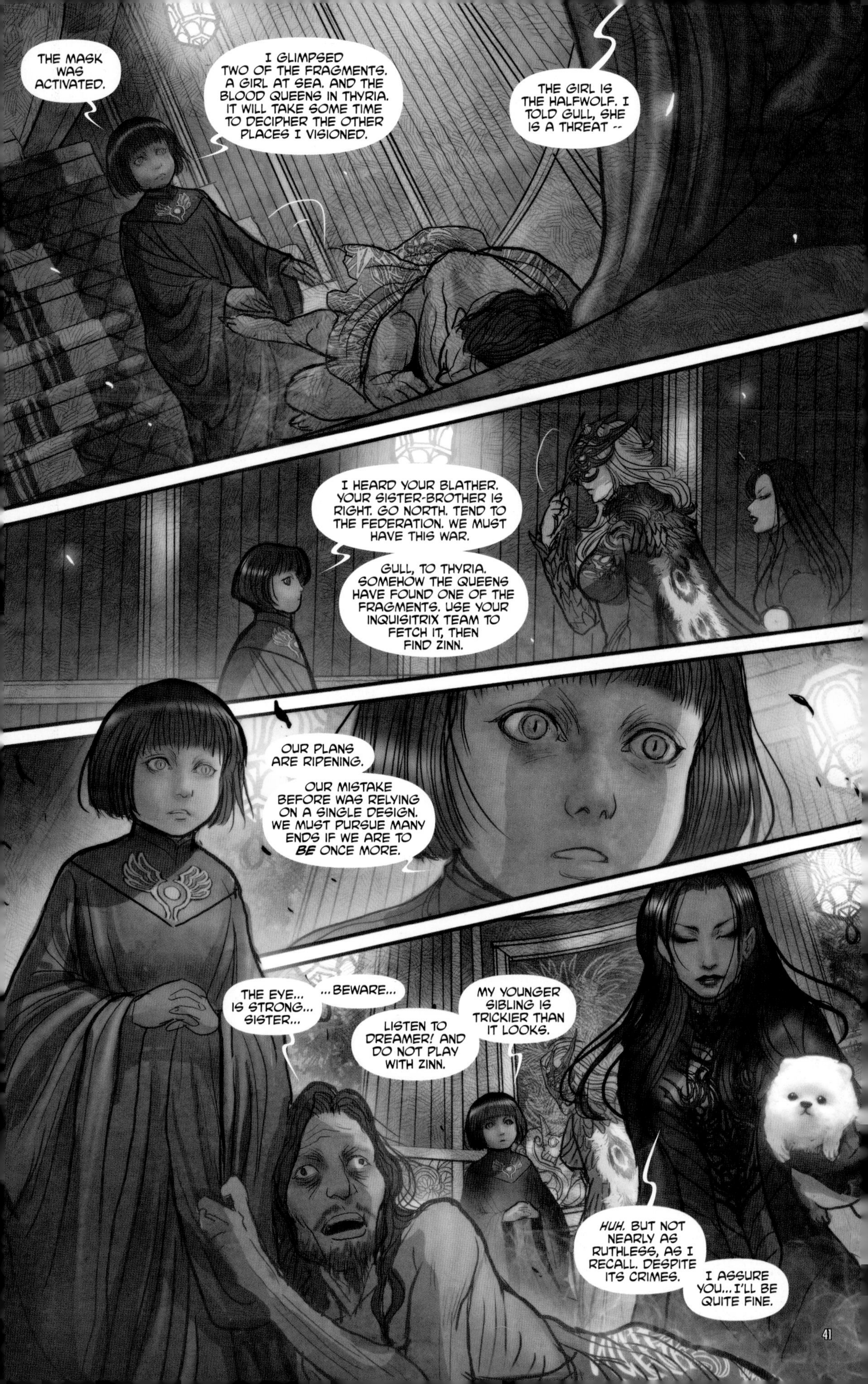
THE MASK WAS ACTIVATED.
I GLIMPSED TWO OF THE FRAGMENTS. A GIRL AT SEA. AND THE BLOOD QUEENS IN THYRIA. IT WILL TAKE SOME TIME TO DECIPHER THE OTHER PLACES I VISIONED.
THE GIRL IS THE HALFWOLF. I TOLD GULL, SHE IS A THREAT --
I HEARD YOUR BLATHER. YOUR SISTER-BROTHER IS RIGHT. GO NORTH. TEND TO THE FEDERATION. WE MUST HAVE THIS WAR.
GULL, TO THYRIA. SOMEHOW THE QUEENS HAVE FOUND ONE OF THE FRAGMENTS. USE YOUR INQUISITRIX TEAM TO FETCH IT, THEN FIND ZINN.
OUR PLANS ARE RIPENING.
OUR MISTAKE BEFORE WAS RELYING ON A SINGLE DESIGN. WE MUST PURSUE MANY ENDS IF WE ARE TO ***BE*** ONCE MORE.
THE EYE... IS STRONG... SISTER...
...BEWARE...
LISTEN TO DREAMER! AND DO NOT PLAY WITH ZINN.
MY YOUNGER SIBLING IS TRICKIER THAN IT LOOKS.
HUH. BUT NOT NEARLY AS RUTHLESS, AS I RECALL. DESPITE ITS CRIMES.
I ASSURE YOU... I'LL BE QUITE FINE.

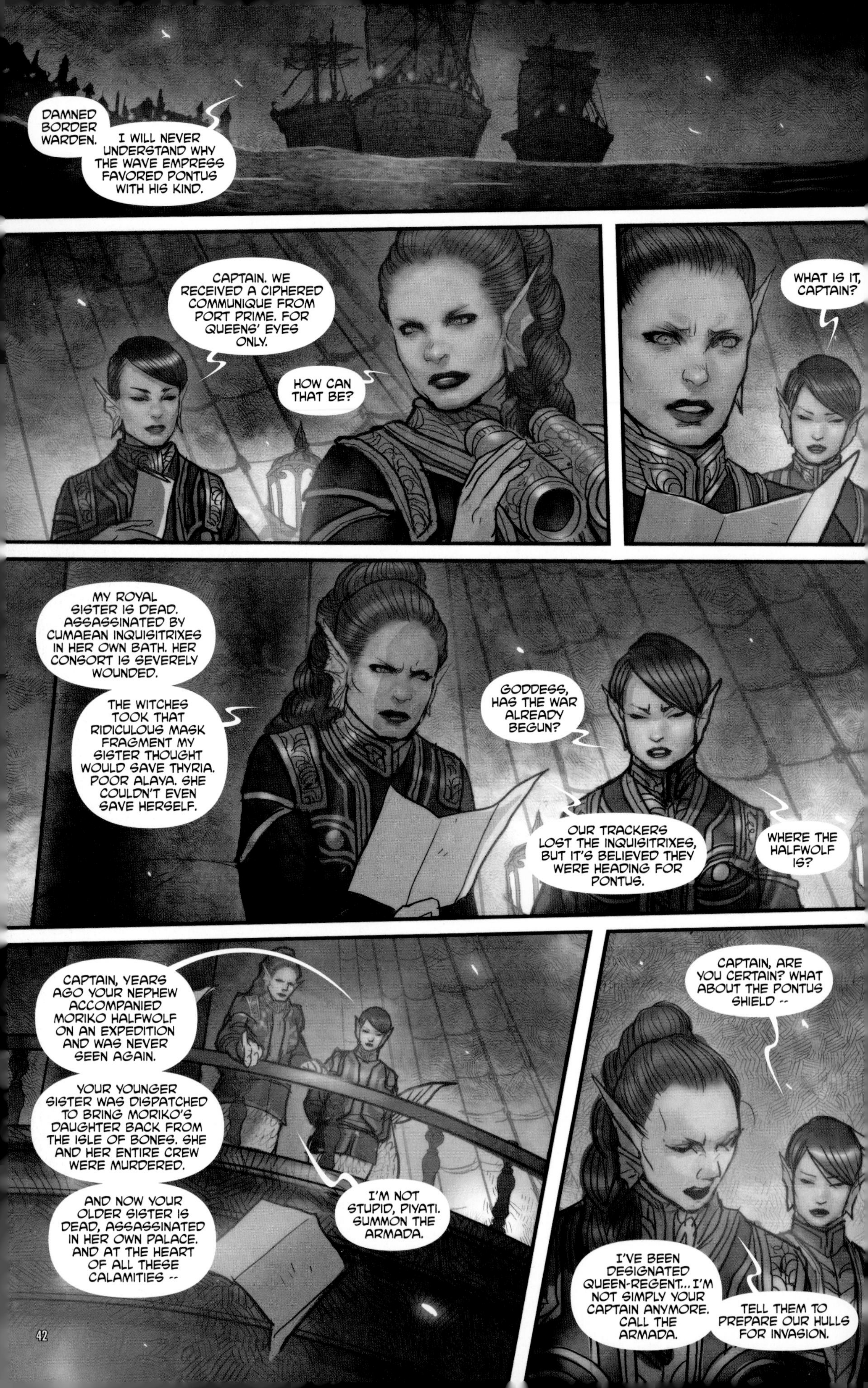
DAMNED BORDER WARDEN.
I WILL NEVER UNDERSTAND WHY THE WAVE EMPRESS FAVORED PONTUS WITH HIS KIND.
CAPTAIN. WE RECEIVED A CIPHERED COMMUNIQUE FROM PORT PRIME. FOR QUEENS' EYES ONLY.
HOW CAN THAT BE?
WHAT IS IT, CAPTAIN?
MY ROYAL SISTER IS DEAD. ASSASSINATED BY CUMAEAN INQUISITRIXES IN HER OWN BATH. HER CONSORT IS SEVERELY WOUNDED.
THE WITCHES TOOK THAT RIDICULOUS MASK FRAGMENT MY SISTER THOUGHT WOULD SAVE THYRIA. POOR ALAYA. SHE COULDN'T EVEN SAVE HERSELF.
GODDESS, HAS THE WAR ALREADY BEGUN?
OUR TRACKERS LOST THE INQUISITRIXES, BUT IT'S BELIEVED THEY WERE HEADING FOR PONTUS.
WHERE THE HALFWOLF IS?
CAPTAIN, YEARS AGO YOUR NEPHEW ACCOMPANIED MORIKO HALFWOLF ON AN EXPEDITION AND WAS NEVER SEEN AGAIN.
YOUR YOUNGER SISTER WAS DISPATCHED TO BRING MORIKO'S DAUGHTER BACK FROM THE ISLE OF BONES. SHE AND HER ENTIRE CREW WERE MURDERED.
AND NOW YOUR OLDER SISTER IS DEAD, ASSASSINATED IN HER OWN PALACE. AND AT THE HEART OF ALL THESE CALAMITIES --
I'M NOT STUPID, PIYATI. SUMMON THE ARMADA.
CAPTAIN, ARE YOU CERTAIN? WHAT ABOUT THE PONTUS SHIELD --
I'VE BEEN DESIGNATED QUEEN-REGENT... I'M NOT SIMPLY YOUR CAPTAIN ANYMORE. CALL THE ARMADA.
TELL THEM TO PREPARE OUR HULLS FOR INVASION.

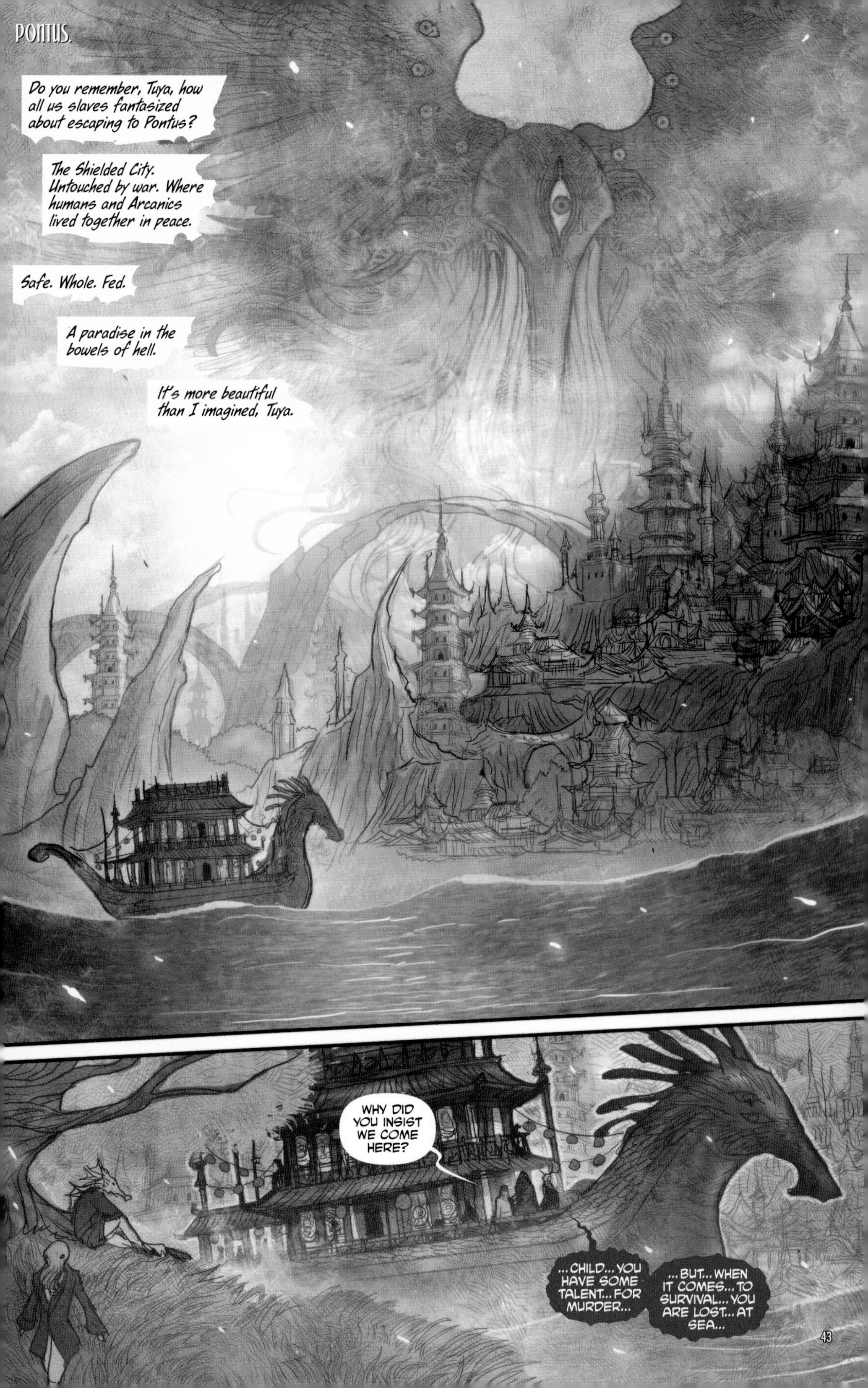
Do you remember, Tuya, how all us slaves fantasized about escaping to Pontus?
The Shielded City. Untouched by war. Where humans and Arcanics lived together in peace.
Safe. Whole. Fed.
A paradise in the bowels of hell.
It's more beautiful than I imagined, Tuya.
WHY DID YOU INSIST WE COME HERE?
...CHILD... YOU HAVE SOME TALENT... FOR MURDER...
...BUT... WHEN IT COMES... TO SURVIVAL... YOU ARE LOST... AT SEA...

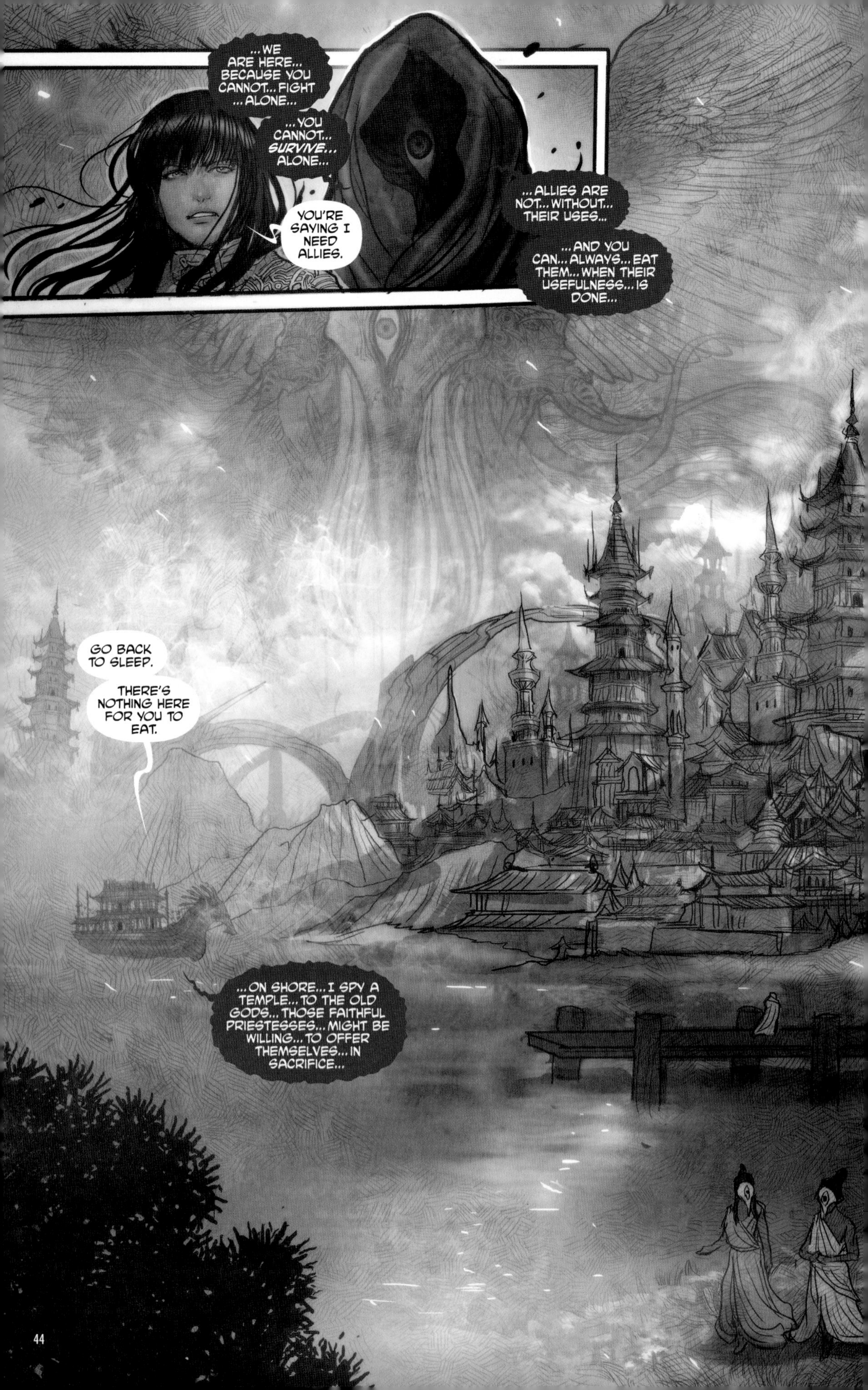
...WE ARE HERE... BECAUSE YOU CANNOT... FIGHT ...ALONE...
...YOU CANNOT... SURVIVE... ALONE...
YOU'RE SAYING I NEED ALLIES.
...ALLIES ARE NOT... WITHOUT... THEIR USES...
...AND YOU CAN... ALWAYS... EAT THEM... WHEN THEIR USEFULNESS... IS DONE...
GO BACK TO SLEEP.
THERE'S NOTHING HERE FOR YOU TO EAT.
...ON SHORE... I SPY A TEMPLE... TO THE OLD GODS... THOSE FAITHFUL PRIESTESSES... MIGHT BE WILLING... TO OFFER THEMSELVES... IN SACRIFICE...

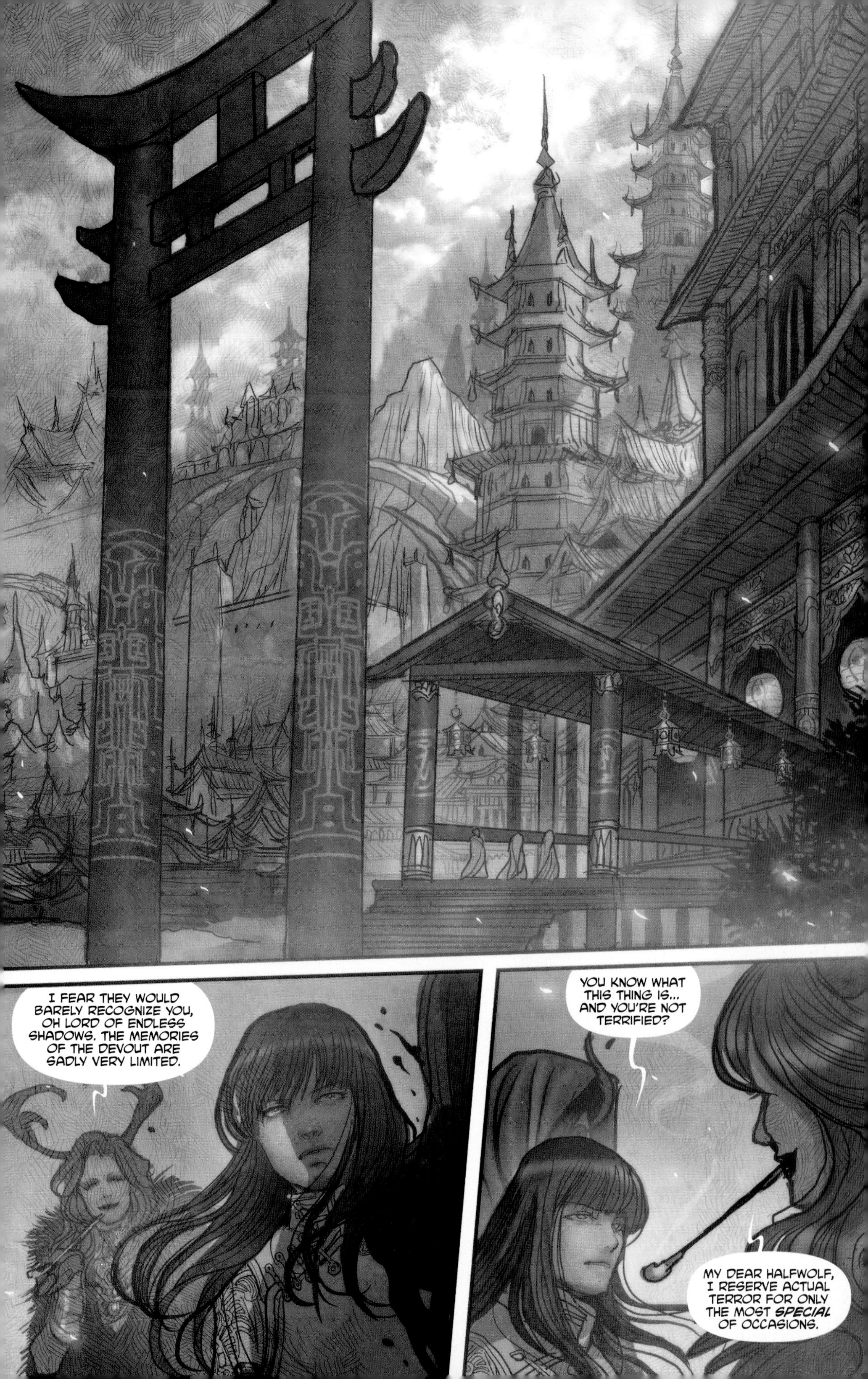
I FEAR THEY WOULD BARELY RECOGNIZE YOU, OH LORD OF ENDLESS SHADOWS. THE MEMORIES OF THE DEVOUT ARE SADLY VERY LIMITED.
YOU KNOW WHAT THIS THING IS... AND YOU'RE NOT TERRIFIED?
MY DEAR HALFWOLF, I RESERVE ACTUAL TERROR FOR ONLY THE MOST *SPECIAL* OF OCCASIONS.

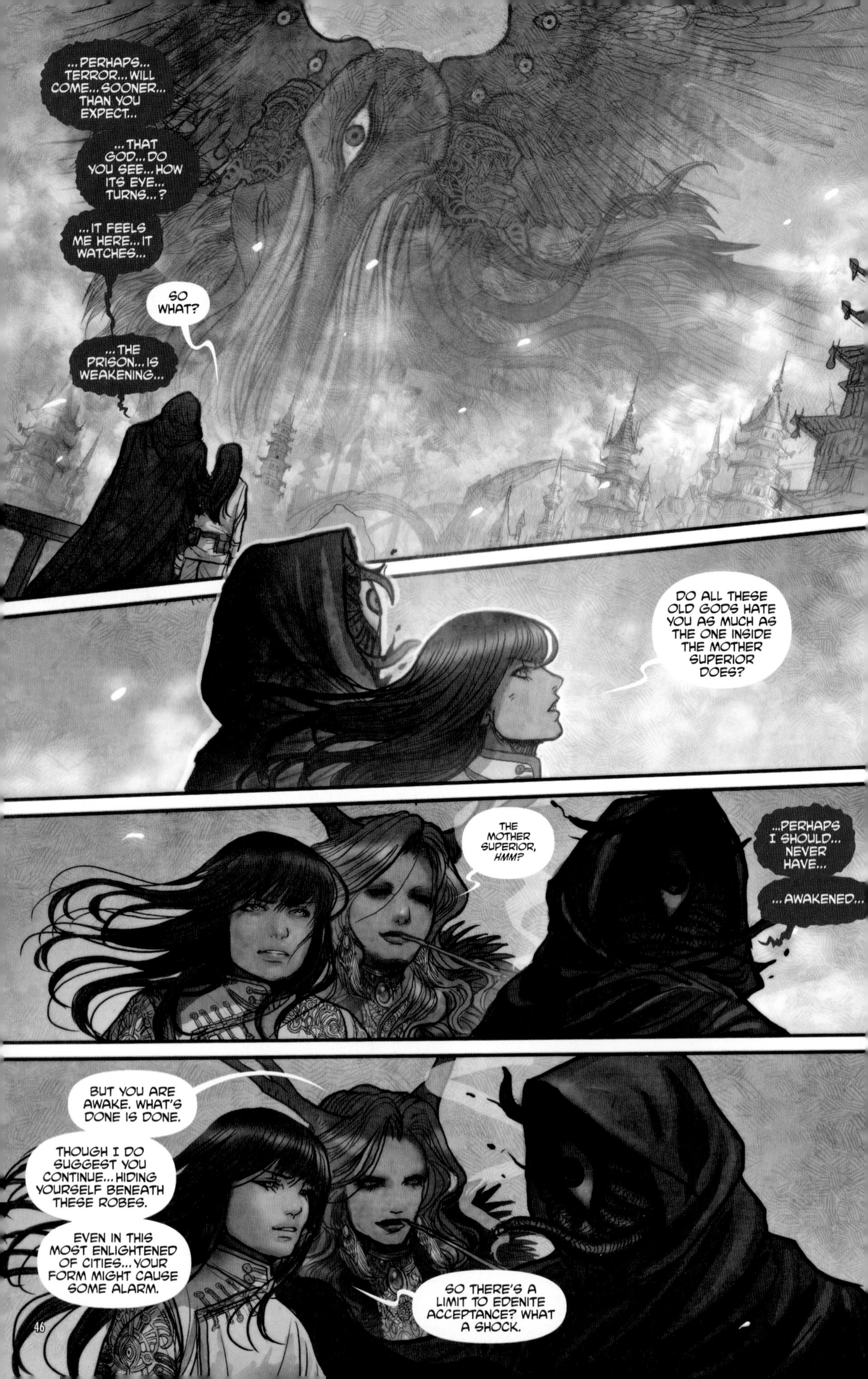

...PERHAPS... TERROR... WILL COME... SOONER... THAN YOU EXPECT...
...THAT GOD... DO YOU SEE... HOW ITS EYE... TURNS...?
...IT FEELS ME HERE... IT WATCHES...
SO WHAT?
...THE PRISON... IS WEAKENING...
DO ALL THESE OLD GODS HATE YOU AS MUCH AS THE ONE INSIDE THE MOTHER SUPERIOR DOES?
THE MOTHER SUPERIOR, HMM?
...PERHAPS I SHOULD... NEVER HAVE...
...AWAKENED...
BUT YOU ARE AWAKE. WHAT'S DONE IS DONE.
THOUGH I DO SUGGEST YOU CONTINUE... HIDING YOURSELF BENEATH THESE ROBES.
EVEN IN THIS MOST ENLIGHTENED OF CITIES... YOUR FORM MIGHT CAUSE SOME ALARM.
SO THERE'S A LIMIT TO EDENITE ACCEPTANCE? WHAT A SHOCK.

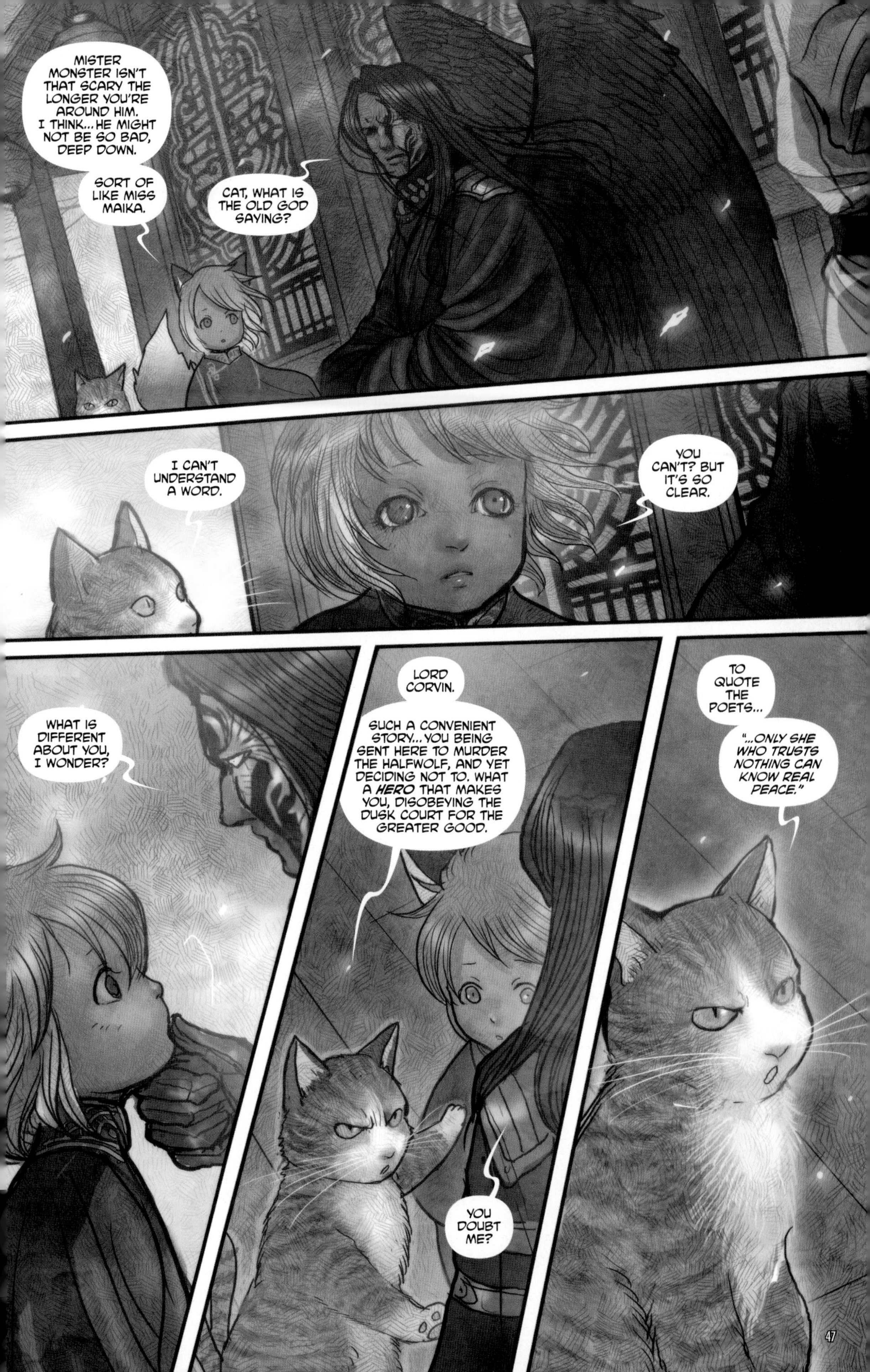
MISTER MONSTER ISN'T THAT SCARY THE LONGER YOU'RE AROUND HIM. I THINK... HE MIGHT NOT BE SO BAD, DEEP DOWN.
SORT OF LIKE MISS MAIKA.
CAT, WHAT IS THE OLD GOD SAYING?
I CAN'T UNDERSTAND A WORD.
YOU CAN'T? BUT IT'S SO CLEAR.
WHAT IS DIFFERENT ABOUT YOU, I WONDER?
LORD CORVIN.
SUCH A CONVENIENT STORY... YOU BEING SENT HERE TO MURDER THE HALFWOLF, AND YET DECIDING NOT TO. WHAT A *HERO* THAT MAKES YOU, DISOBEYING THE DUSK COURT FOR THE GREATER GOOD.
YOU DOUBT ME?
TO QUOTE THE POETS...
"...ONLY SHE WHO TRUSTS NOTHING CAN KNOW REAL PEACE."

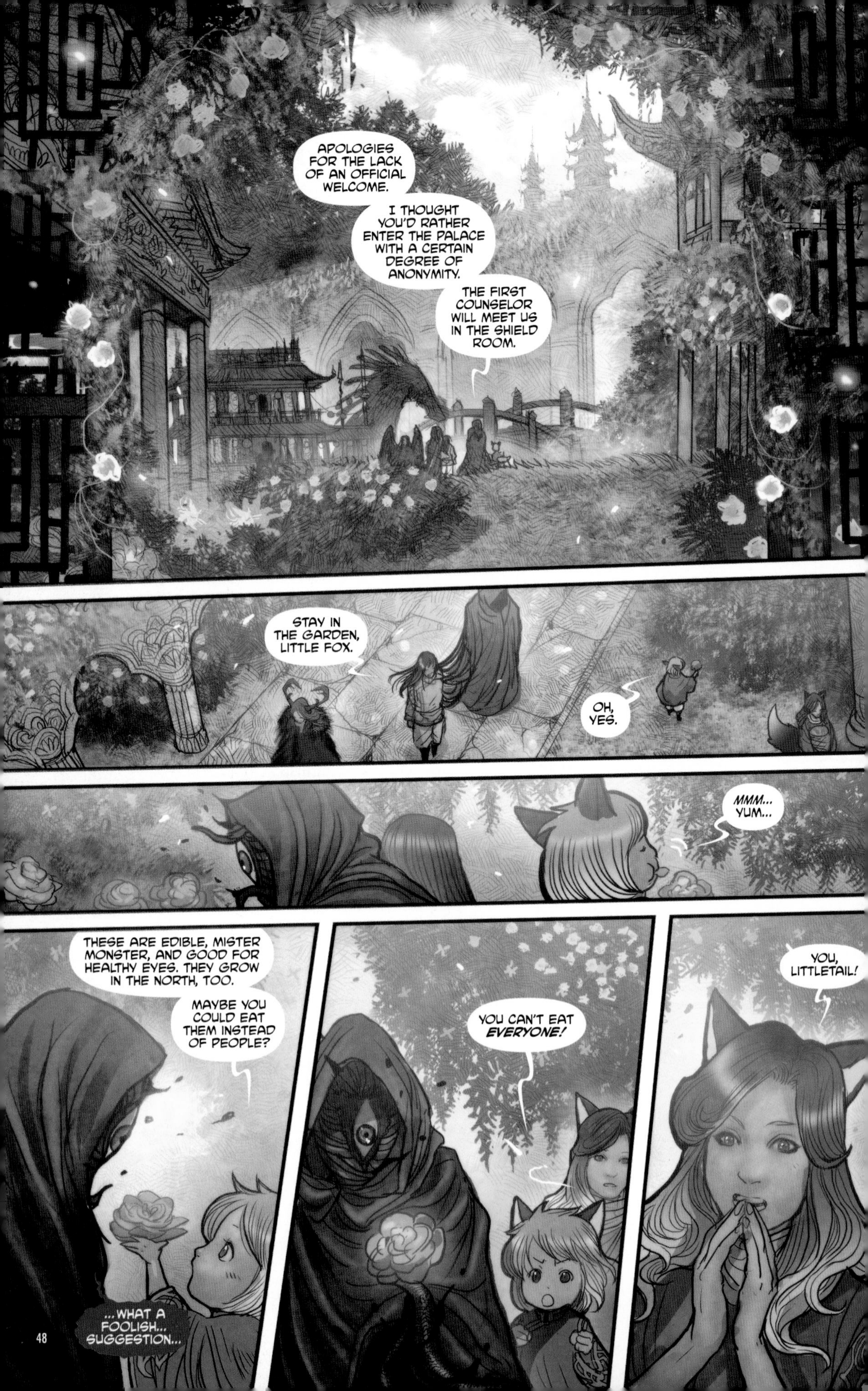
APOLOGIES FOR THE LACK OF AN OFFICIAL WELCOME.
I THOUGHT YOU'D RATHER ENTER THE PALACE WITH A CERTAIN DEGREE OF ANONYMITY.
THE FIRST COUNSELOR WILL MEET US IN THE SHIELD ROOM.
STAY IN THE GARDEN, LITTLE FOX.
OH, YES.
MMM... YUM...
THESE ARE EDIBLE, MISTER MONSTER, AND GOOD FOR HEALTHY EYES. THEY GROW IN THE NORTH, TOO.
MAYBE YOU COULD EAT THEM INSTEAD OF PEOPLE?
...WHAT A FOOLISH... SUGGESTION...
YOU CAN'T EAT *EVERYONE!*
YOU, LITTLETAIL!

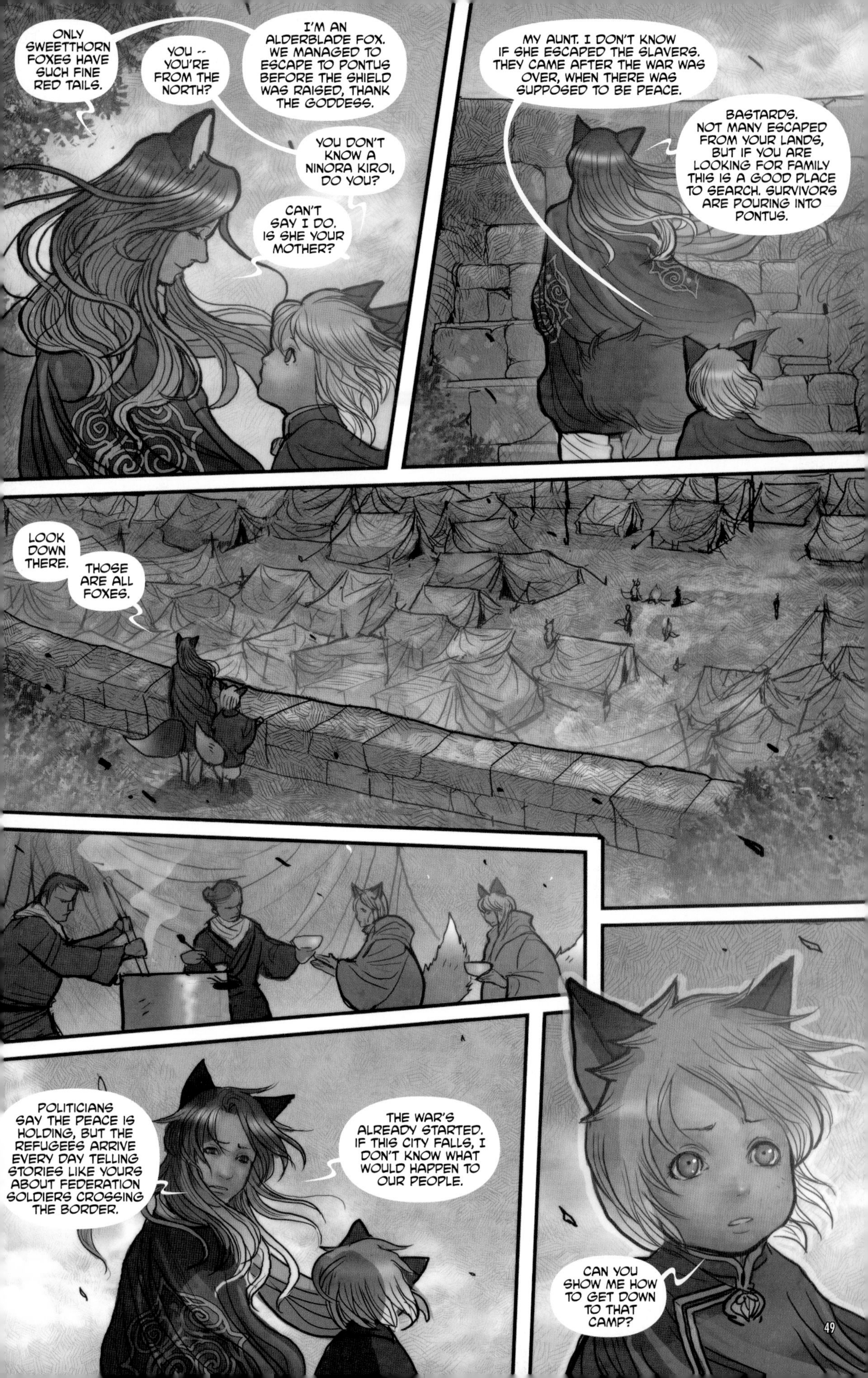
ONLY SWEETTHORN FOXES HAVE SUCH FINE RED TAILS.
YOU -- YOU'RE FROM THE NORTH?
I'M AN ALDERBLADE FOX. WE MANAGED TO ESCAPE TO PONTUS BEFORE THE SHIELD WAS RAISED, THANK THE GODDESS.
YOU DON'T KNOW A NINORA KIROI, DO YOU?
CAN'T SAY I DO. IS SHE YOUR MOTHER?
MY AUNT. I DON'T KNOW IF SHE ESCAPED THE SLAVERS. THEY CAME AFTER THE WAR WAS OVER, WHEN THERE WAS SUPPOSED TO BE PEACE.
BASTARDS. NOT MANY ESCAPED FROM YOUR LANDS, BUT IF YOU ARE LOOKING FOR FAMILY THIS IS A GOOD PLACE TO SEARCH. SURVIVORS ARE POURING INTO PONTUS.
LOOK DOWN THERE.
THOSE ARE ALL FOXES.
POLITICIANS SAY THE PEACE IS HOLDING, BUT THE REFUGEES ARRIVE EVERY DAY TELLING STORIES LIKE YOURS ABOUT FEDERATION SOLDIERS CROSSING THE BORDER.
THE WAR'S ALREADY STARTED. IF THIS CITY FALLS, I DON'T KNOW WHAT WOULD HAPPEN TO OUR PEOPLE.
CAN YOU SHOW ME HOW TO GET DOWN TO THAT CAMP?

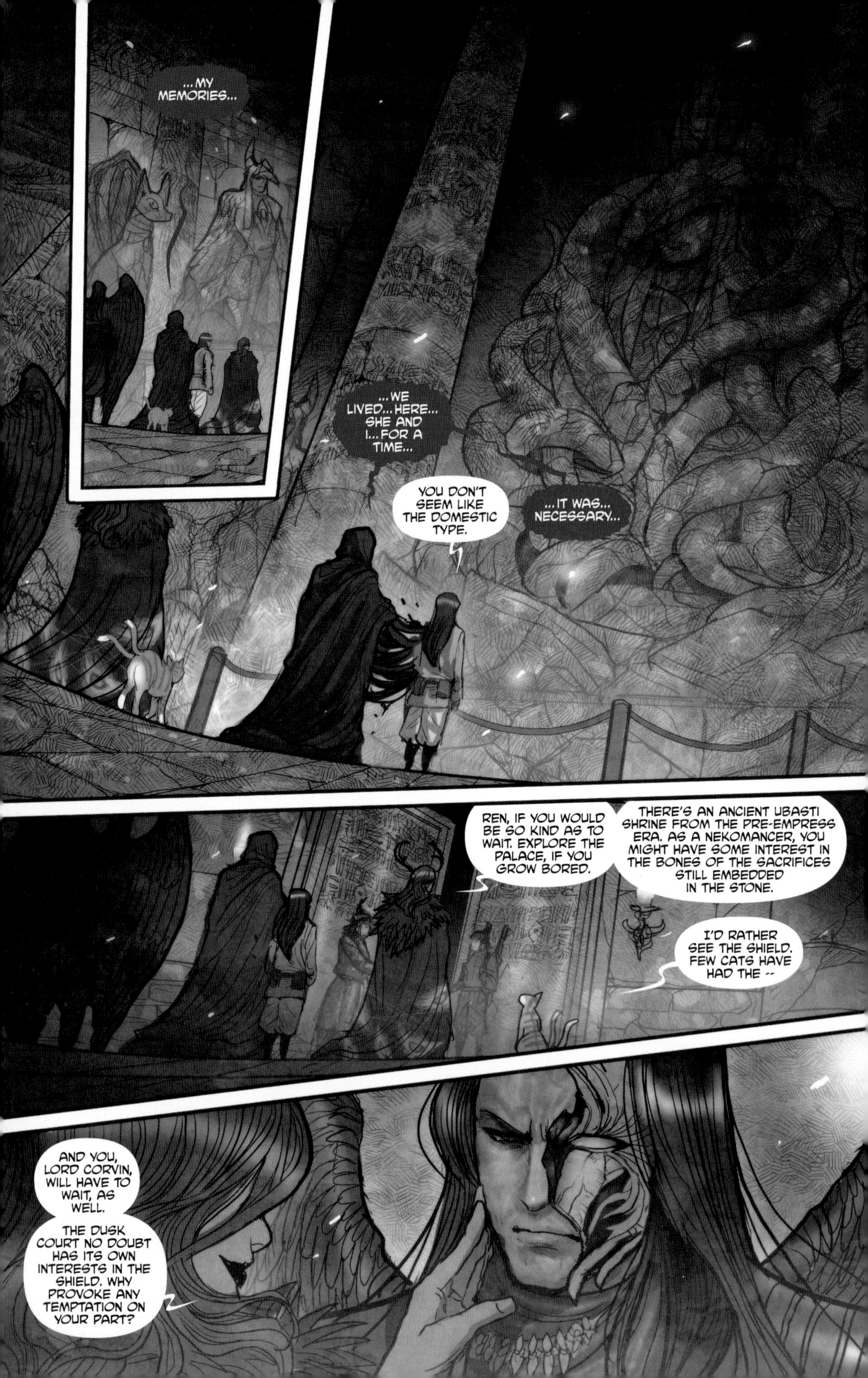
...MY MEMORIES...
...WE LIVED... HERE... SHE AND I... FOR A TIME...
YOU DON'T SEEM LIKE THE DOMESTIC TYPE.
...IT WAS... NECESSARY...
REN, IF YOU WOULD BE SO KIND AS TO WAIT. EXPLORE THE PALACE, IF YOU GROW BORED.
THERE'S AN ANCIENT UBASTI SHRINE FROM THE PRE-EMPRESS ERA. AS A NEKOMANCER, YOU MIGHT HAVE SOME INTEREST IN THE BONES OF THE SACRIFICES STILL EMBEDDED IN THE STONE.
I'D RATHER SEE THE SHIELD. FEW CATS HAVE HAD THE --
AND YOU, LORD CORVIN, WILL HAVE TO WAIT, AS WELL.
THE DUSK COURT NO DOUBT HAS ITS OWN INTERESTS IN THE SHIELD. WHY PROVOKE ANY TEMPTATION ON YOUR PART?

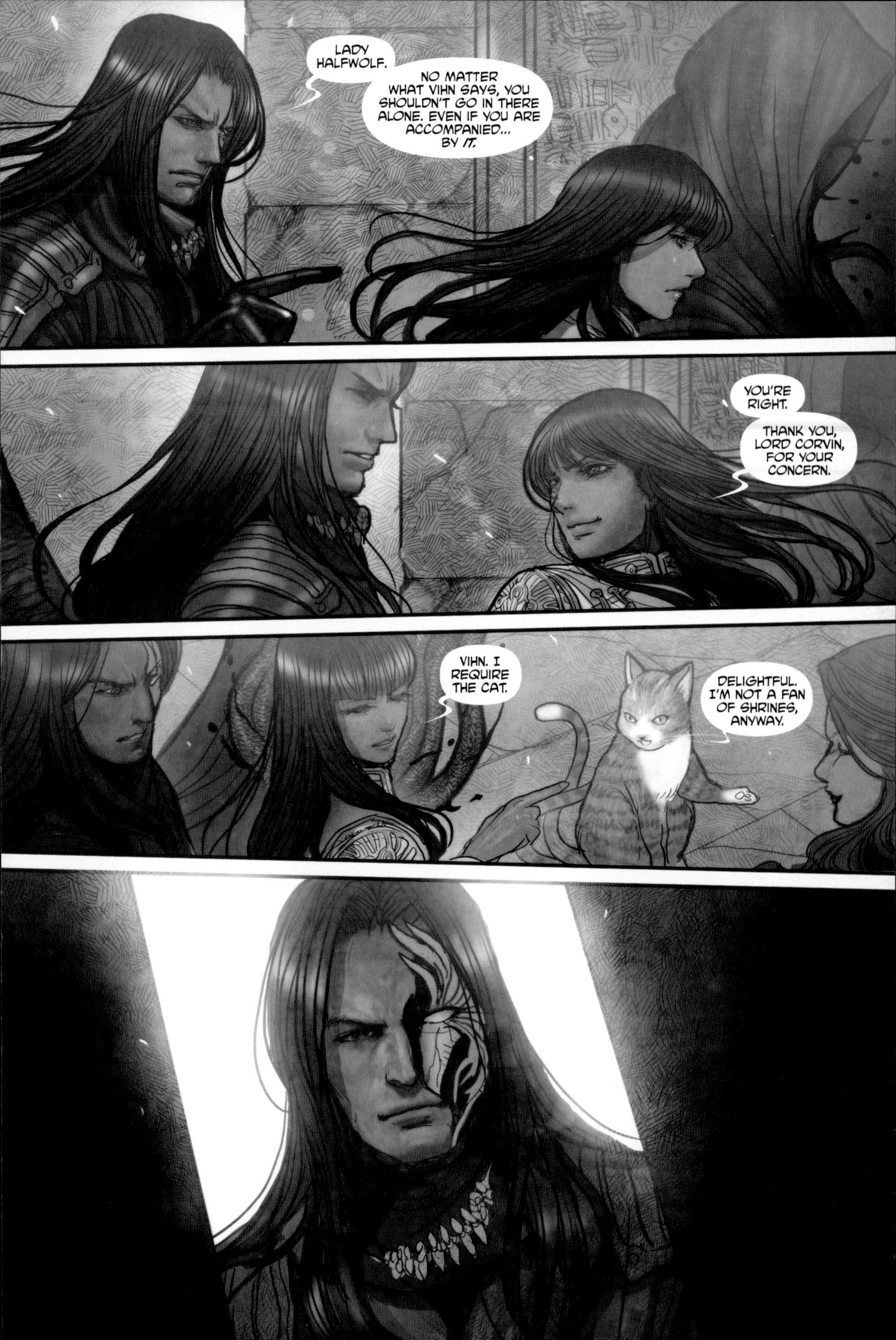
LADY HALFWOLF.
NO MATTER WHAT VIHN SAYS, YOU SHOULDN'T GO IN THERE ALONE. EVEN IF YOU ARE ACCOMPANIED... BY IT.
YOU'RE RIGHT.
THANK YOU, LORD CORVIN, FOR YOUR CONCERN.
VIHN. I REQUIRE THE CAT.
DELIGHTFUL. I'M NOT A FAN OF SHRINES, ANYWAY.

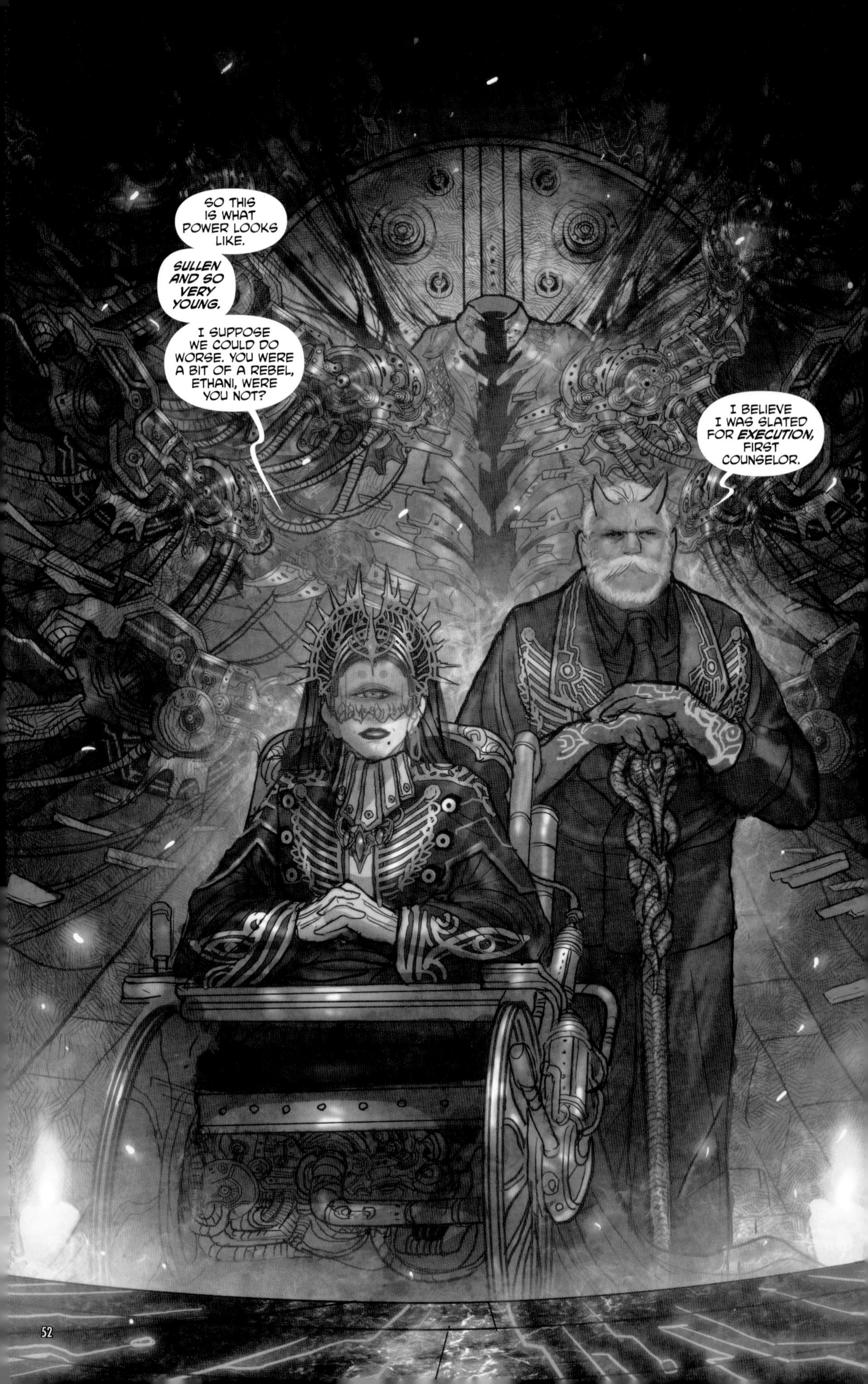
SO THIS IS WHAT POWER LOOKS LIKE.
SULLEN AND SO VERY YOUNG.
I SUPPOSE WE COULD DO WORSE. YOU WERE A BIT OF A REBEL, ETHANI, WERE YOU NOT?
I BELIEVE I WAS SLATED FOR EXECUTION, FIRST COUNSELOR.

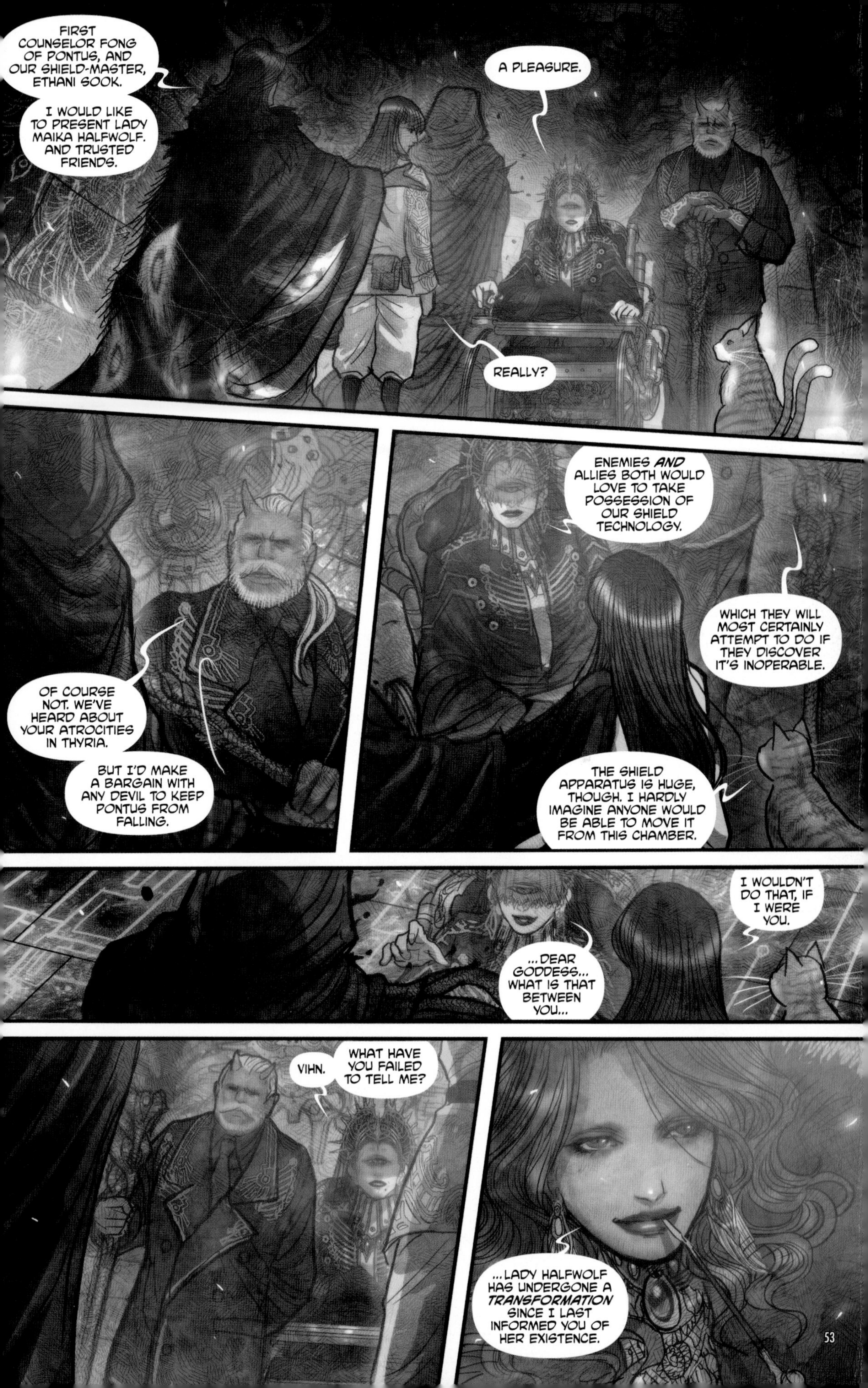

FIRST COUNSELOR FONG OF PONTUS, AND OUR SHIELD-MASTER, ETHANI SOOK.
I WOULD LIKE TO PRESENT LADY MAIKA HALFWOLF. AND TRUSTED FRIENDS.
A PLEASURE.
REALLY?
OF COURSE NOT. WE'VE HEARD ABOUT YOUR ATROCITIES IN THYRIA.
BUT I'D MAKE A BARGAIN WITH ANY DEVIL TO KEEP PONTUS FROM FALLING.
ENEMIES AND ALLIES BOTH WOULD LOVE TO TAKE POSSESSION OF OUR SHIELD TECHNOLOGY.
WHICH THEY WILL MOST CERTAINLY ATTEMPT TO DO IF THEY DISCOVER IT'S INOPERABLE.
THE SHIELD APPARATUS IS HUGE, THOUGH. I HARDLY IMAGINE ANYONE WOULD BE ABLE TO MOVE IT FROM THIS CHAMBER.
I WOULDN'T DO THAT, IF I WERE YOU.
...DEAR GODDESS... WHAT IS THAT BETWEEN YOU...
VIHN.
WHAT HAVE YOU FAILED TO TELL ME?
...LADY HALFWOLF HAS UNDERGONE A TRANSFORMATION SINCE I LAST INFORMED YOU OF HER EXISTENCE.

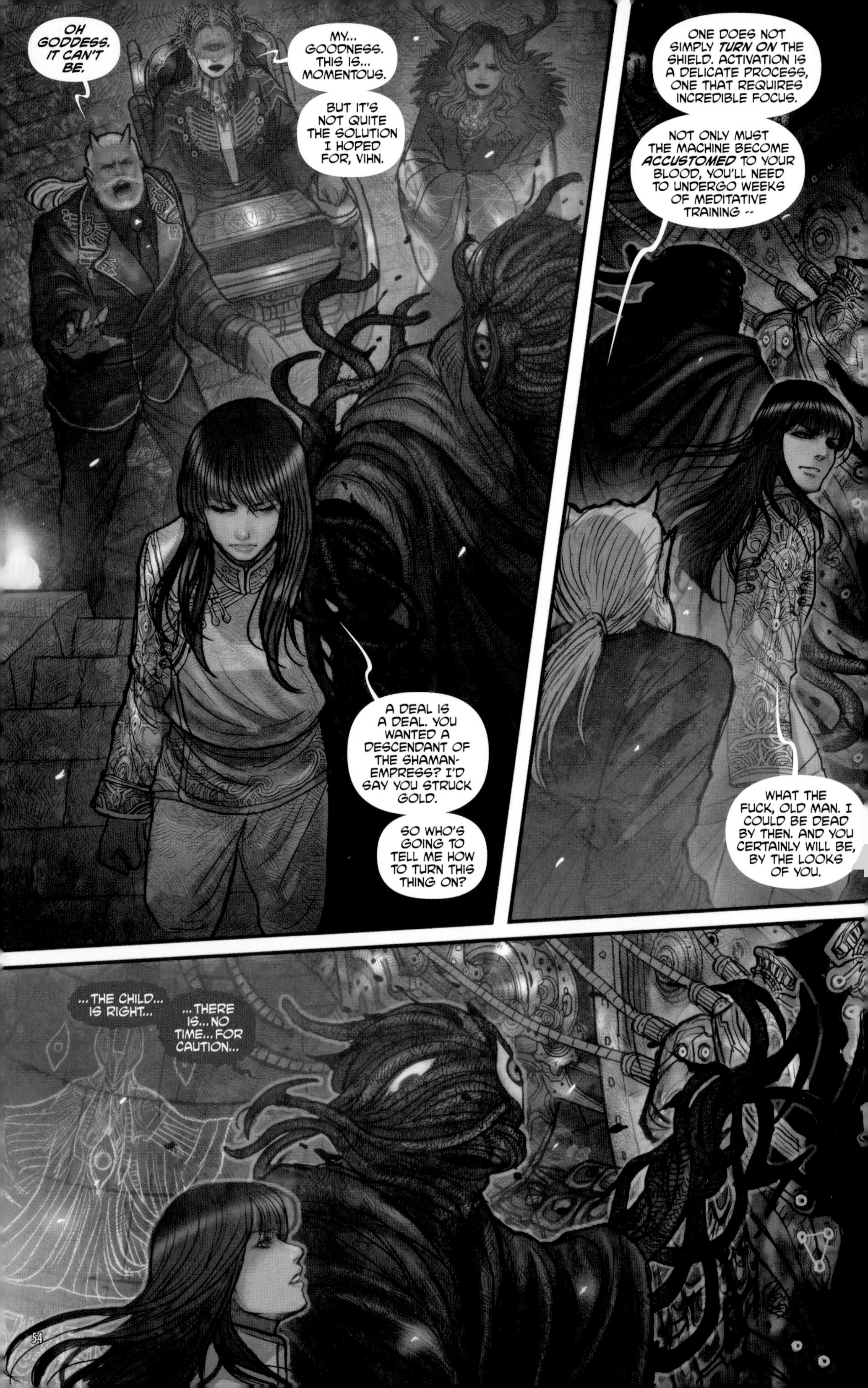
OH GODDESS. IT CAN'T BE.
MY... GOODNESS. THIS IS... MOMENTOUS.
BUT IT'S NOT QUITE THE SOLUTION I HOPED FOR, VIHN.
A DEAL IS A DEAL. YOU WANTED A DESCENDANT OF THE SHAMAN-EMPRESS? I'D SAY YOU STRUCK GOLD.
SO WHO'S GOING TO TELL ME HOW TO TURN THIS THING ON?
ONE DOES NOT SIMPLY TURN ON THE SHIELD. ACTIVATION IS A DELICATE PROCESS, ONE THAT REQUIRES INCREDIBLE FOCUS.
NOT ONLY MUST THE MACHINE BECOME ACCUSTOMED TO YOUR BLOOD, YOU'LL NEED TO UNDERGO WEEKS OF MEDITATIVE TRAINING --
WHAT THE FUCK, OLD MAN. I COULD BE DEAD BY THEN. AND YOU CERTAINLY WILL BE, BY THE LOOKS OF YOU.
...THE CHILD... IS RIGHT...
...THERE IS... NO TIME... FOR CAUTION...

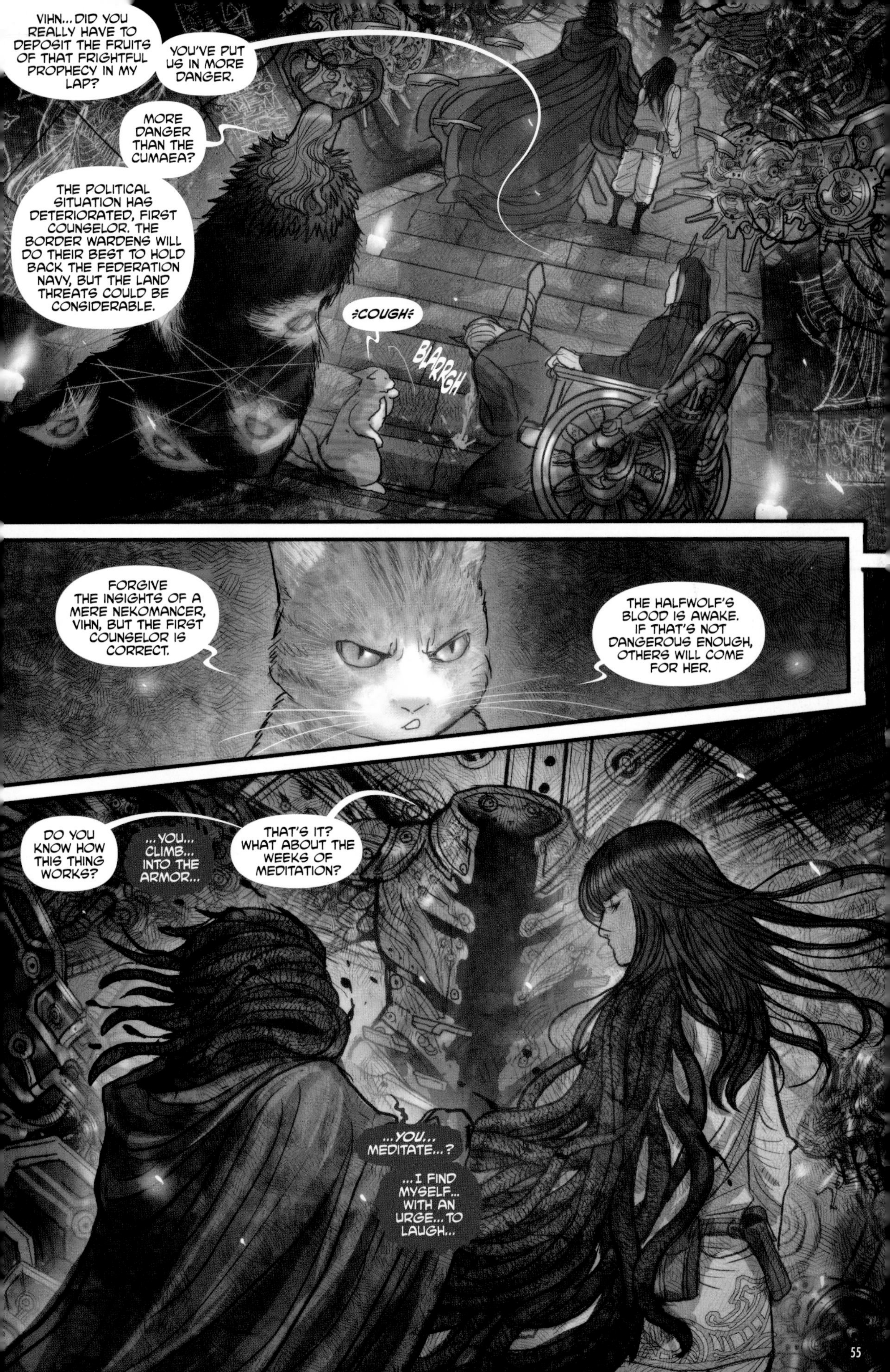
VIHN... DID YOU REALLY HAVE TO DEPOSIT THE FRUITS OF THAT FRIGHTFUL PROPHECY IN MY LAP?
YOU'VE PUT US IN MORE DANGER.
MORE DANGER THAN THE CUMAEA?
THE POLITICAL SITUATION HAS DETERIORATED, FIRST COUNSELOR. THE BORDER WARDENS WILL DO THEIR BEST TO HOLD BACK THE FEDERATION NAVY, BUT THE LAND THREATS COULD BE CONSIDERABLE.
COUGH
BLARRGH
FORGIVE THE INSIGHTS OF A MERE NEKOMANCER, VIHN, BUT THE FIRST COUNSELOR IS CORRECT.
THE HALFWOLF'S BLOOD IS AWAKE. IF THAT'S NOT DANGEROUS ENOUGH, OTHERS WILL COME FOR HER.
DO YOU KNOW HOW THIS THING WORKS?
...YOU... CLIMB... INTO THE ARMOR...
THAT'S IT? WHAT ABOUT THE WEEKS OF MEDITATION?
...YOU... MEDITATE...?
...I FIND MYSELF... WITH AN URGE... TO LAUGH...

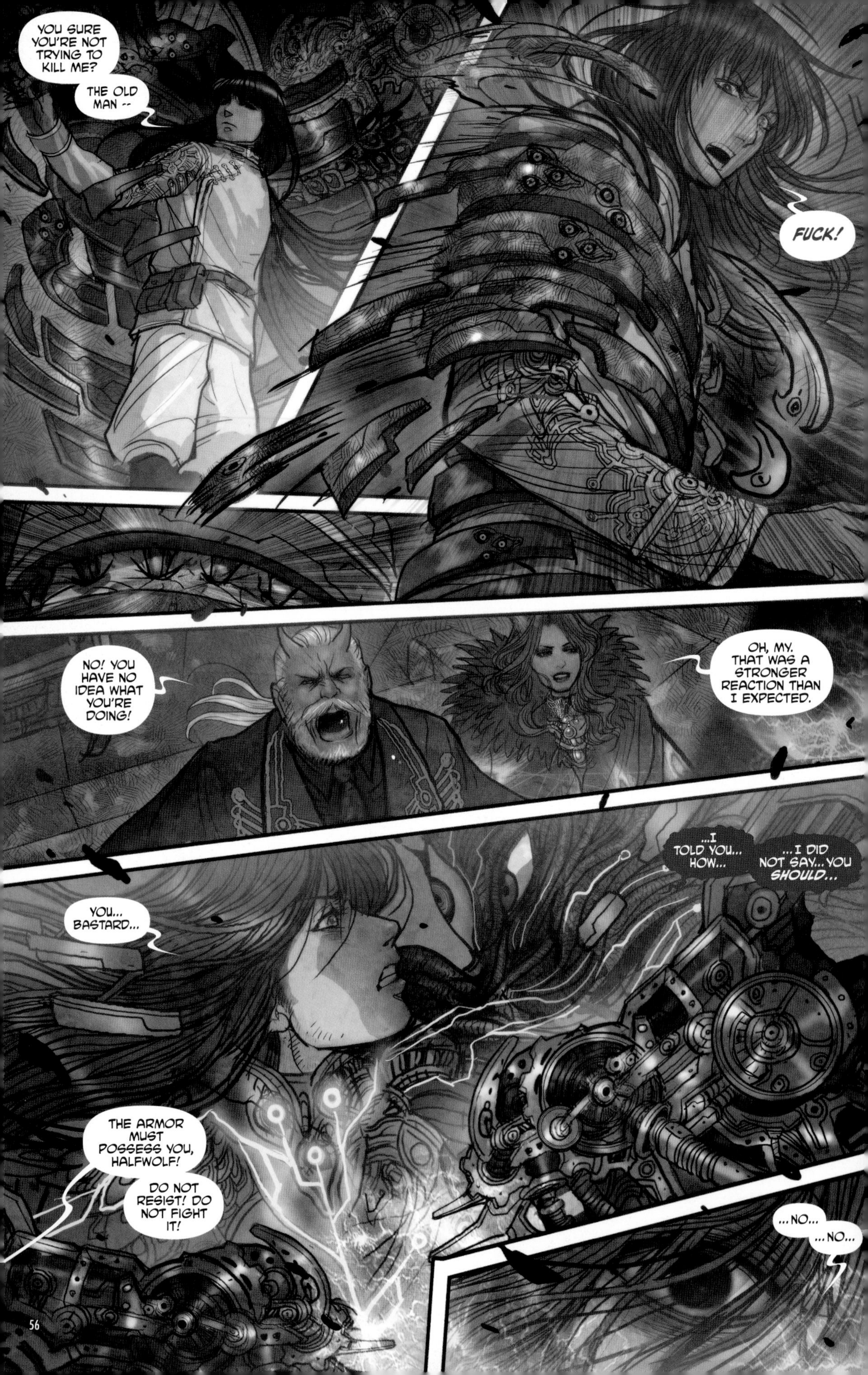

YOU SURE YOU'RE NOT TRYING TO KILL ME?
THE OLD MAN --
FUCK!
NO! YOU HAVE NO IDEA WHAT YOU'RE DOING!
OH, MY. THAT WAS A STRONGER REACTION THAN I EXPECTED.
...I TOLD YOU... HOW...
...I DID NOT SAY... YOU SHOULD...
YOU... BASTARD...
THE ARMOR MUST POSSESS YOU, HALFWOLF!
DO NOT RESIST! DO NOT FIGHT IT!
...NO...
...NO...

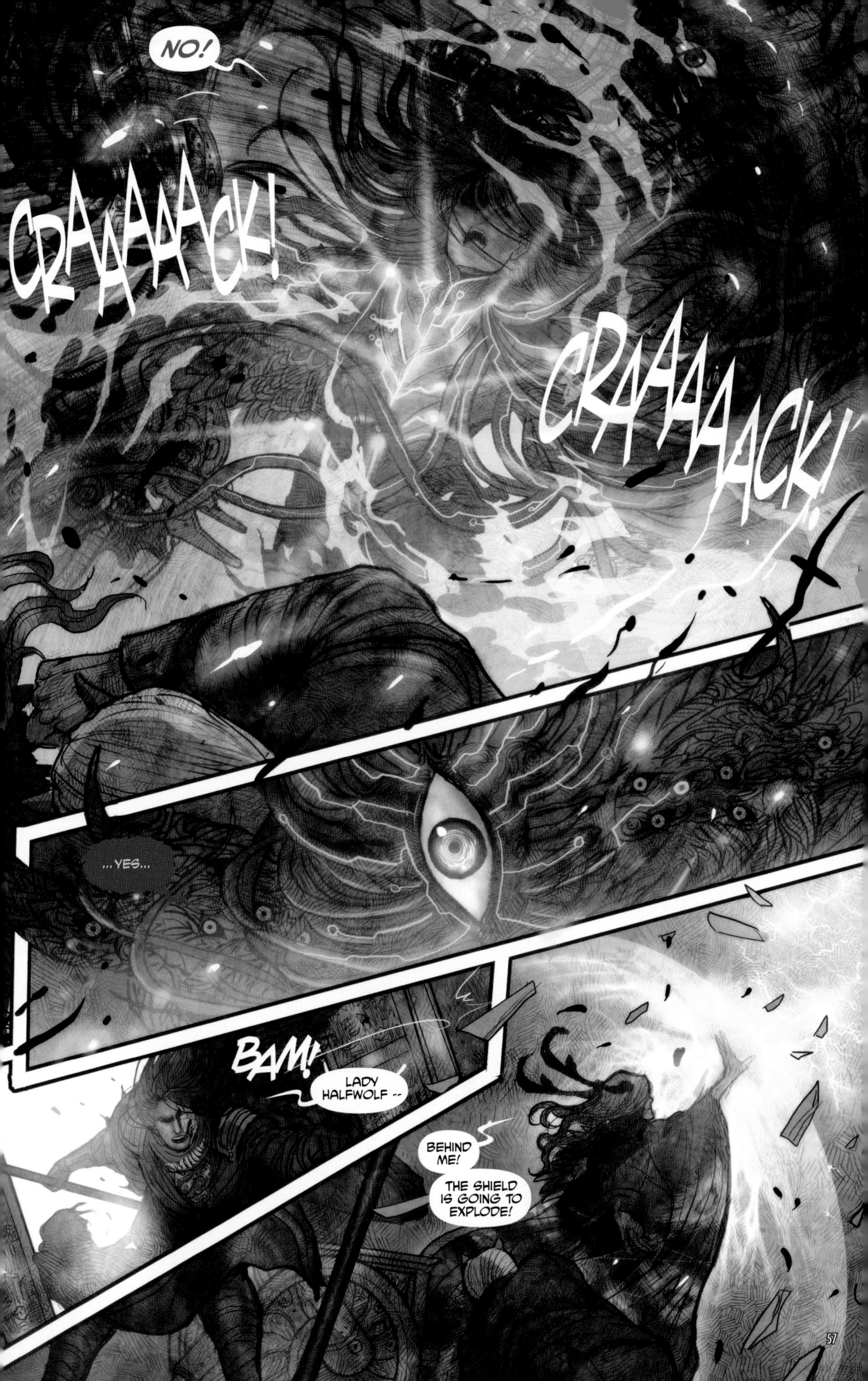
NO!
CRAAAAACK!
CRAAAAACK!
...YES...
BAM!
LADY HALFWOLF --
BEHIND ME!
THE SHIELD IS GOING TO EXPLODE!

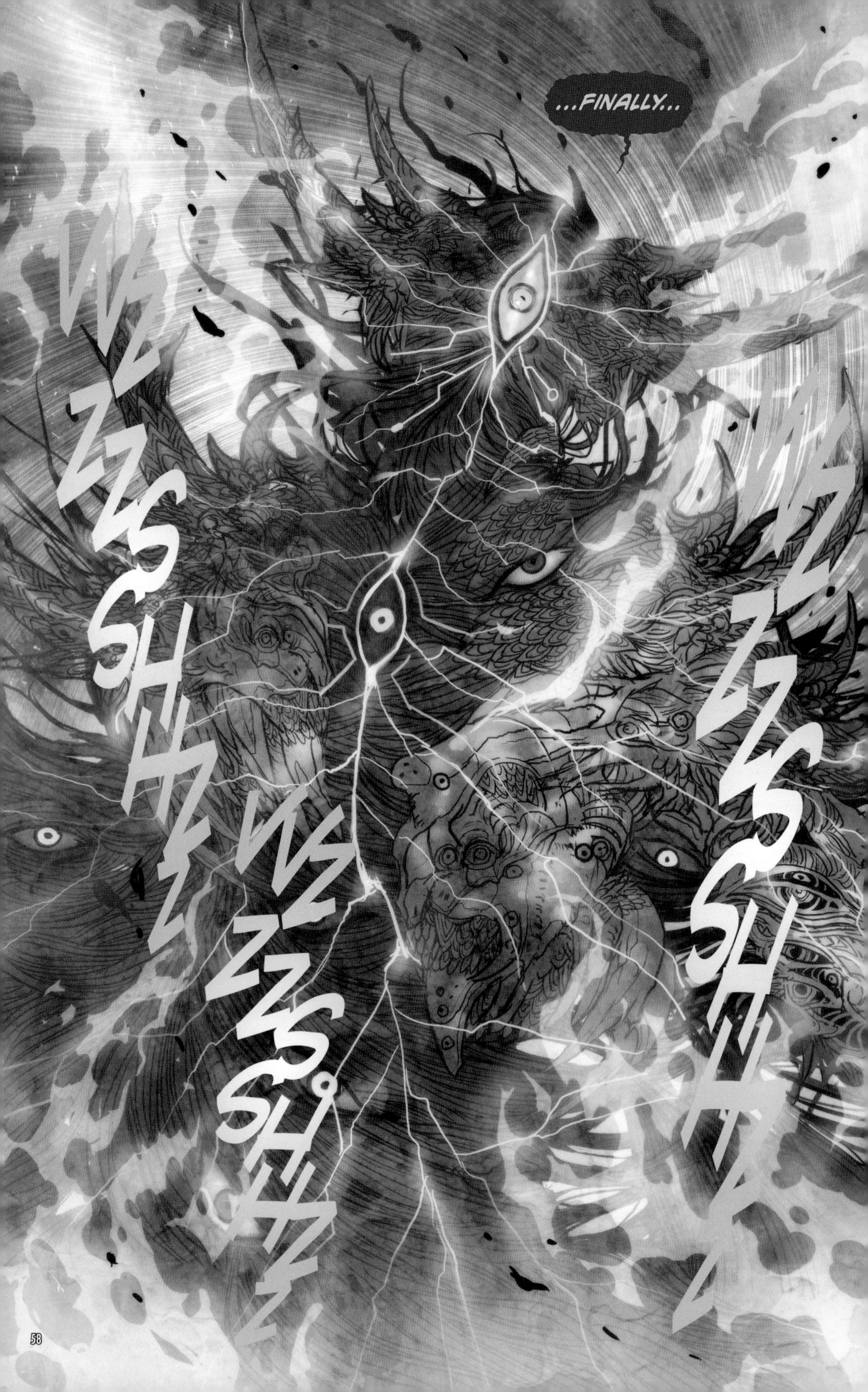
...FINALLY...

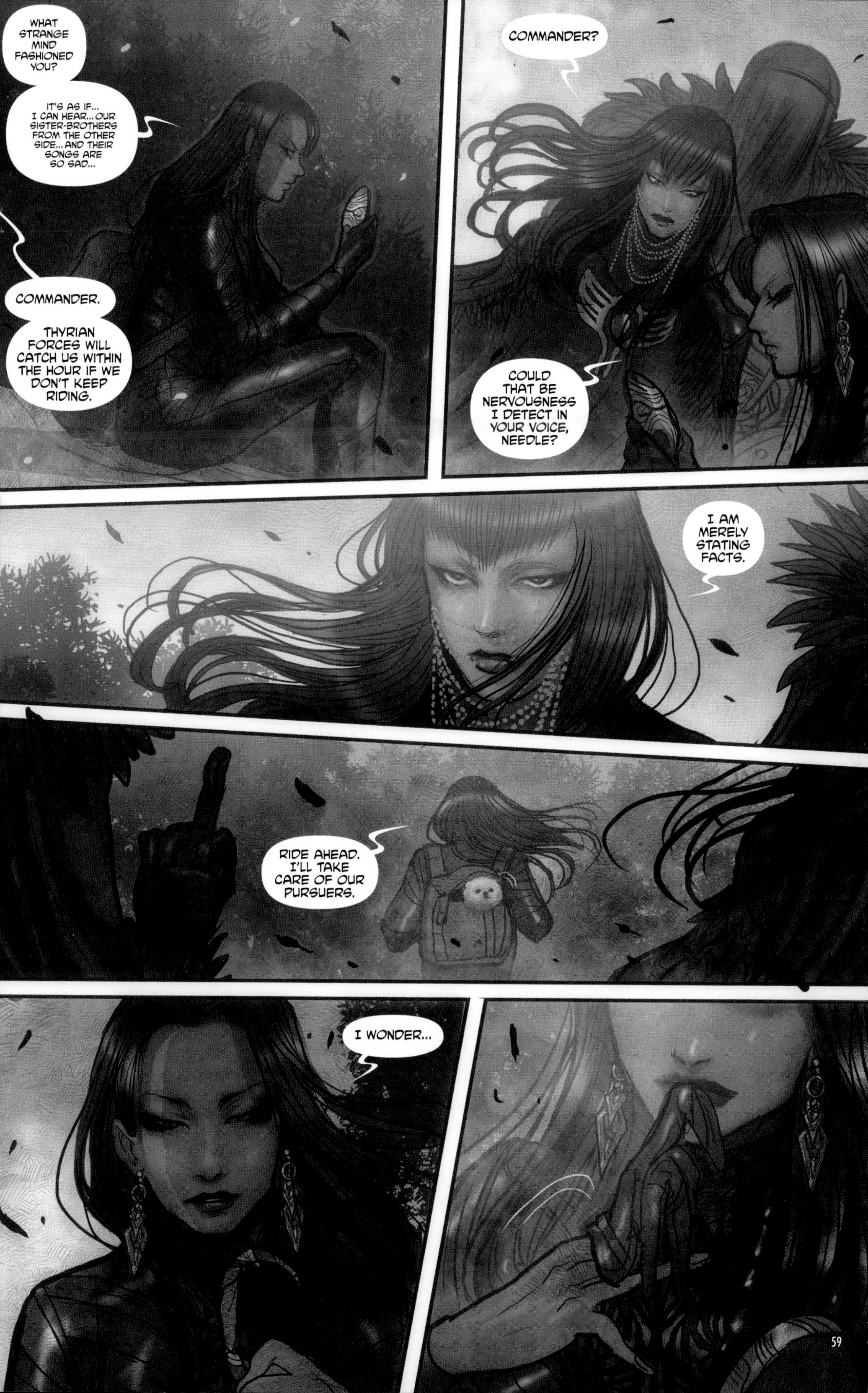
WHAT STRANGE MIND FASHIONED YOU?
IT'S AS IF... I CAN HEAR...OUR SISTER-BROTHERS FROM THE OTHER SIDE... AND THEIR SONGS ARE SO SAD...
COMMANDER.
THYRIAN FORCES WILL CATCH US WITHIN THE HOUR IF WE DON'T KEEP RIDING.
COMMANDER?
COULD THAT BE NERVOUSNESS I DETECT IN YOUR VOICE, NEEDLE?
I AM MERELY STATING FACTS.
RIDE AHEAD. I'LL TAKE CARE OF OUR PURSUERS.
I WONDER...

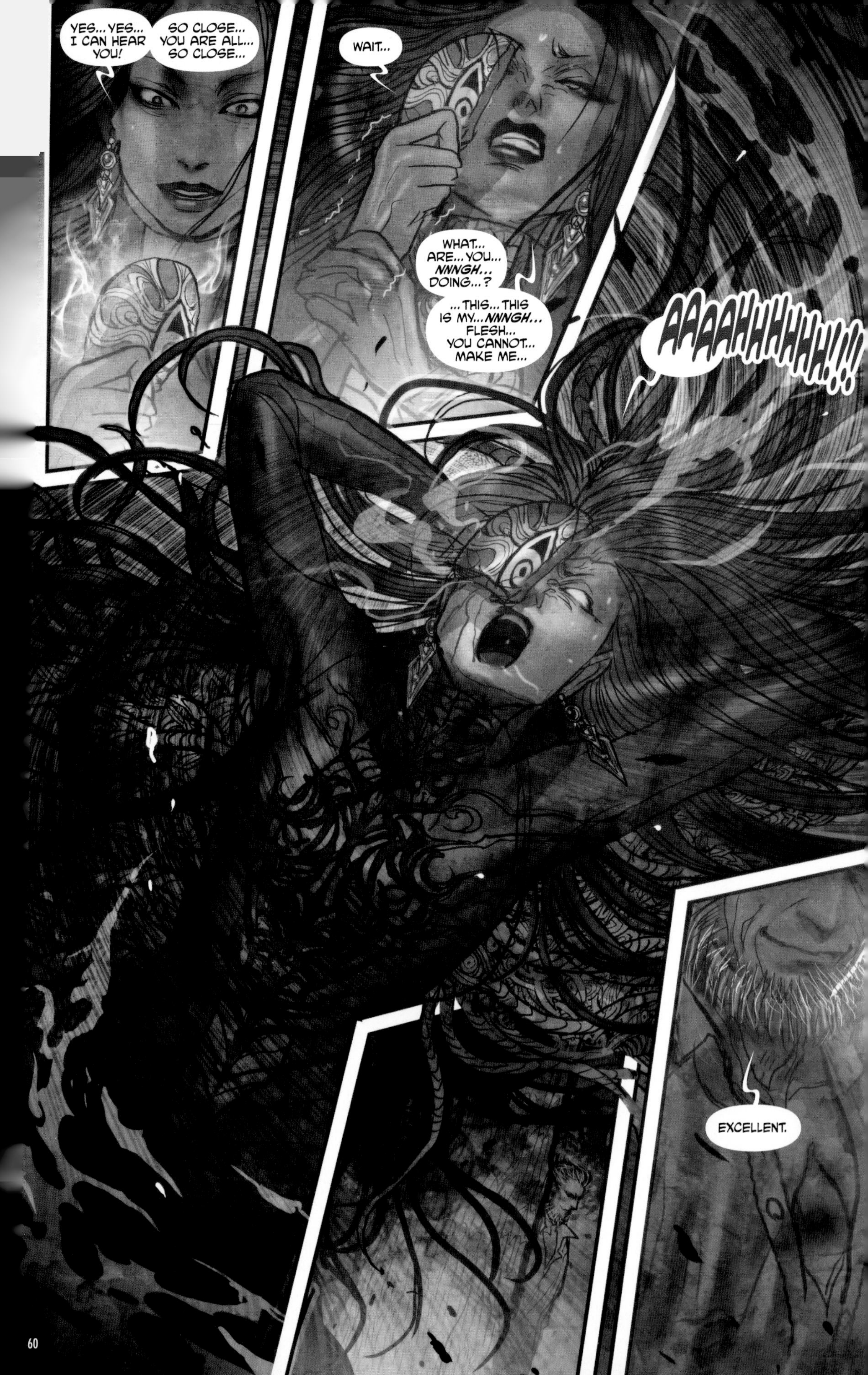
YES... YES... I CAN HEAR YOU!
SO CLOSE... YOU ARE ALL... SO CLOSE...
WAIT...
WHAT... ARE... YOU... NNNGH... DOING...?
...THIS... THIS IS MY... NNNGH... FLESH... YOU CANNOT... MAKE ME...
AAAAHHHHHH!!!!
EXCELLENT.

An excerpt of a lecture from the esteemed **Professor Tam Tam**, former First Record-Keeper of the Is'hami Temple, and learned contemporary of Namron Black Claw...

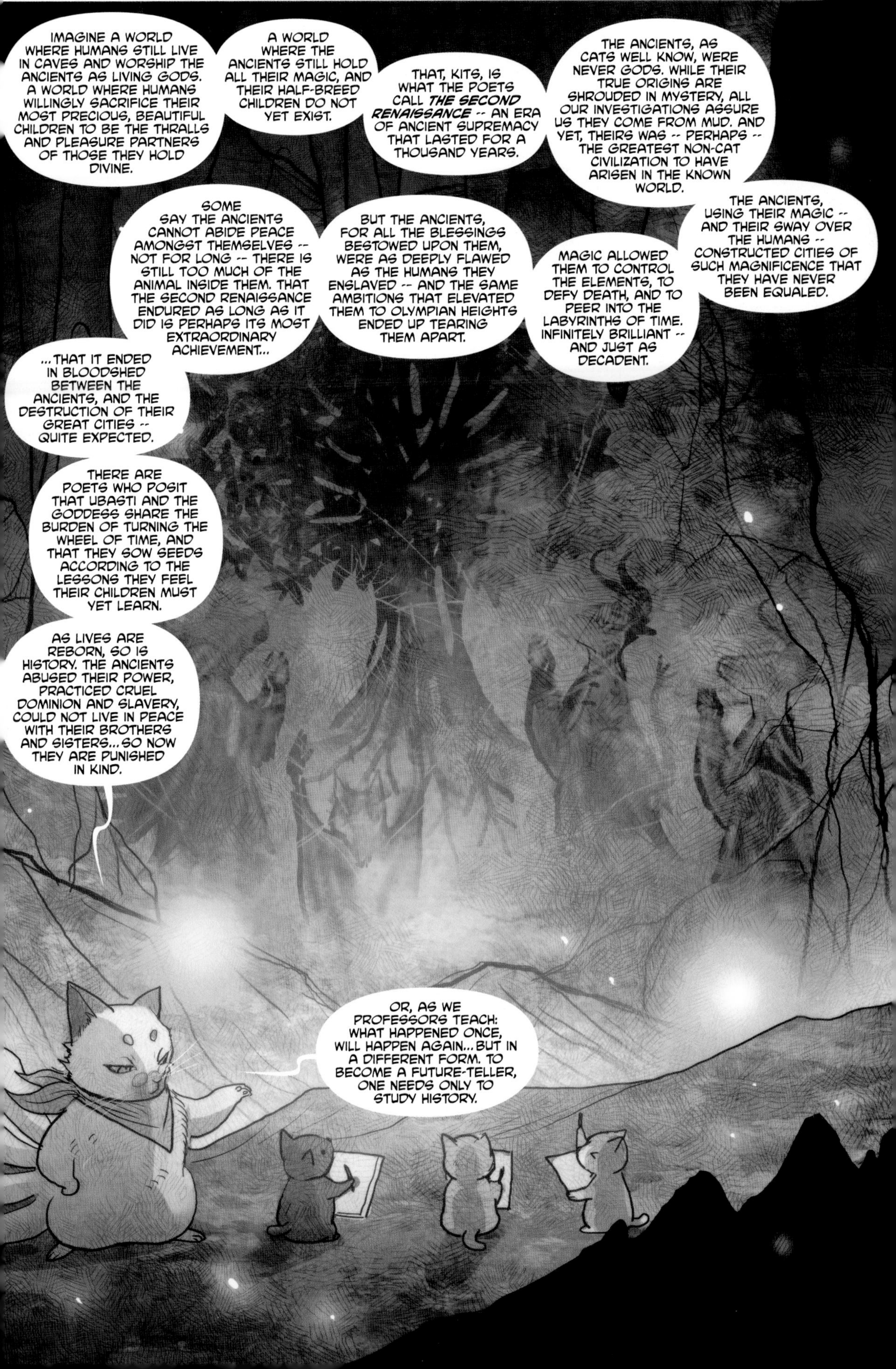
IMAGINE A WORLD WHERE HUMANS STILL LIVE IN CAVES AND WORSHIP THE ANCIENTS AS LIVING GODS. A WORLD WHERE HUMANS WILLINGLY SACRIFICE THEIR MOST PRECIOUS, BEAUTIFUL CHILDREN TO BE THE THRALLS AND PLEASURE PARTNERS OF THOSE THEY HOLD DIVINE.
A WORLD WHERE THE ANCIENTS STILL HOLD ALL THEIR MAGIC, AND THEIR HALF-BREED CHILDREN DO NOT YET EXIST.
THAT, KITS, IS WHAT THE POETS CALL *THE SECOND RENAISSANCE* -- AN ERA OF ANCIENT SUPREMACY THAT LASTED FOR A THOUSAND YEARS.
THE ANCIENTS, AS CATS WELL KNOW, WERE NEVER GODS. WHILE THEIR TRUE ORIGINS ARE SHROUDED IN MYSTERY, ALL OUR INVESTIGATIONS ASSURE US THEY COME FROM MUD. AND YET, THEIRS WAS -- PERHAPS -- THE GREATEST NON-CAT CIVILIZATION TO HAVE ARISEN IN THE KNOWN WORLD.
THE ANCIENTS, USING THEIR MAGIC -- AND THEIR SWAY OVER THE HUMANS -- CONSTRUCTED CITIES OF SUCH MAGNIFICENCE THAT THEY HAVE NEVER BEEN EQUALED.
MAGIC ALLOWED THEM TO CONTROL THE ELEMENTS, TO DEFY DEATH, AND TO PEER INTO THE LABYRINTHS OF TIME. INFINITELY BRILLIANT -- AND JUST AS DECADENT.
BUT THE ANCIENTS, FOR ALL THE BLESSINGS BESTOWED UPON THEM, WERE AS DEEPLY FLAWED AS THE HUMANS THEY ENSLAVED -- AND THE SAME AMBITIONS THAT ELEVATED THEM TO OLYMPIAN HEIGHTS ENDED UP TEARING THEM APART.
SOME SAY THE ANCIENTS CANNOT ABIDE PEACE AMONGST THEMSELVES -- NOT FOR LONG -- THERE IS STILL TOO MUCH OF THE ANIMAL INSIDE THEM. THAT THE SECOND RENAISSANCE ENDURED AS LONG AS IT DID IS PERHAPS ITS MOST EXTRAORDINARY ACHIEVEMENT...
...THAT IT ENDED IN BLOODSHED BETWEEN THE ANCIENTS, AND THE DESTRUCTION OF THEIR GREAT CITIES -- QUITE EXPECTED.
THERE ARE POETS WHO POSIT THAT UBASTI AND THE GODDESS SHARE THE BURDEN OF TURNING THE WHEEL OF TIME, AND THAT THEY SOW SEEDS ACCORDING TO THE LESSONS THEY FEEL THEIR CHILDREN MUST YET LEARN.
AS LIVES ARE REBORN, SO IS HISTORY. THE ANCIENTS ABUSED THEIR POWER, PRACTICED CRUEL DOMINION AND SLAVERY, COULD NOT LIVE IN PEACE WITH THEIR BROTHERS AND SISTERS... SO NOW THEY ARE PUNISHED IN KIND.
OR, AS WE PROFESSORS TEACH: WHAT HAPPENED ONCE, WILL HAPPEN AGAIN... BUT IN A DIFFERENT FORM. TO BECOME A FUTURE-TELLER, ONE NEEDS ONLY TO STUDY HISTORY.

CHAPTER FIFTEEN

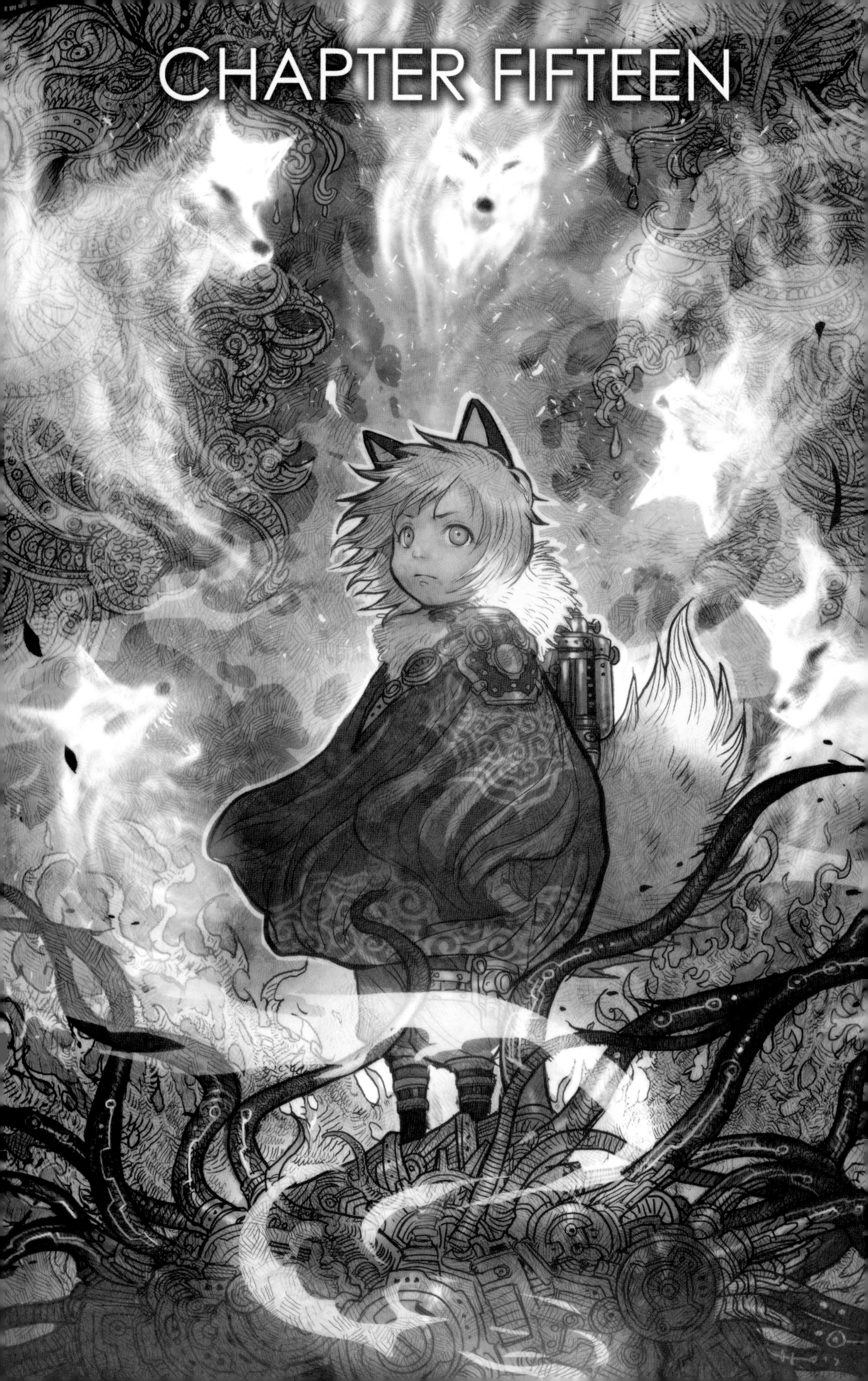

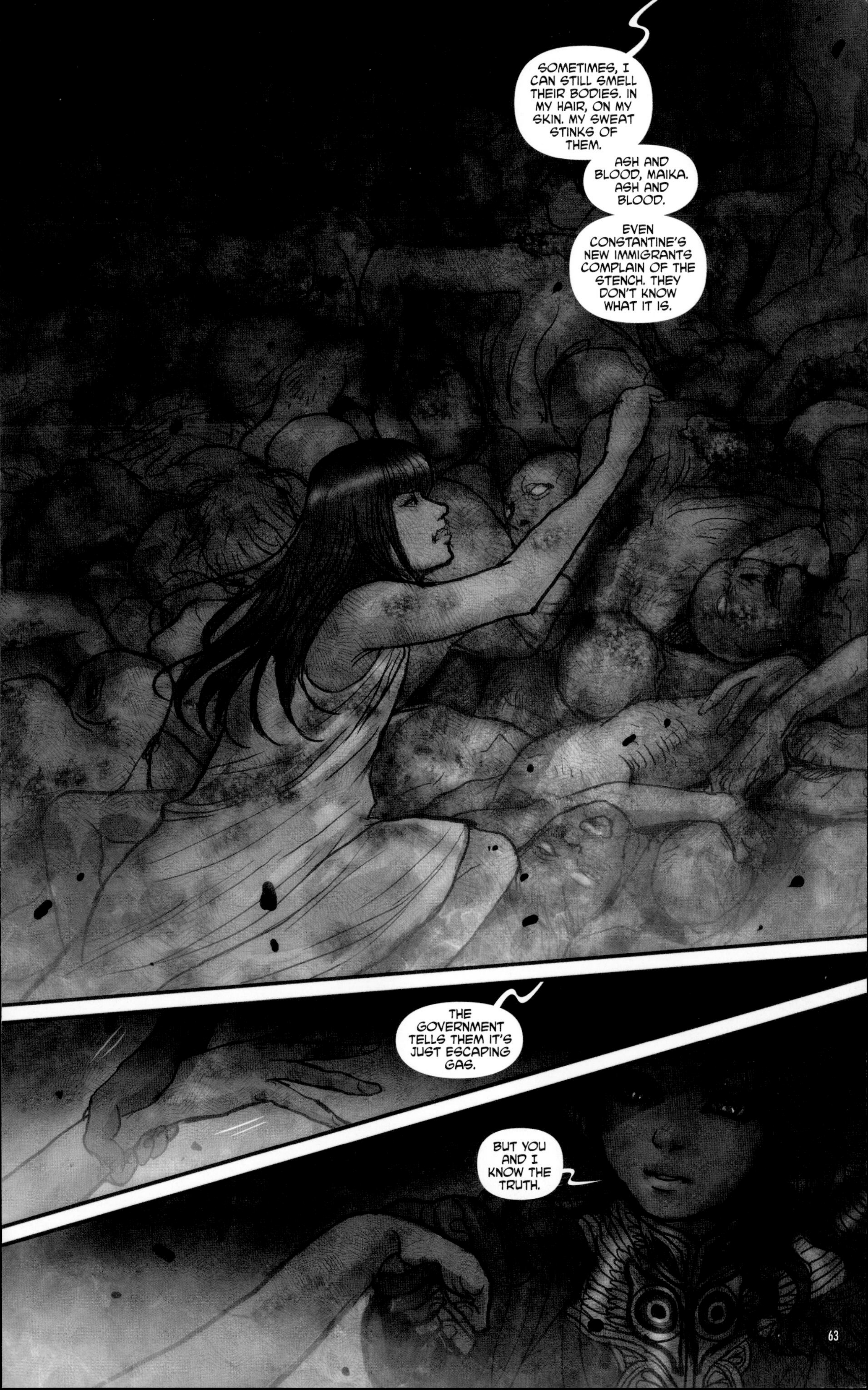
SOMETIMES, I CAN STILL SMELL THEIR BODIES. IN MY HAIR, ON MY SKIN. MY SWEAT STINKS OF THEM.
ASH AND BLOOD, MAIKA. ASH AND BLOOD.
EVEN CONSTANTINE'S NEW IMMIGRANTS COMPLAIN OF THE STENCH. THEY DON'T KNOW WHAT IT IS.
THE GOVERNMENT TELLS THEM IT'S JUST ESCAPING GAS.
BUT YOU AND I KNOW THE TRUTH.

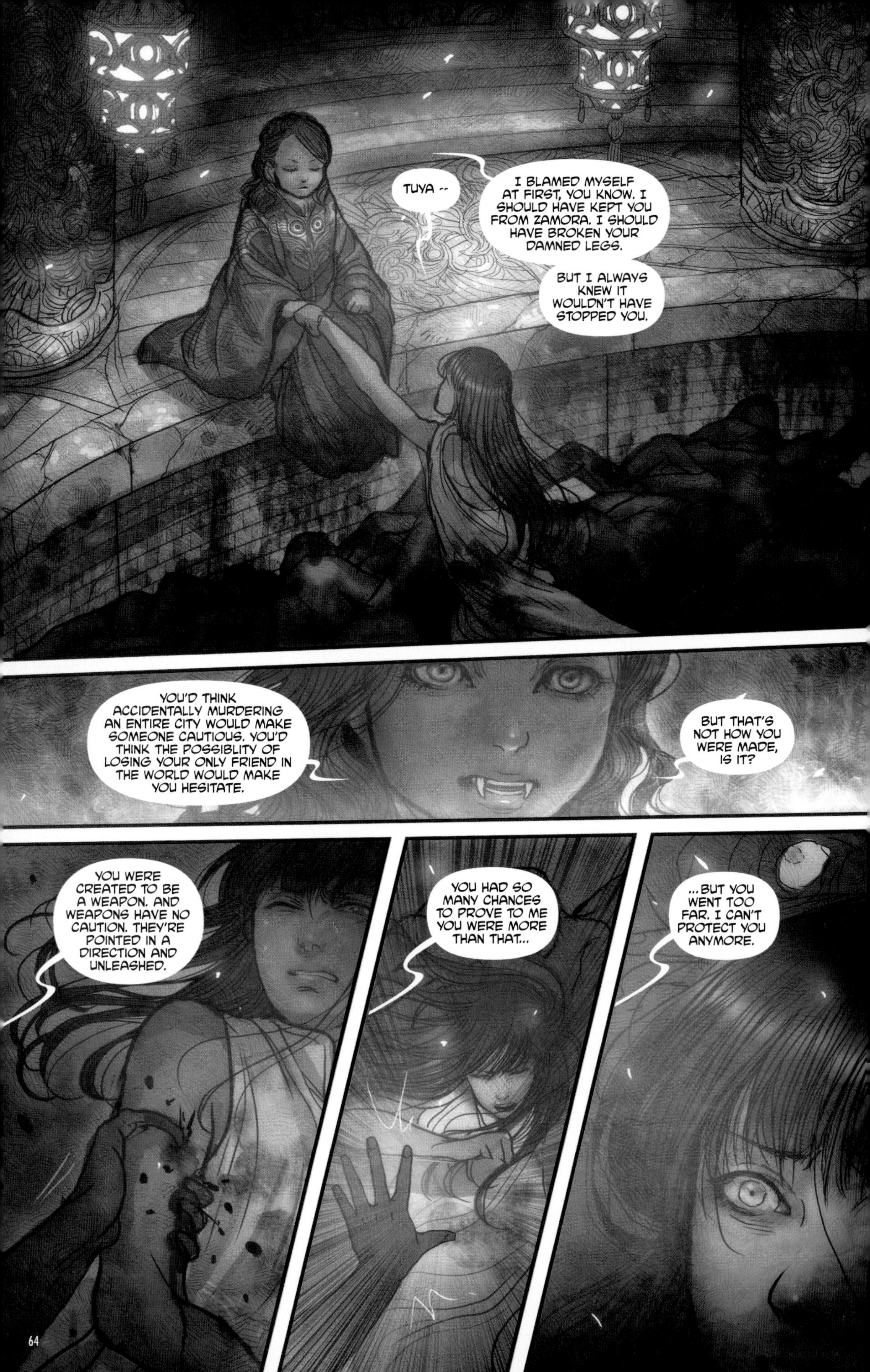
TUYA --
I BLAMED MYSELF AT FIRST, YOU KNOW. I SHOULD HAVE KEPT YOU FROM ZAMORA. I SHOULD HAVE BROKEN YOUR DAMNED LEGS.
BUT I ALWAYS KNEW IT WOULDN'T HAVE STOPPED YOU.
YOU'D THINK ACCIDENTALLY MURDERING AN ENTIRE CITY WOULD MAKE SOMEONE CAUTIOUS. YOU'D THINK THE POSSIBLITY OF LOSING YOUR ONLY FRIEND IN THE WORLD WOULD MAKE YOU HESITATE.
BUT THAT'S NOT HOW YOU WERE MADE, IS IT?
YOU WERE CREATED TO BE A WEAPON. AND WEAPONS HAVE NO CAUTION. THEY'RE POINTED IN A DIRECTION AND UNLEASHED.
YOU HAD SO MANY CHANCES TO PROVE TO ME YOU WERE MORE THAN THAT...
...BUT YOU WENT TOO FAR. I CAN'T PROTECT YOU ANYMORE.

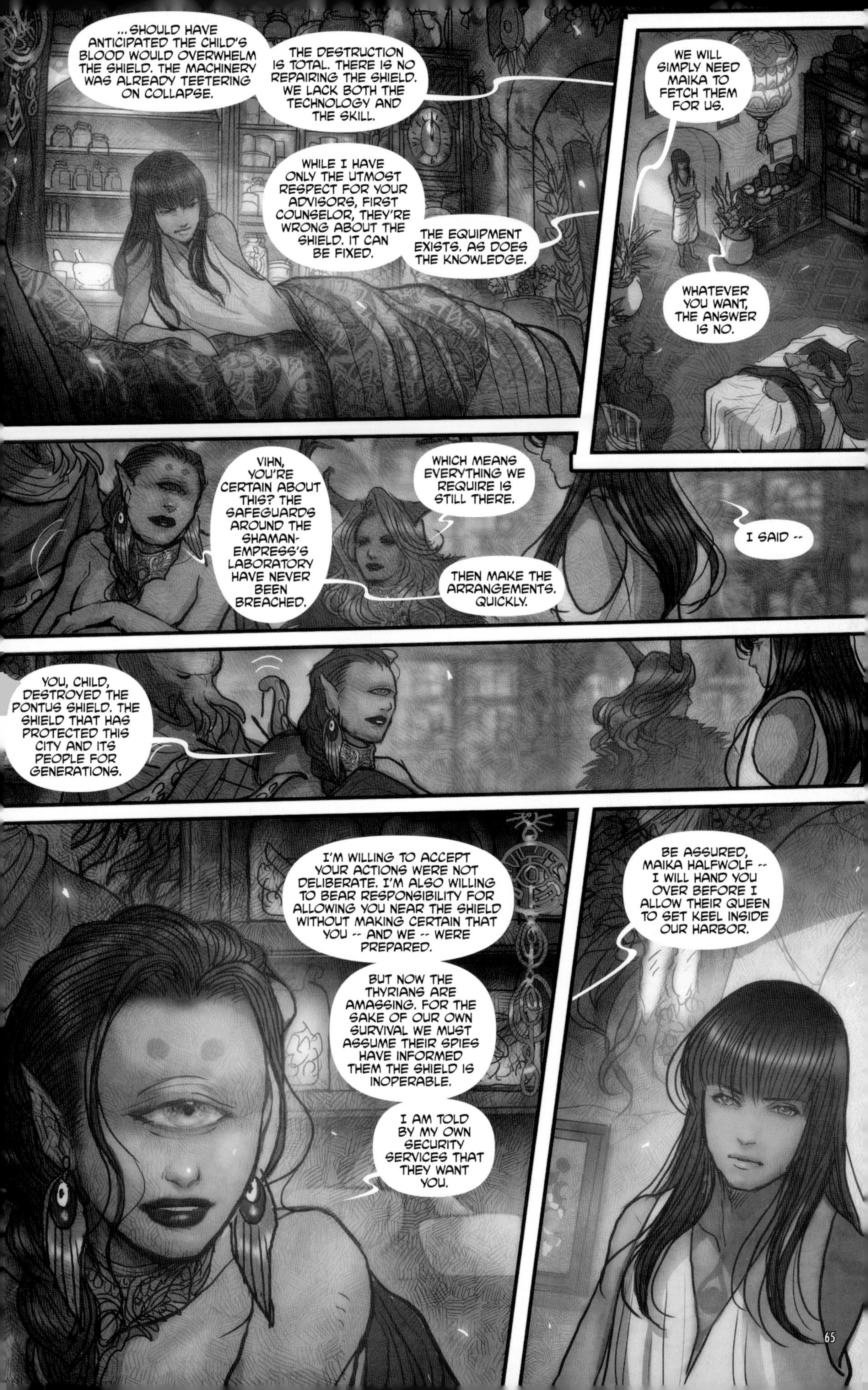
...SHOULD HAVE ANTICIPATED THE CHILD'S BLOOD WOULD OVERWHELM THE SHIELD. THE MACHINERY WAS ALREADY TEETERING ON COLLAPSE.
THE DESTRUCTION IS TOTAL. THERE IS NO REPAIRING THE SHIELD. WE LACK BOTH THE TECHNOLOGY AND THE SKILL.
WHILE I HAVE ONLY THE UTMOST RESPECT FOR YOUR ADVISORS, FIRST COUNSELOR, THEY'RE WRONG ABOUT THE SHIELD. IT CAN BE FIXED.
THE EQUIPMENT EXISTS. AS DOES THE KNOWLEDGE.
WE WILL SIMPLY NEED MAIKA TO FETCH THEM FOR US.
WHATEVER YOU WANT, THE ANSWER IS NO.
VIHN, YOU'RE CERTAIN ABOUT THIS? THE SAFEGUARDS AROUND THE SHAMAN-EMPRESS'S LABORATORY HAVE NEVER BEEN BREACHED.
WHICH MEANS EVERYTHING WE REQUIRE IS STILL THERE.
THEN MAKE THE ARRANGEMENTS. QUICKLY.
I SAID --
YOU, CHILD, DESTROYED THE PONTUS SHIELD. THE SHIELD THAT HAS PROTECTED THIS CITY AND ITS PEOPLE FOR GENERATIONS.
I'M WILLING TO ACCEPT YOUR ACTIONS WERE NOT DELIBERATE. I'M ALSO WILLING TO BEAR RESPONSIBILITY FOR ALLOWING YOU NEAR THE SHIELD WITHOUT MAKING CERTAIN THAT YOU -- AND WE -- WERE PREPARED.
BUT NOW THE THYRIANS ARE AMASSING. FOR THE SAKE OF OUR OWN SURVIVAL WE MUST ASSUME THEIR SPIES HAVE INFORMED THEM THE SHIELD IS INOPERABLE.
I AM TOLD BY MY OWN SECURITY SERVICES THAT THEY WANT YOU.
BE ASSURED, MAIKA HALFWOLF -- I WILL HAND YOU OVER BEFORE I ALLOW THEIR QUEEN TO SET KEEL INSIDE OUR HARBOR.

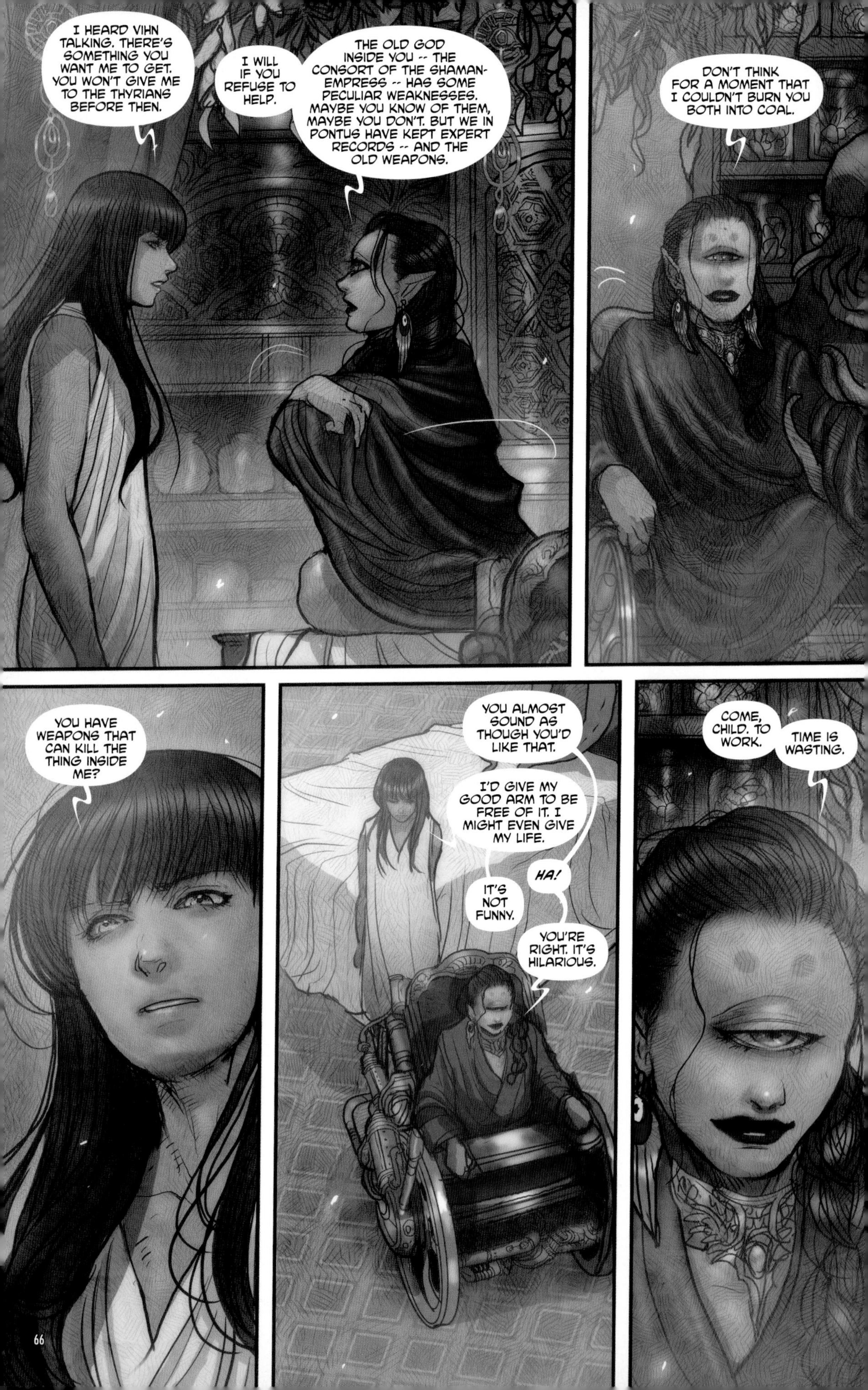
I HEARD VIHN TALKING. THERE'S SOMETHING YOU WANT ME TO GET. YOU WON'T GIVE ME TO THE THYRIANS BEFORE THEN.
I WILL IF YOU REFUSE TO HELP.
THE OLD GOD INSIDE YOU -- THE CONSORT OF THE SHAMAN-EMPRESS -- HAS SOME PECULIAR WEAKNESSES. MAYBE YOU KNOW OF THEM, MAYBE YOU DON'T. BUT WE IN PONTUS HAVE KEPT EXPERT RECORDS -- AND THE OLD WEAPONS.
DON'T THINK FOR A MOMENT THAT I COULDN'T BURN YOU BOTH INTO COAL.
YOU HAVE WEAPONS THAT CAN KILL THE THING INSIDE ME?
YOU ALMOST SOUND AS THOUGH YOU'D LIKE THAT.
I'D GIVE MY GOOD ARM TO BE FREE OF IT. I MIGHT EVEN GIVE MY LIFE.
HA!
IT'S NOT FUNNY.
YOU'RE RIGHT. IT'S HILARIOUS.
COME, CHILD. TO WORK.
TIME IS WASTING.

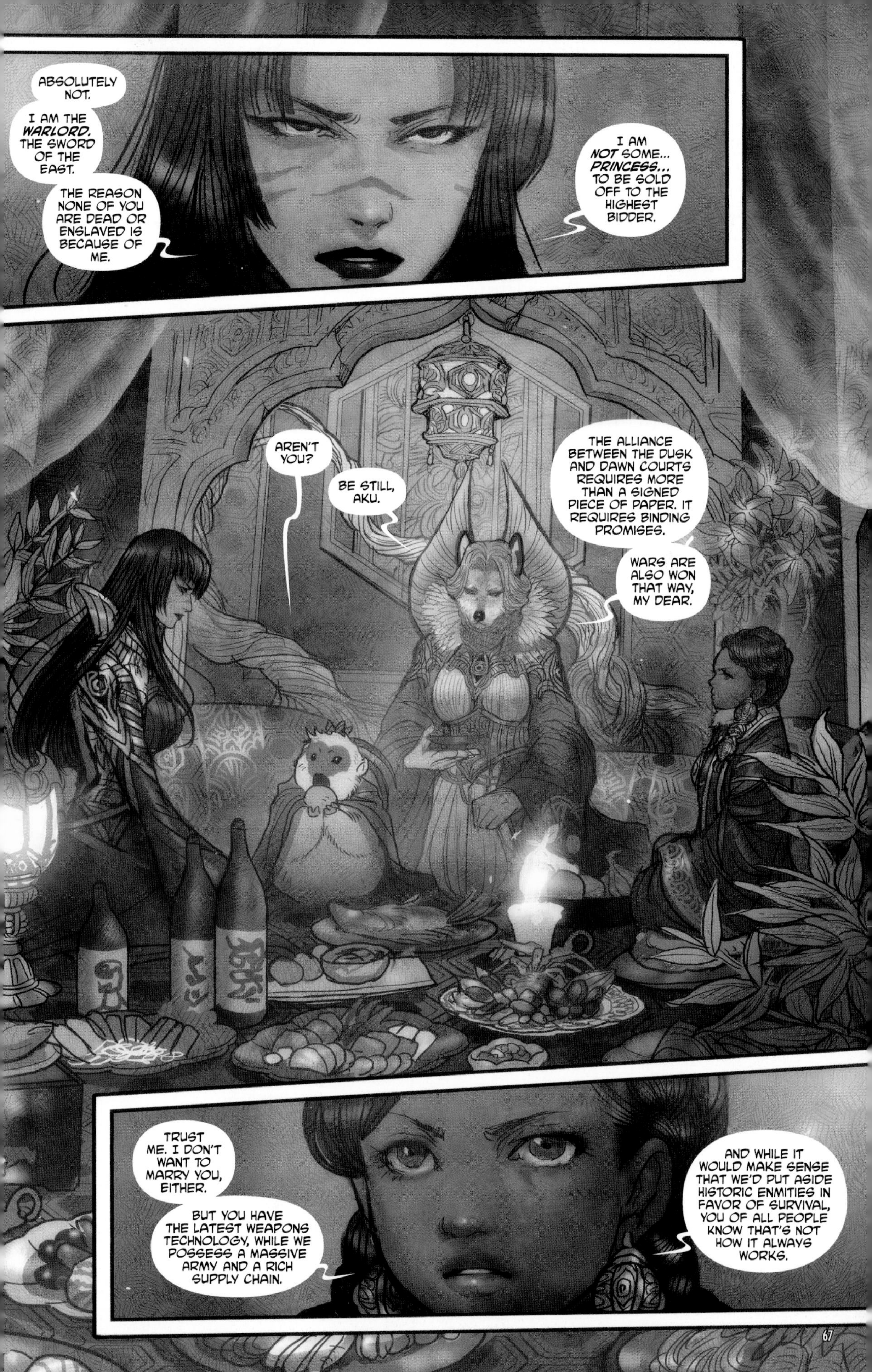
ABSOLUTELY NOT.
I AM THE WARLORD, THE SWORD OF THE EAST.
THE REASON NONE OF YOU ARE DEAD OR ENSLAVED IS BECAUSE OF ME.
I AM NOT SOME... PRINCESS... TO BE SOLD OFF TO THE HIGHEST BIDDER.
AREN'T YOU?
BE STILL, AKU.
THE ALLIANCE BETWEEN THE DUSK AND DAWN COURTS REQUIRES MORE THAN A SIGNED PIECE OF PAPER. IT REQUIRES BINDING PROMISES.
WARS ARE ALSO WON THAT WAY, MY DEAR.
TRUST ME. I DON'T WANT TO MARRY YOU, EITHER.
BUT YOU HAVE THE LATEST WEAPONS TECHNOLOGY, WHILE WE POSSESS A MASSIVE ARMY AND A RICH SUPPLY CHAIN.
AND WHILE IT WOULD MAKE SENSE THAT WE'D PUT ASIDE HISTORIC ENMITIES IN FAVOR OF SURVIVAL, YOU OF ALL PEOPLE KNOW THAT'S NOT HOW IT ALWAYS WORKS.

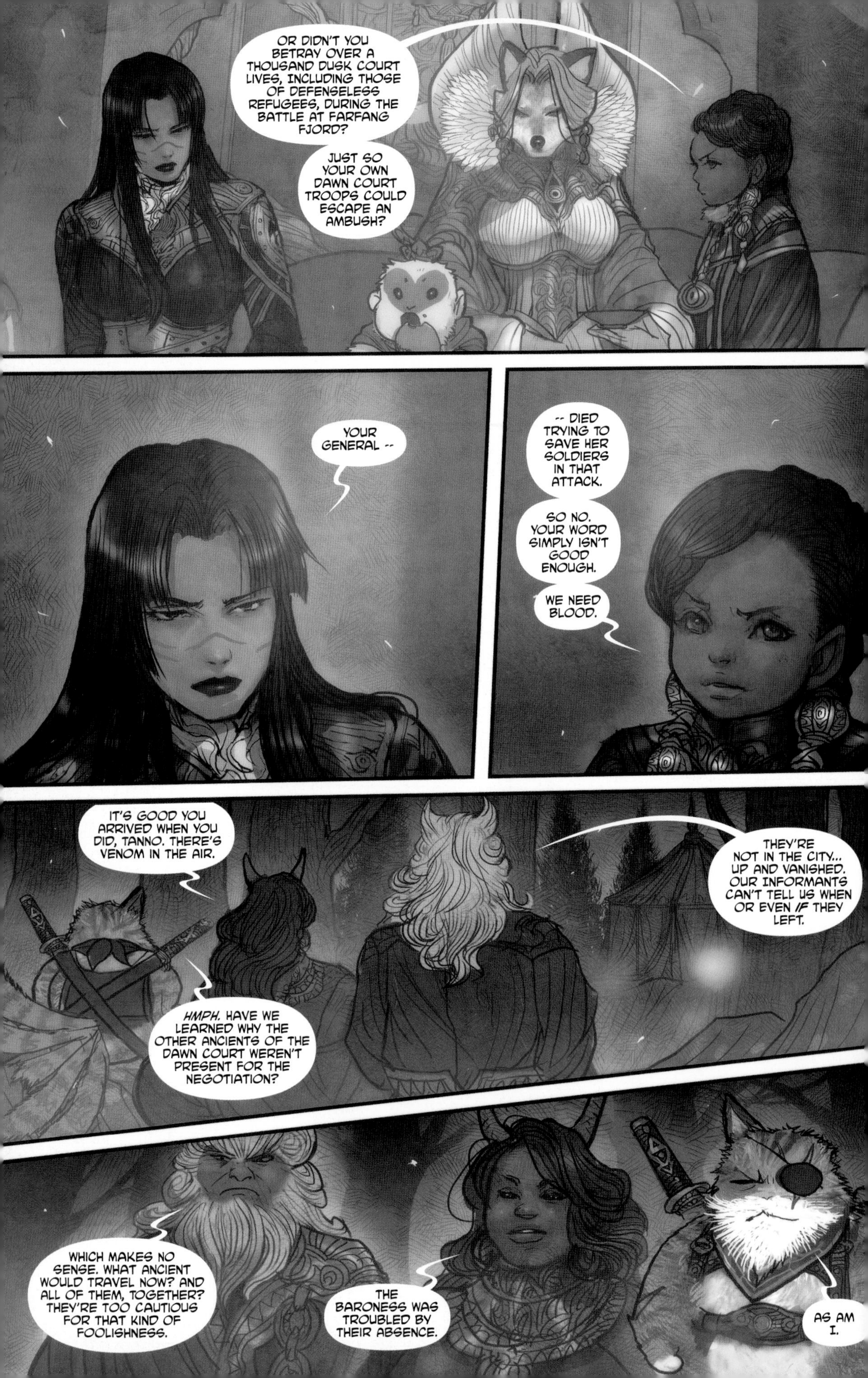
OR DIDN'T YOU BETRAY OVER A THOUSAND DUSK COURT LIVES, INCLUDING THOSE OF DEFENSELESS REFUGEES, DURING THE BATTLE AT FARFANG FJORD?
JUST SO YOUR OWN DAWN COURT TROOPS COULD ESCAPE AN AMBUSH?
YOUR GENERAL --
-- DIED TRYING TO SAVE HER SOLDIERS IN THAT ATTACK.
SO NO. YOUR WORD SIMPLY ISN'T GOOD ENOUGH.
WE NEED BLOOD.
IT'S GOOD YOU ARRIVED WHEN YOU DID, TANNO. THERE'S VENOM IN THE AIR.
THEY'RE NOT IN THE CITY... UP AND VANISHED. OUR INFORMANTS CAN'T TELL US WHEN OR EVEN *IF* THEY LEFT.
HMPH. HAVE WE LEARNED WHY THE OTHER ANCIENTS OF THE DAWN COURT WEREN'T PRESENT FOR THE NEGOTIATION?
WHICH MAKES NO SENSE. WHAT ANCIENT WOULD TRAVEL NOW? AND ALL OF THEM, TOGETHER? THEY'RE TOO CAUTIOUS FOR THAT KIND OF FOOLISHNESS.
THE BARONESS WAS TROUBLED BY THEIR ABSENCE.
AS AM I.

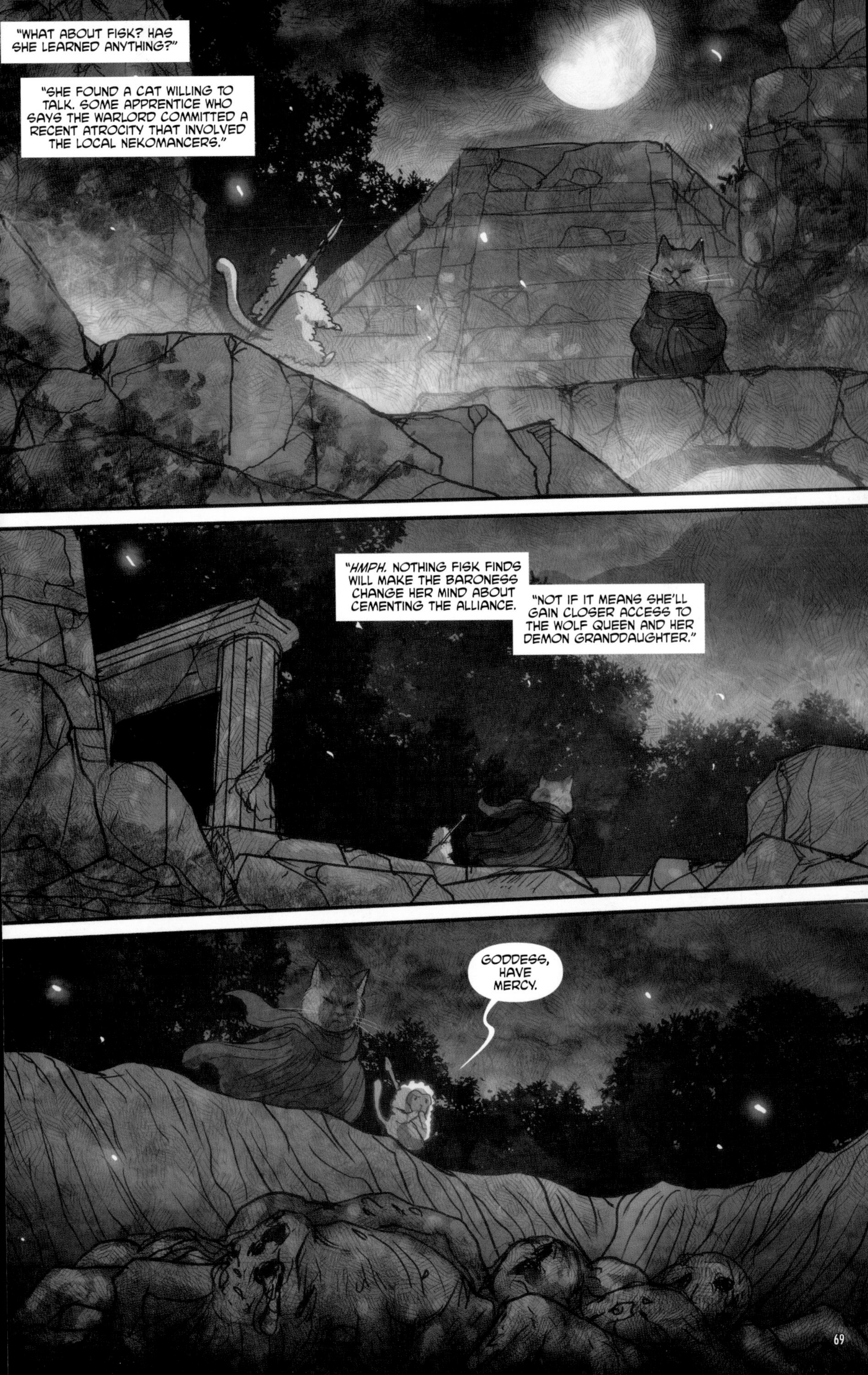
"WHAT ABOUT FISK? HAS SHE LEARNED ANYTHING?"
"SHE FOUND A CAT WILLING TO TALK. SOME APPRENTICE WHO SAYS THE WARLORD COMMITTED A RECENT ATROCITY THAT INVOLVED THE LOCAL NEKOMANCERS."
"*HMPH.* NOTHING FISK FINDS WILL MAKE THE BARONESS CHANGE HER MIND ABOUT CEMENTING THE ALLIANCE.
"NOT IF IT MEANS SHE'LL GAIN CLOSER ACCESS TO THE WOLF QUEEN AND HER DEMON GRANDDAUGHTER."
GODDESS, HAVE MERCY.

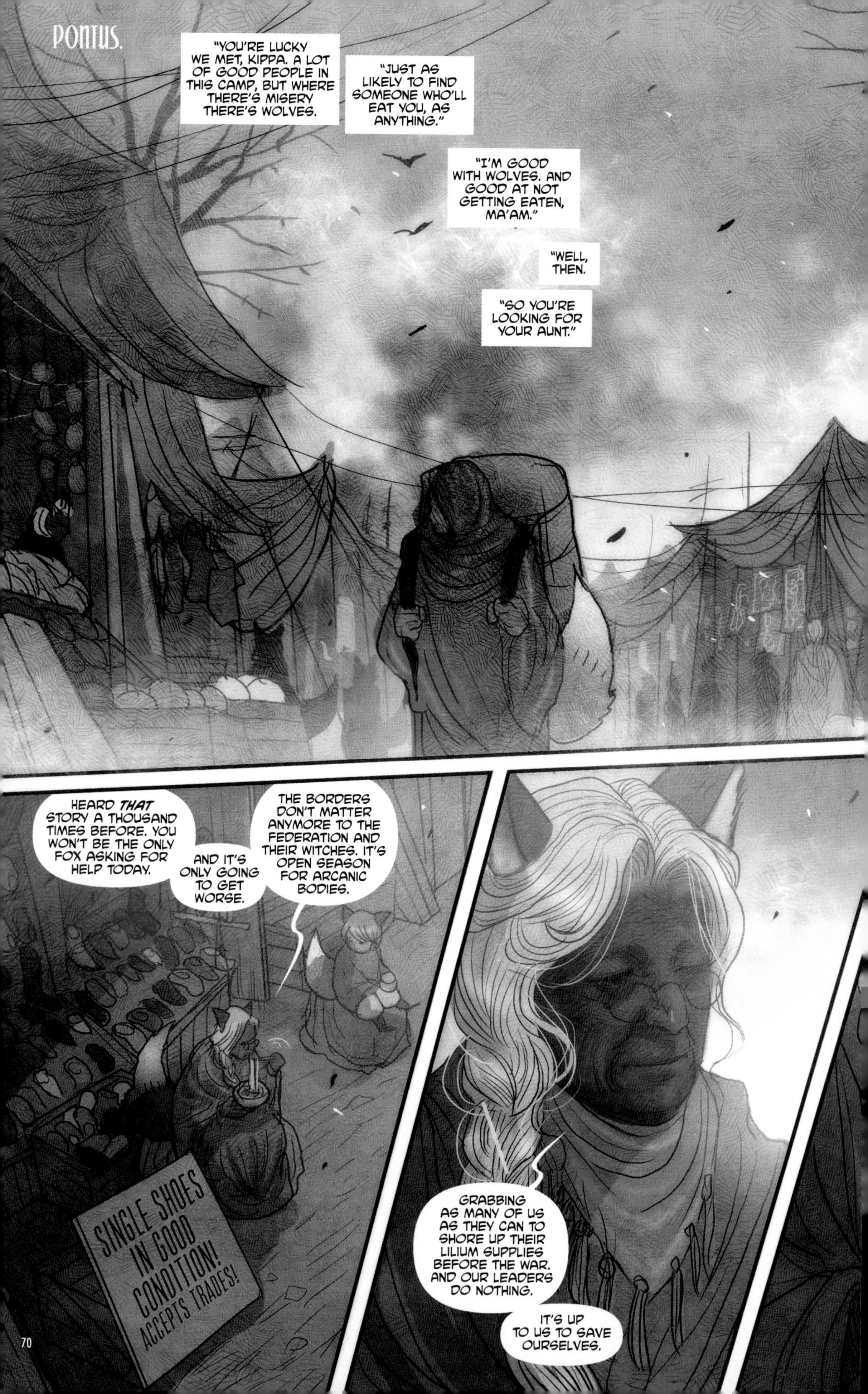
PONTUS.
"YOU'RE LUCKY WE MET, KIPPA. A LOT OF GOOD PEOPLE IN THIS CAMP, BUT WHERE THERE'S MISERY THERE'S WOLVES.
"JUST AS LIKELY TO FIND SOMEONE WHO'LL EAT YOU, AS ANYTHING."
"I'M GOOD WITH WOLVES. AND GOOD AT NOT GETTING EATEN, MA'AM."
"WELL, THEN.
"SO YOU'RE LOOKING FOR YOUR AUNT."
HEARD *THAT* STORY A THOUSAND TIMES BEFORE. YOU WON'T BE THE ONLY FOX ASKING FOR HELP TODAY.
AND IT'S ONLY GOING TO GET WORSE.
THE BORDERS DON'T MATTER ANYMORE TO THE FEDERATION AND THEIR WITCHES. IT'S OPEN SEASON FOR ARCANIC BODIES.
SINGLE SHOES IN GOOD CONDITION! ACCEPTS TRADES!
GRABBING AS MANY OF US AS THEY CAN TO SHORE UP THEIR LILIUM SUPPLIES BEFORE THE WAR. AND OUR LEADERS DO NOTHING.
IT'S UP TO US TO SAVE OURSELVES.

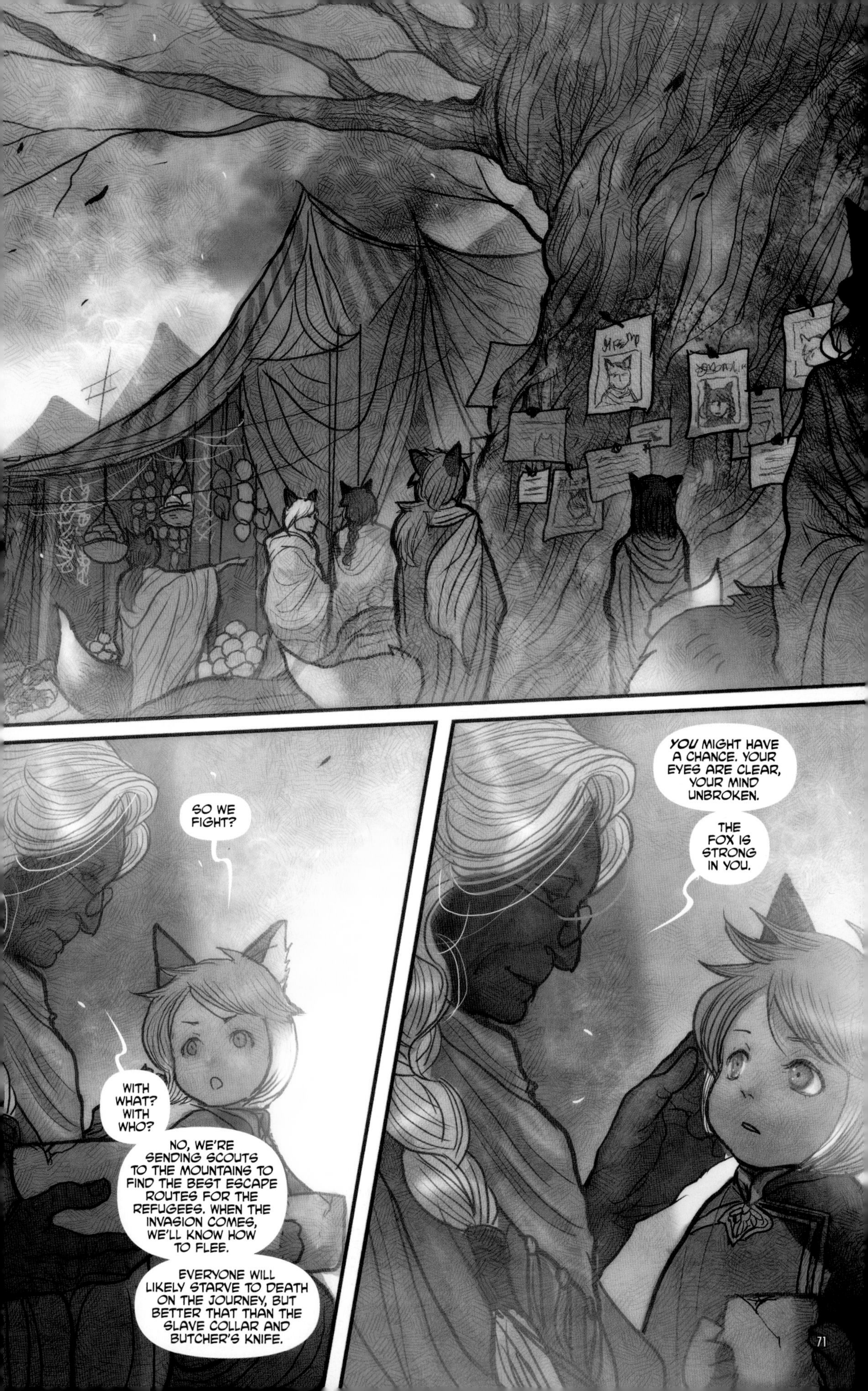
SO WE FIGHT?
WITH WHAT? WITH WHO?
NO, WE'RE SENDING SCOUTS TO THE MOUNTAINS TO FIND THE BEST ESCAPE ROUTES FOR THE REFUGEES. WHEN THE INVASION COMES, WE'LL KNOW HOW TO FLEE.
EVERYONE WILL LIKELY STARVE TO DEATH ON THE JOURNEY, BUT BETTER THAT THAN THE SLAVE COLLAR AND BUTCHER'S KNIFE.
YOU MIGHT HAVE A CHANCE. YOUR EYES ARE CLEAR, YOUR MIND UNBROKEN.
THE FOX IS STRONG IN YOU.

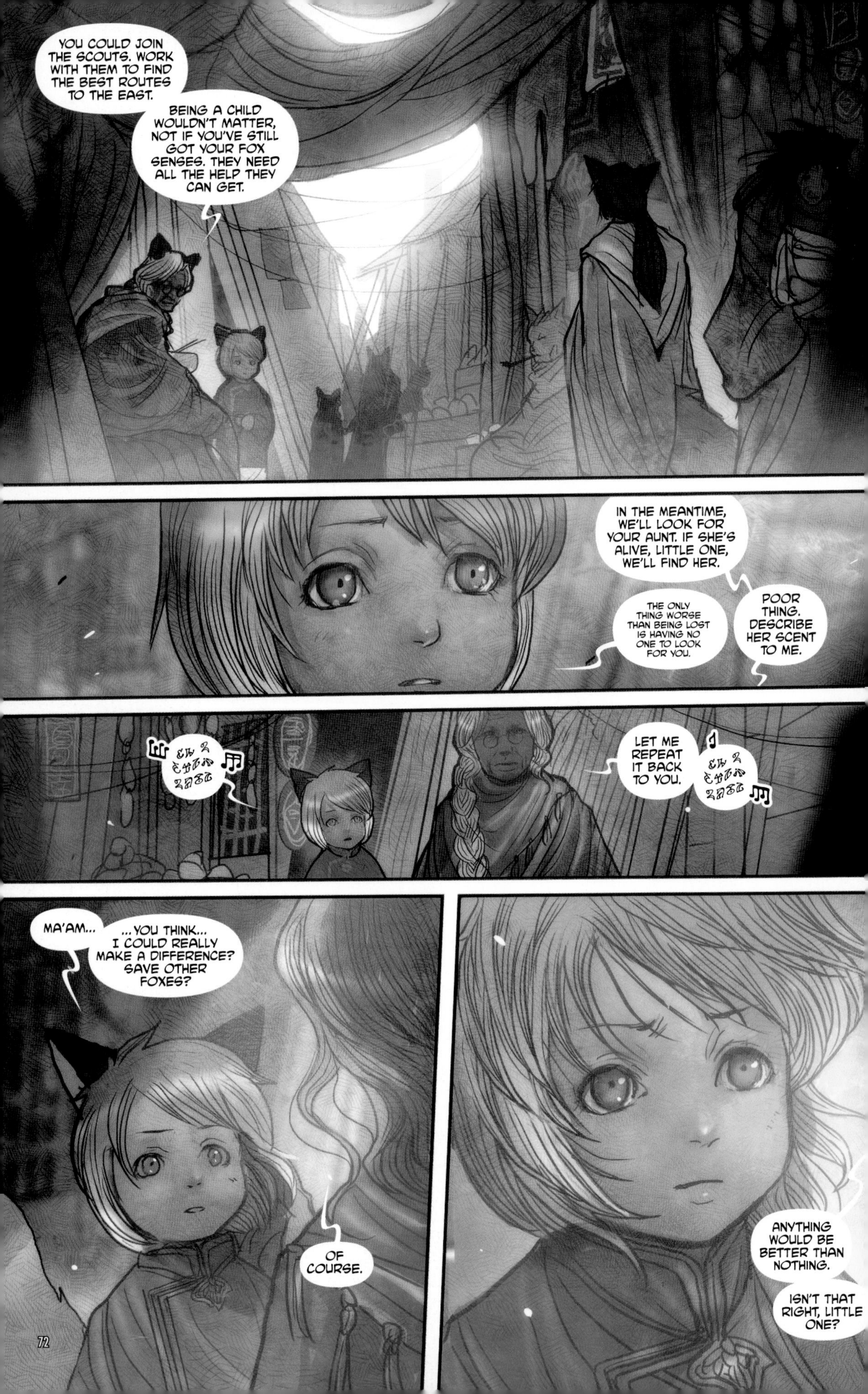
YOU COULD JOIN THE SCOUTS. WORK WITH THEM TO FIND THE BEST ROUTES TO THE EAST.
BEING A CHILD WOULDN'T MATTER, NOT IF YOU'VE STILL GOT YOUR FOX SENSES. THEY NEED ALL THE HELP THEY CAN GET.
IN THE MEANTIME, WE'LL LOOK FOR YOUR AUNT. IF SHE'S ALIVE, LITTLE ONE, WE'LL FIND HER.
POOR THING. DESCRIBE HER SCENT TO ME.
THE ONLY THING WORSE THAN BEING LOST IS HAVING NO ONE TO LOOK FOR YOU.
LET ME REPEAT IT BACK TO YOU.
MA'AM...
...YOU THINK... I COULD REALLY MAKE A DIFFERENCE? SAVE OTHER FOXES?
OF COURSE.
ANYTHING WOULD BE BETTER THAN NOTHING.
ISN'T THAT RIGHT, LITTLE ONE?

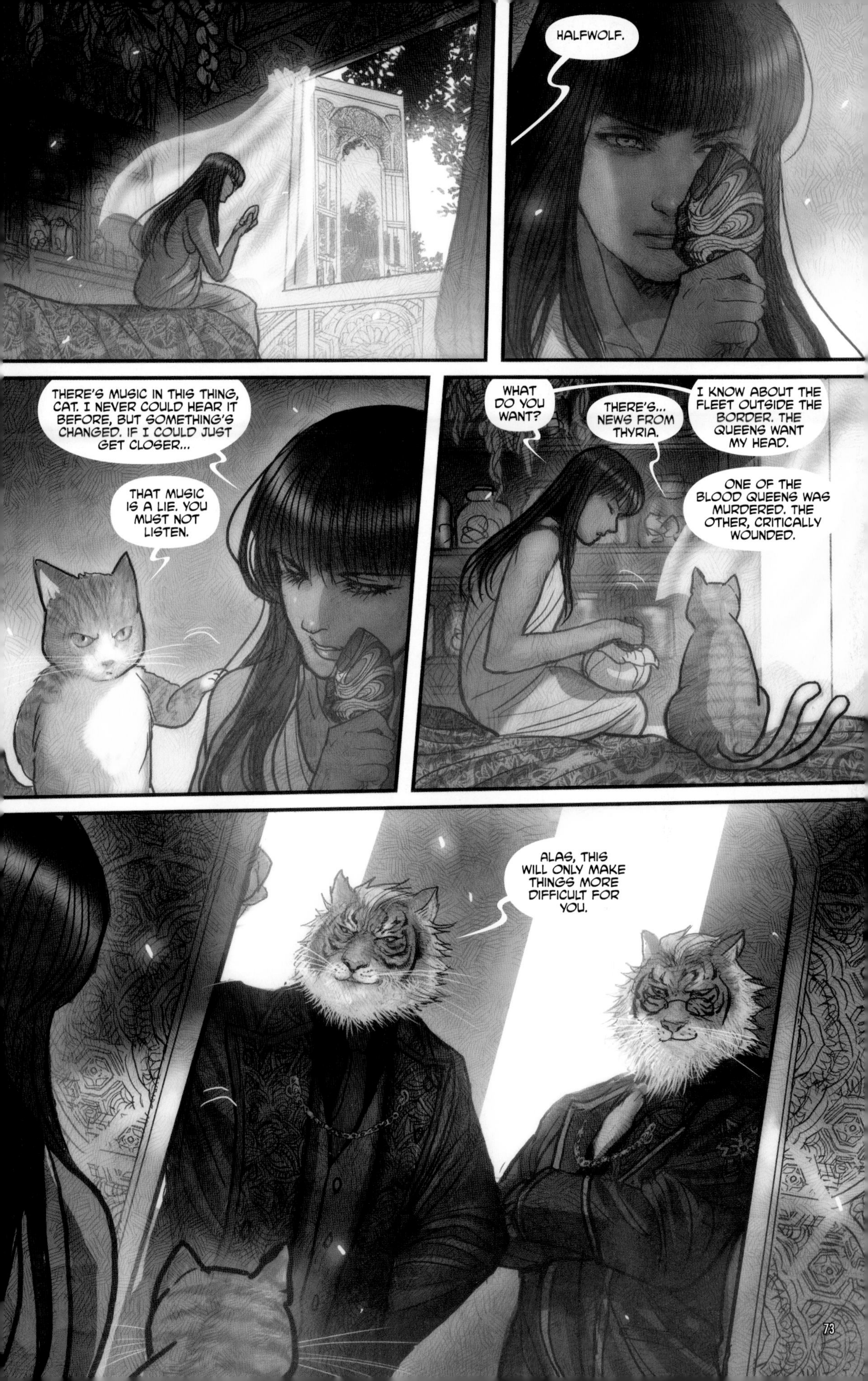
HALFWOLF.
THERE'S MUSIC IN THIS THING, CAT. I NEVER COULD HEAR IT BEFORE, BUT SOMETHING'S CHANGED. IF I COULD JUST GET CLOSER...
THAT MUSIC IS A LIE. YOU MUST NOT LISTEN.
WHAT DO YOU WANT?
THERE'S... NEWS FROM THYRIA.
I KNOW ABOUT THE FLEET OUTSIDE THE BORDER. THE QUEENS WANT MY HEAD.
ONE OF THE BLOOD QUEENS WAS MURDERED. THE OTHER, CRITICALLY WOUNDED.
ALAS, THIS WILL ONLY MAKE THINGS MORE DIFFICULT FOR YOU.

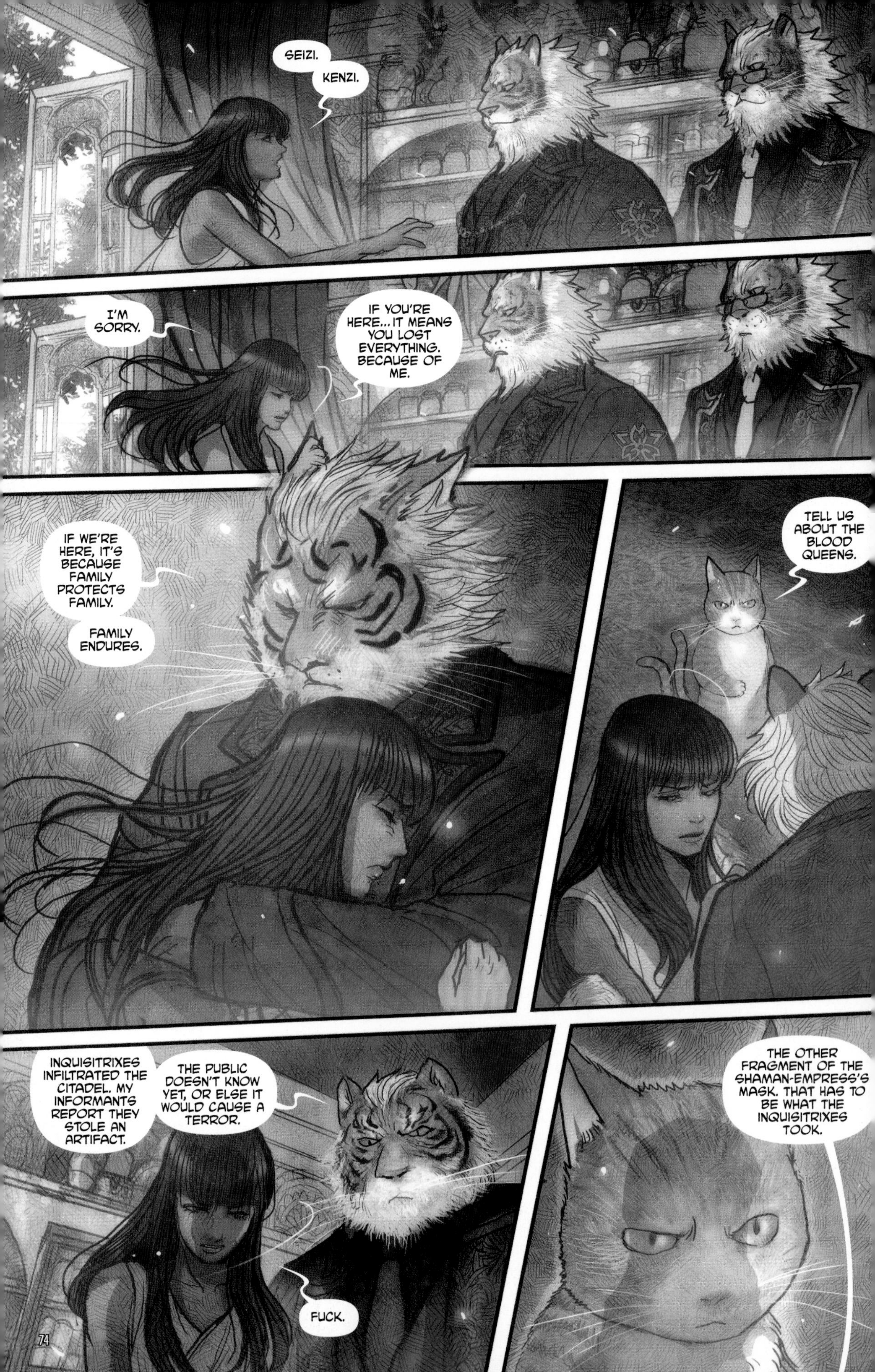
SEIZI.
KENZI.
I'M SORRY.
IF YOU'RE HERE... IT MEANS YOU LOST EVERYTHING. BECAUSE OF ME.
IF WE'RE HERE, IT'S BECAUSE FAMILY PROTECTS FAMILY.
FAMILY ENDURES.
TELL US ABOUT THE BLOOD QUEENS.
INQUISITRIXES INFILTRATED THE CITADEL. MY INFORMANTS REPORT THEY STOLE AN ARTIFACT.
THE PUBLIC DOESN'T KNOW YET, OR ELSE IT WOULD CAUSE A TERROR.
FUCK.
THE OTHER FRAGMENT OF THE SHAMAN-EMPRESS'S MASK. THAT HAS TO BE WHAT THE INQUISITRIXES TOOK.

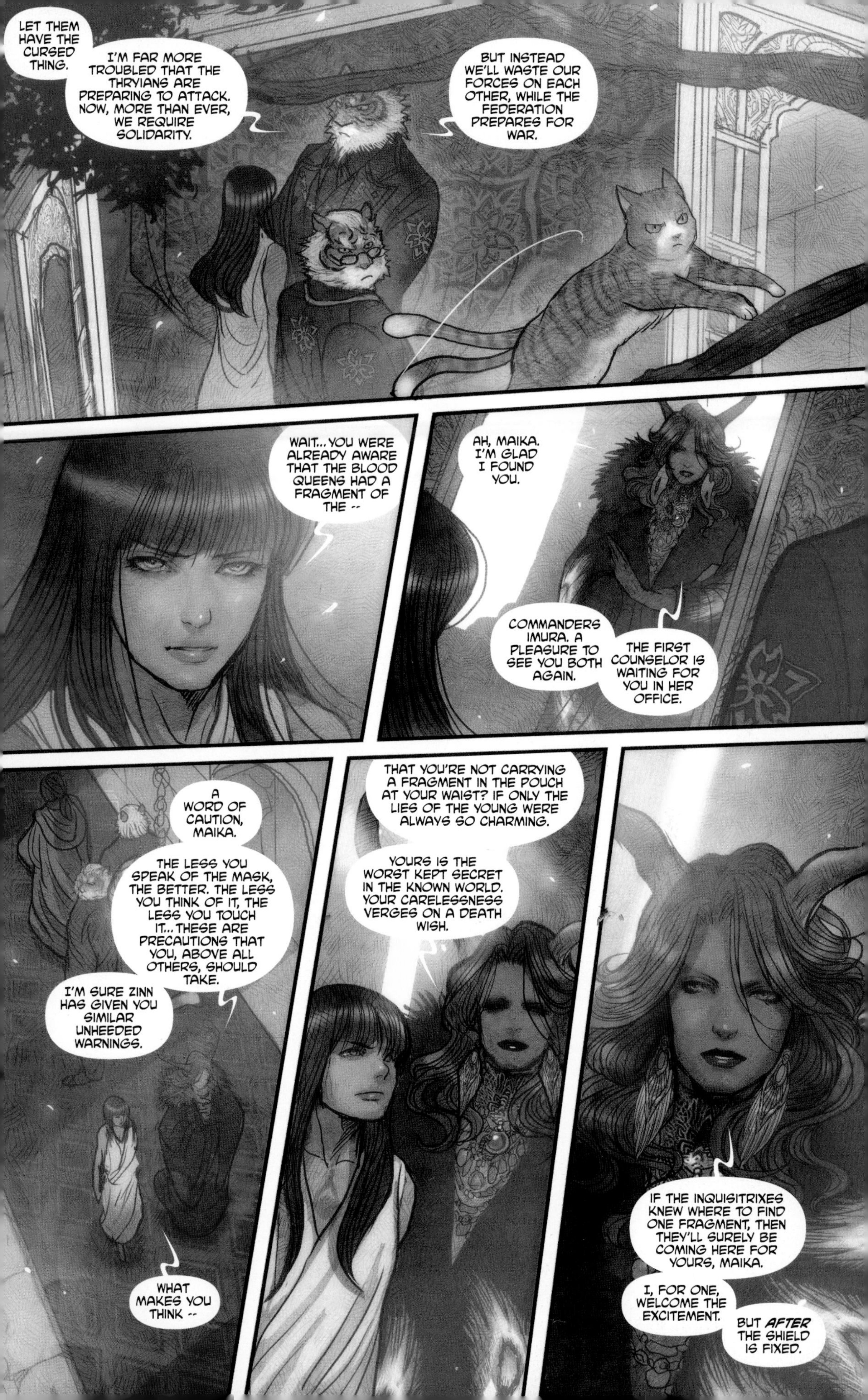
LET THEM HAVE THE CURSED THING.
I'M FAR MORE TROUBLED THAT THE THRYIANS ARE PREPARING TO ATTACK. NOW, MORE THAN EVER, WE REQUIRE SOLIDARITY.
BUT INSTEAD WE'LL WASTE OUR FORCES ON EACH OTHER, WHILE THE FEDERATION PREPARES FOR WAR.
WAIT... YOU WERE ALREADY AWARE THAT THE BLOOD QUEENS HAD A FRAGMENT OF THE --
AH, MAIKA. I'M GLAD I FOUND YOU.
COMMANDERS IMURA. A PLEASURE TO SEE YOU BOTH AGAIN.
THE FIRST COUNSELOR IS WAITING FOR YOU IN HER OFFICE.
A WORD OF CAUTION, MAIKA.
THE LESS YOU SPEAK OF THE MASK, THE BETTER. THE LESS YOU THINK OF IT, THE LESS YOU TOUCH IT... THESE ARE PRECAUTIONS THAT YOU, ABOVE ALL OTHERS, SHOULD TAKE.
I'M SURE ZINN HAS GIVEN YOU SIMILAR UNHEEDED WARNINGS.
WHAT MAKES YOU THINK --
THAT YOU'RE NOT CARRYING A FRAGMENT IN THE POUCH AT YOUR WAIST? IF ONLY THE LIES OF THE YOUNG WERE ALWAYS SO CHARMING.
YOURS IS THE WORST KEPT SECRET IN THE KNOWN WORLD. YOUR CARELESSNESS VERGES ON A DEATH WISH.
IF THE INQUISITRIXES KNEW WHERE TO FIND ONE FRAGMENT, THEN THEY'LL SURELY BE COMING HERE FOR YOURS, MAIKA.
I, FOR ONE, WELCOME THE EXCITEMENT.
BUT *AFTER* THE SHIELD IS FIXED.

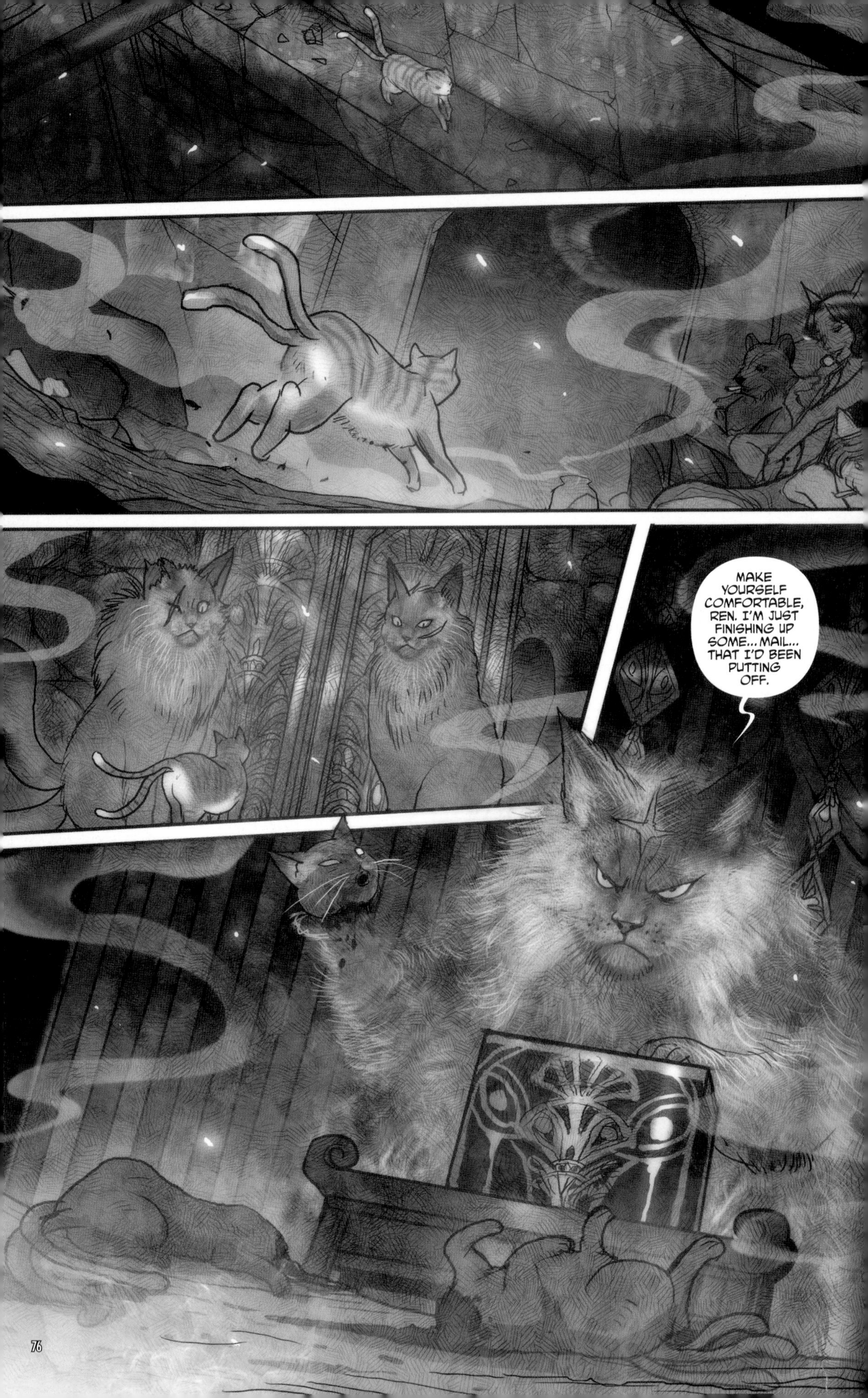
MAKE YOURSELF COMFORTABLE, REN. I'M JUST FINISHING UP SOME... MAIL... THAT I'D BEEN PUTTING OFF.

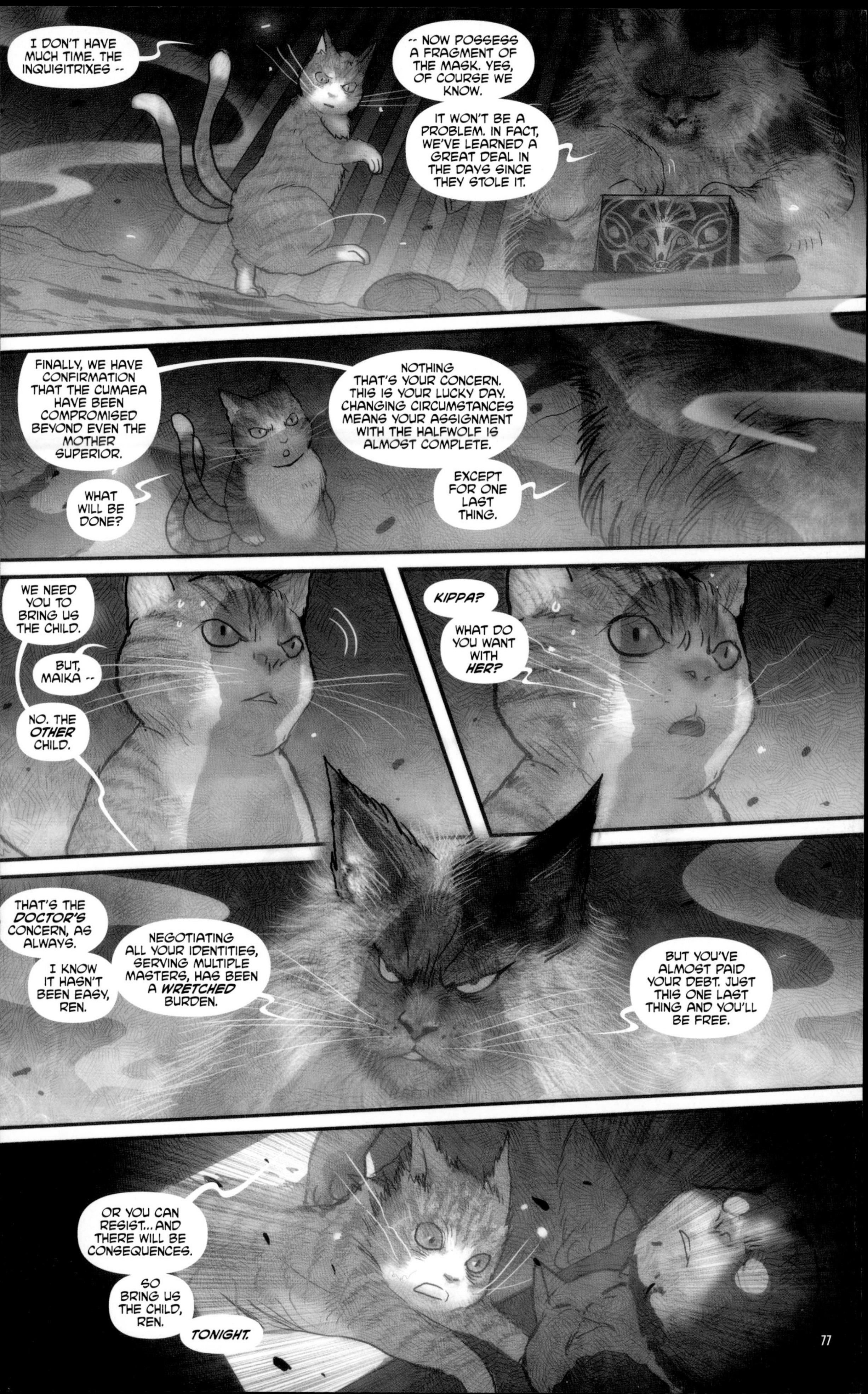
I DON'T HAVE MUCH TIME. THE INQUISITRIXES --
-- NOW POSSESS A FRAGMENT OF THE MASK. YES, OF COURSE WE KNOW.
IT WON'T BE A PROBLEM. IN FACT, WE'VE LEARNED A GREAT DEAL IN THE DAYS SINCE THEY STOLE IT.
FINALLY, WE HAVE CONFIRMATION THAT THE CUMAEA HAVE BEEN COMPROMISED BEYOND EVEN THE MOTHER SUPERIOR.
WHAT WILL BE DONE?
NOTHING THAT'S YOUR CONCERN. THIS IS YOUR LUCKY DAY. CHANGING CIRCUMSTANCES MEANS YOUR ASSIGNMENT WITH THE HALFWOLF IS ALMOST COMPLETE.
EXCEPT FOR ONE LAST THING.
WE NEED YOU TO BRING US THE CHILD.
BUT, MAIKA --
NO. THE *OTHER* CHILD.
KIPPA?
WHAT DO YOU WANT WITH *HER?*
THAT'S THE *DOCTOR'S* CONCERN, AS ALWAYS.
I KNOW IT HASN'T BEEN EASY, REN.
NEGOTIATING ALL YOUR IDENTITIES, SERVING MULTIPLE MASTERS, HAS BEEN A *WRETCHED* BURDEN.
BUT YOU'VE ALMOST PAID YOUR DEBT. JUST THIS ONE LAST THING AND YOU'LL BE FREE.
OR YOU CAN RESIST... AND THERE WILL BE CONSEQUENCES.
SO BRING US THE CHILD, REN.
TONIGHT.

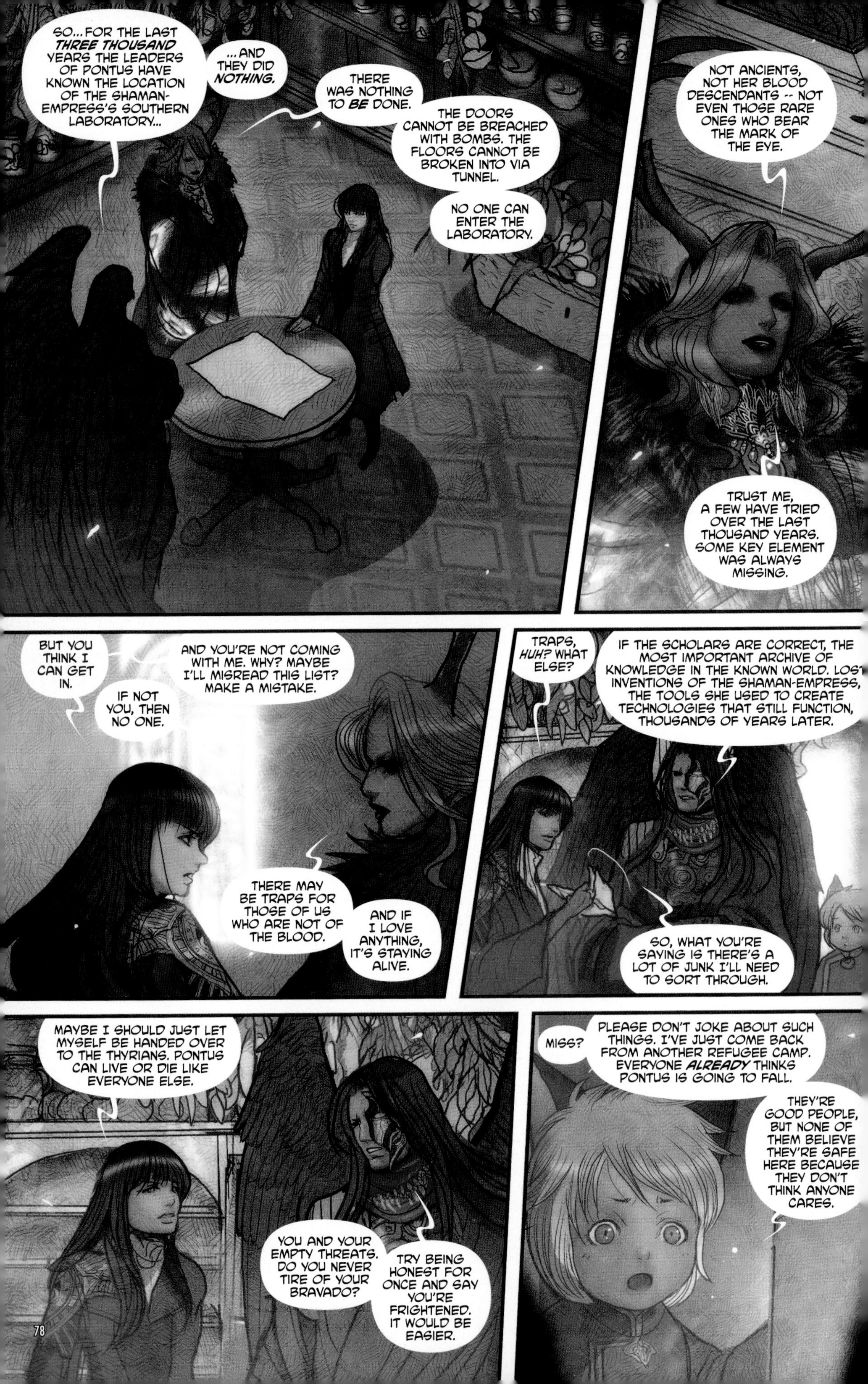
SO... FOR THE LAST THREE THOUSAND YEARS THE LEADERS OF PONTUS HAVE KNOWN THE LOCATION OF THE SHAMAN-EMPRESS'S SOUTHERN LABORATORY...
...AND THEY DID NOTHING.
THERE WAS NOTHING TO BE DONE.
THE DOORS CANNOT BE BREACHED WITH BOMBS. THE FLOORS CANNOT BE BROKEN INTO VIA TUNNEL.
NO ONE CAN ENTER THE LABORATORY.
NOT ANCIENTS, NOT HER BLOOD DESCENDANTS -- NOT EVEN THOSE RARE ONES WHO BEAR THE MARK OF THE EYE.
TRUST ME, A FEW HAVE TRIED OVER THE LAST THOUSAND YEARS. SOME KEY ELEMENT WAS ALWAYS MISSING.
BUT YOU THINK I CAN GET IN.
IF NOT YOU, THEN NO ONE.
AND YOU'RE NOT COMING WITH ME. WHY? MAYBE I'LL MISREAD THIS LIST? MAKE A MISTAKE.
THERE MAY BE TRAPS FOR THOSE OF US WHO ARE NOT OF THE BLOOD.
AND IF I LOVE ANYTHING, IT'S STAYING ALIVE.
TRAPS, HUH? WHAT ELSE?
IF THE SCHOLARS ARE CORRECT, THE MOST IMPORTANT ARCHIVE OF KNOWLEDGE IN THE KNOWN WORLD. LOST INVENTIONS OF THE SHAMAN-EMPRESS, THE TOOLS SHE USED TO CREATE TECHNOLOGIES THAT STILL FUNCTION, THOUSANDS OF YEARS LATER.
SO, WHAT YOU'RE SAYING IS THERE'S A LOT OF JUNK I'LL NEED TO SORT THROUGH.
MAYBE I SHOULD JUST LET MYSELF BE HANDED OVER TO THE THYRIANS. PONTUS CAN LIVE OR DIE LIKE EVERYONE ELSE.
YOU AND YOUR EMPTY THREATS. DO YOU NEVER TIRE OF YOUR BRAVADO?
TRY BEING HONEST FOR ONCE AND SAY YOU'RE FRIGHTENED. IT WOULD BE EASIER.
MISS?
PLEASE DON'T JOKE ABOUT SUCH THINGS. I'VE JUST COME BACK FROM ANOTHER REFUGEE CAMP. EVERYONE ALREADY THINKS PONTUS IS GOING TO FALL.
THEY'RE GOOD PEOPLE, BUT NONE OF THEM BELIEVE THEY'RE SAFE HERE BECAUSE THEY DON'T THINK ANYONE CARES.

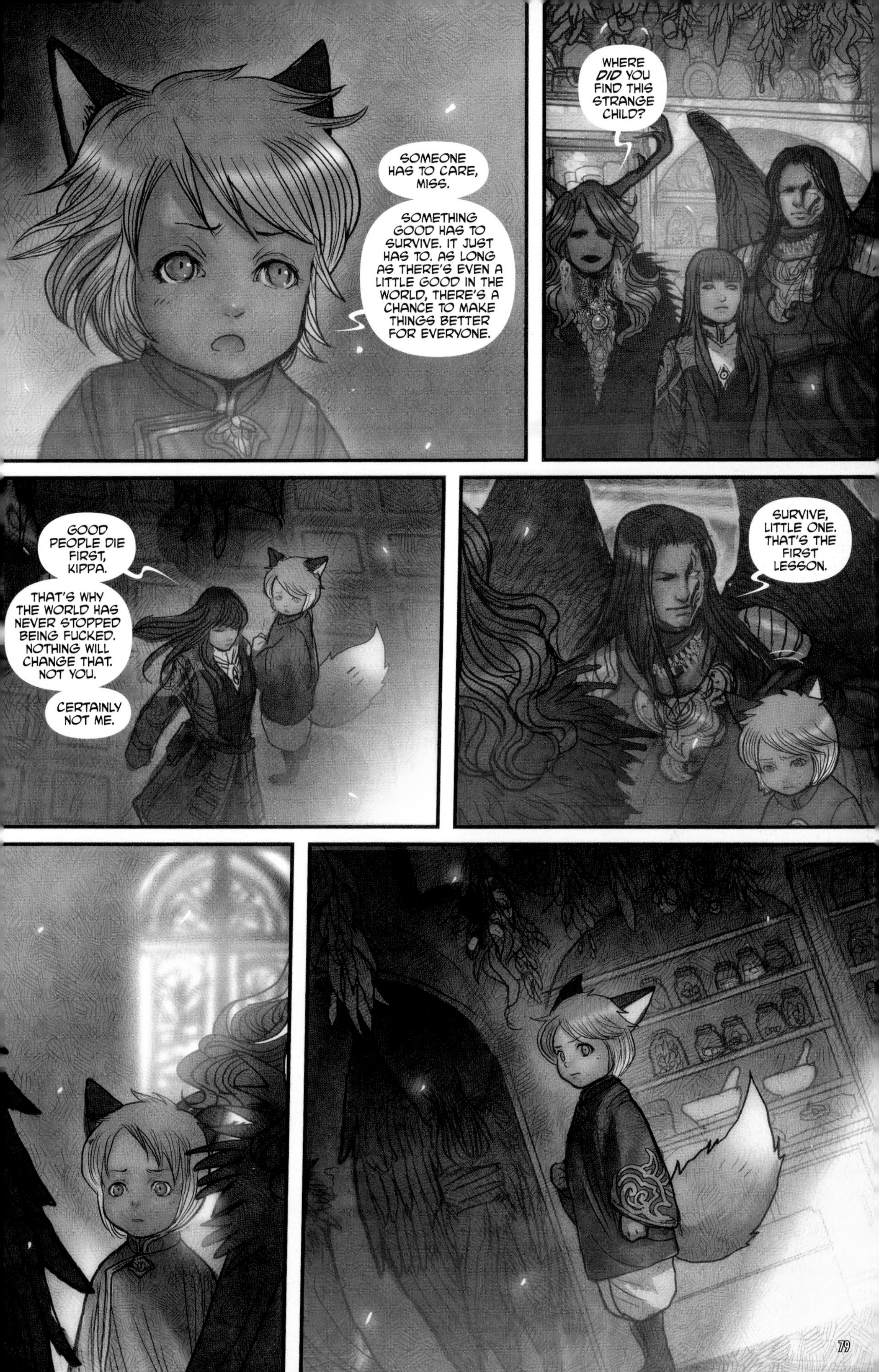
SOMEONE HAS TO CARE, MISS.
SOMETHING GOOD HAS TO SURVIVE. IT JUST HAS TO. AS LONG AS THERE'S EVEN A LITTLE GOOD IN THE WORLD, THERE'S A CHANCE TO MAKE THINGS BETTER FOR EVERYONE.
WHERE *DID* YOU FIND THIS STRANGE CHILD?
GOOD PEOPLE DIE FIRST, KIPPA.
THAT'S WHY THE WORLD HAS NEVER STOPPED BEING FUCKED. NOTHING WILL CHANGE THAT. NOT YOU.
CERTAINLY NOT ME.
SURVIVE, LITTLE ONE. THAT'S THE FIRST LESSON.

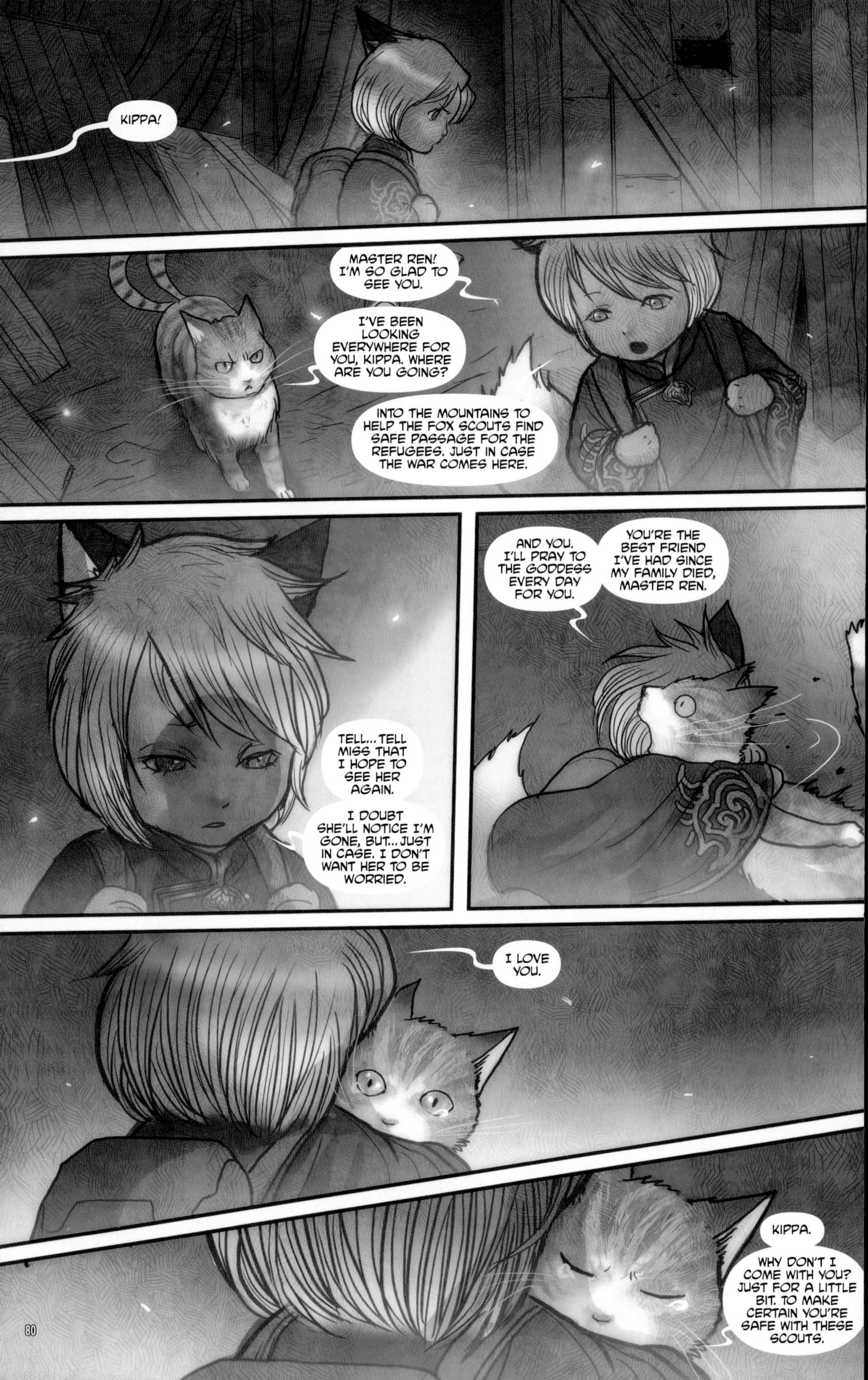
KIPPA!
MASTER REN! I'M SO GLAD TO SEE YOU.
I'VE BEEN LOOKING EVERYWHERE FOR YOU, KIPPA. WHERE ARE YOU GOING?
INTO THE MOUNTAINS TO HELP THE FOX SCOUTS FIND SAFE PASSAGE FOR THE REFUGEES. JUST IN CASE THE WAR COMES HERE.
TELL... TELL MISS THAT I HOPE TO SEE HER AGAIN.
I DOUBT SHE'LL NOTICE I'M GONE, BUT... JUST IN CASE. I DON'T WANT HER TO BE WORRIED.
AND YOU. I'LL PRAY TO THE GODDESS EVERY DAY FOR YOU.
YOU'RE THE BEST FRIEND I'VE HAD SINCE MY FAMILY DIED, MASTER REN.
I LOVE YOU.
KIPPA.
WHY DON'T I COME WITH YOU? JUST FOR A LITTLE BIT. TO MAKE CERTAIN YOU'RE SAFE WITH THESE SCOUTS.

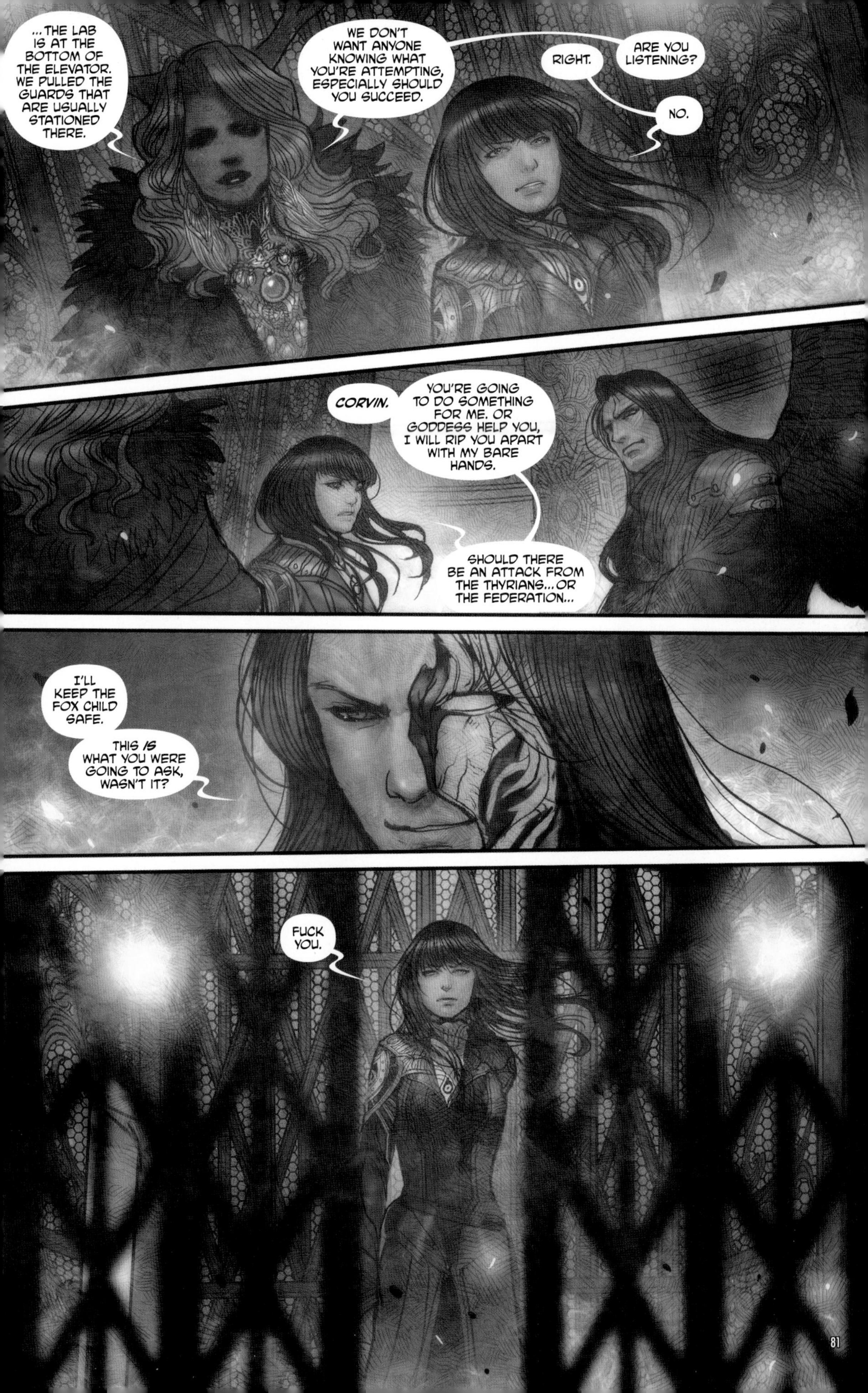
...THE LAB IS AT THE BOTTOM OF THE ELEVATOR. WE PULLED THE GUARDS THAT ARE USUALLY STATIONED THERE.
WE DON'T WANT ANYONE KNOWING WHAT YOU'RE ATTEMPTING, ESPECIALLY SHOULD YOU SUCCEED.
ARE YOU LISTENING?
RIGHT.
NO.
CORVIN.
YOU'RE GOING TO DO SOMETHING FOR ME. OR GODDESS HELP YOU, I WILL RIP YOU APART WITH MY BARE HANDS.
SHOULD THERE BE AN ATTACK FROM THE THYRIANS...OR THE FEDERATION...
I'LL KEEP THE FOX CHILD SAFE.
THIS *IS* WHAT YOU WERE GOING TO ASK, WASN'T IT?
FUCK YOU.

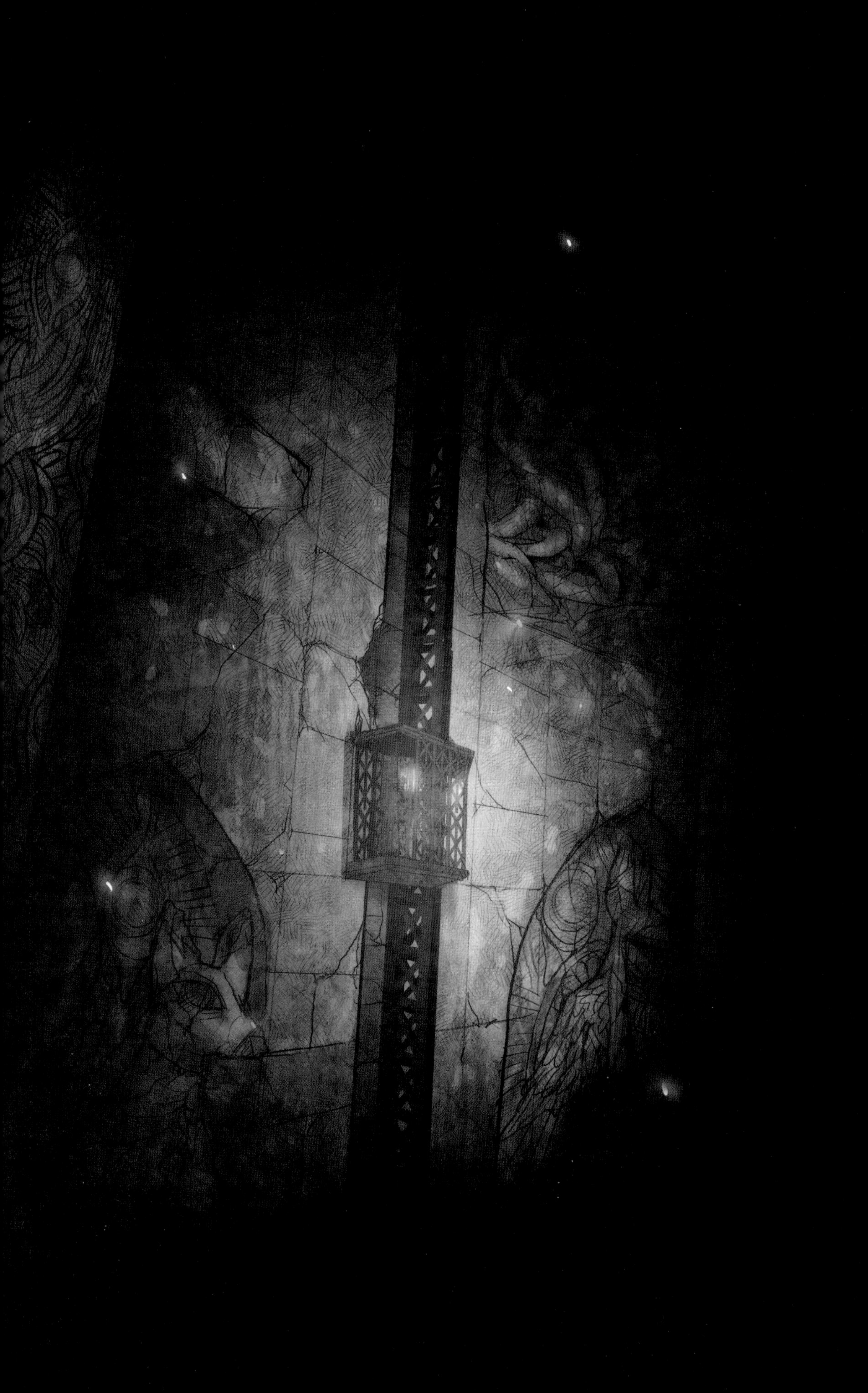

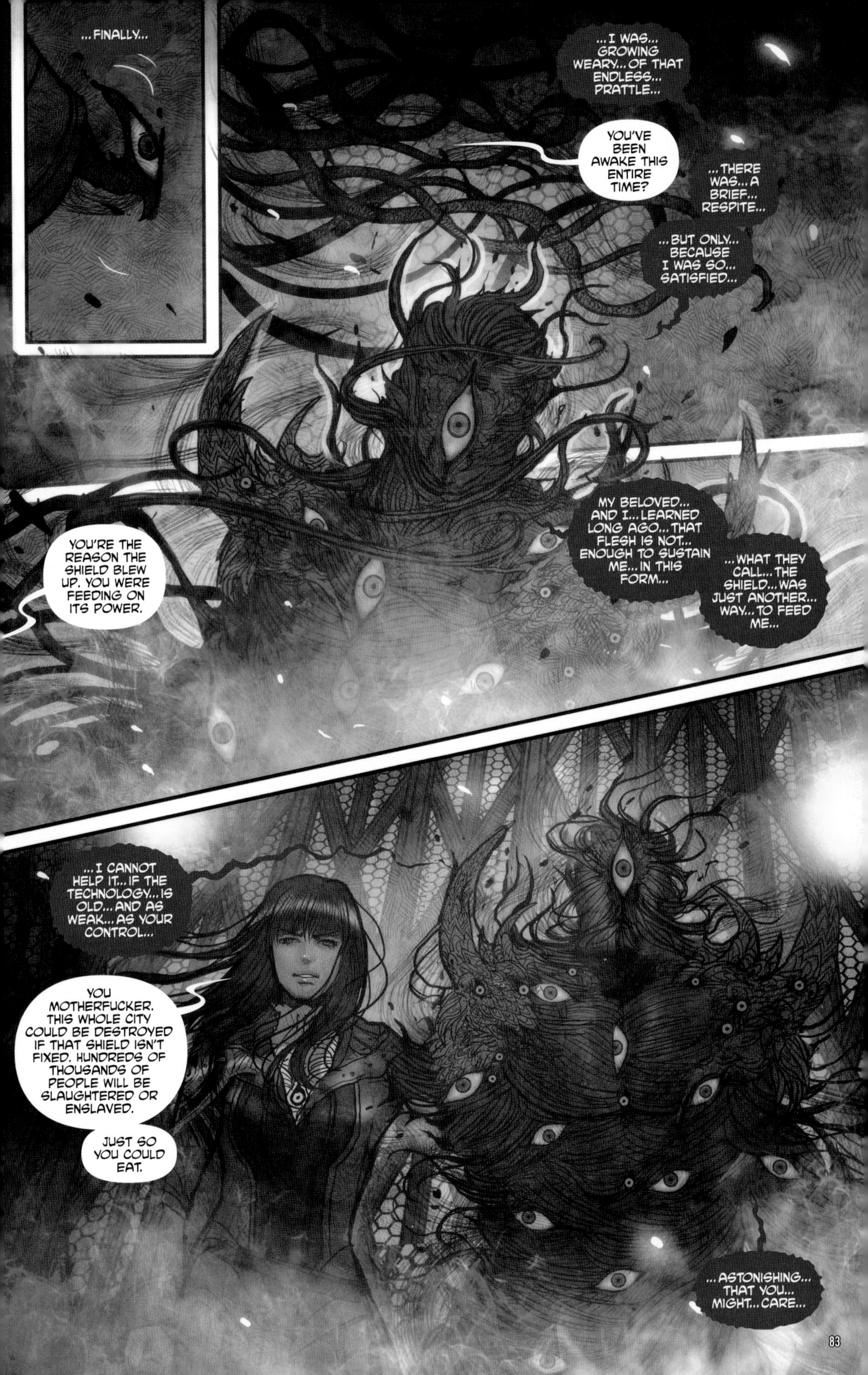
...FINALLY...
...I WAS... GROWING WEARY... OF THAT ENDLESS... PRATTLE...
YOU'VE BEEN AWAKE THIS ENTIRE TIME?
...THERE WAS... A BRIEF... RESPITE...
...BUT ONLY... BECAUSE I WAS SO... SATISFIED...
YOU'RE THE REASON THE SHIELD BLEW UP. YOU WERE FEEDING ON ITS POWER.
MY BELOVED... AND I... LEARNED LONG AGO... THAT FLESH IS NOT... ENOUGH TO SUSTAIN ME... IN THIS FORM...
...WHAT THEY CALL... THE SHIELD... WAS JUST ANOTHER... WAY... TO FEED ME...
...I CANNOT HELP IT... IF THE TECHNOLOGY... IS OLD... AND AS WEAK... AS YOUR CONTROL...
YOU MOTHERFUCKER. THIS WHOLE CITY COULD BE DESTROYED IF THAT SHIELD ISN'T FIXED. HUNDREDS OF THOUSANDS OF PEOPLE WILL BE SLAUGHTERED OR ENSLAVED.
JUST SO YOU COULD EAT.
...ASTONISHING... THAT YOU... MIGHT... CARE...

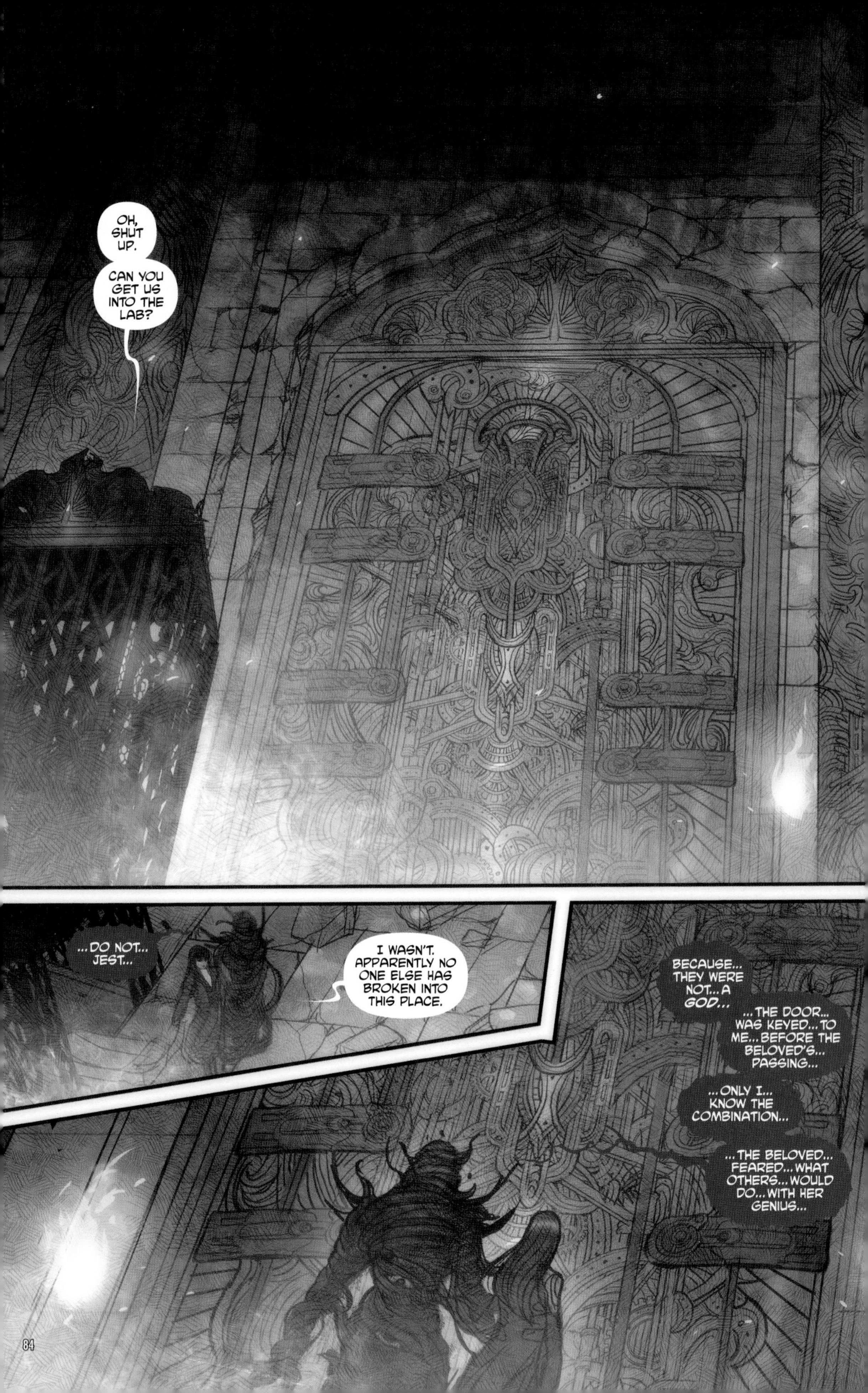
OH, SHUT UP.
CAN YOU GET US INTO THE LAB?
...DO NOT... JEST...
I WASN'T. APPARENTLY NO ONE ELSE HAS BROKEN INTO THIS PLACE.
BECAUSE... THEY WERE NOT... A *GOD*...
...THE DOOR... WAS KEYED... TO ME... BEFORE THE BELOVED'S... PASSING...
...ONLY I... KNOW THE COMBINATION...
...THE BELOVED... FEARED... WHAT OTHERS... WOULD DO... WITH HER GENIUS...

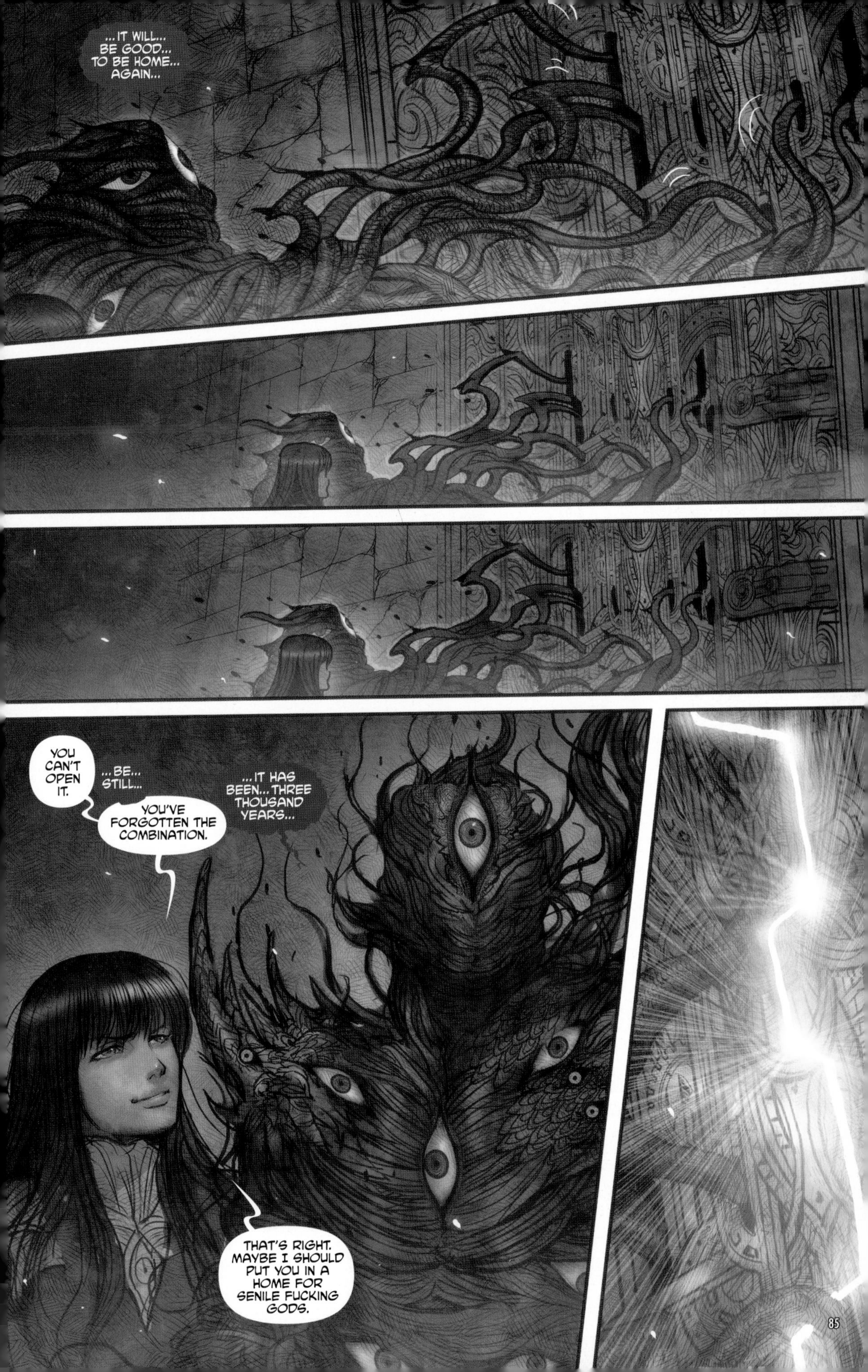
...IT WILL... BE GOOD... TO BE HOME... AGAIN...
YOU CAN'T OPEN IT.
...BE... STILL...
YOU'VE FORGOTTEN THE COMBINATION.
...IT HAS BEEN... THREE THOUSAND YEARS...
THAT'S RIGHT. MAYBE I SHOULD PUT YOU IN A HOME FOR SENILE FUCKING GODS.

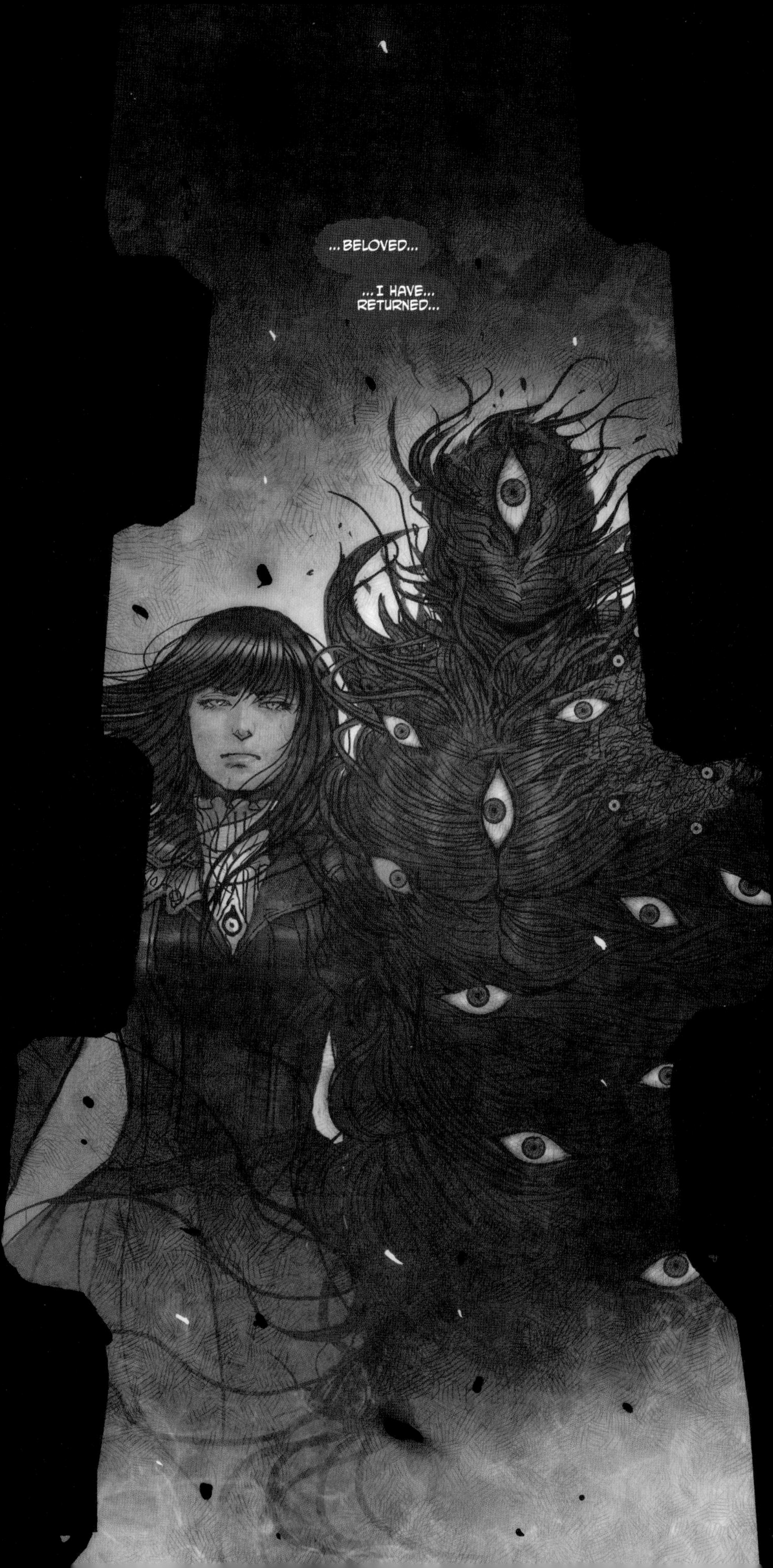
...BELOVED...
...I HAVE... RETURNED...

An excerpt of a lecture from the esteemed **Professor Tam Tam,** former First Record-Keeper of the Is'hami Temple, and learned contemporary of Namron Black Claw...

Ah, the Old Gods.

We've discussed them before – their immense power, their destructive natures – how they are the very opposite of divine. Invaders, some Poets claim. Demonic entities from another world, whose unending hunger was an abomination.

Thank Ubasti they were banished. And yet...and yet...how quickly the truth was forgotten.

According to our records, the first cult of the Old Gods emerged almost four thousand years ago, well inland from the coast where humans already worshipped the Wave Empress and her Siren children.

Humans were the logical fools to fall prey to the Old Gods – having never battled them, as the Ancients had – and afflicted by a poverty of spirit unmatched by even the most crude animal. How easily fooled they were by such otherwordly magnificence, whispering empty prayers, making blood sacrifices to demons that would consume them in a heartbeat if they were able.

And yet, in the end, Arcanics fared little better.

The fault rests with one of the Ancients, a changeling trickster who disguised herself to live among mortal humans and Arcanics. She was, perhaps, a little too fond of telling stories, and not wary enough of her own charisma.

Her most famous (and improbable) tale was about an Old God who escapes to the known world in search of redemption, and falls in love with a powerful queen. Against all good sense, this frivolity spread like wildfire – and rewrote history. Suddenly, the Old Gods were creatures of tragedy and romance, longing to walk amongst mortals, and share their wisdom.

And that was enough, kits, to become a religion. Benign, yes, based on a philosophy of love and compassion, and mercy. Looking to the Old Gods as guides to an enlightened life.

But cats have never been fooled. We have never forgotten the horror.

The horror that Ubasti promises will come again.

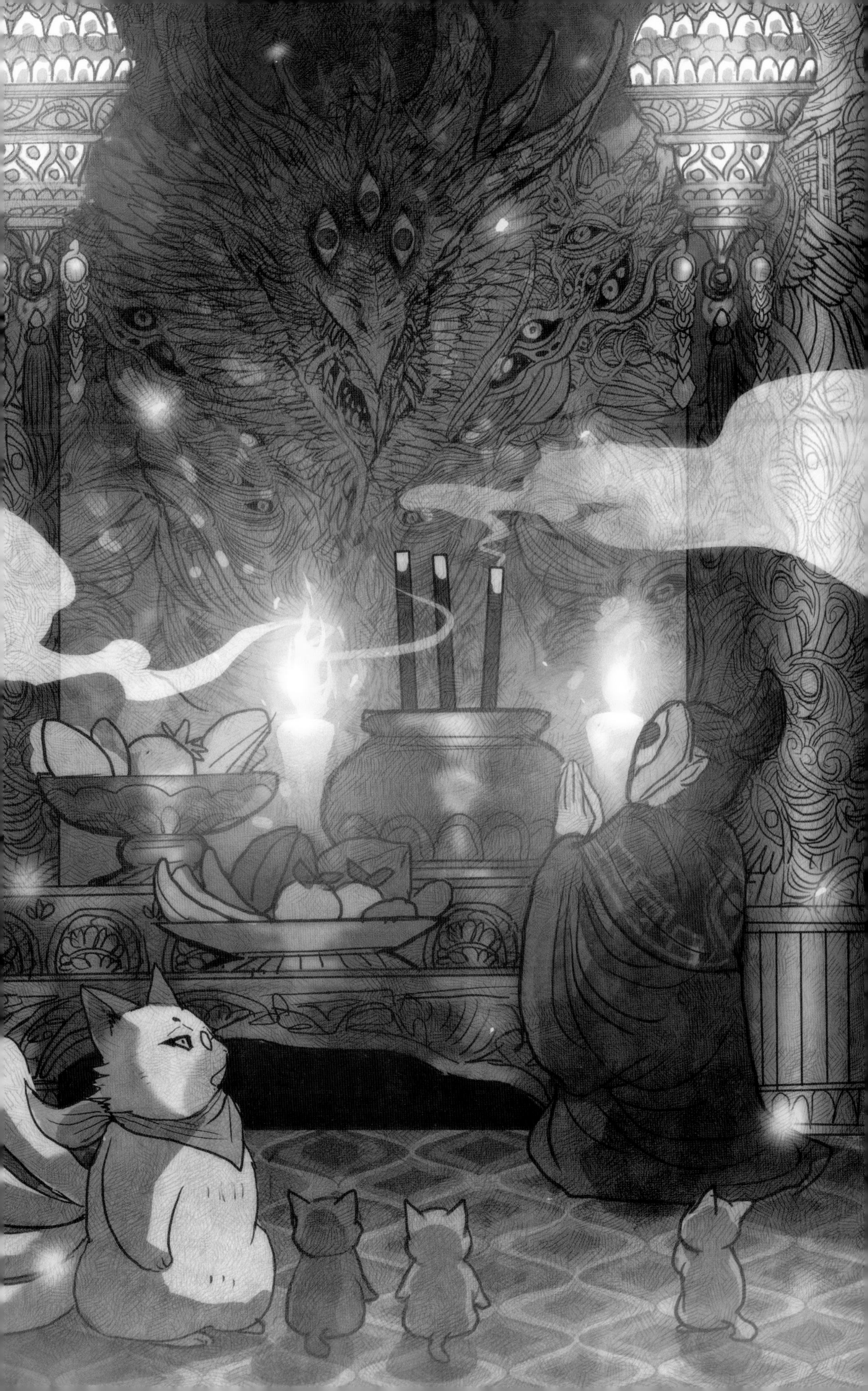

CHAPTER SIXTEEN

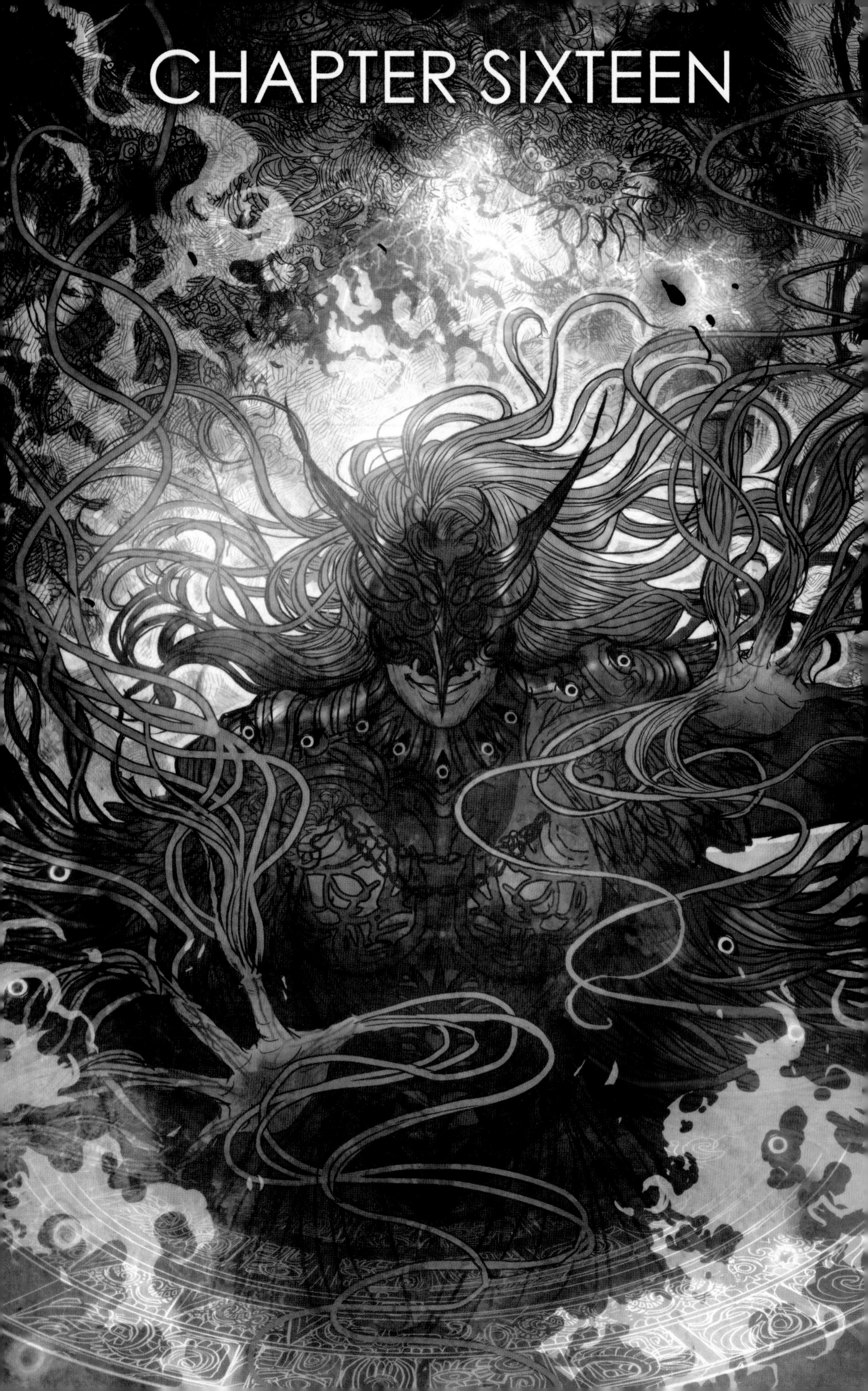

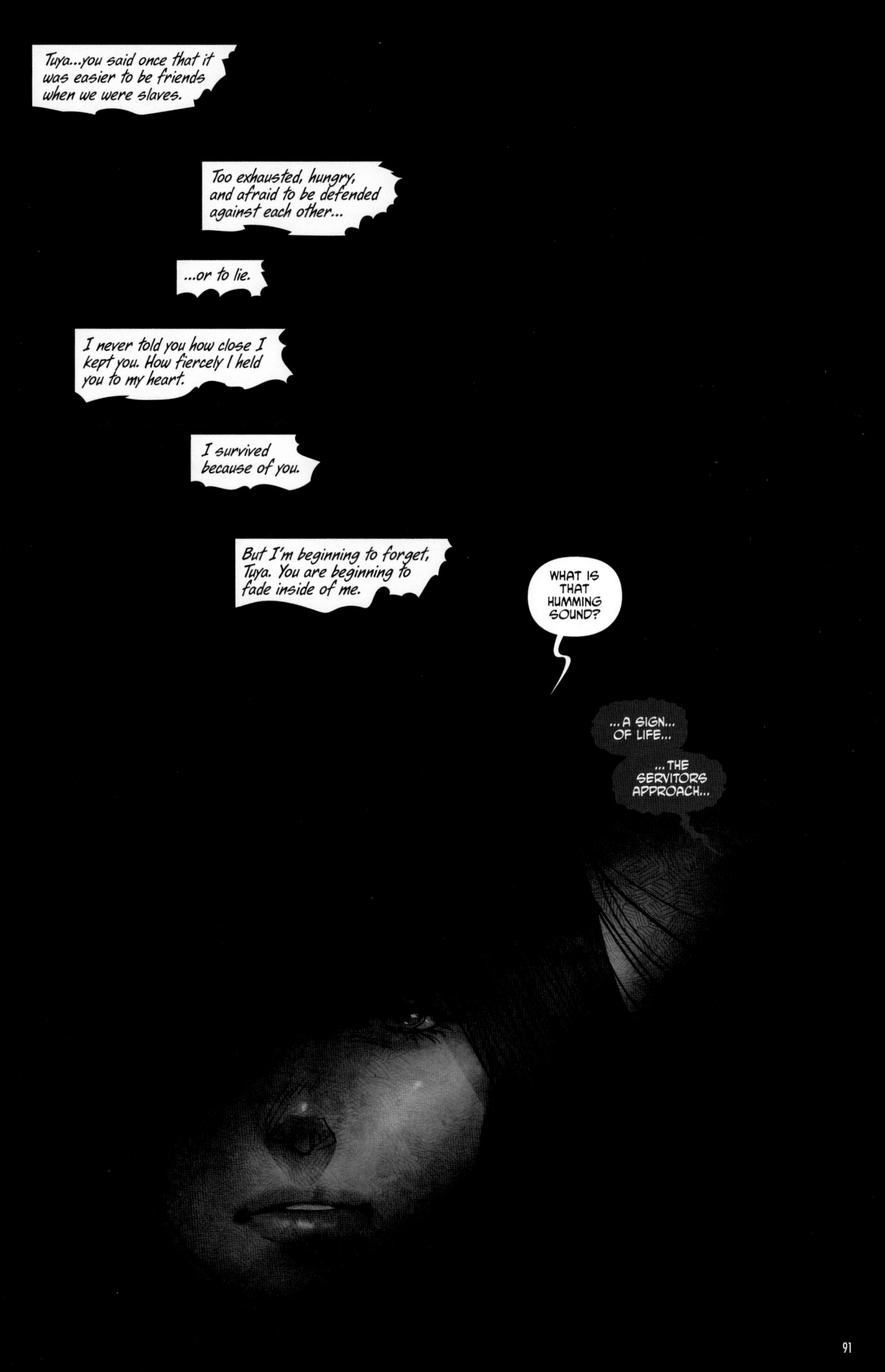
Tuya...you said once that it was easier to be friends when we were slaves.
Too exhausted, hungry, and afraid to be defended against each other...
...or to lie.
I never told you how close I kept you. How fiercely I held you to my heart.
I survived because of you.
But I'm beginning to forget, Tuya. You are beginning to fade inside of me.
WHAT IS THAT HUMMING SOUND?
...A SIGN... OF LIFE...
...THE SERVITORS APPROACH...

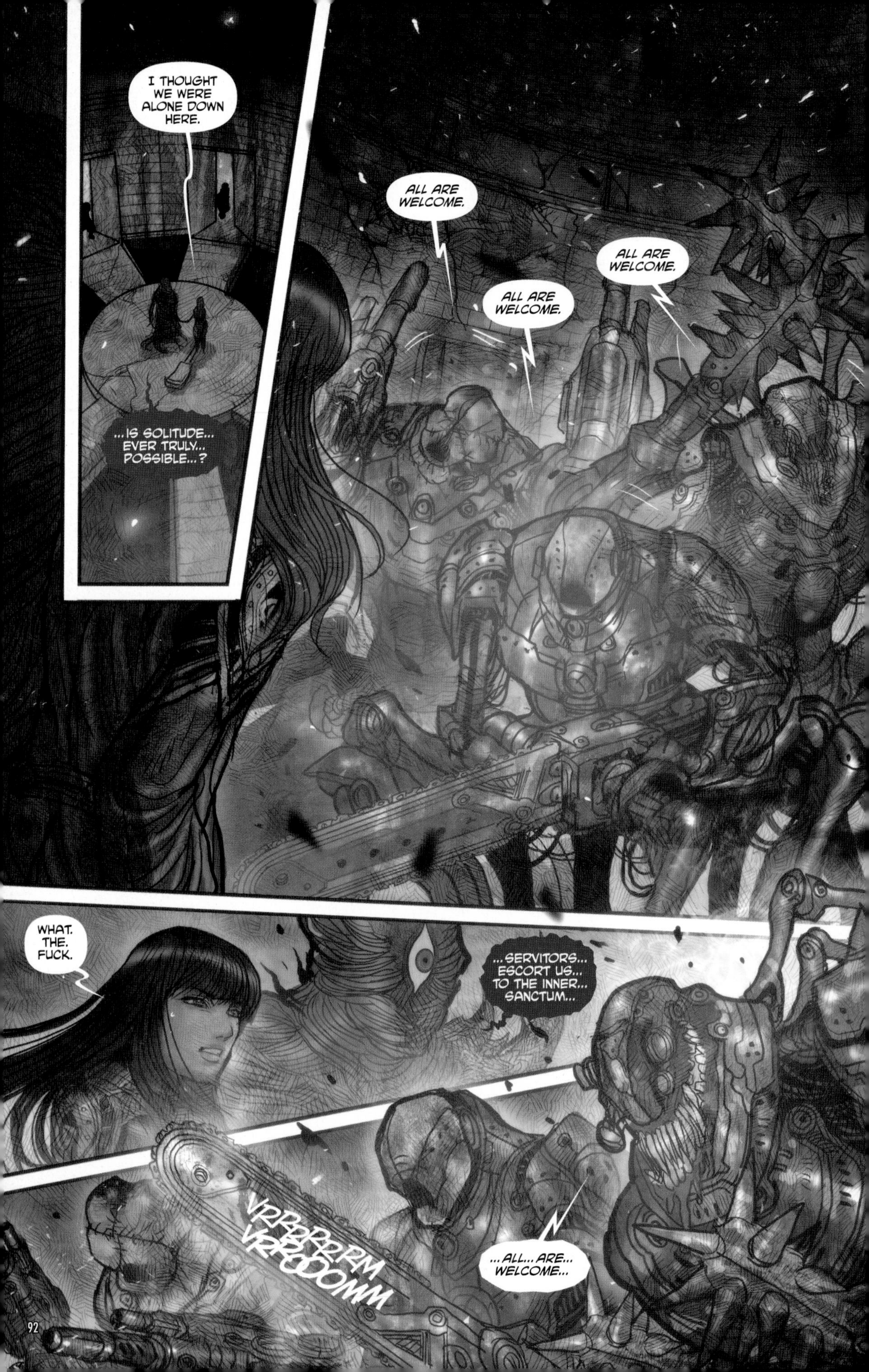
I THOUGHT WE WERE ALONE DOWN HERE.
...IS SOLITUDE... EVER TRULY... POSSIBLE...?
ALL ARE WELCOME.
ALL ARE WELCOME.
ALL ARE WELCOME.
WHAT. THE. FUCK.
...SERVITORS... ESCORT US... TO THE INNER... SANCTUM...
VRRRRRRRM VRROOOMM
...ALL... ARE... WELCOME...

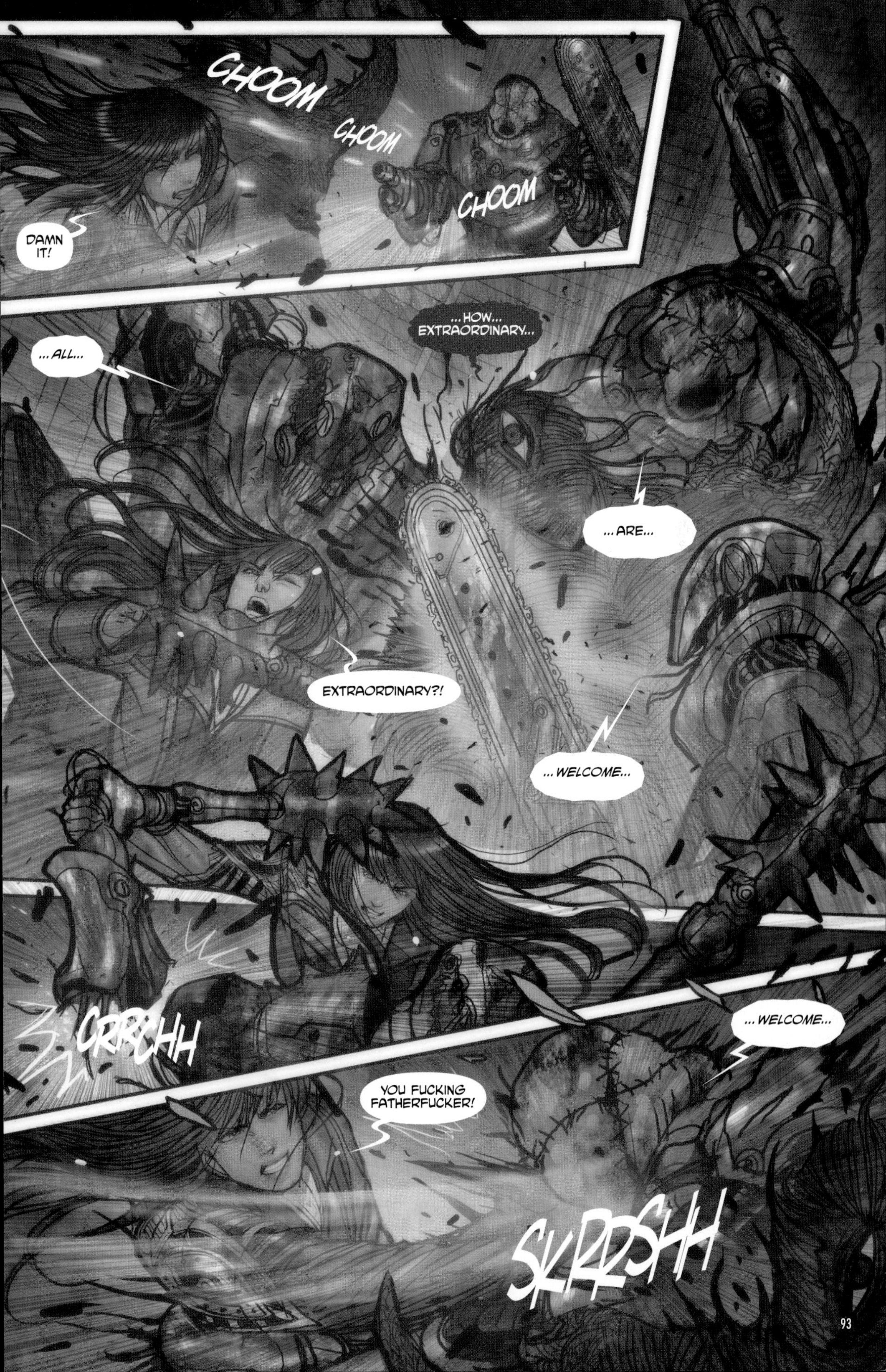
CHOOM
CHOOM
CHOOM
DAMN IT!
...ALL...
...HOW... EXTRAORDINARY...
...ARE...
EXTRAORDINARY?!
...WELCOME...
CRRRCHH
...WELCOME...
YOU FUCKING FATHERFUCKER!
SKRRSHH

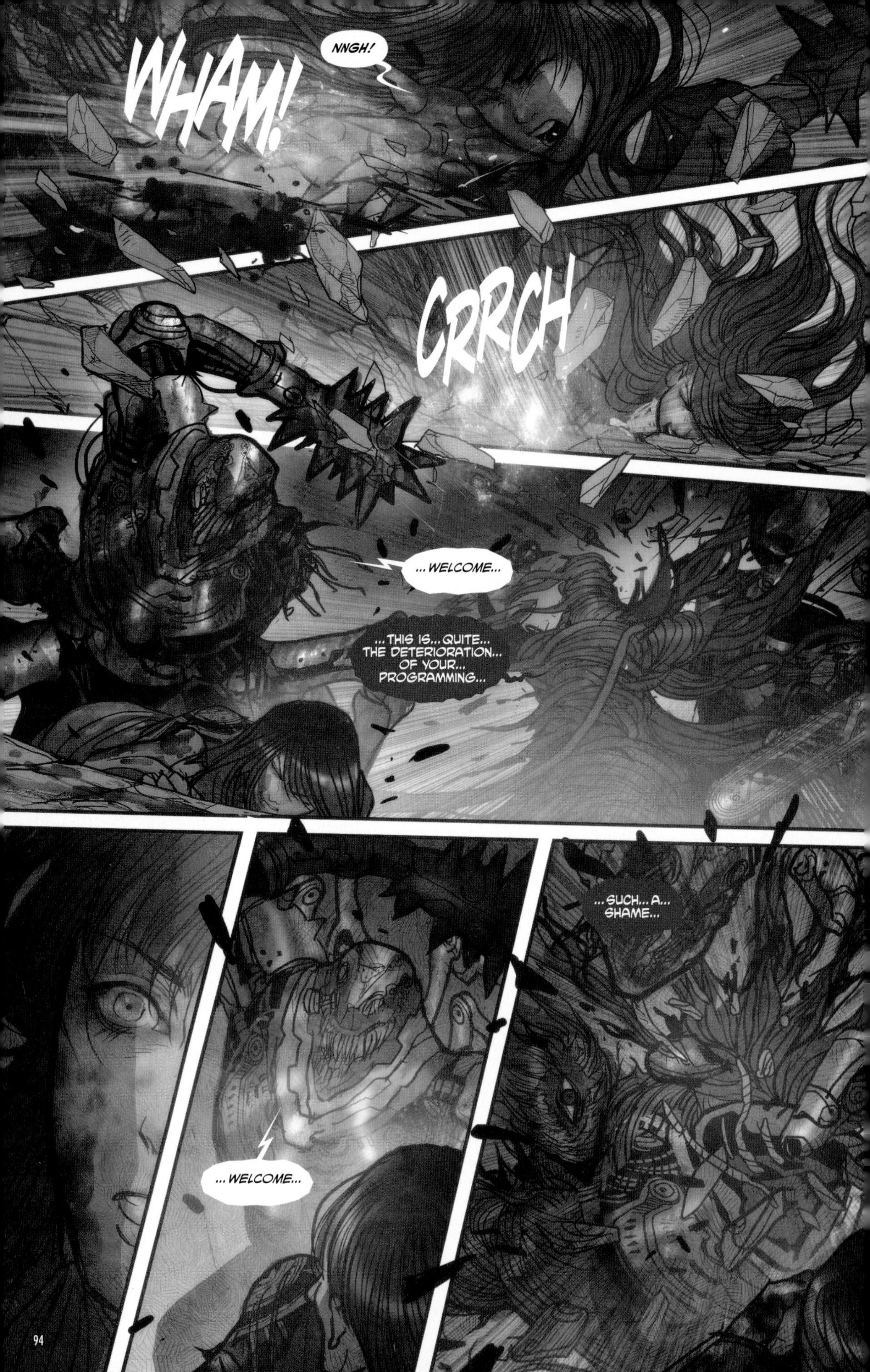
WHAM!
NNGH!
CRRCH
...WELCOME...
...THIS IS... QUITE... THE DETERIORATION... OF YOUR... PROGRAMMING...
...WELCOME...
...SUCH... A... SHAME...

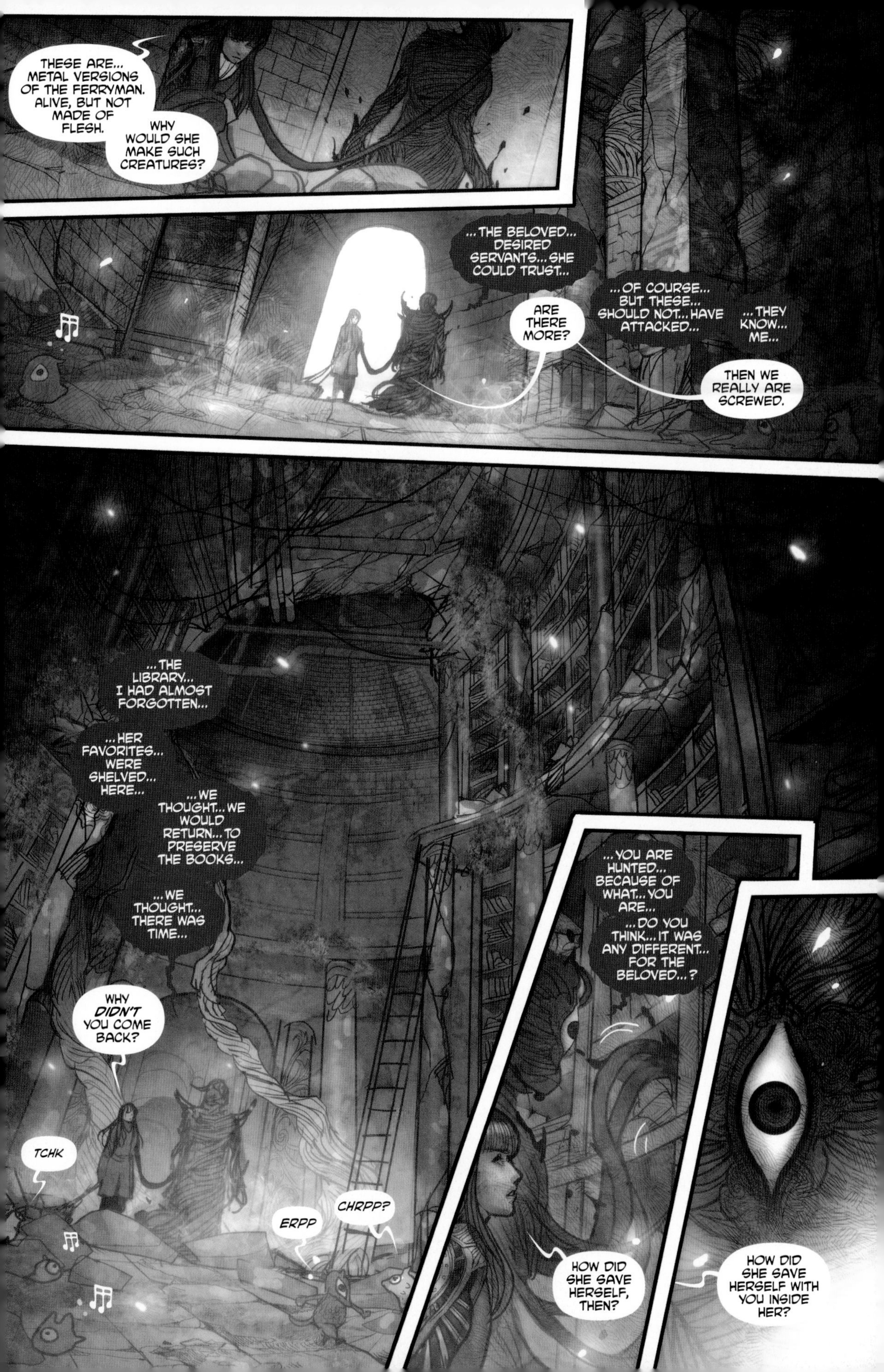
THESE ARE... METAL VERSIONS OF THE FERRYMAN. ALIVE, BUT NOT MADE OF FLESH.
WHY WOULD SHE MAKE SUCH CREATURES?
...THE BELOVED... DESIRED SERVANTS... SHE COULD TRUST...
ARE THERE MORE?
...OF COURSE... BUT THESE... SHOULD NOT... HAVE ATTACKED...
...THEY KNOW... ME...
THEN WE REALLY ARE SCREWED.
...THE LIBRARY... I HAD ALMOST FORGOTTEN...
...HER FAVORITES... WERE SHELVED... HERE...
...WE THOUGHT... WE WOULD RETURN... TO PRESERVE THE BOOKS...
...WE THOUGHT... THERE WAS TIME...
WHY DIDN'T YOU COME BACK?
TCHK
ERPP
CHRPP?
...YOU ARE HUNTED... BECAUSE OF WHAT... YOU ARE...
...DO YOU THINK... IT WAS ANY DIFFERENT... FOR THE BELOVED...?
HOW DID SHE SAVE HERSELF, THEN?
HOW DID SHE SAVE HERSELF WITH YOU INSIDE HER?

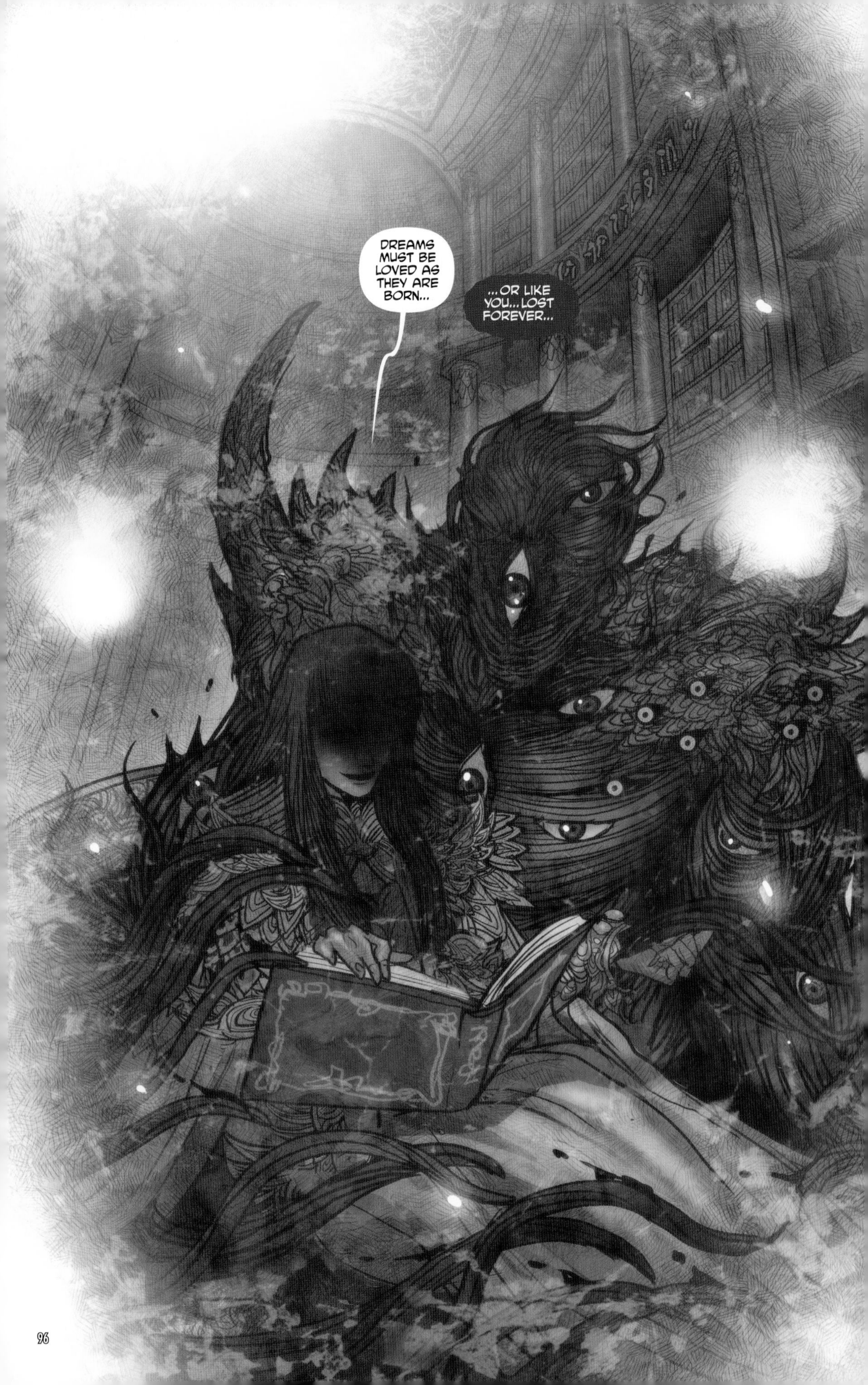
DREAMS MUST BE LOVED AS THEY ARE BORN...
...OR LIKE YOU...LOST FOREVER...

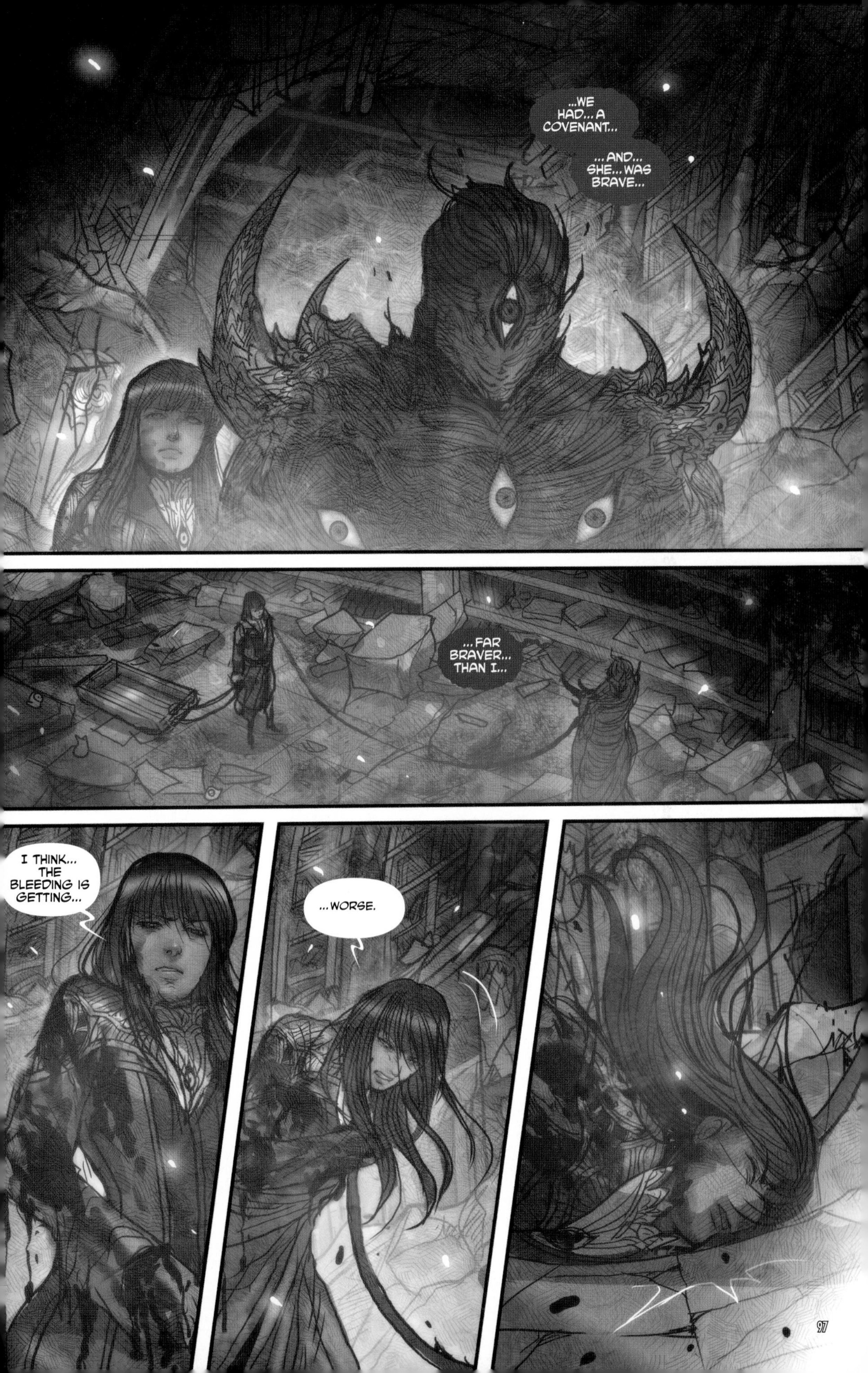
...WE HAD... A COVENANT...
...AND... SHE... WAS BRAVE...
...FAR BRAVER... THAN I...
I THINK... THE BLEEDING IS GETTING...
...WORSE.

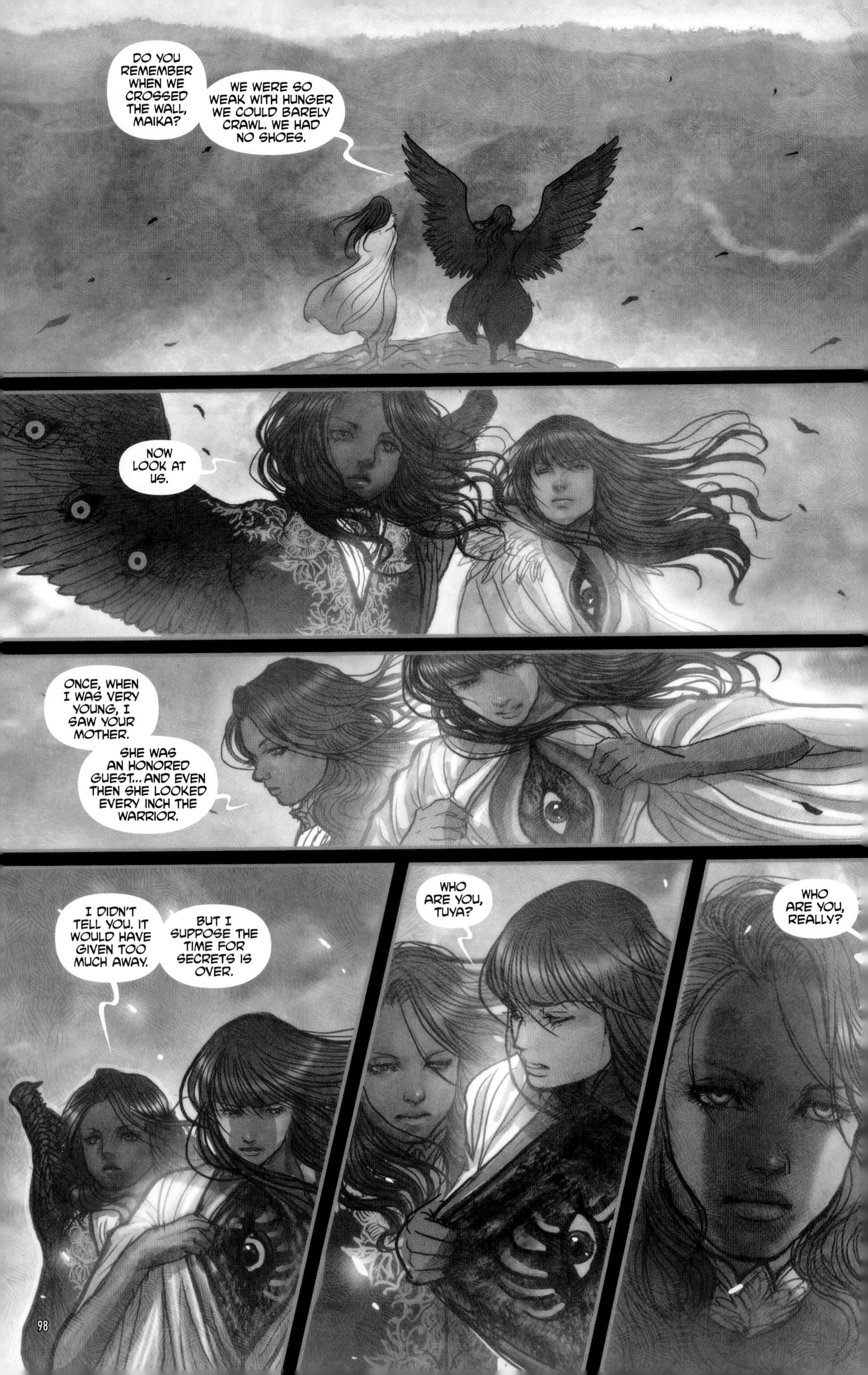
DO YOU REMEMBER WHEN WE CROSSED THE WALL, MAIKA?
WE WERE SO WEAK WITH HUNGER WE COULD BARELY CRAWL. WE HAD NO SHOES.
NOW LOOK AT US.
ONCE, WHEN I WAS VERY YOUNG, I SAW YOUR MOTHER.
SHE WAS AN HONORED GUEST... AND EVEN THEN SHE LOOKED EVERY INCH THE WARRIOR.
I DIDN'T TELL YOU. IT WOULD HAVE GIVEN TOO MUCH AWAY.
BUT I SUPPOSE THE TIME FOR SECRETS IS OVER.
WHO ARE YOU, TUYA?
WHO ARE YOU, REALLY?

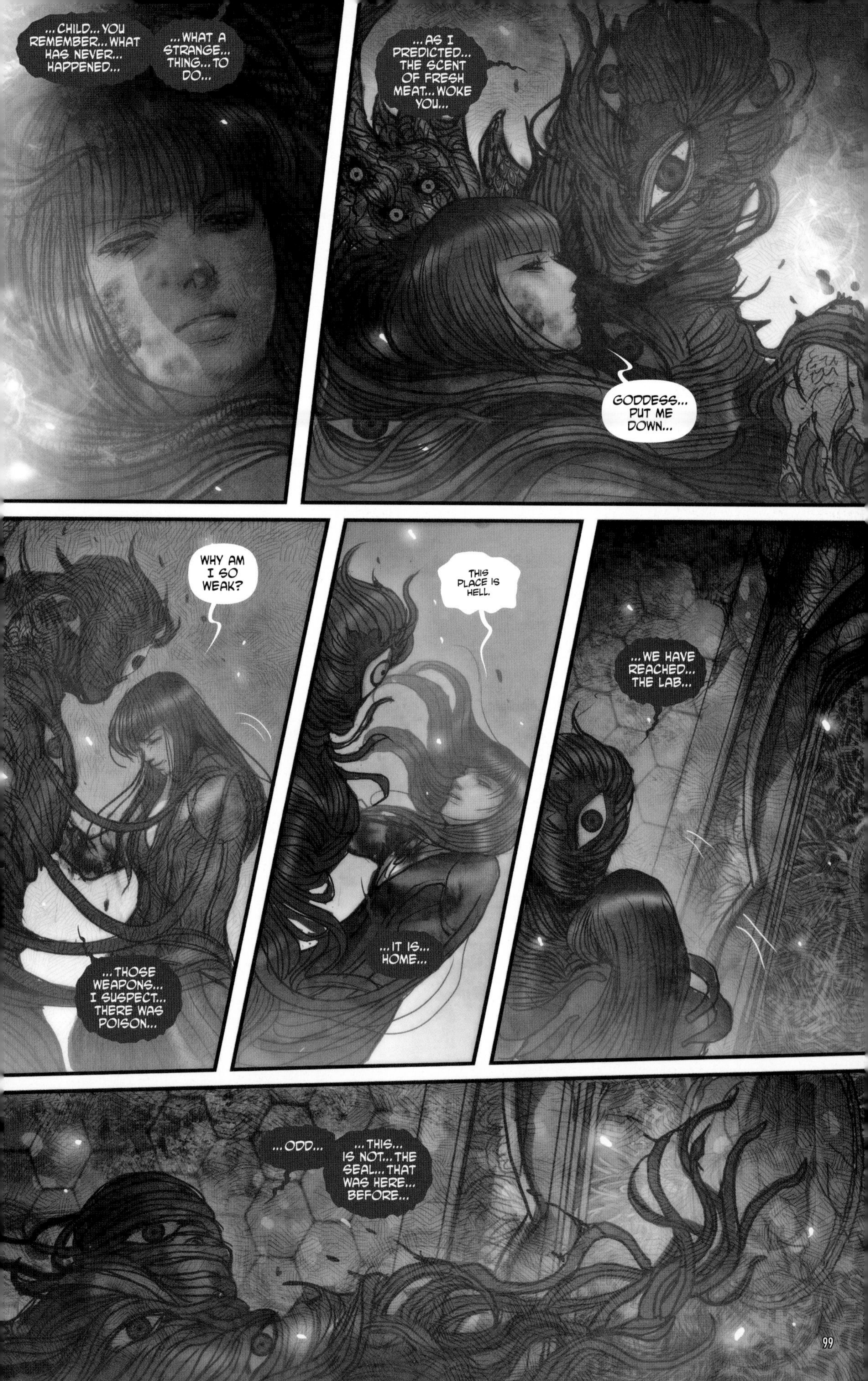
...CHILD...YOU REMEMBER...WHAT HAS NEVER... HAPPENED...
...WHAT A STRANGE... THING...TO DO...
...AS I PREDICTED... THE SCENT OF FRESH MEAT...WOKE YOU...
GODDESS... PUT ME DOWN...
WHY AM I SO WEAK?
...THOSE WEAPONS... I SUSPECT... THERE WAS POISON...
THIS PLACE IS HELL.
...IT IS... HOME...
...WE HAVE REACHED... THE LAB...
...ODD...
...THIS... IS NOT...THE SEAL...THAT WAS HERE... BEFORE...

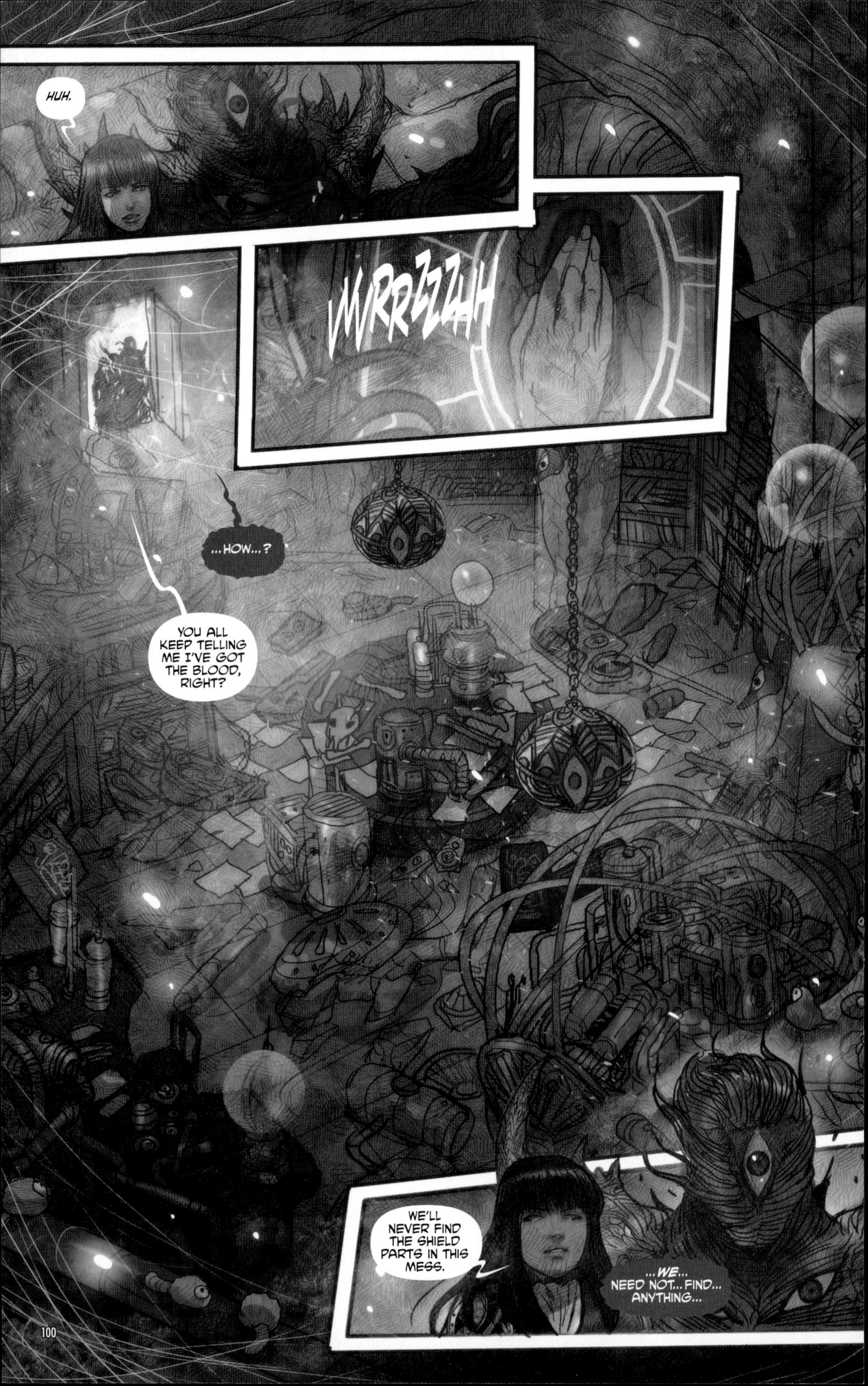
HUH.
VVVRRZZZHH
...HOW...?
YOU ALL KEEP TELLING ME I'VE GOT THE BLOOD, RIGHT?
WE'LL NEVER FIND THE SHIELD PARTS IN THIS MESS.
...WE... NEED NOT... FIND... ANYTHING...

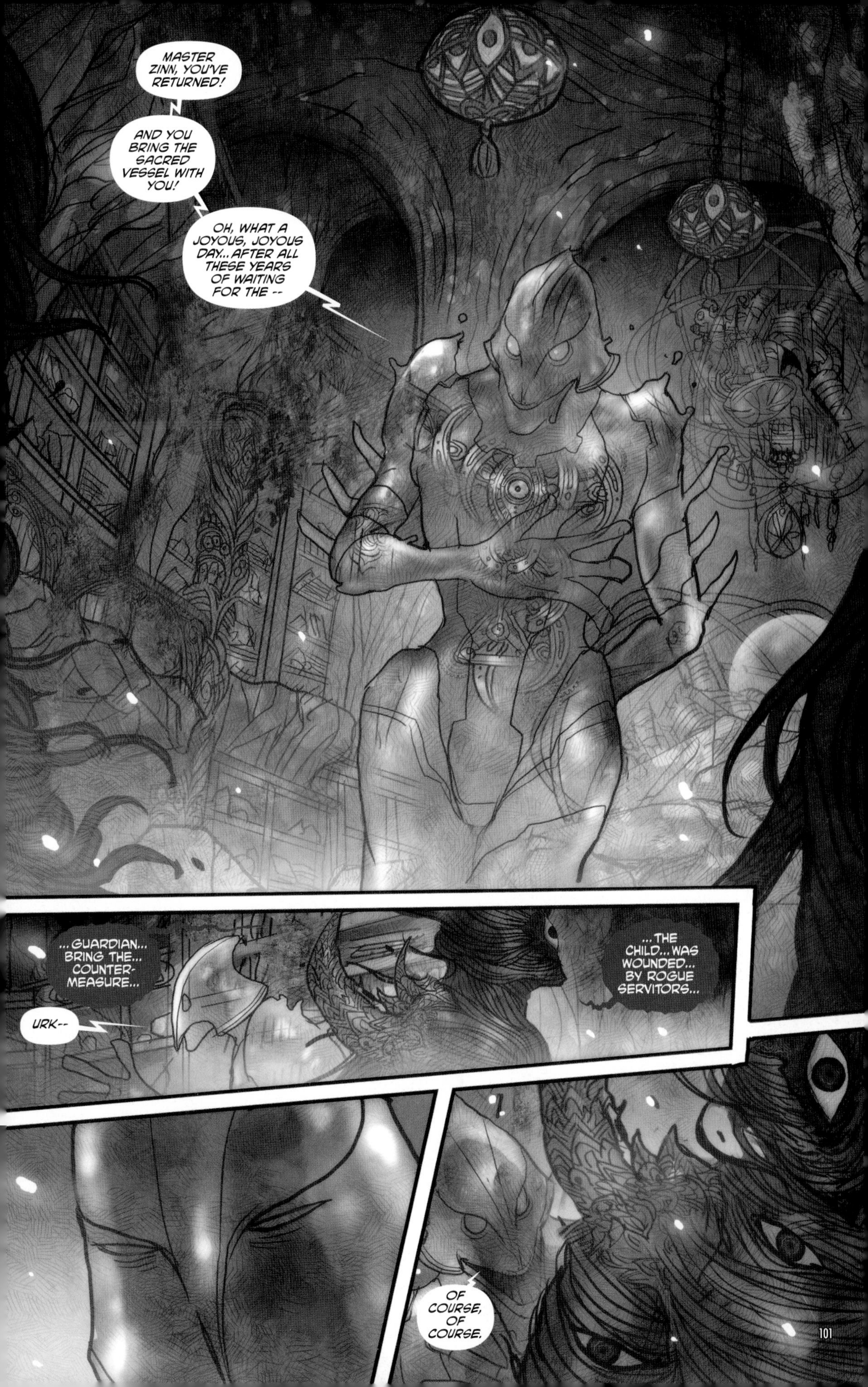
MASTER ZINN, YOU'VE RETURNED!
AND YOU BRING THE SACRED VESSEL WITH YOU!
OH, WHAT A JOYOUS, JOYOUS DAY... AFTER ALL THESE YEARS OF WAITING FOR THE --
...GUARDIAN... BRING THE... COUNTER-MEASURE...
URK--
...THE CHILD... WAS WOUNDED... BY ROGUE SERVITORS...
OF COURSE, OF COURSE.

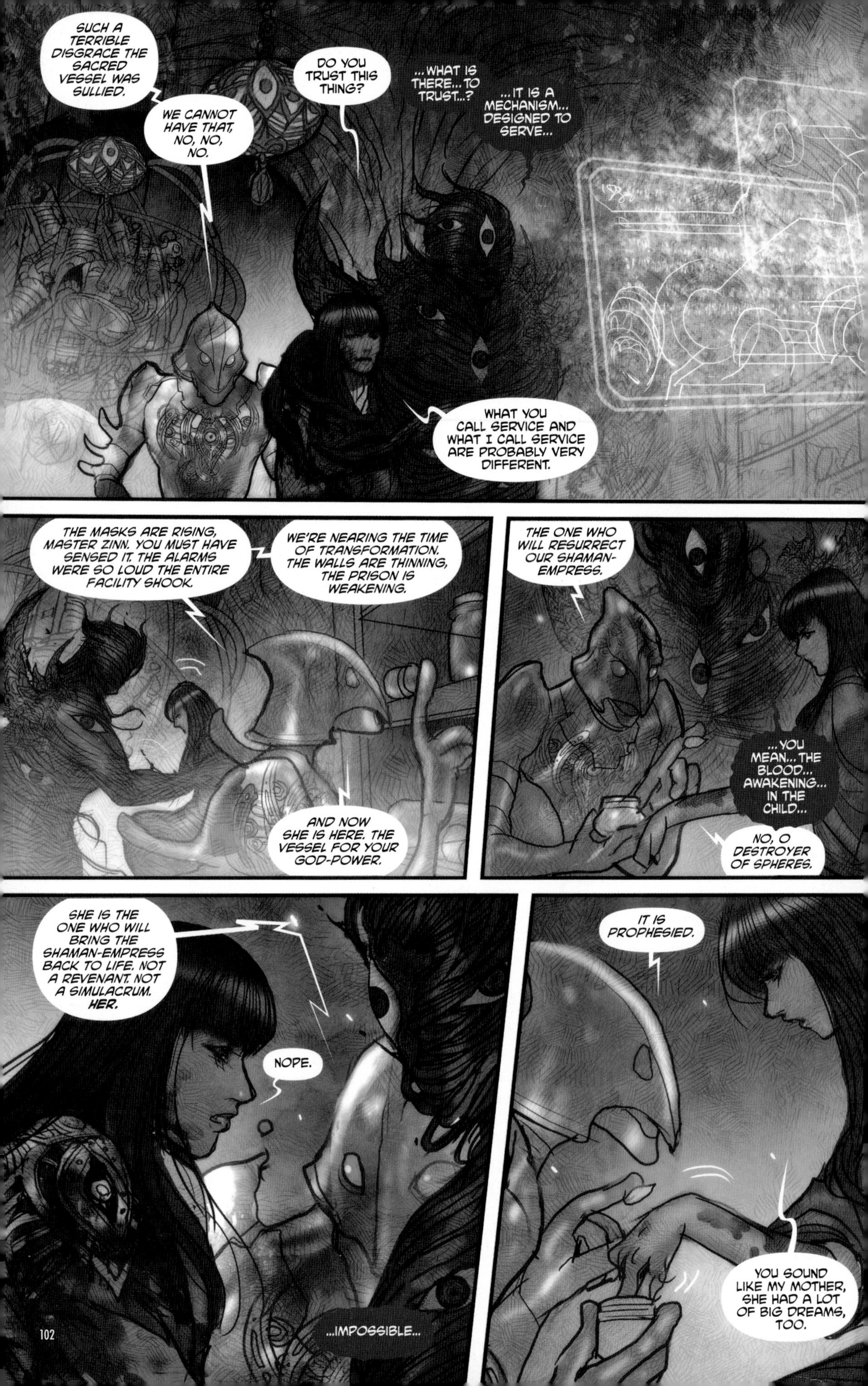
SUCH A TERRIBLE DISGRACE THE SACRED VESSEL WAS SULLIED.
WE CANNOT HAVE THAT, NO, NO, NO.
DO YOU TRUST THIS THING?
...WHAT IS THERE...TO TRUST...?
...IT IS A MECHANISM... DESIGNED TO SERVE...
WHAT YOU CALL SERVICE AND WHAT I CALL SERVICE ARE PROBABLY VERY DIFFERENT.
THE MASKS ARE RISING, MASTER ZINN. YOU MUST HAVE SENSED IT. THE ALARMS WERE SO LOUD THE ENTIRE FACILITY SHOOK.
WE'RE NEARING THE TIME OF TRANSFORMATION. THE WALLS ARE THINNING, THE PRISON IS WEAKENING.
AND NOW SHE IS HERE. THE VESSEL FOR YOUR GOD-POWER.
THE ONE WHO WILL RESURRECT OUR SHAMAN-EMPRESS.
...YOU MEAN... THE BLOOD... AWAKENING... IN THE CHILD...
NO, O DESTROYER OF SPHERES.
SHE IS THE ONE WHO WILL BRING THE SHAMAN-EMPRESS BACK TO LIFE. NOT A REVENANT. NOT A SIMULACRUM. HER.
NOPE.
...IMPOSSIBLE...
IT IS PROPHESIED.
YOU SOUND LIKE MY MOTHER, SHE HAD A LOT OF BIG DREAMS, TOO.

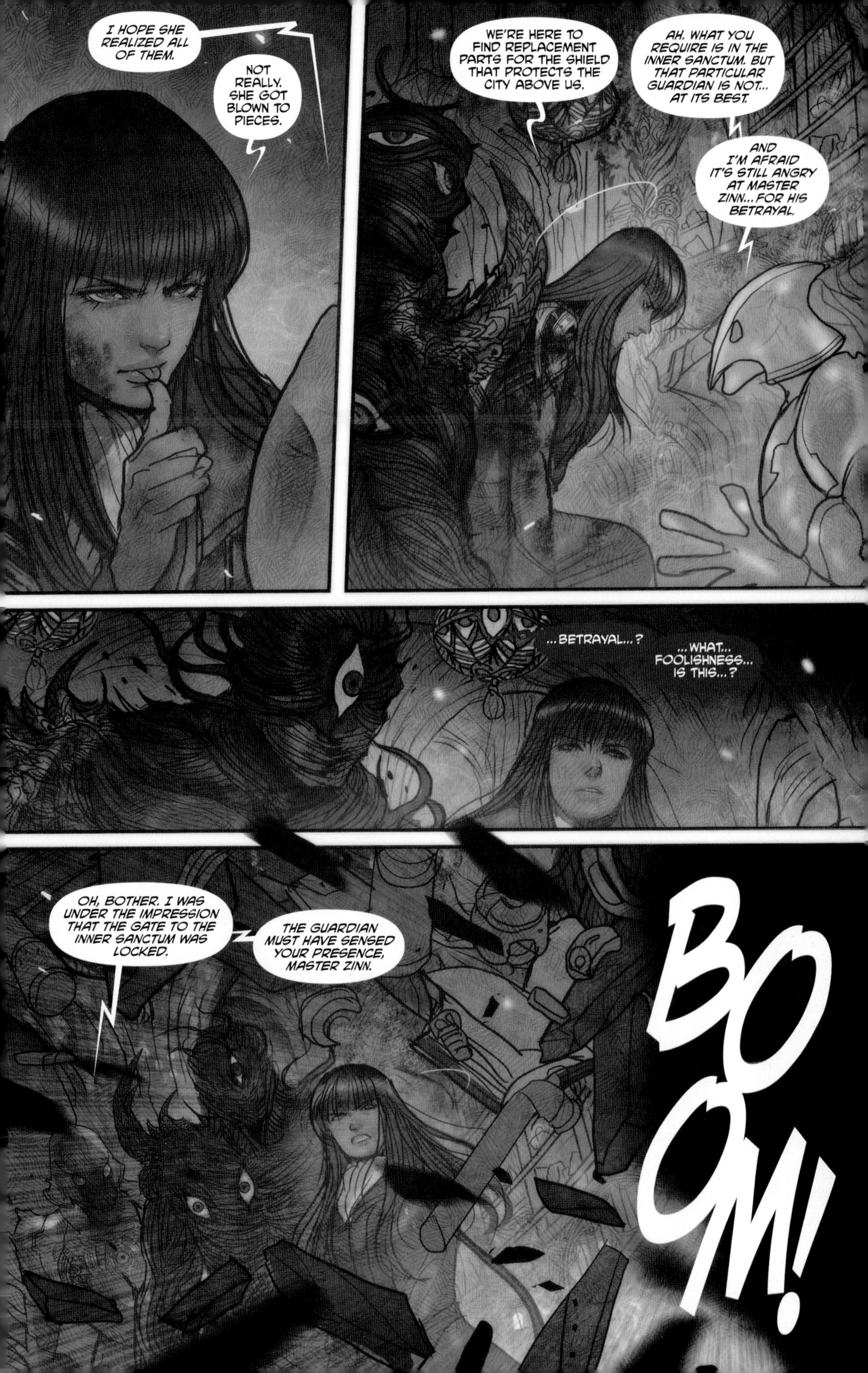
I HOPE SHE REALIZED ALL OF THEM.
NOT REALLY. SHE GOT BLOWN TO PIECES.
WE'RE HERE TO FIND REPLACEMENT PARTS FOR THE SHIELD THAT PROTECTS THE CITY ABOVE US.
AH. WHAT YOU REQUIRE IS IN THE INNER SANCTUM. BUT THAT PARTICULAR GUARDIAN IS NOT... AT ITS BEST.
AND I'M AFRAID IT'S STILL ANGRY AT MASTER ZINN... FOR HIS BETRAYAL.
...BETRAYAL...?
...WHAT... FOOLISHNESS... IS THIS...?
OH, BOTHER. I WAS UNDER THE IMPRESSION THAT THE GATE TO THE INNER SANCTUM WAS LOCKED.
THE GUARDIAN MUST HAVE SENSED YOUR PRESENCE, MASTER ZINN.
BOOOM!

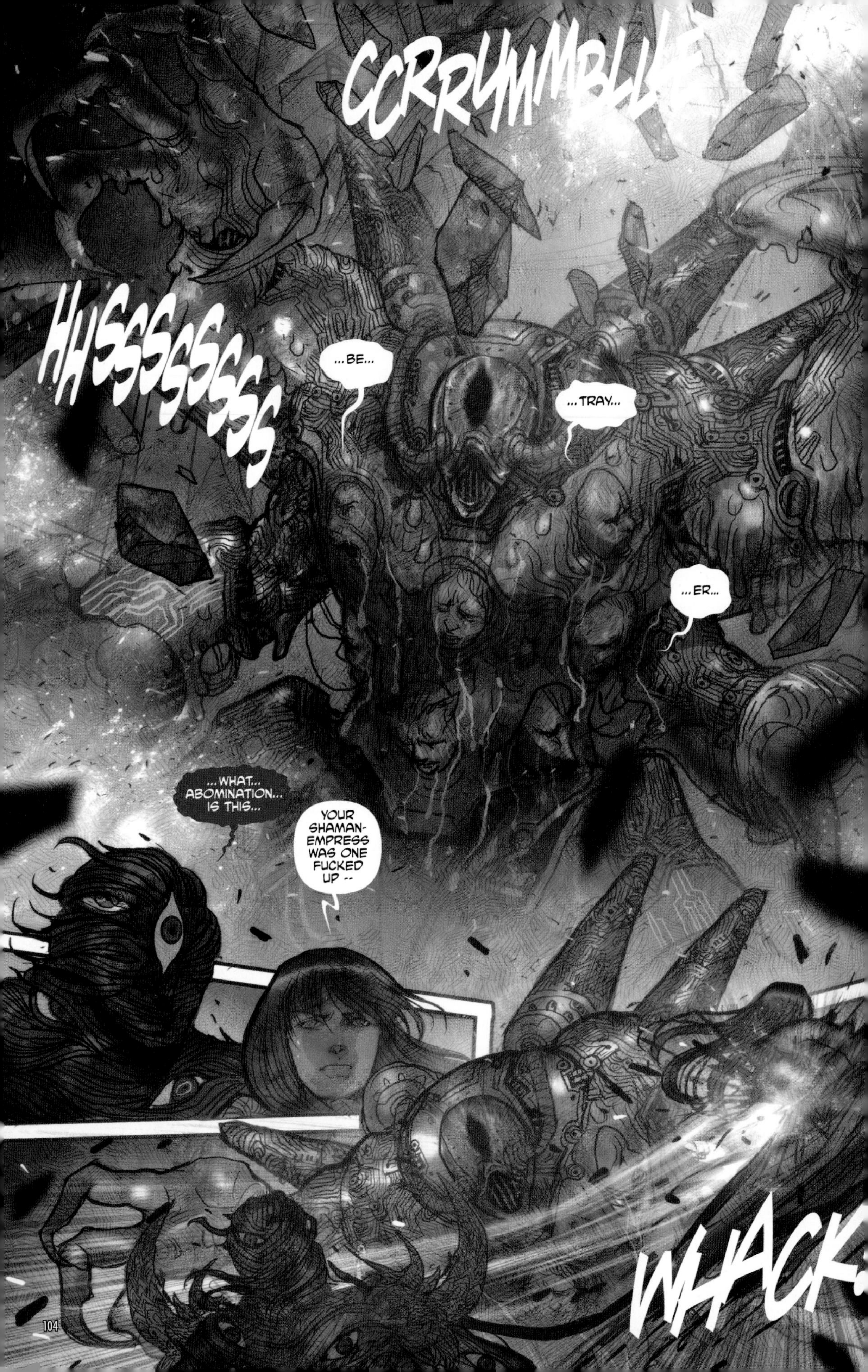
CCRRUMMBLLE
HHSSSSSSSSS
...BE...
...TRAY...
...ER...
...WHAT... ABOMINATION... IS THIS...
YOUR SHAMAN-EMPRESS WAS ONE FUCKED UP --
WHACK!

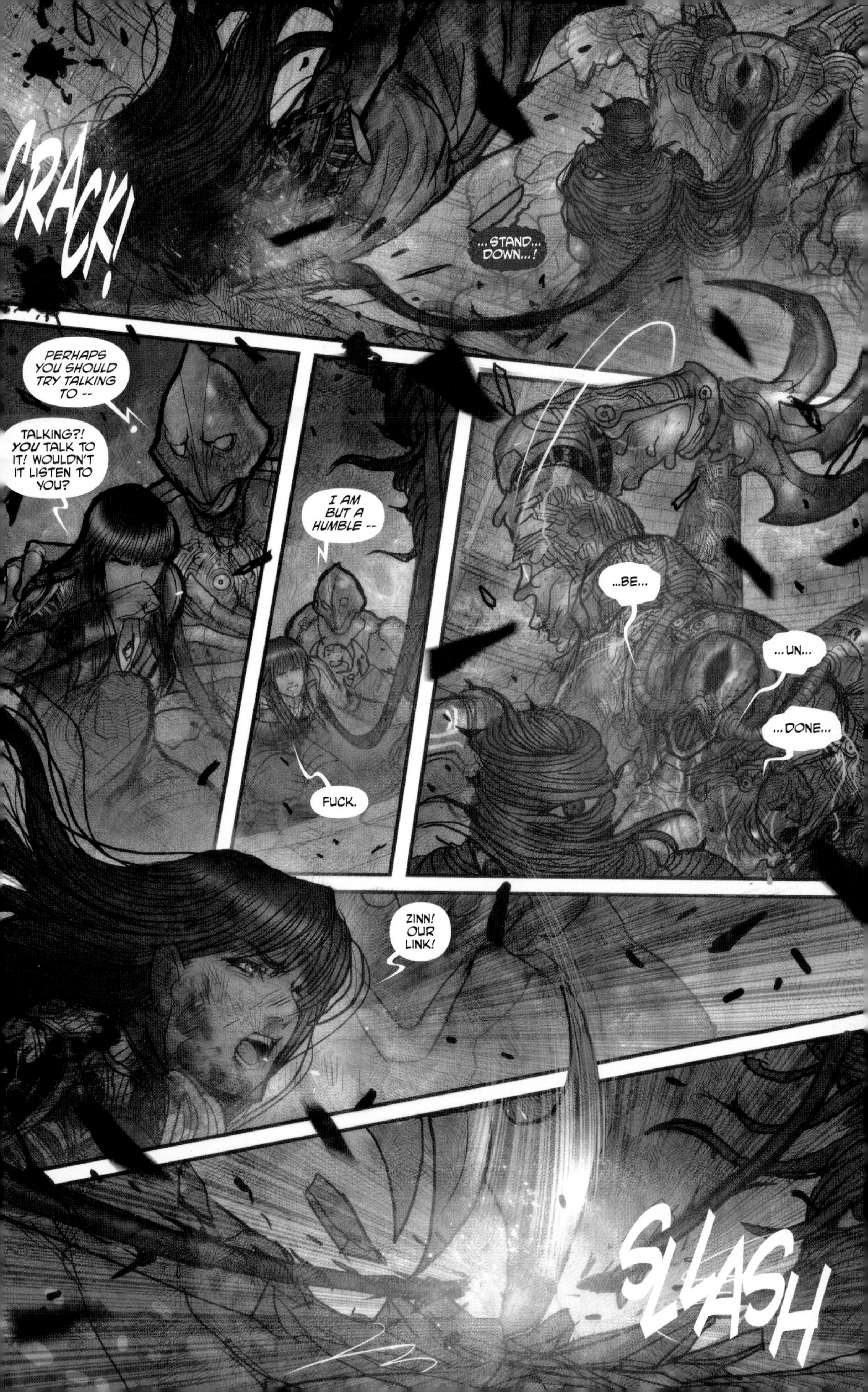
CRACK!
...STAND... DOWN...!
PERHAPS YOU SHOULD TRY TALKING TO --
TALKING?! YOU TALK TO IT! WOULDN'T IT LISTEN TO YOU?
I AM BUT A HUMBLE --
FUCK.
...BE...
...UN...
...DONE...
ZINN! OUR LINK!
SLLASH

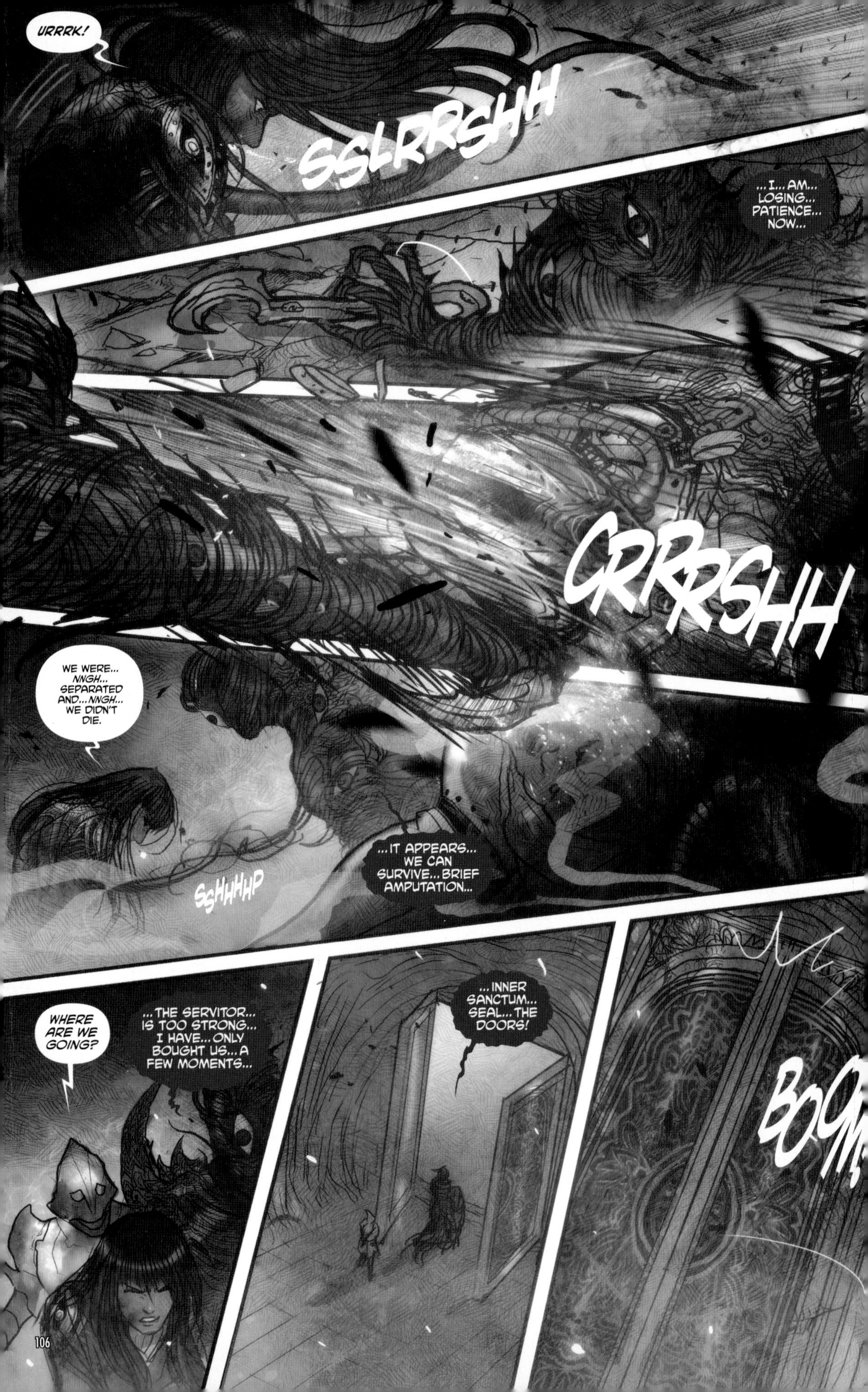
URRRK!
SSLRRSHH
...I... AM... LOSING... PATIENCE... NOW...
CRRRSHH
WE WERE... NNGH... SEPARATED AND... NNGH... WE DIDN'T DIE.
SSHHHHP
...IT APPEARS... WE CAN SURVIVE... BRIEF AMPUTATION...
WHERE ARE WE GOING?
...THE SERVITOR... IS TOO STRONG... I HAVE... ONLY BOUGHT US... A FEW MOMENTS...
...INNER SANCTUM... SEAL... THE DOORS!
BOOM

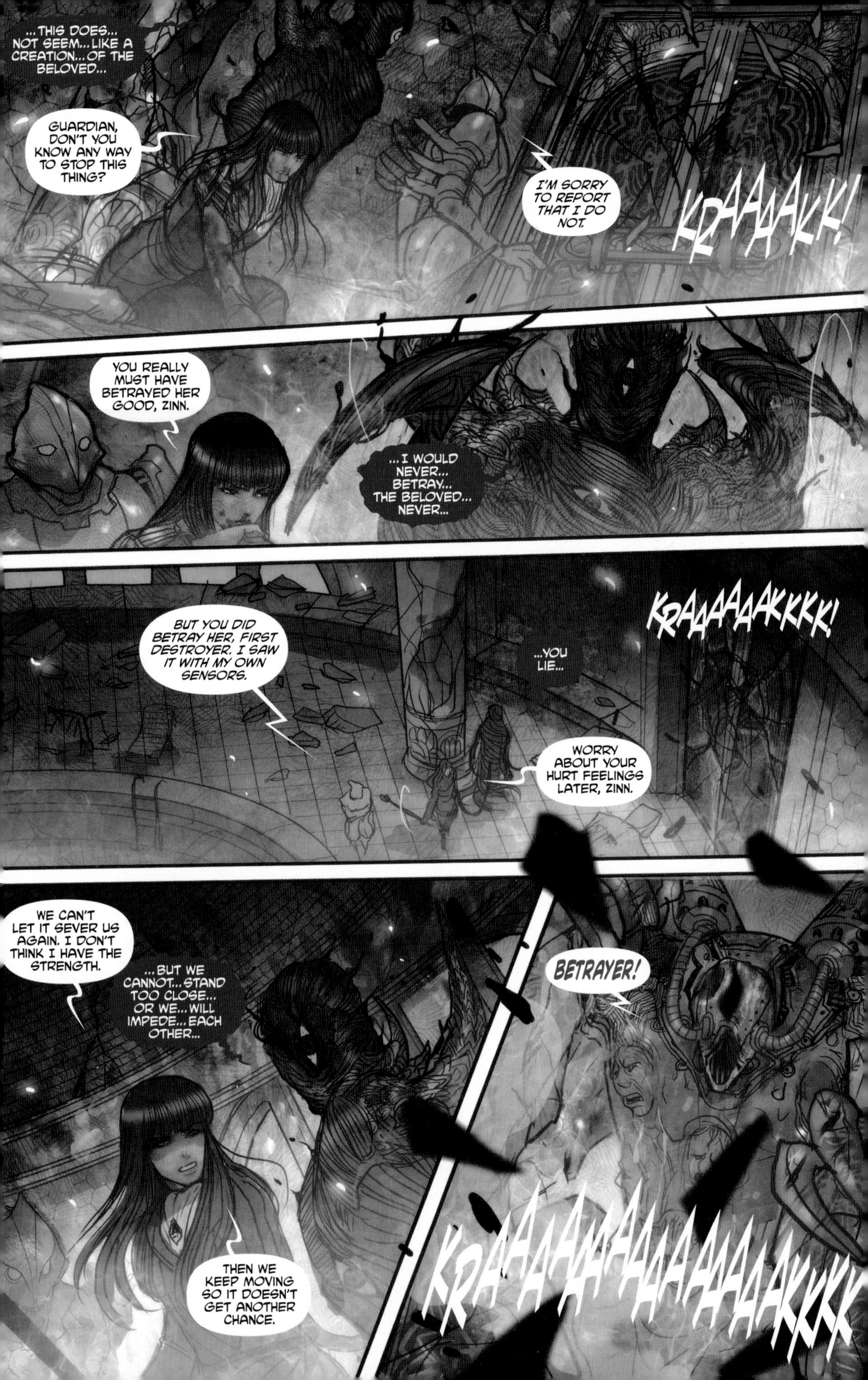
...THIS DOES... NOT SEEM... LIKE A CREATION... OF THE BELOVED...
GUARDIAN, DON'T YOU KNOW ANY WAY TO STOP THIS THING?
I'M SORRY TO REPORT THAT I DO NOT.
KRAAAAKK!
YOU REALLY MUST HAVE BETRAYED HER GOOD, ZINN.
...I WOULD NEVER... BETRAY... THE BELOVED... NEVER...
BUT YOU DID BETRAY HER, FIRST DESTROYER. I SAW IT WITH MY OWN SENSORS.
...YOU LIE...
KRAAAAAKKKK!
WORRY ABOUT YOUR HURT FEELINGS LATER, ZINN.
WE CAN'T LET IT SEVER US AGAIN. I DON'T THINK I HAVE THE STRENGTH.
...BUT WE CANNOT... STAND TOO CLOSE... OR WE... WILL IMPEDE... EACH OTHER...
THEN WE KEEP MOVING SO IT DOESN'T GET ANOTHER CHANCE.
BETRAYER!
KRAAAAAAAAAAAAAAKKKK

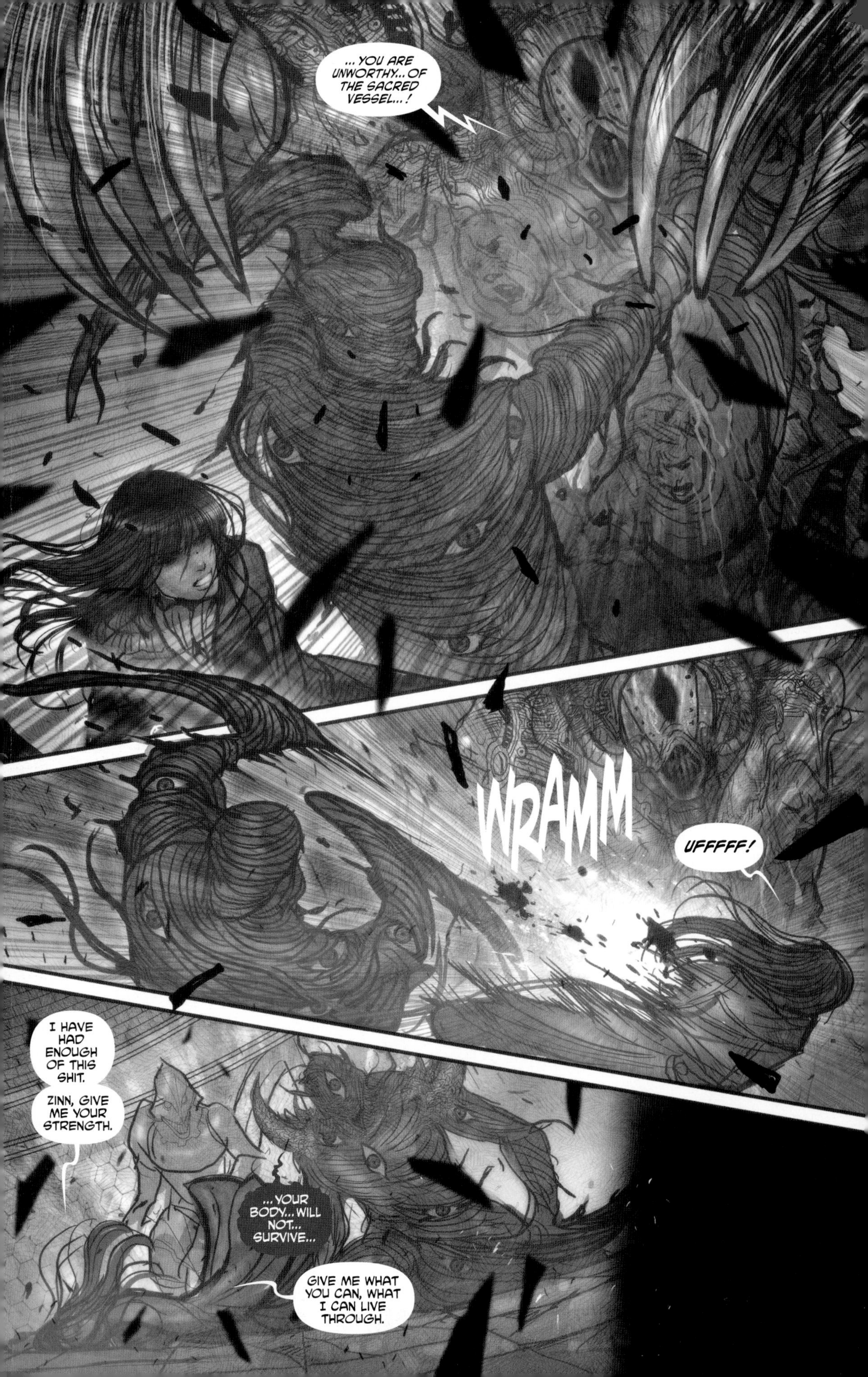
...YOU ARE UNWORTHY...OF THE SACRED VESSEL...!
WRAMM
UFFFFF!
I HAVE HAD ENOUGH OF THIS SHIT.
ZINN, GIVE ME YOUR STRENGTH.
...YOUR BODY...WILL NOT... SURVIVE...
GIVE ME WHAT YOU CAN, WHAT I CAN LIVE THROUGH.

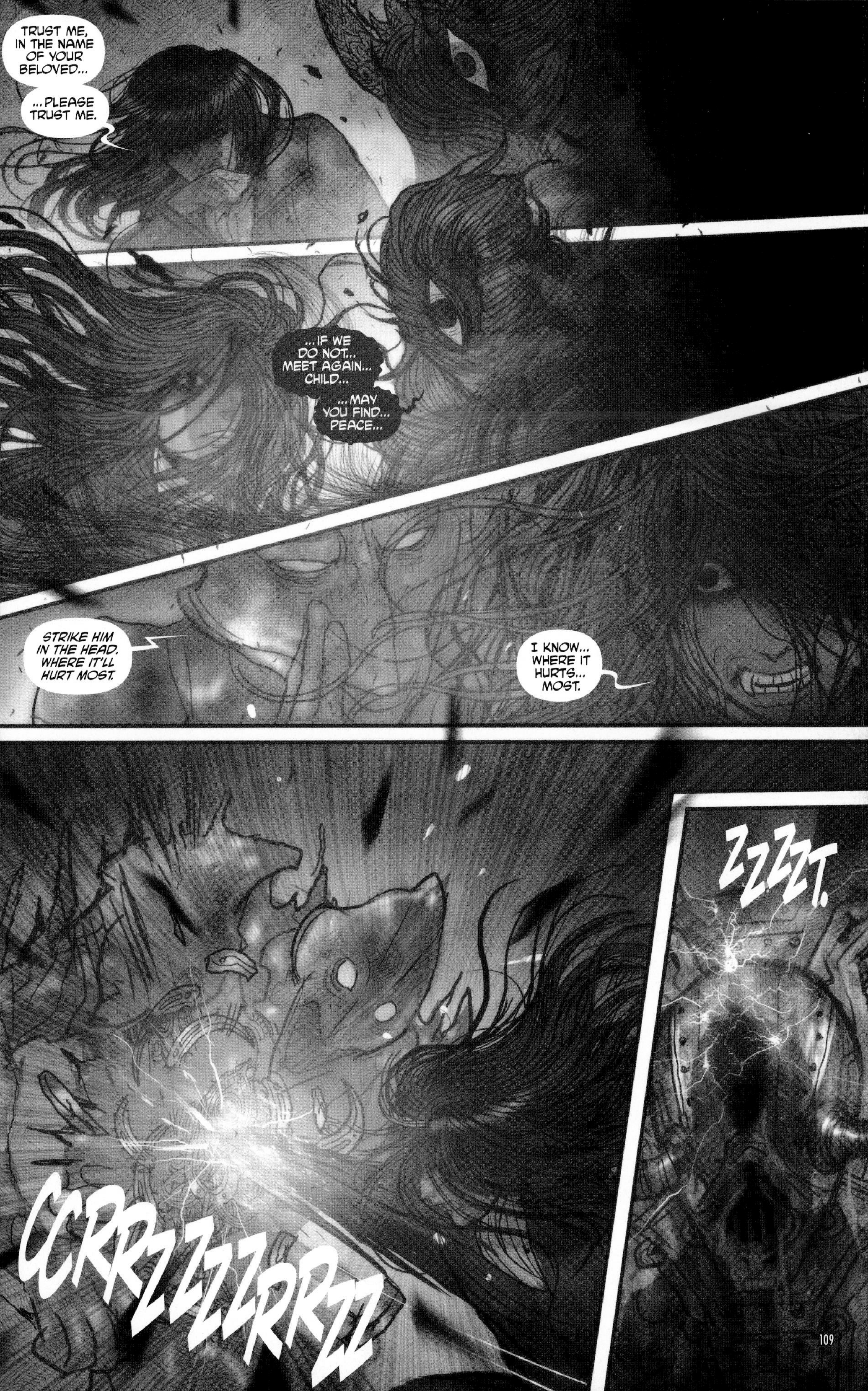
TRUST ME, IN THE NAME OF YOUR BELOVED...
...PLEASE TRUST ME.
...IF WE DO NOT... MEET AGAIN... CHILD...
...MAY YOU FIND... PEACE...
STRIKE HIM IN THE HEAD. WHERE IT'LL HURT MOST.
I KNOW... WHERE IT HURTS... MOST.
ZZZZT.
CCRRZZZZZRRRZZ

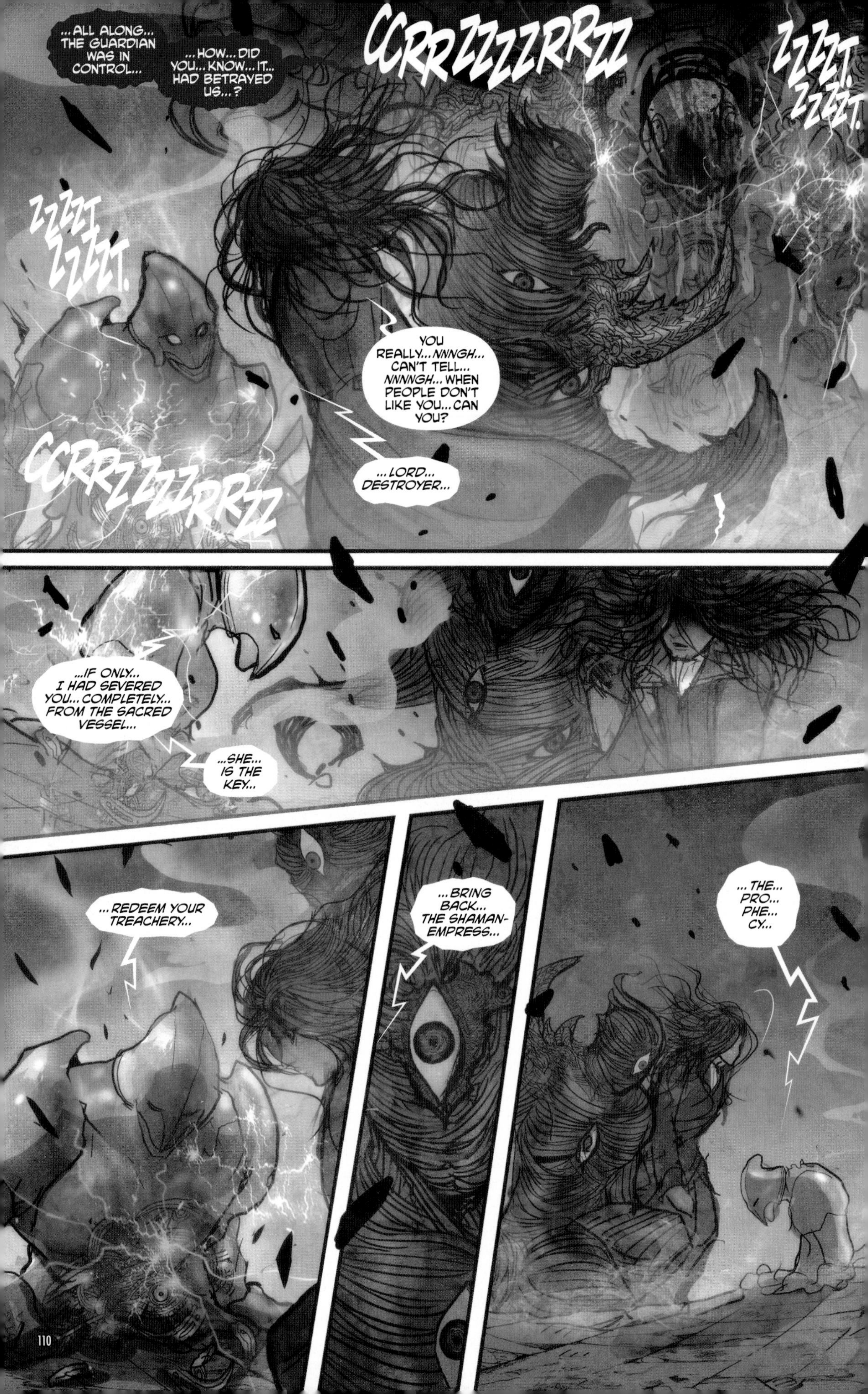
...ALL ALONG... THE GUARDIAN WAS IN CONTROL...
...HOW... DID YOU... KNOW... IT... HAD BETRAYED US...?
CCRRZZZZZRRZZ
ZZZZT. ZZZZT.
ZZZZT ZZZZT.
YOU REALLY... NNNGH... CAN'T TELL... NNNGH... WHEN PEOPLE DON'T LIKE YOU... CAN YOU?
...LORD... DESTROYER...
CCRRZZZZZRRZZ
...IF ONLY... I HAD SEVERED YOU... COMPLETELY... FROM THE SACRED VESSEL...
...SHE... IS THE KEY...
...REDEEM YOUR TREACHERY...
...BRING BACK... THE SHAMAN-EMPRESS...
...THE... PRO... PHE... CY...

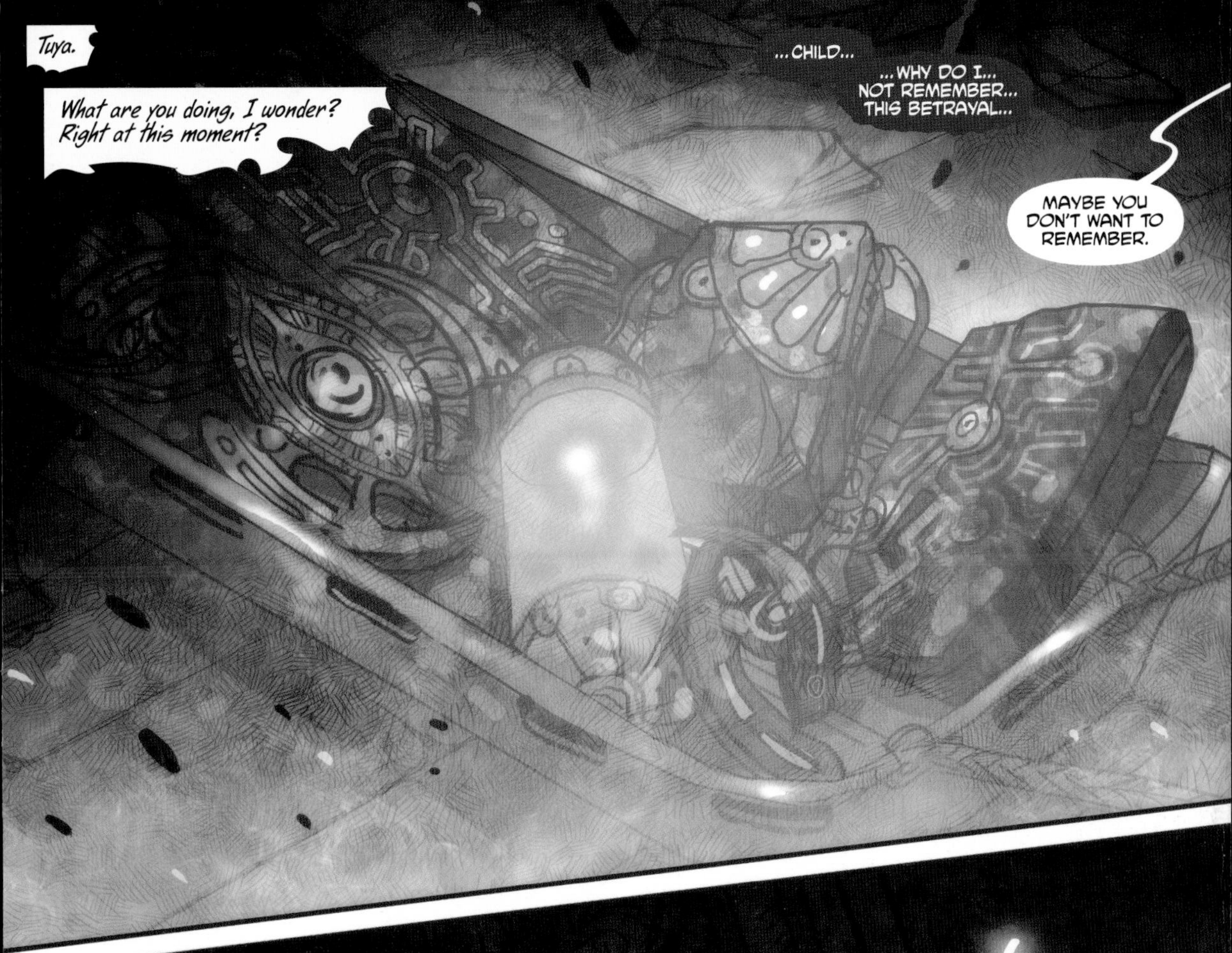
Tuya.
What are you doing, I wonder? Right at this moment?
...CHILD...
...WHY DO I... NOT REMEMBER... THIS BETRAYAL...
MAYBE YOU DON'T WANT TO REMEMBER.

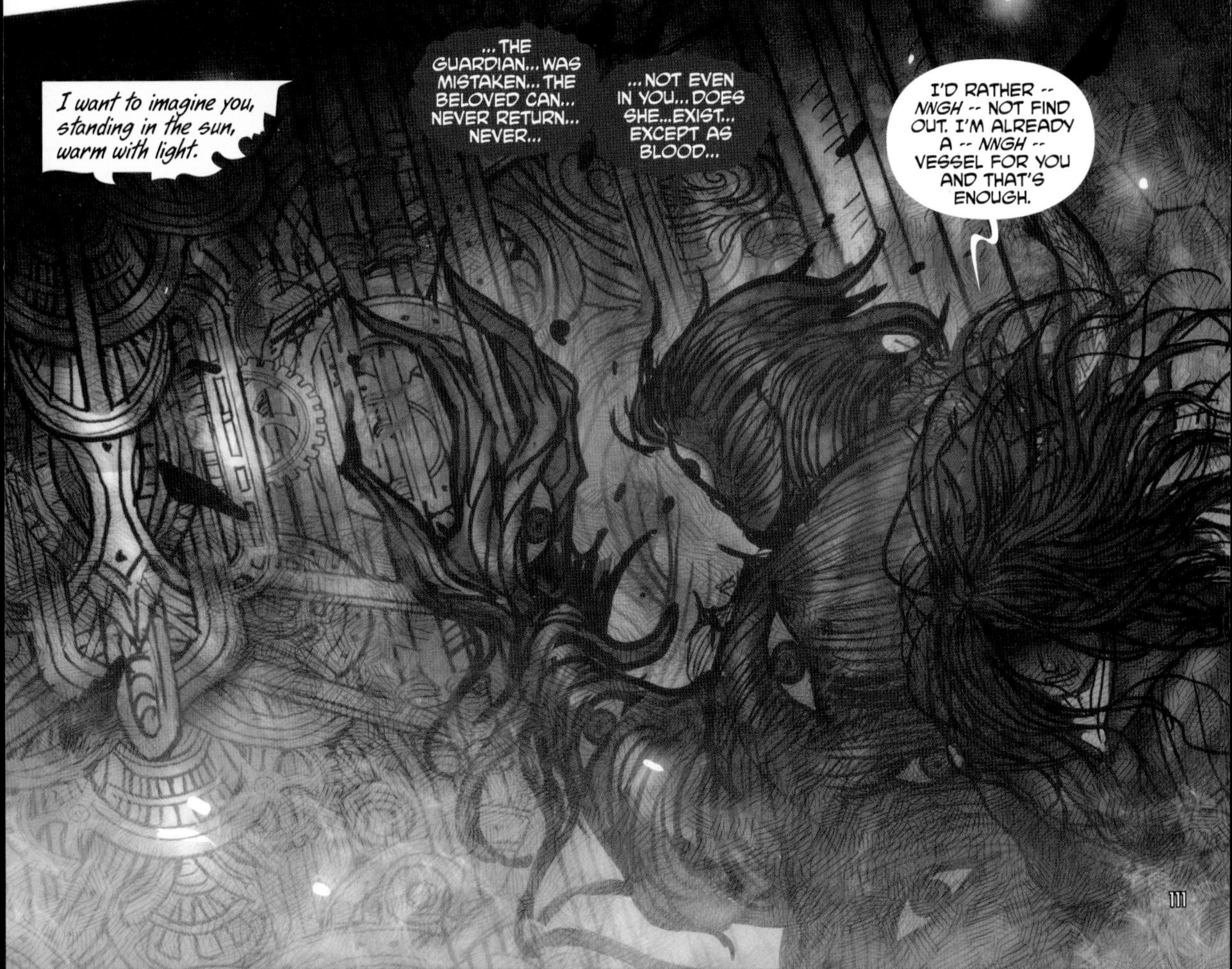
I want to imagine you, standing in the sun, warm with light.
...THE GUARDIAN...WAS MISTAKEN...THE BELOVED CAN... NEVER RETURN... NEVER...
...NOT EVEN IN YOU...DOES SHE...EXIST... EXCEPT AS BLOOD...
I'D RATHER -- *NNGH* -- NOT FIND OUT. I'M ALREADY A -- *NNGH* -- VESSEL FOR YOU AND THAT'S ENOUGH.

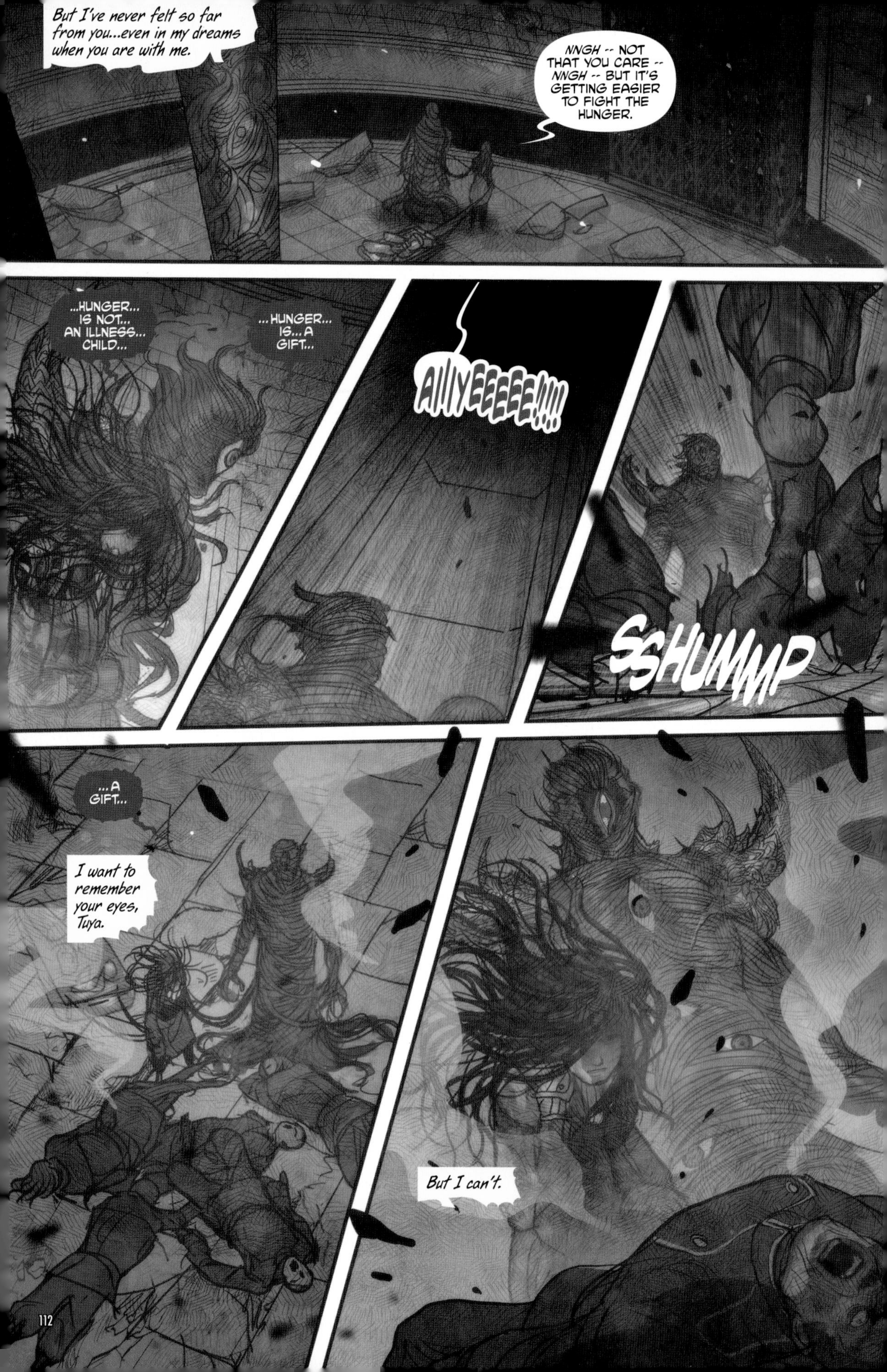
But I've never felt so far from you...even in my dreams when you are with me.
NNGH -- NOT THAT YOU CARE -- NNGH -- BUT IT'S GETTING EASIER TO FIGHT THE HUNGER.
...HUNGER... IS NOT... AN ILLNESS... CHILD...
...HUNGER... IS... A GIFT...
AIIIYEEEEE!!!!
SSHUMMP
...A GIFT...
I want to remember your eyes, Tuya.
But I can't.

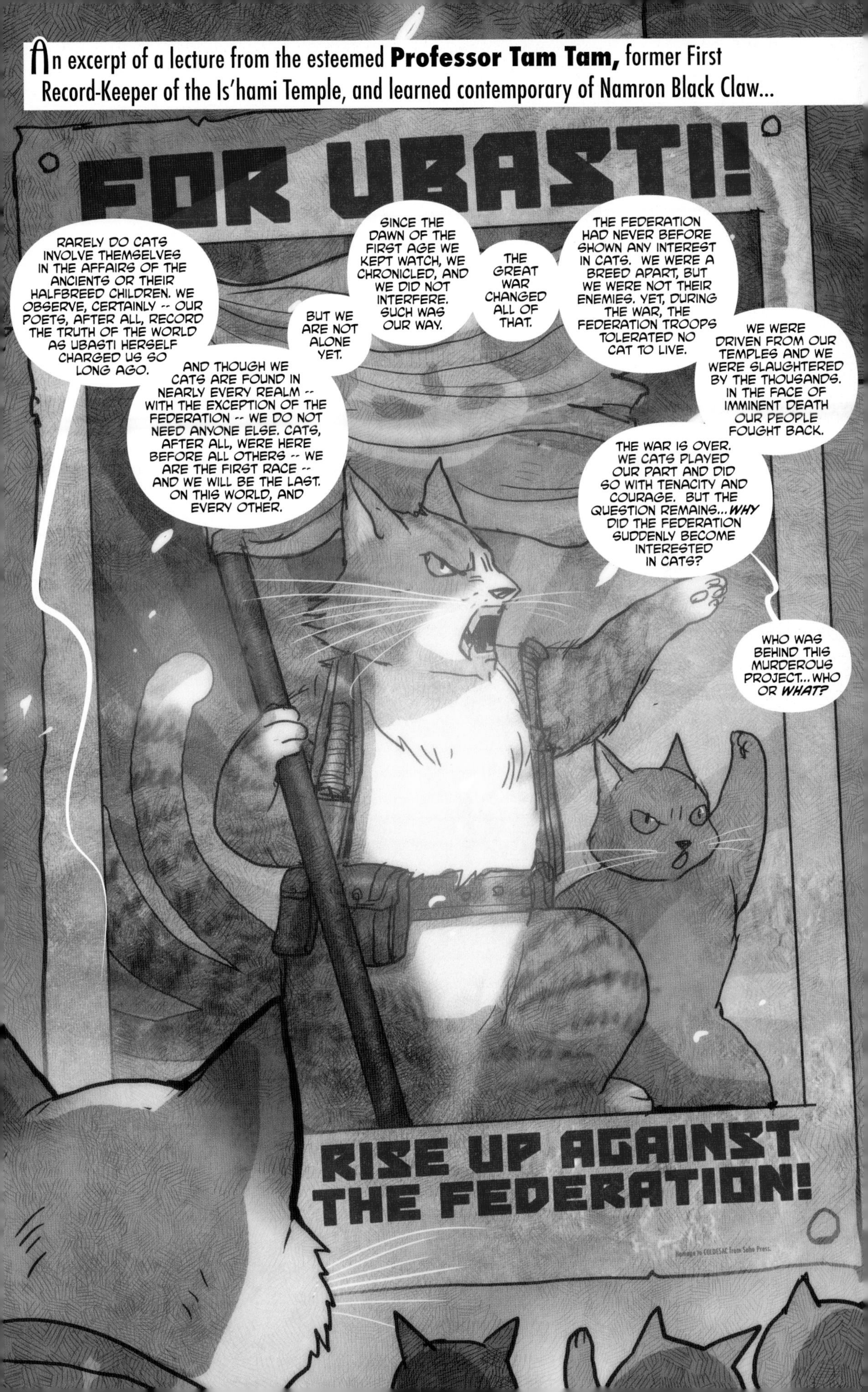
An excerpt of a lecture from the esteemed **Professor Tam Tam,** former First Record-Keeper of the Is'hami Temple, and learned contemporary of Namron Black Claw...
FOR UBASTI!
RARELY DO CATS INVOLVE THEMSELVES IN THE AFFAIRS OF THE ANCIENTS OR THEIR HALFBREED CHILDREN. WE OBSERVE, CERTAINLY -- OUR POETS, AFTER ALL, RECORD THE TRUTH OF THE WORLD AS UBASTI HERSELF CHARGED US SO LONG AGO.
AND THOUGH WE CATS ARE FOUND IN NEARLY EVERY REALM -- WITH THE EXCEPTION OF THE FEDERATION -- WE DO NOT NEED ANYONE ELSE. CATS, AFTER ALL, WERE HERE BEFORE ALL OTHERS -- WE ARE THE FIRST RACE -- AND WE WILL BE THE LAST. ON THIS WORLD, AND EVERY OTHER.
BUT WE ARE NOT ALONE YET.
SINCE THE DAWN OF THE FIRST AGE WE KEPT WATCH, WE CHRONICLED, AND WE DID NOT INTERFERE. SUCH WAS OUR WAY.
THE GREAT WAR CHANGED ALL OF THAT.
THE FEDERATION HAD NEVER BEFORE SHOWN ANY INTEREST IN CATS. WE WERE A BREED APART, BUT WE WERE NOT THEIR ENEMIES. YET, DURING THE WAR, THE FEDERATION TROOPS TOLERATED NO CAT TO LIVE.
WE WERE DRIVEN FROM OUR TEMPLES AND WE WERE SLAUGHTERED BY THE THOUSANDS. IN THE FACE OF IMMINENT DEATH OUR PEOPLE FOUGHT BACK.
THE WAR IS OVER. WE CATS PLAYED OUR PART AND DID SO WITH TENACITY AND COURAGE. BUT THE QUESTION REMAINS... *WHY* DID THE FEDERATION SUDDENLY BECOME INTERESTED IN CATS?
WHO WAS BEHIND THIS MURDEROUS PROJECT... WHO OR *WHAT?*
RISE UP AGAINST THE FEDERATION!
Homage to CULDESAC from Soba Press.

CHAPTER SEVENTEEN

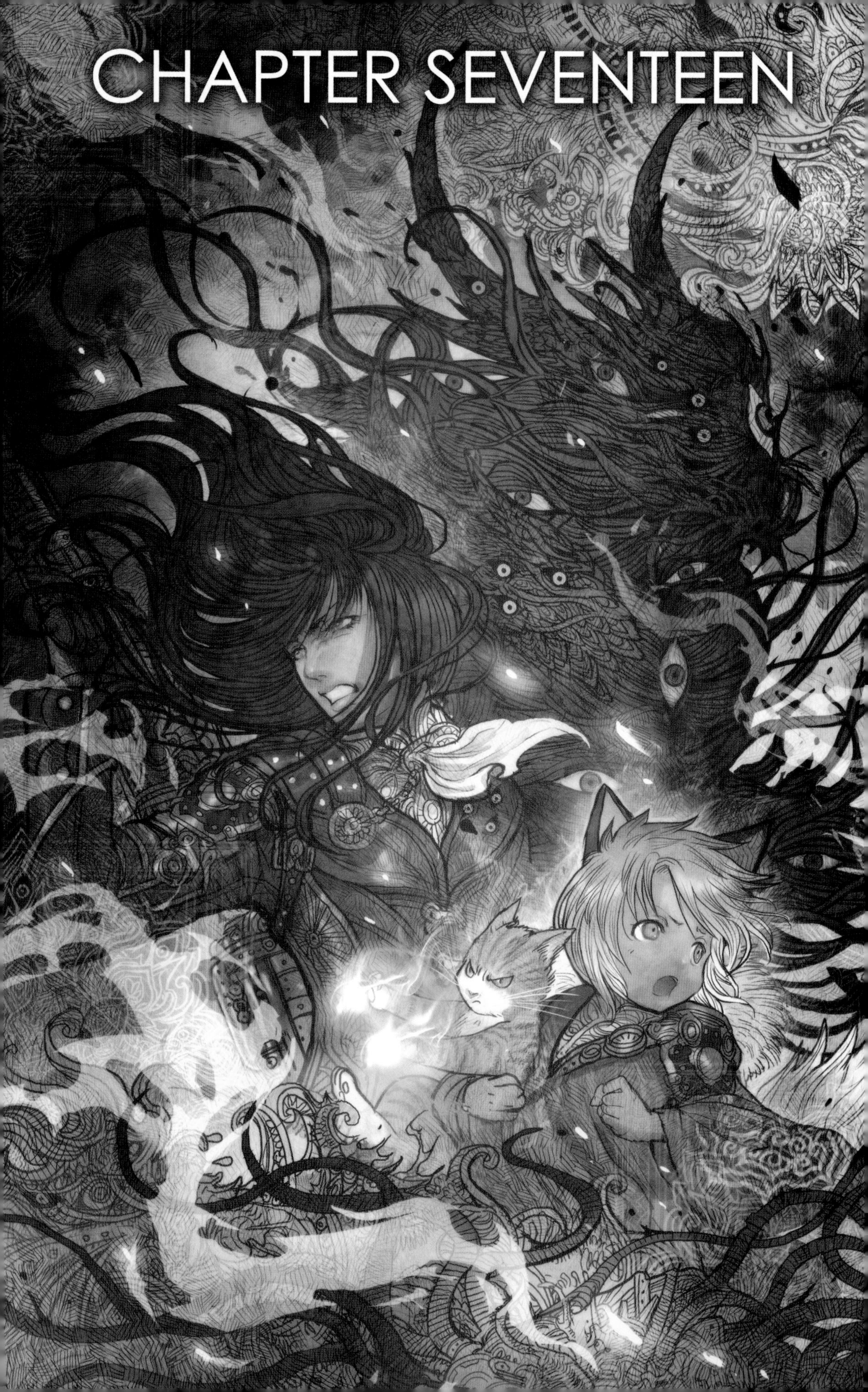

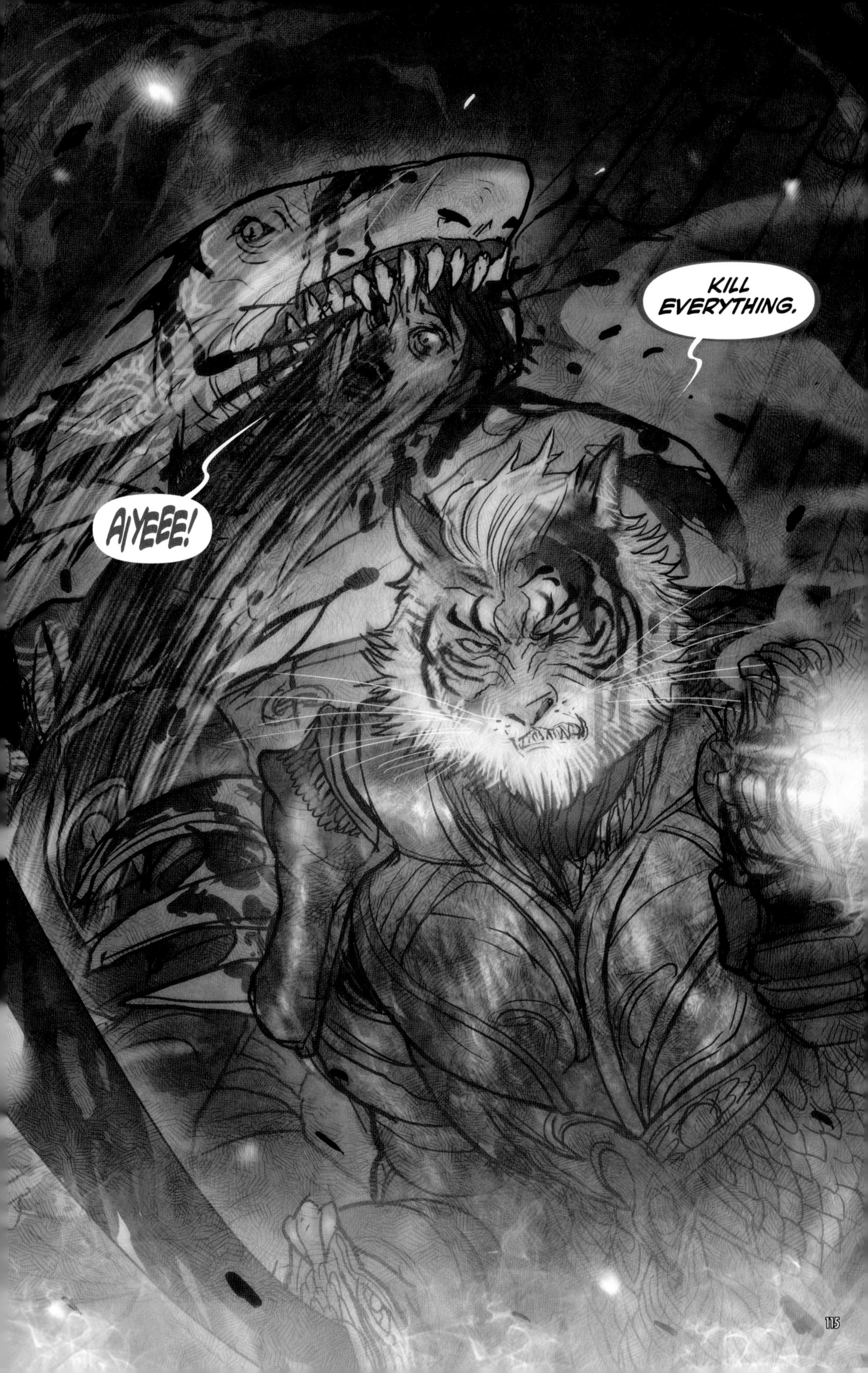
KILL EVERYTHING.
AIYEEE!

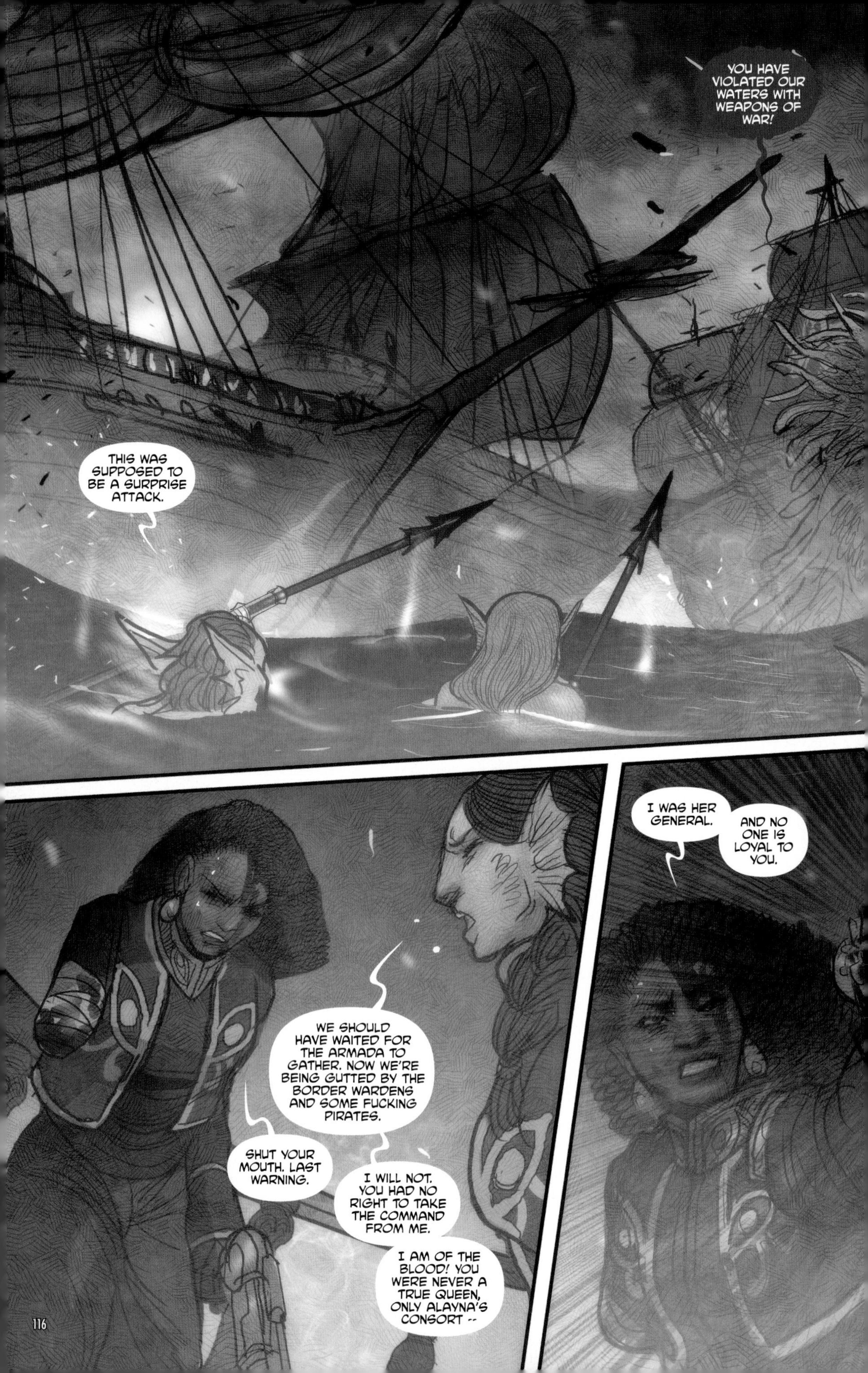
YOU HAVE VIOLATED OUR WATERS WITH WEAPONS OF WAR!
THIS WAS SUPPOSED TO BE A SURPRISE ATTACK.
WE SHOULD HAVE WAITED FOR THE ARMADA TO GATHER. NOW WE'RE BEING GUTTED BY THE BORDER WARDENS AND SOME FUCKING PIRATES.
SHUT YOUR MOUTH. LAST WARNING.
I WILL NOT. YOU HAD NO RIGHT TO TAKE THE COMMAND FROM ME.
I AM OF THE BLOOD! YOU WERE NEVER A TRUE QUEEN, ONLY ALAYNA'S CONSORT --
I WAS HER GENERAL.
AND NO ONE IS LOYAL TO YOU.

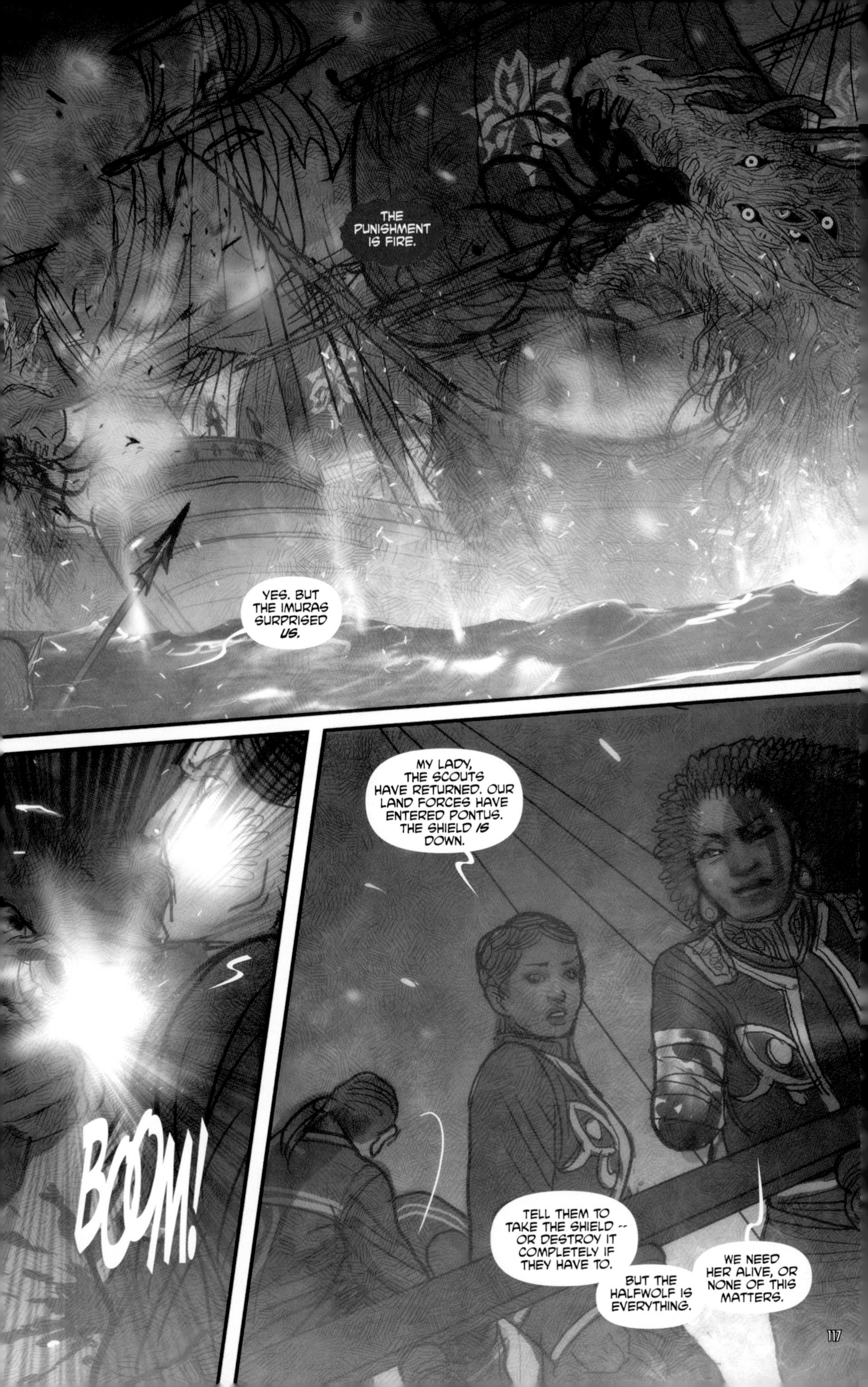
THE PUNISHMENT IS FIRE.
YES. BUT THE IMURAS SURPRISED *US.*
BOOM!
MY LADY, THE SCOUTS HAVE RETURNED. OUR LAND FORCES HAVE ENTERED PONTUS. THE SHIELD *IS* DOWN.
TELL THEM TO TAKE THE SHIELD -- OR DESTROY IT COMPLETELY IF THEY HAVE TO.
BUT THE HALFWOLF IS EVERYTHING.
WE NEED HER ALIVE, OR NONE OF THIS MATTERS.

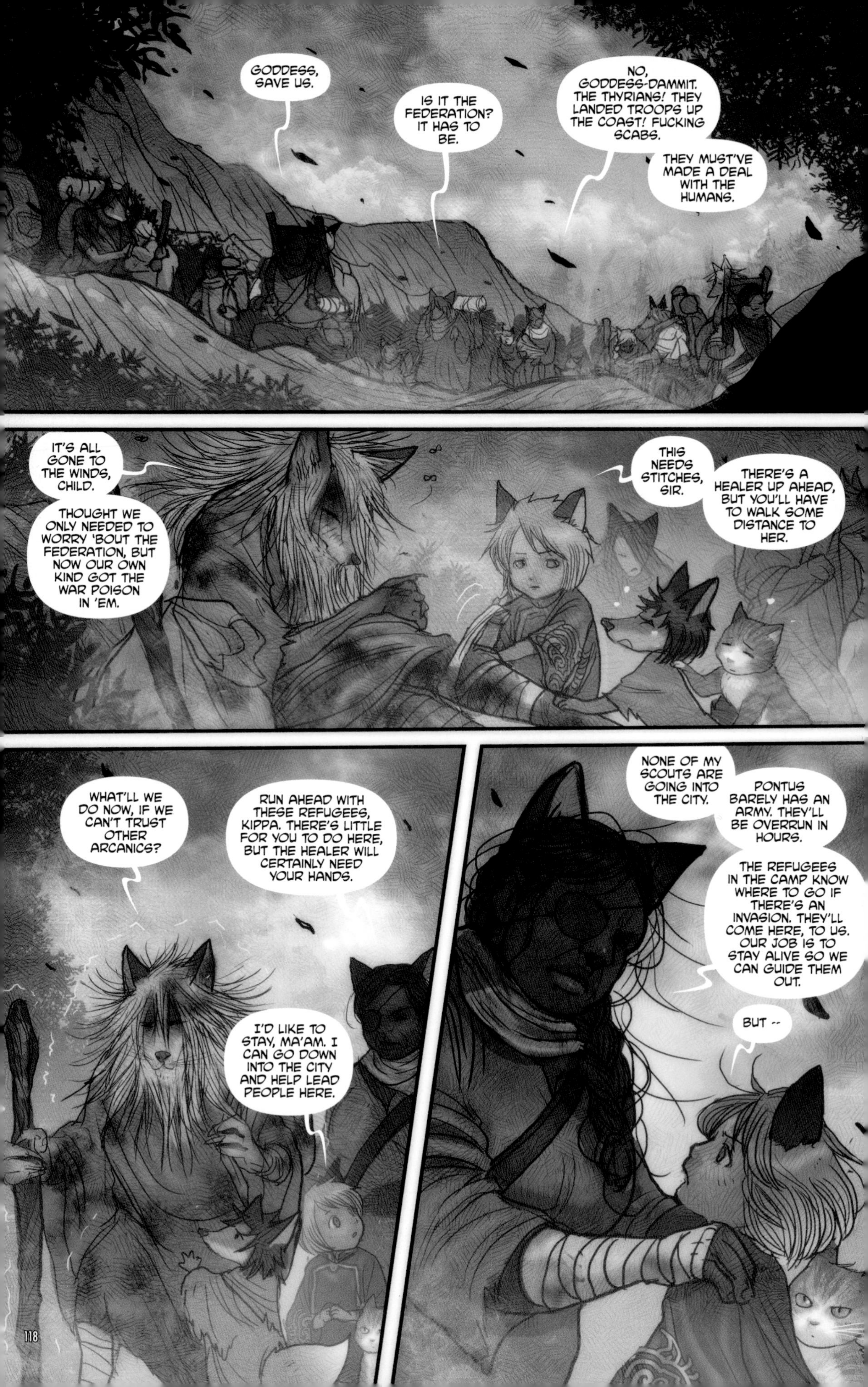
GODDESS, SAVE US.
IS IT THE FEDERATION? IT HAS TO BE.
NO, GODDESS-DAMMIT. THE THYRIANS! THEY LANDED TROOPS UP THE COAST! FUCKING SCABS.
THEY MUST'VE MADE A DEAL WITH THE HUMANS.
IT'S ALL GONE TO THE WINDS, CHILD.
THOUGHT WE ONLY NEEDED TO WORRY 'BOUT THE FEDERATION, BUT NOW OUR OWN KIND GOT THE WAR POISON IN 'EM.
THIS NEEDS STITCHES, SIR.
THERE'S A HEALER UP AHEAD, BUT YOU'LL HAVE TO WALK SOME DISTANCE TO HER.
WHAT'LL WE DO NOW, IF WE CAN'T TRUST OTHER ARCANICS?
RUN AHEAD WITH THESE REFUGEES, KIPPA. THERE'S LITTLE FOR YOU TO DO HERE, BUT THE HEALER WILL CERTAINLY NEED YOUR HANDS.
I'D LIKE TO STAY, MA'AM. I CAN GO DOWN INTO THE CITY AND HELP LEAD PEOPLE HERE.
NONE OF MY SCOUTS ARE GOING INTO THE CITY.
PONTUS BARELY HAS AN ARMY. THEY'LL BE OVERRUN IN HOURS.
THE REFUGEES IN THE CAMP KNOW WHERE TO GO IF THERE'S AN INVASION. THEY'LL COME HERE, TO US. OUR JOB IS TO STAY ALIVE SO WE CAN GUIDE THEM OUT.
BUT --

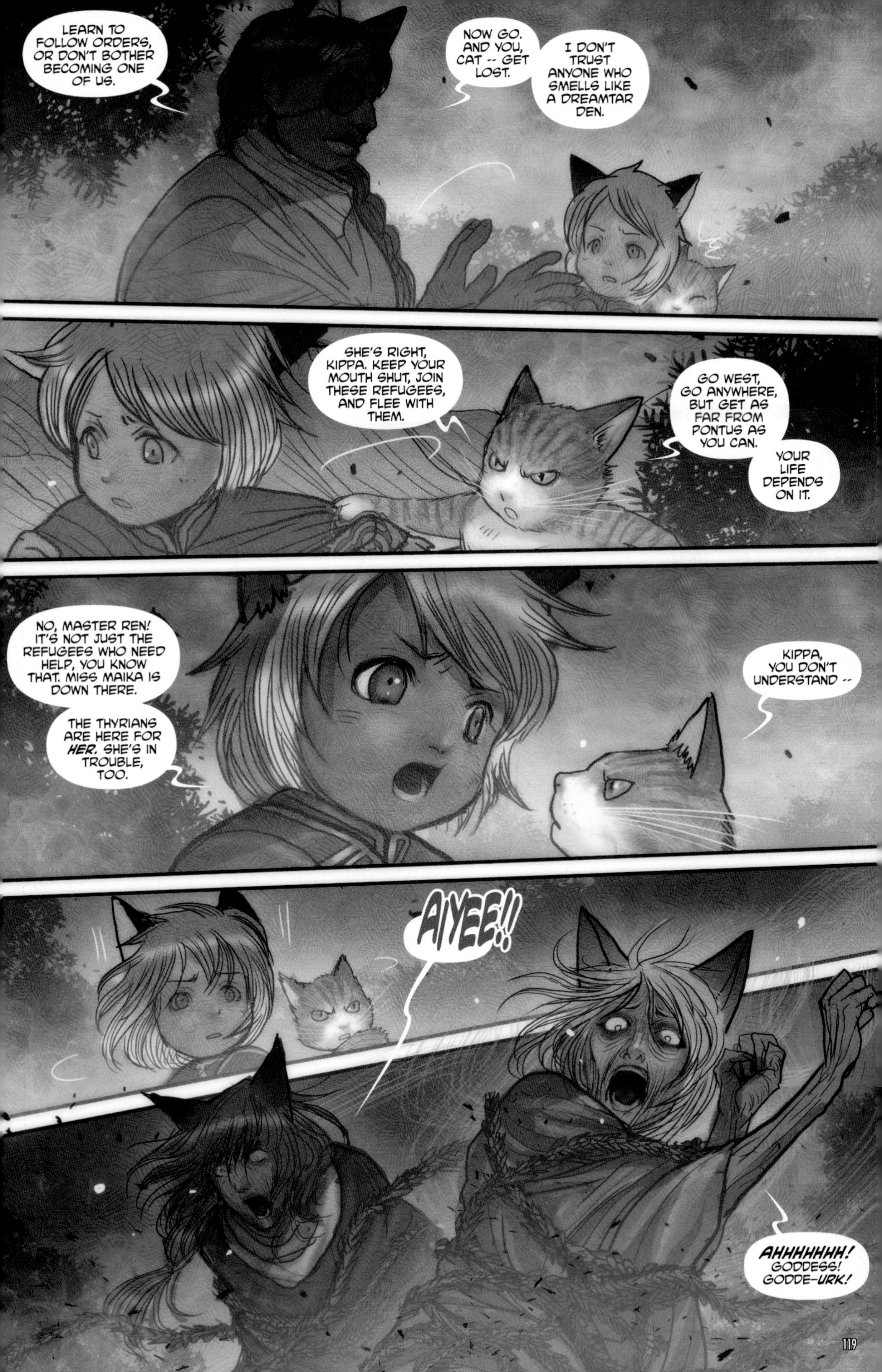
LEARN TO FOLLOW ORDERS, OR DON'T BOTHER BECOMING ONE OF US.
NOW GO. AND YOU, CAT -- GET LOST.
I DON'T TRUST ANYONE WHO SMELLS LIKE A DREAMTAR DEN.
SHE'S RIGHT, KIPPA. KEEP YOUR MOUTH SHUT, JOIN THESE REFUGEES, AND FLEE WITH THEM.
GO WEST, GO ANYWHERE, BUT GET AS FAR FROM PONTUS AS YOU CAN.
YOUR LIFE DEPENDS ON IT.
NO, MASTER REN! IT'S NOT JUST THE REFUGEES WHO NEED HELP, YOU KNOW THAT. MISS MAIKA IS DOWN THERE.
THE THYRIANS ARE HERE FOR HER. SHE'S IN TROUBLE, TOO.
KIPPA, YOU DON'T UNDERSTAND --
AIYEE!!
AHHHHHHH! GODDESS! GODDE-URK!

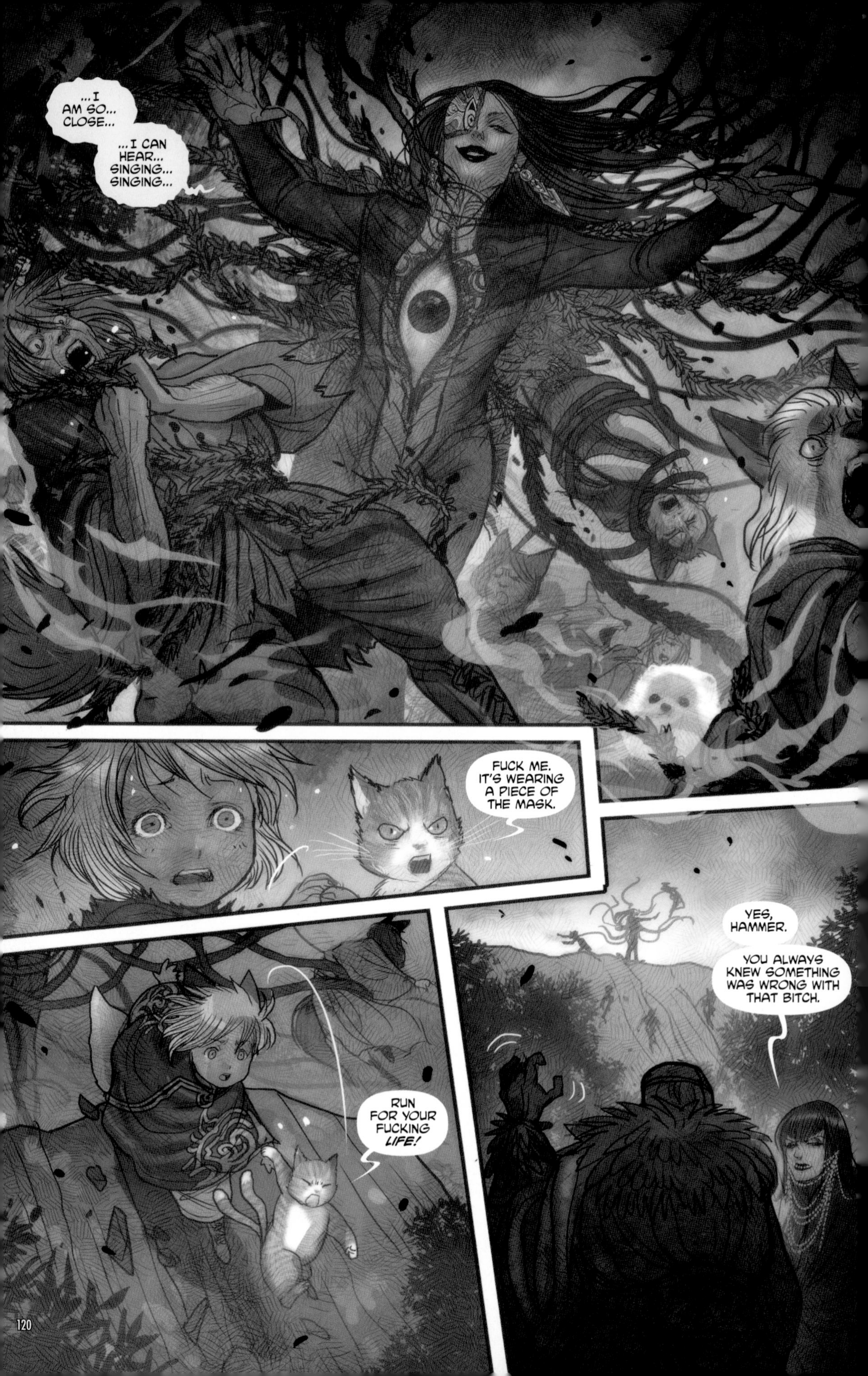
...I AM SO... CLOSE...
...I CAN HEAR... SINGING... SINGING...
FUCK ME. IT'S WEARING A PIECE OF THE MASK.
YES, HAMMER.
YOU ALWAYS KNEW SOMETHING WAS WRONG WITH THAT BITCH.
RUN FOR YOUR FUCKING *LIFE!*

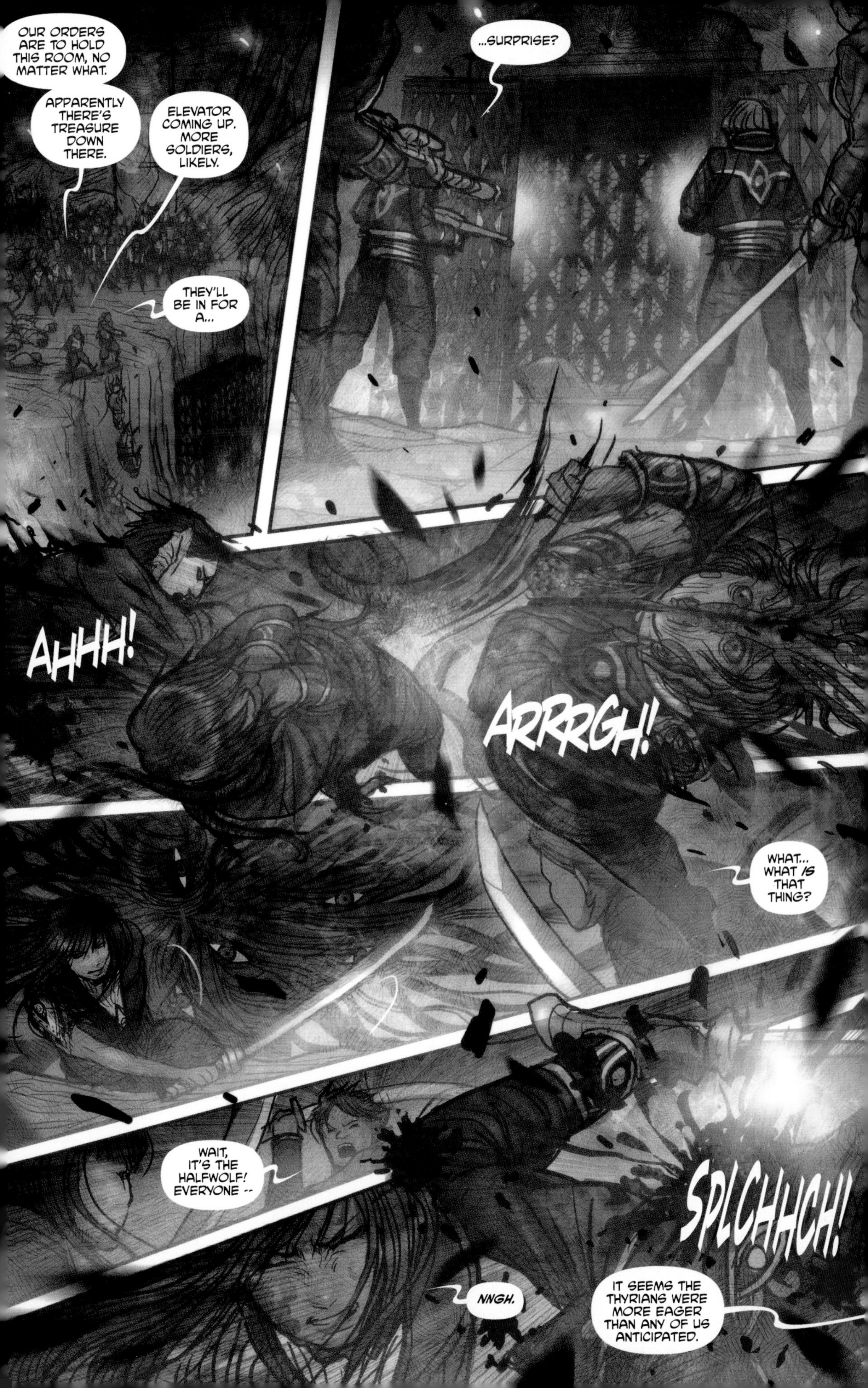

OUR ORDERS ARE TO HOLD THIS ROOM, NO MATTER WHAT.
APPARENTLY THERE'S TREASURE DOWN THERE.
ELEVATOR COMING UP. MORE SOLDIERS, LIKELY.
THEY'LL BE IN FOR A...
...SURPRISE?
AHHH!
ARRRGH!
WHAT... WHAT IS THAT THING?
WAIT, IT'S THE HALFWOLF! EVERYONE --
SPLCHHCH!
NNGH.
IT SEEMS THE THYRIANS WERE MORE EAGER THAN ANY OF US ANTICIPATED.

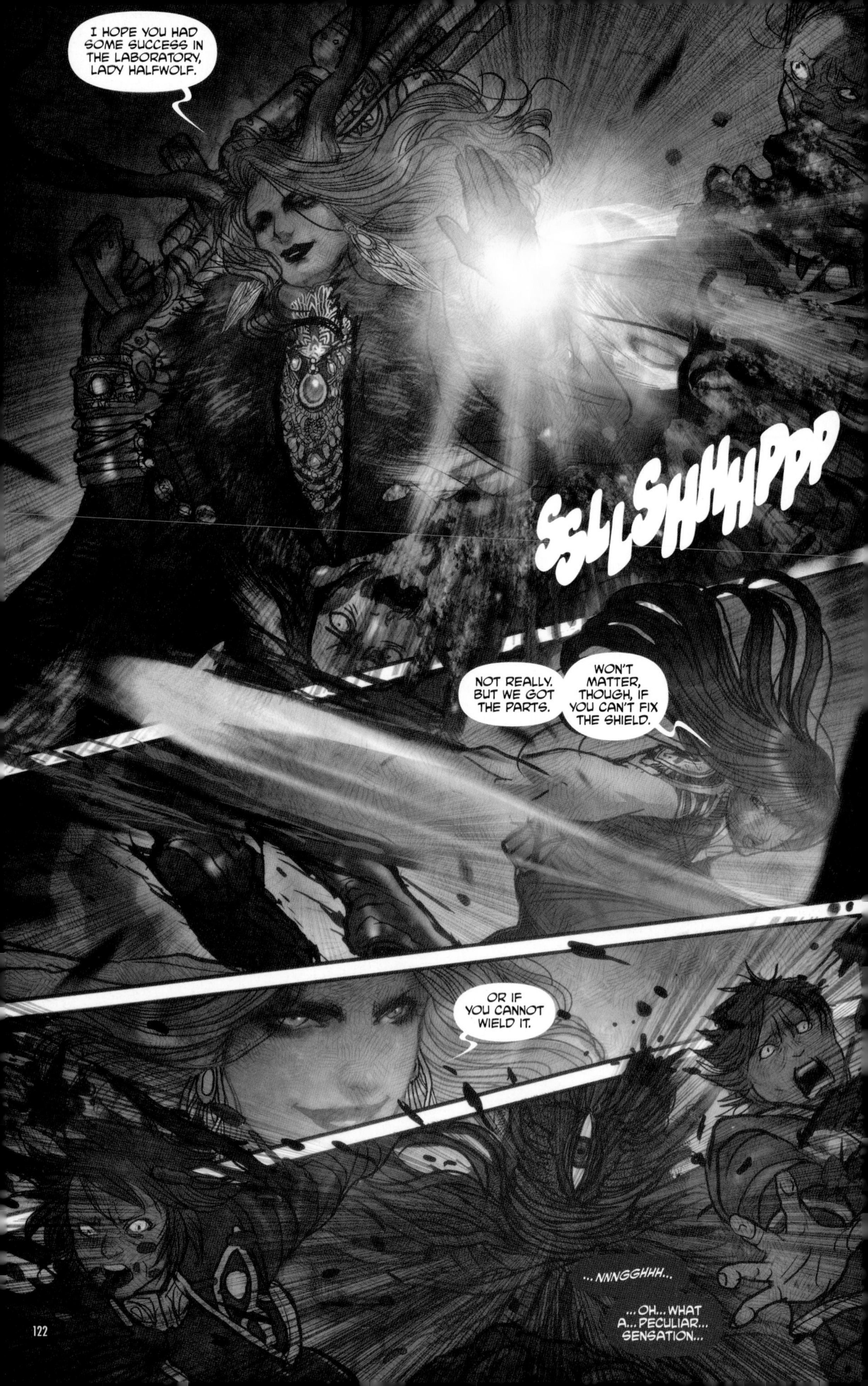

I HOPE YOU HAD SOME SUCCESS IN THE LABORATORY, LADY HALFWOLF.
SSLLSHHHHPPP
NOT REALLY. BUT WE GOT THE PARTS.
WON'T MATTER, THOUGH, IF YOU CAN'T FIX THE SHIELD.
OR IF YOU CANNOT WIELD IT.
...NNNGGHHH...
...OH...WHAT A...PECULIAR... SENSATION...

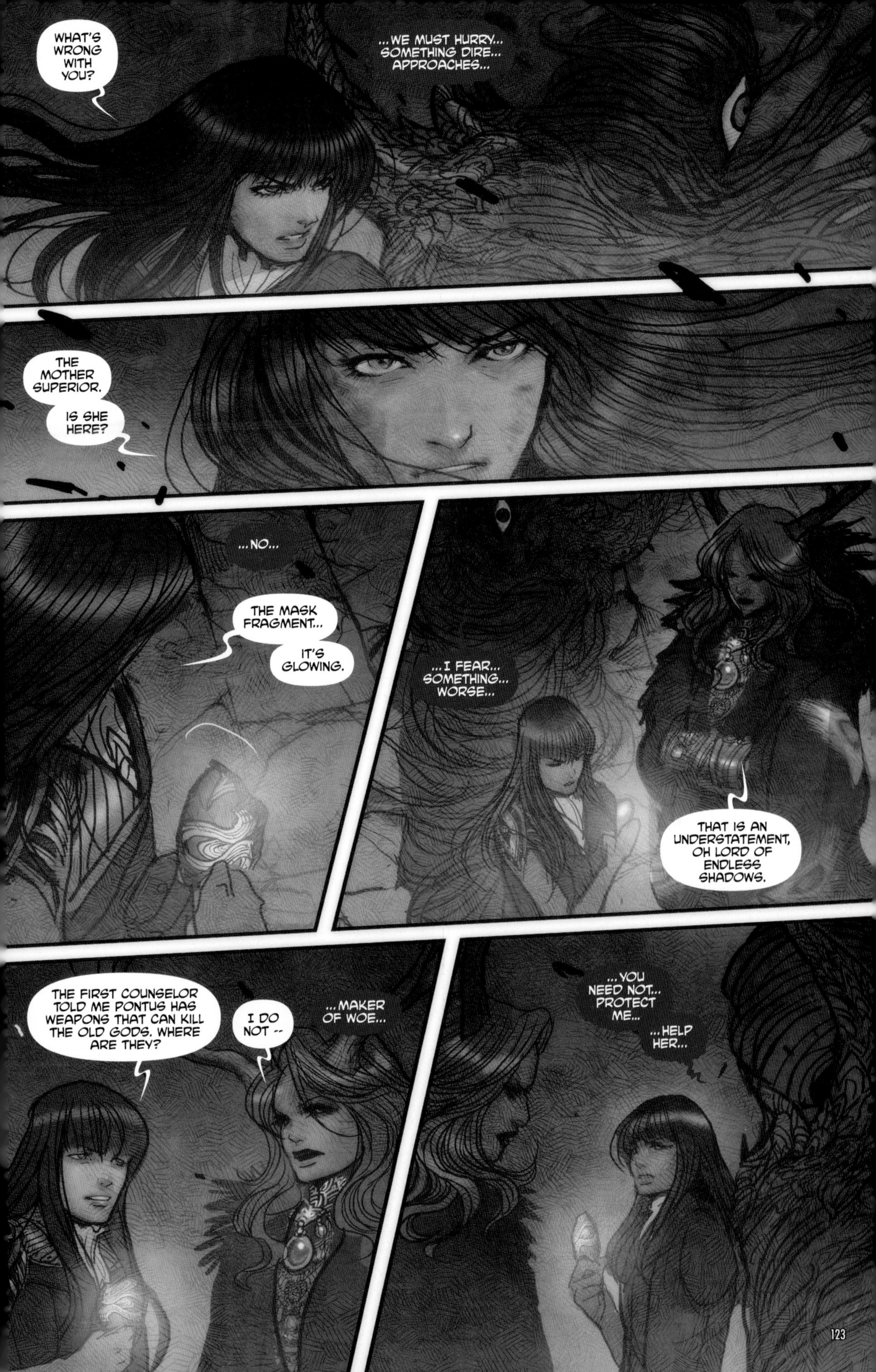
WHAT'S WRONG WITH YOU?
...WE MUST HURRY... SOMETHING DIRE... APPROACHES...
THE MOTHER SUPERIOR.
IS SHE HERE?
...NO...
THE MASK FRAGMENT...
IT'S GLOWING.
...I FEAR... SOMETHING... WORSE...
THAT IS AN UNDERSTATEMENT, OH LORD OF ENDLESS SHADOWS.
THE FIRST COUNSELOR TOLD ME PONTUS HAS WEAPONS THAT CAN KILL THE OLD GODS. WHERE ARE THEY?
I DO NOT --
...MAKER OF WOE...
...YOU NEED NOT... PROTECT ME...
...HELP HER...

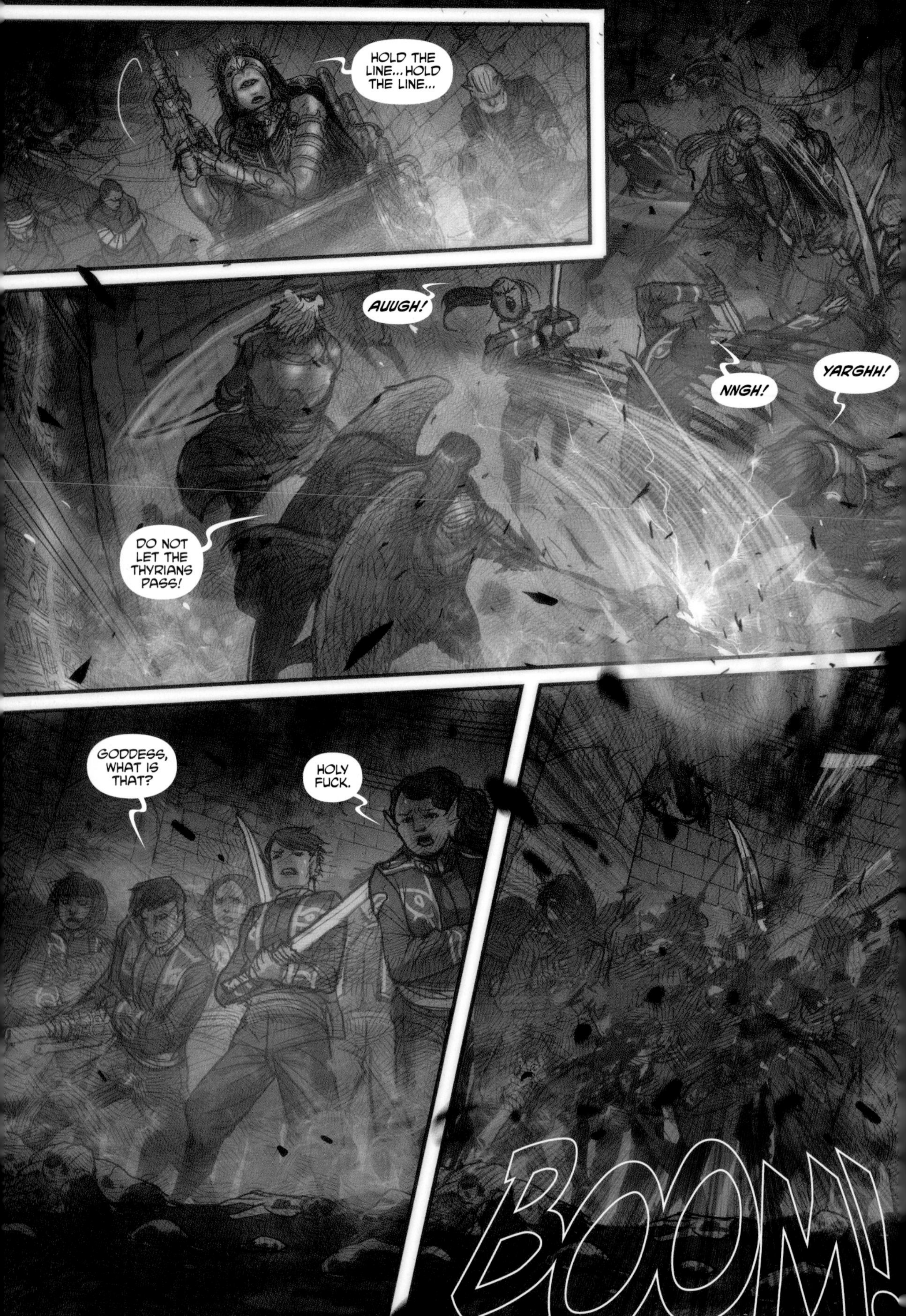
HOLD THE LINE... HOLD THE LINE...
AUUGH!
NNGH!
YARGHH!
DO NOT LET THE THYRIANS PASS!
GODDESS, WHAT IS THAT?
HOLY FUCK.
BOOM!

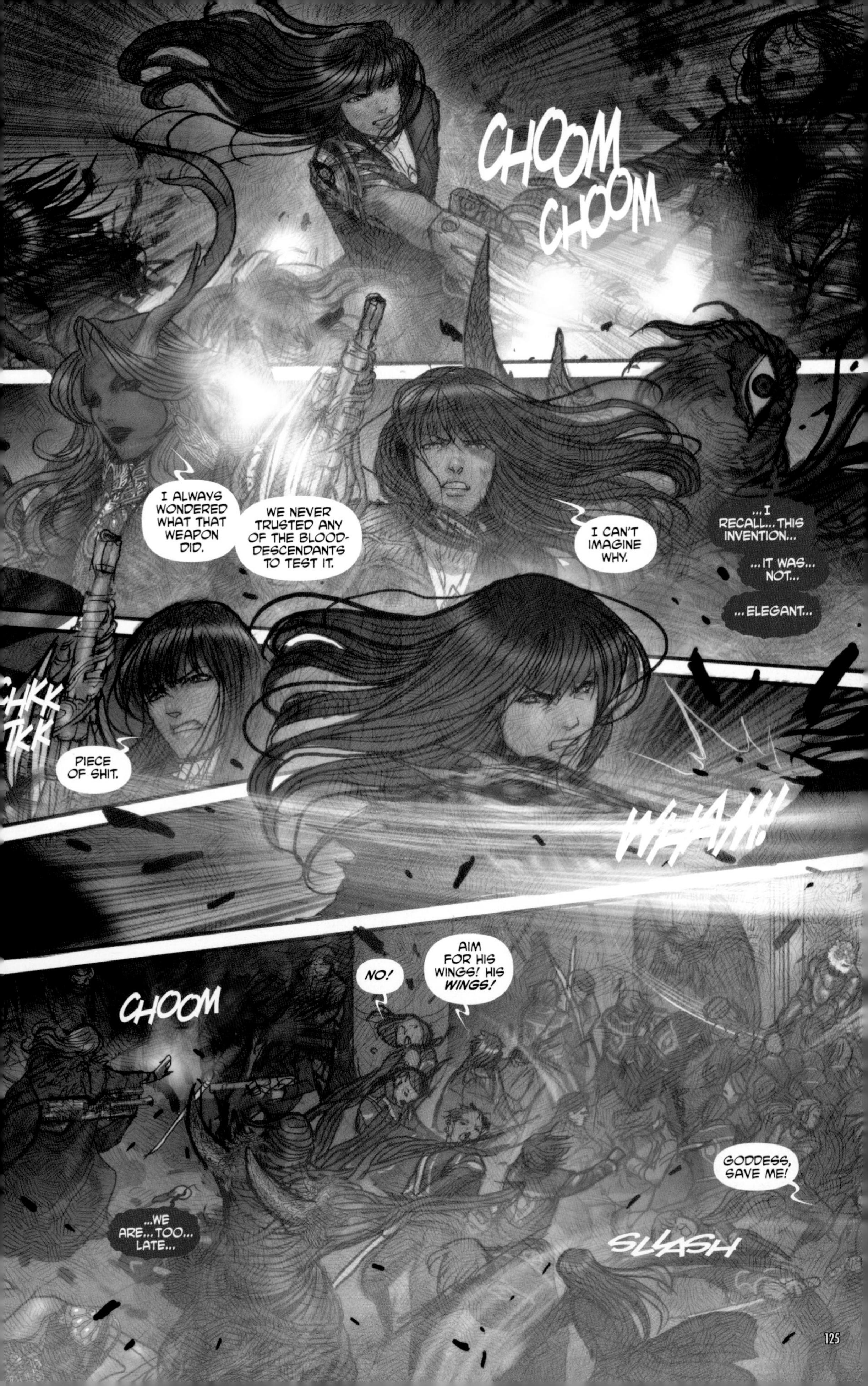
CHOOM CHOOM
I ALWAYS WONDERED WHAT THAT WEAPON DID.
WE NEVER TRUSTED ANY OF THE BLOOD-DESCENDANTS TO TEST IT.
I CAN'T IMAGINE WHY.
...I RECALL...THIS INVENTION...
...IT WAS... NOT...
...ELEGANT...
CHKK TKK
PIECE OF SHIT.
WHAM!
CHOOM
NO!
AIM FOR HIS WINGS! HIS WINGS!
GODDESS, SAVE ME!
...WE ARE...TOO... LATE...
SLASH

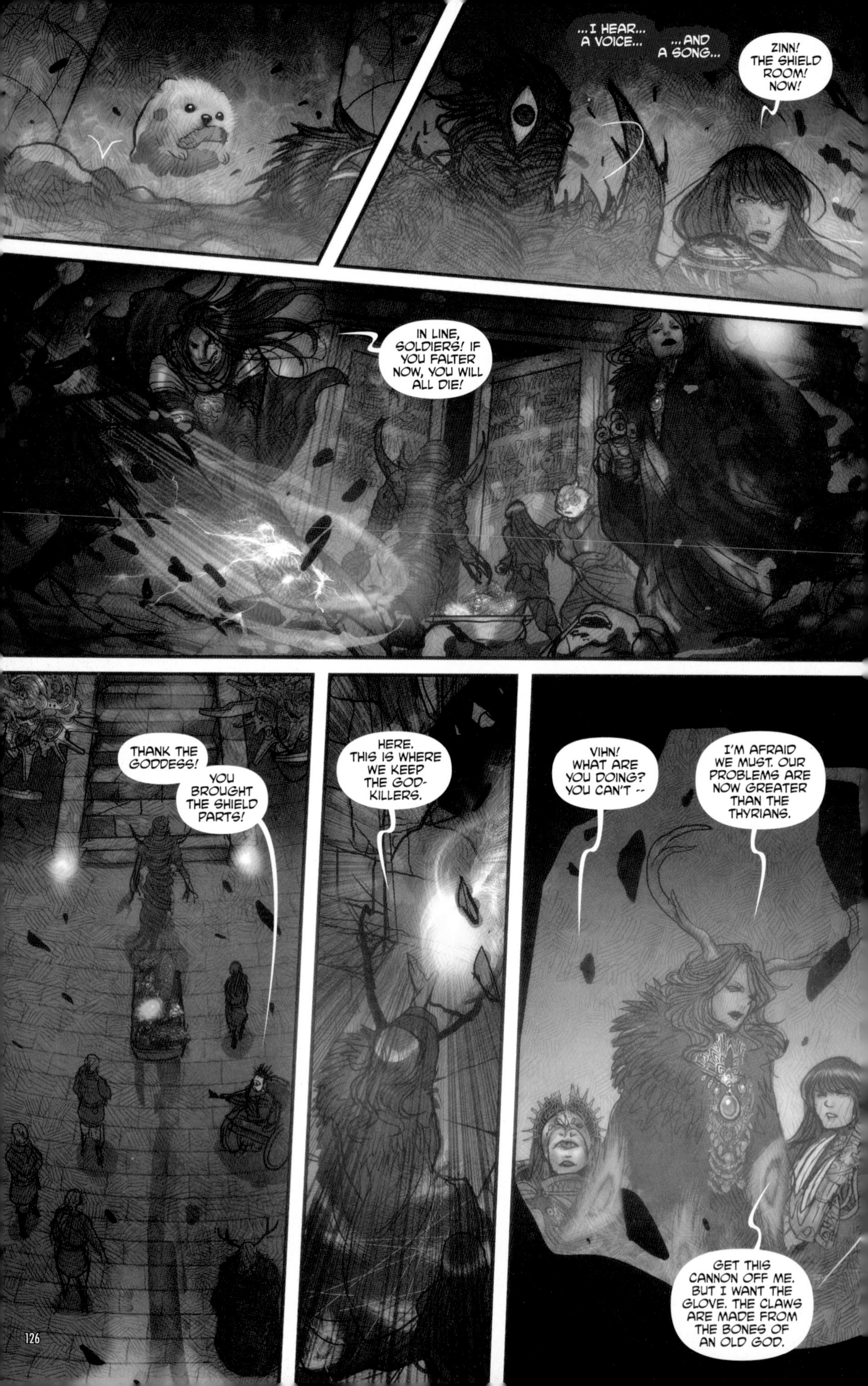
...I HEAR... A VOICE...
...AND A SONG...
ZINN! THE SHIELD ROOM! NOW!
IN LINE, SOLDIERS! IF YOU FALTER NOW, YOU WILL ALL DIE!
THANK THE GODDESS!
YOU BROUGHT THE SHIELD PARTS!
HERE. THIS IS WHERE WE KEEP THE GOD-KILLERS.
VIHN! WHAT ARE YOU DOING? YOU CAN'T --
I'M AFRAID WE MUST. OUR PROBLEMS ARE NOW GREATER THAN THE THYRIANS.
GET THIS CANNON OFF ME. BUT I WANT THE GLOVE. THE CLAWS ARE MADE FROM THE BONES OF AN OLD GOD.

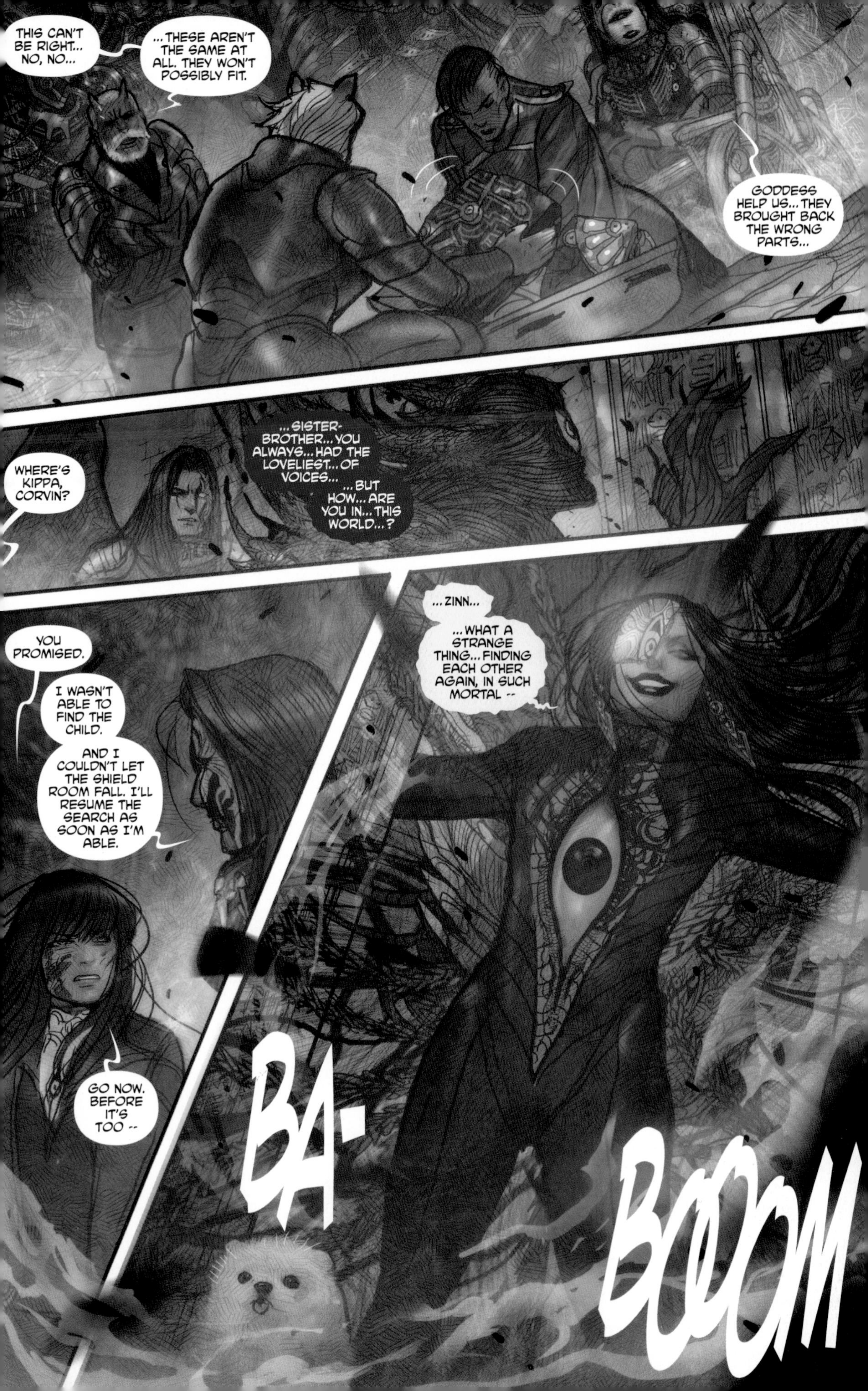
THIS CAN'T BE RIGHT... NO, NO...
...THESE AREN'T THE SAME AT ALL. THEY WON'T POSSIBLY FIT.
GODDESS HELP US... THEY BROUGHT BACK THE WRONG PARTS...
WHERE'S KIPPA, CORVIN?
...SISTER-BROTHER... YOU ALWAYS... HAD THE LOVELIEST... OF VOICES...
...BUT HOW... ARE YOU IN... THIS WORLD...?
YOU PROMISED.
I WASN'T ABLE TO FIND THE CHILD.
AND I COULDN'T LET THE SHIELD ROOM FALL. I'LL RESUME THE SEARCH AS SOON AS I'M ABLE.
...ZINN...
...WHAT A STRANGE THING... FINDING EACH OTHER AGAIN, IN SUCH MORTAL --
GO NOW. BEFORE IT'S TOO --
BA-
BOOOM

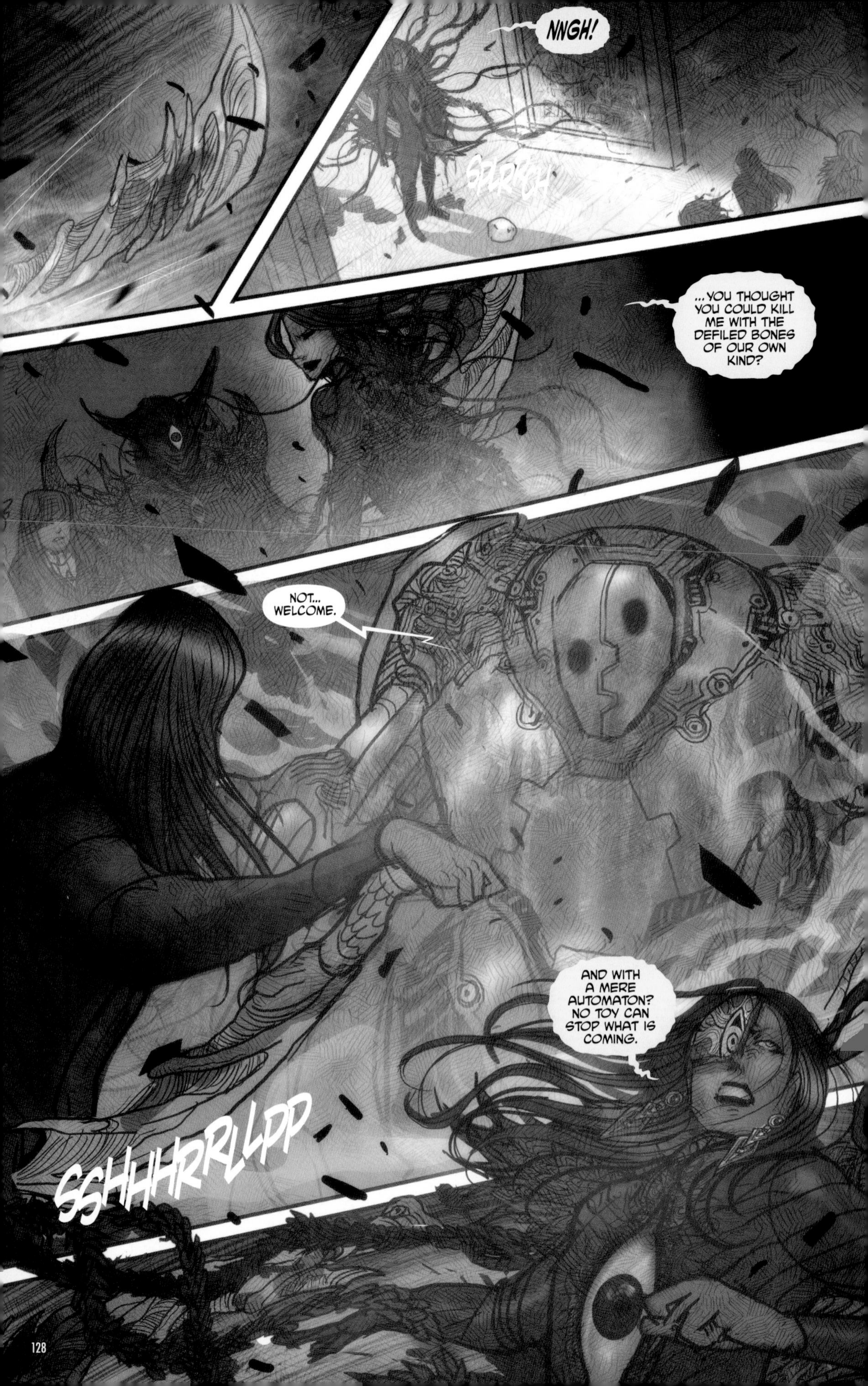
NNGH!
SPLRTCH
...YOU THOUGHT YOU COULD KILL ME WITH THE DEFILED BONES OF OUR OWN KIND?
NOT... WELCOME.
AND WITH A MERE AUTOMATON? NO TOY CAN STOP WHAT IS COMING.
SSHHHRRLLPP

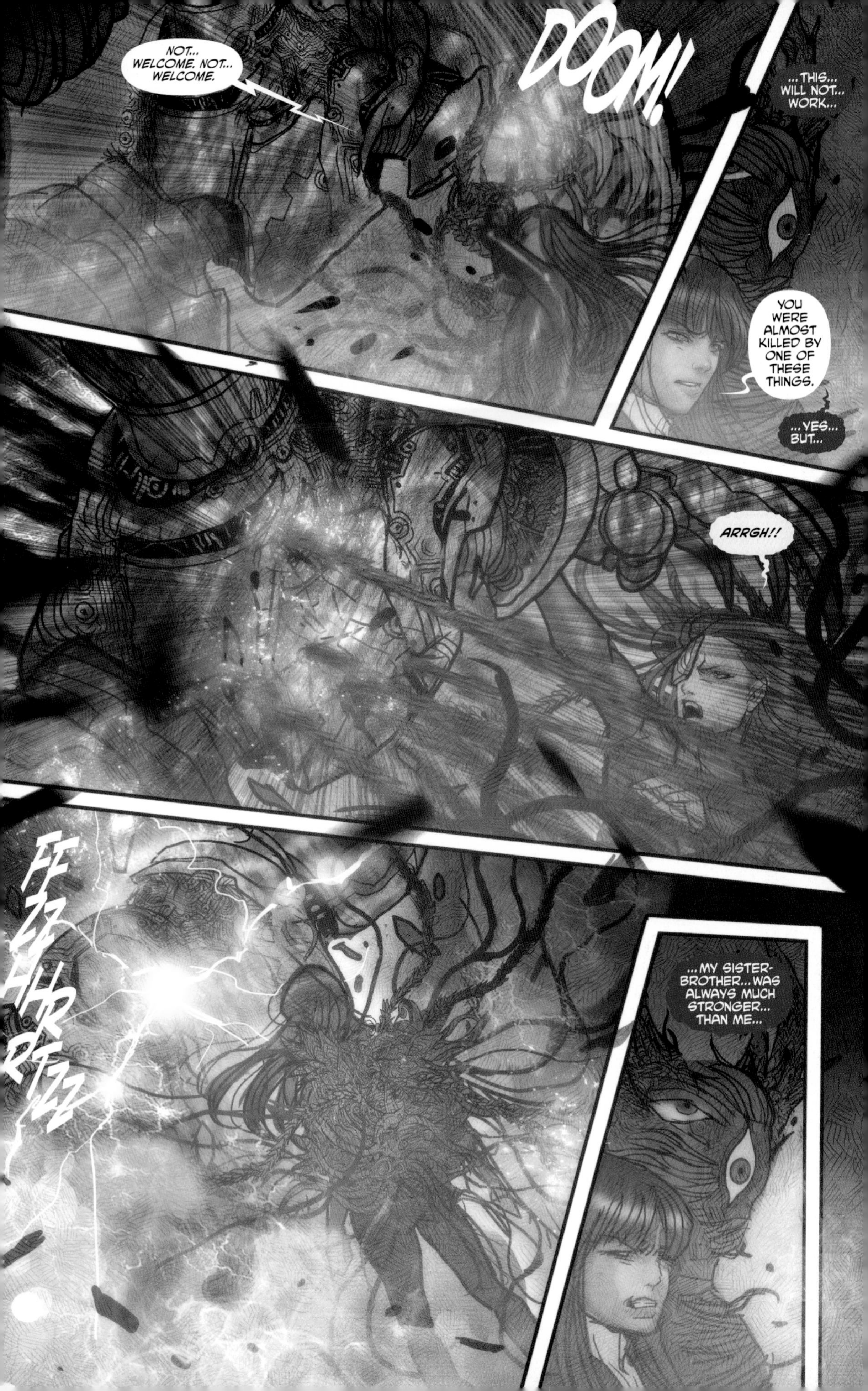
NOT... WELCOME. NOT... WELCOME.
DOOM!!
...THIS... WILL NOT... WORK...
YOU WERE ALMOST KILLED BY ONE OF THESE THINGS.
...YES... BUT...
ARRGH!!
FFZZZHHRRTZZZ
...MY SISTER-BROTHER...WAS ALWAYS MUCH STRONGER... THAN ME...

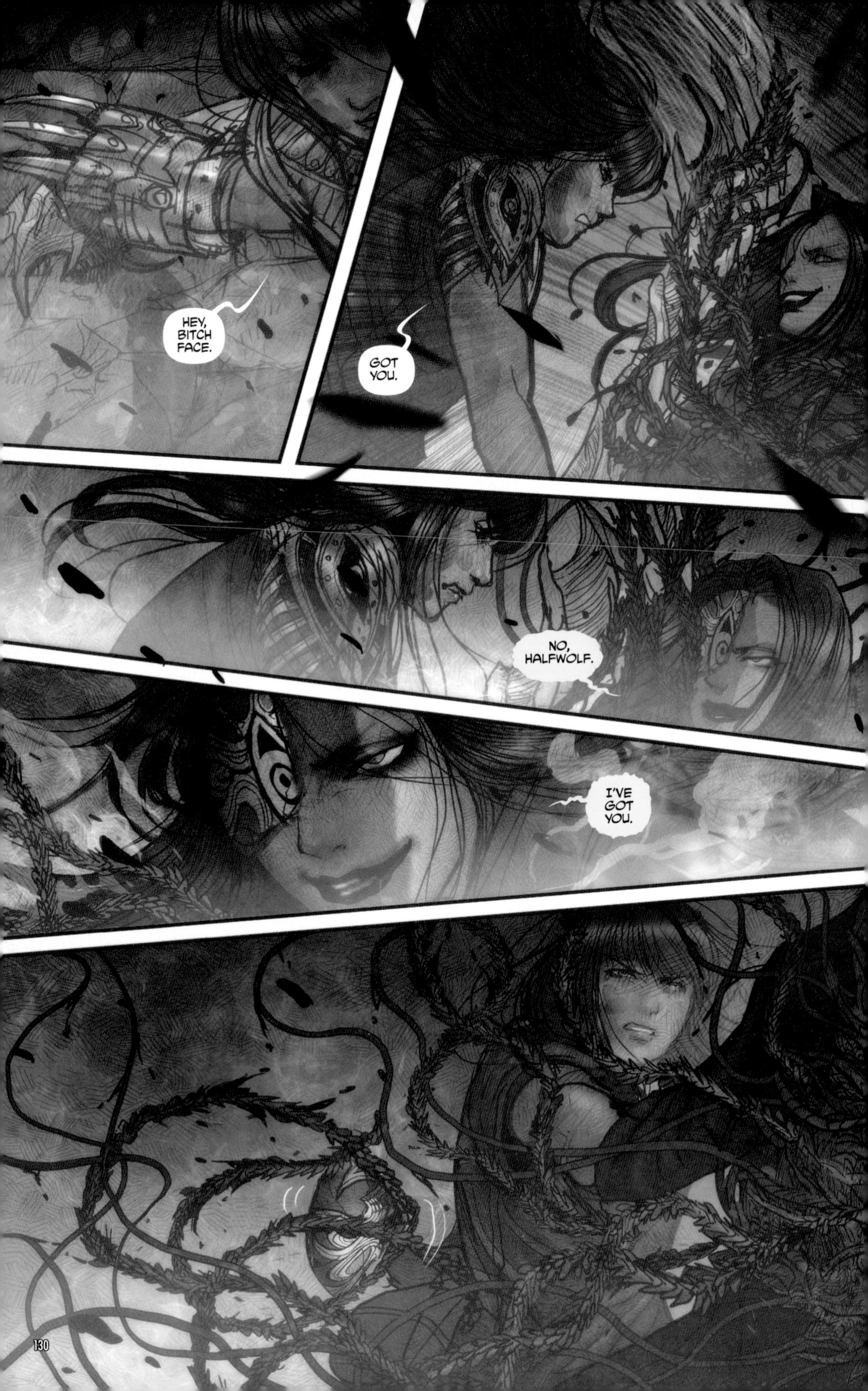
HEY, BITCH FACE.
GOT YOU.
NO, HALFWOLF.
I'VE GOT YOU.

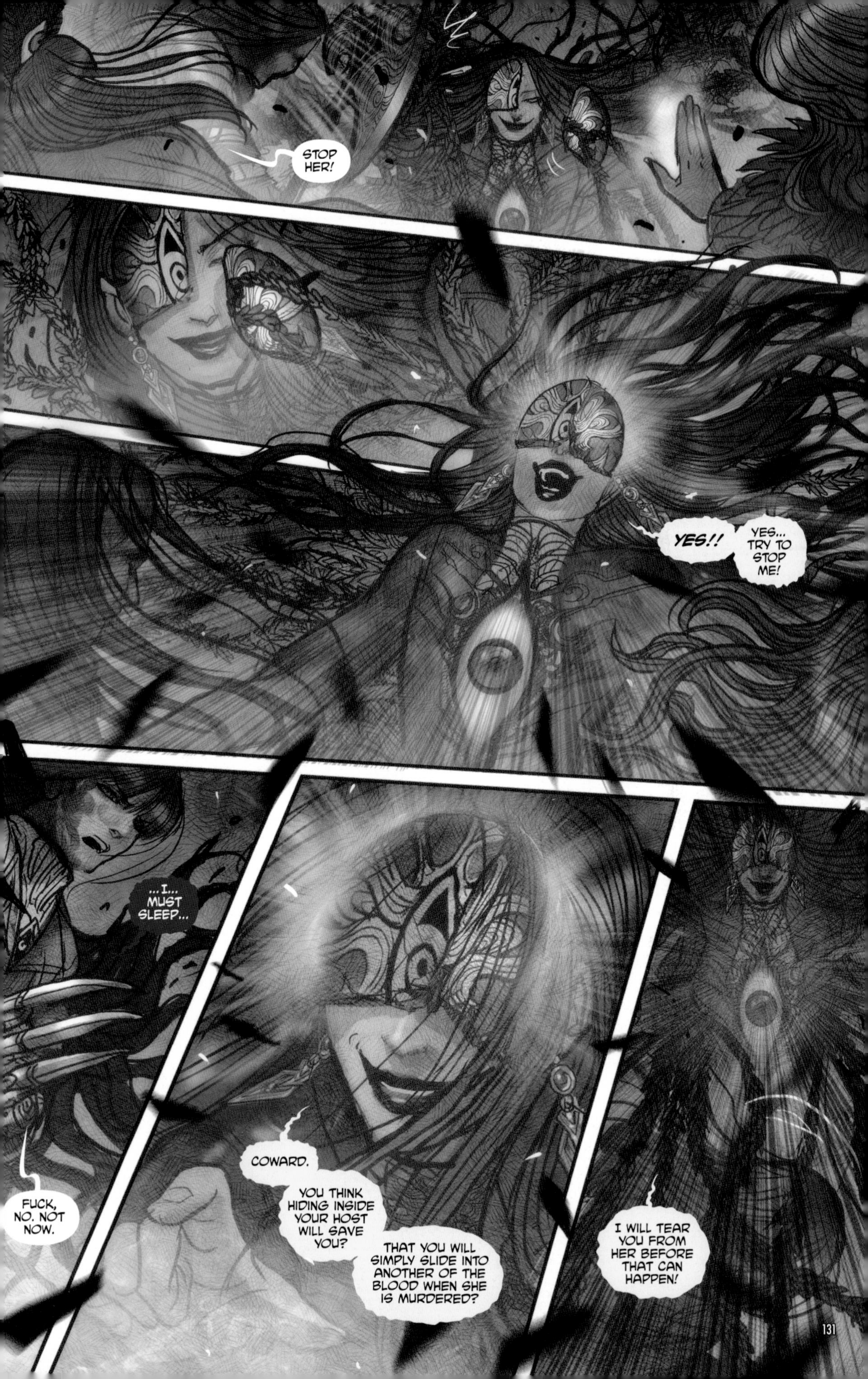
STOP HER!
YES!!
YES... TRY TO STOP ME!
...I... MUST SLEEP...
FUCK, NO. NOT NOW.
COWARD.
YOU THINK HIDING INSIDE YOUR HOST WILL SAVE YOU?
THAT YOU WILL SIMPLY SLIDE INTO ANOTHER OF THE BLOOD WHEN SHE IS MURDERED?
I WILL TEAR YOU FROM HER BEFORE THAT CAN HAPPEN!

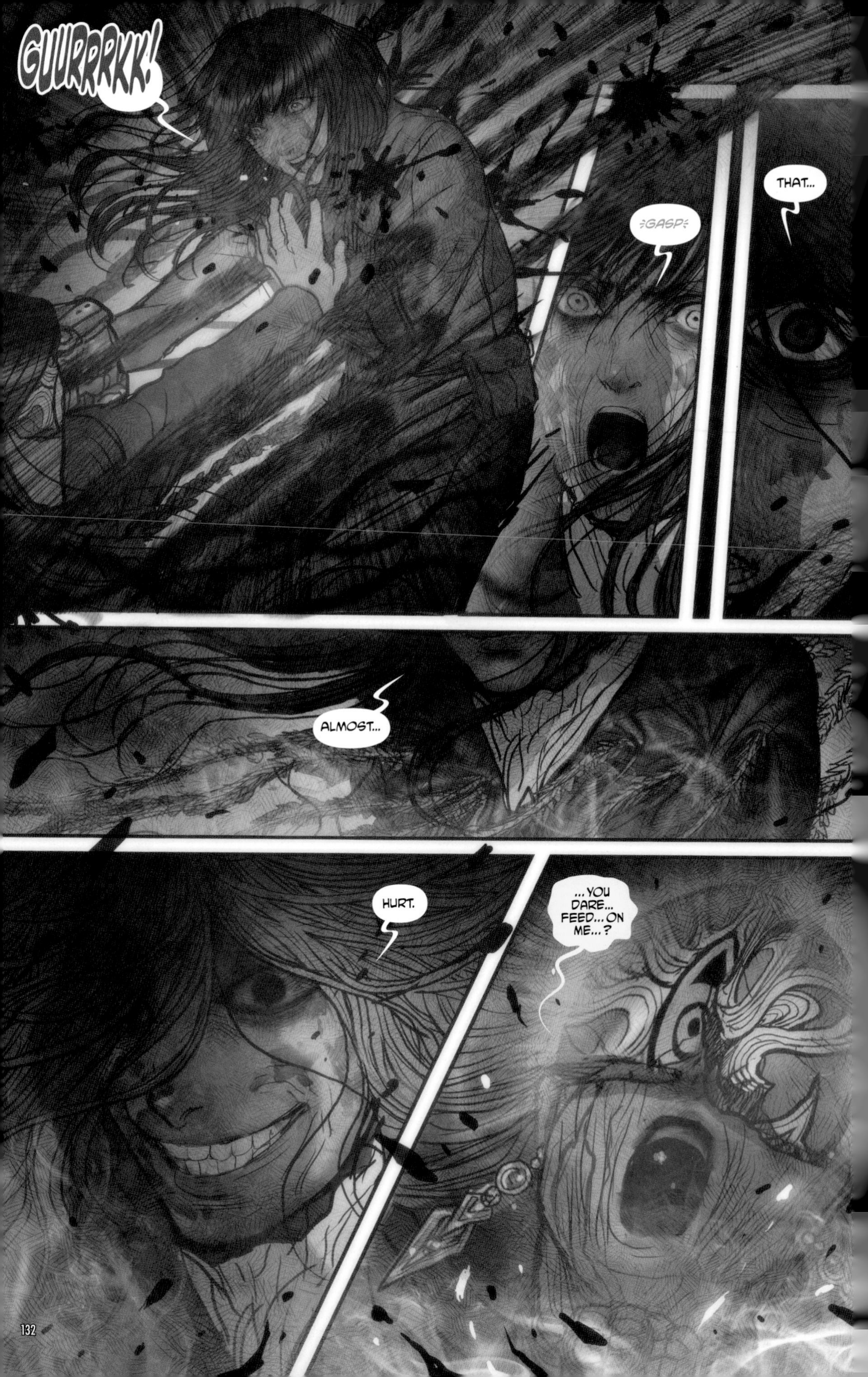
GUURRRKK!
≈GASP≈
THAT...
ALMOST...
HURT.
...YOU DARE... FEED... ON ME...?

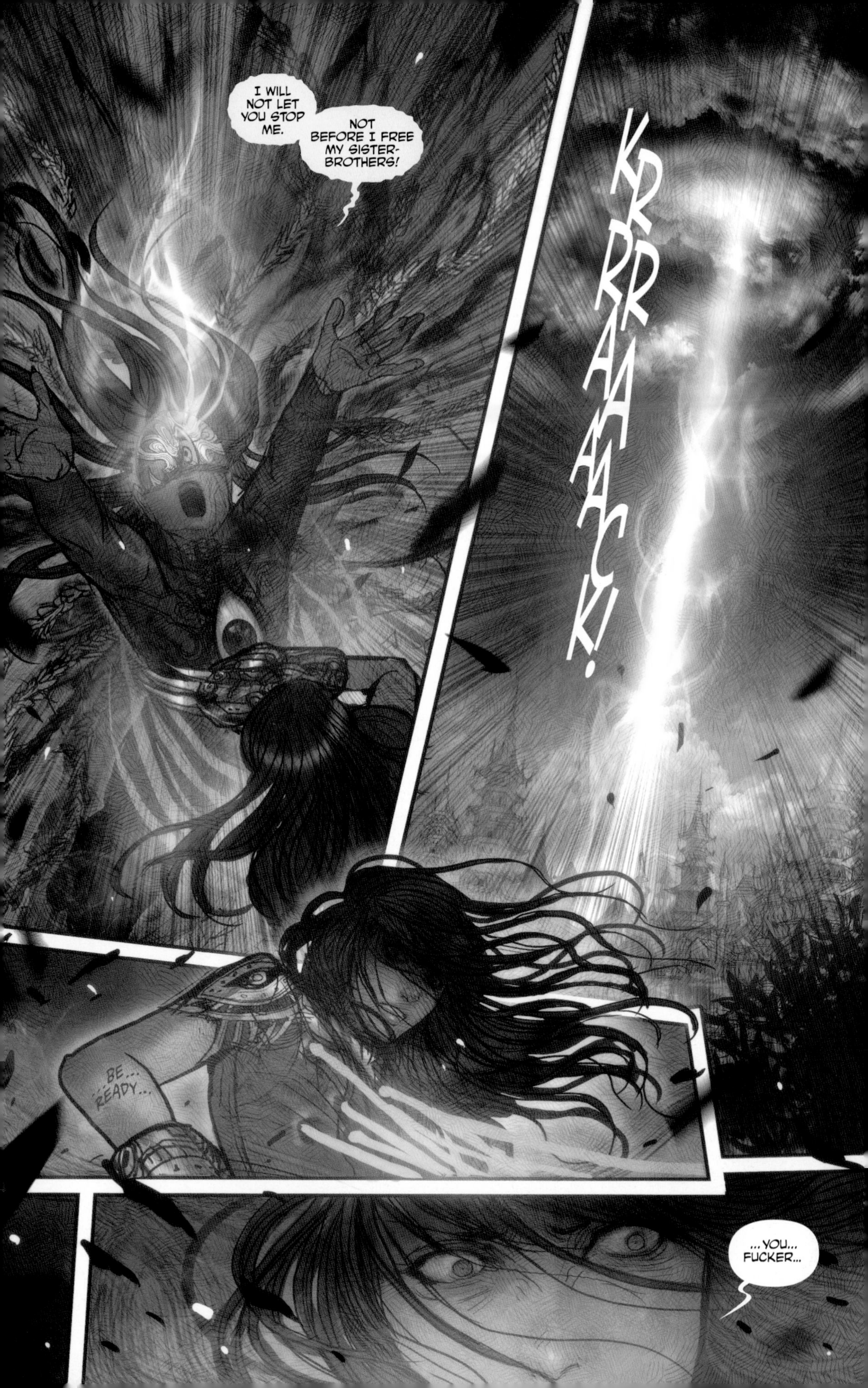
I WILL NOT LET YOU STOP ME.
NOT BEFORE I FREE MY SISTER-BROTHERS!
KRRRAAAACK!
...BE... READY...
...YOU... FUCKER...

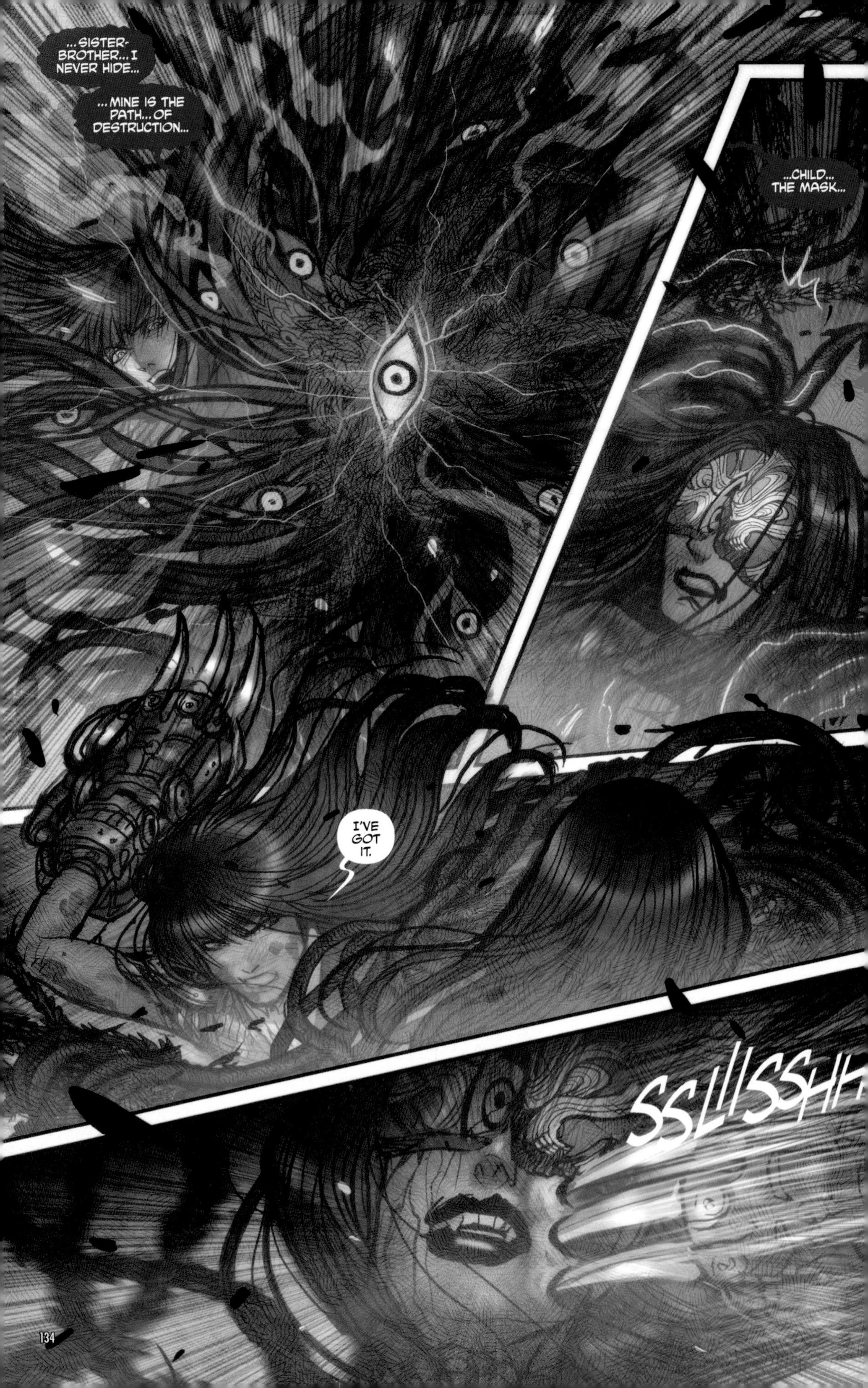
...SISTER-BROTHER... I NEVER HIDE...
...MINE IS THE PATH... OF DESTRUCTION...
...CHILD... THE MASK...
I'VE GOT IT.
SSLIISSHH

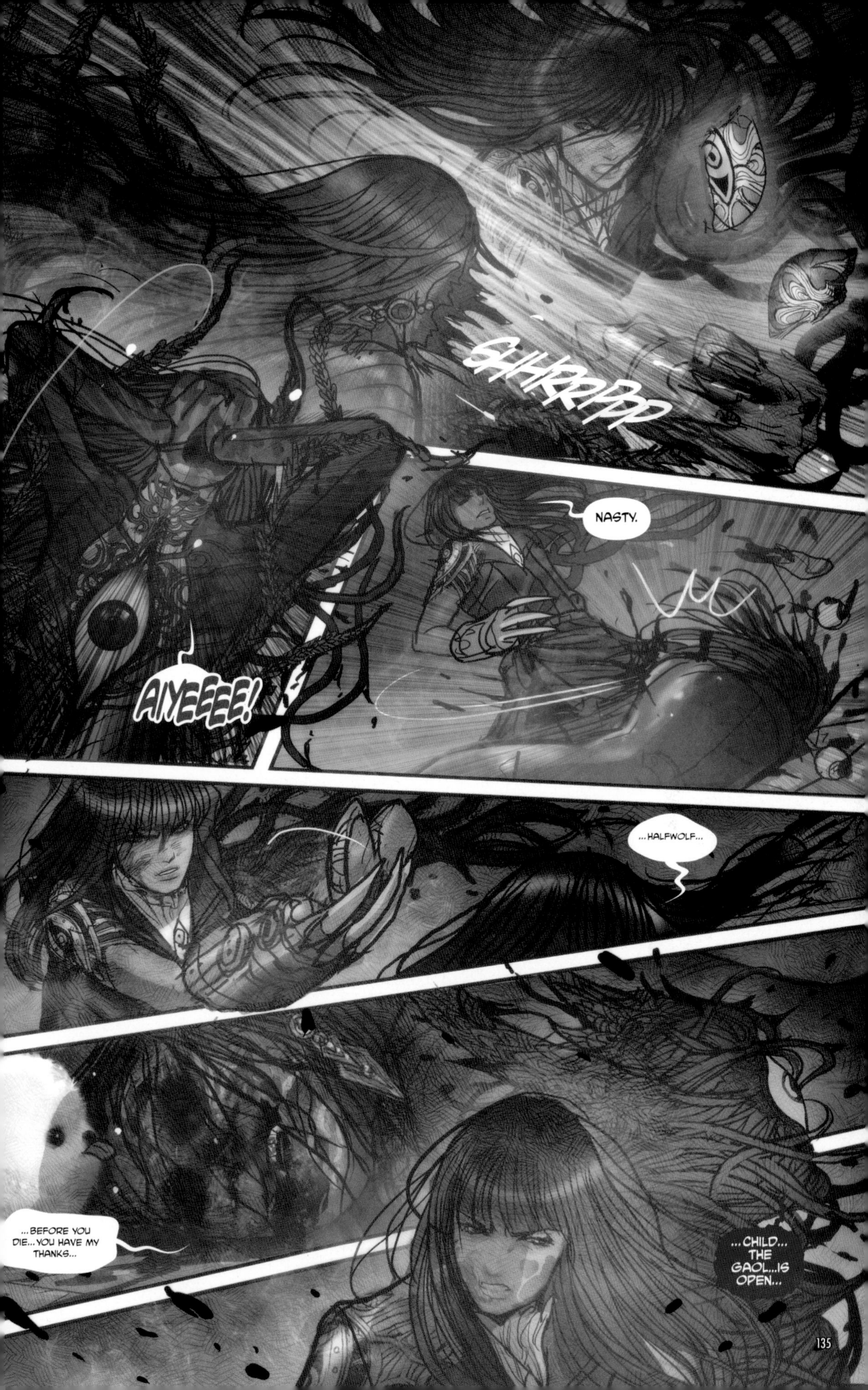
SHHRIPPP
NASTY.
AIYEEEE!
...HALFWOLF...
...BEFORE YOU DIE...YOU HAVE MY THANKS...
...CHILD... THE GAOL...IS OPEN...

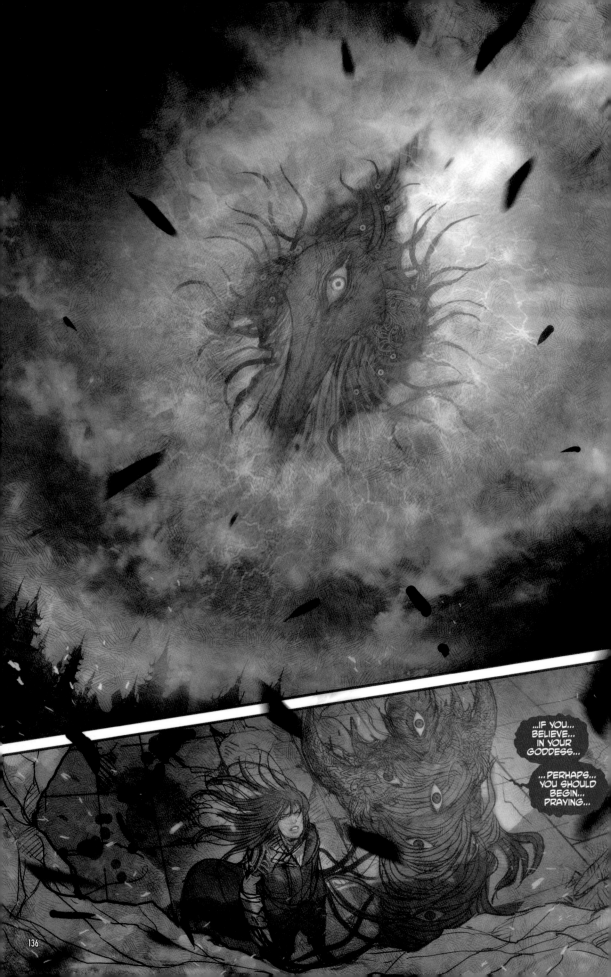

...IF YOU... BELIEVE... IN YOUR GODDESS...

...PERHAPS... YOU SHOULD BEGIN... PRAYING...

An excerpt of a lecture from the esteemed **Professor Tam Tam,** former First Record-Keeper of the Is'hami Temple, and learned contemporary of Namron Black Claw...

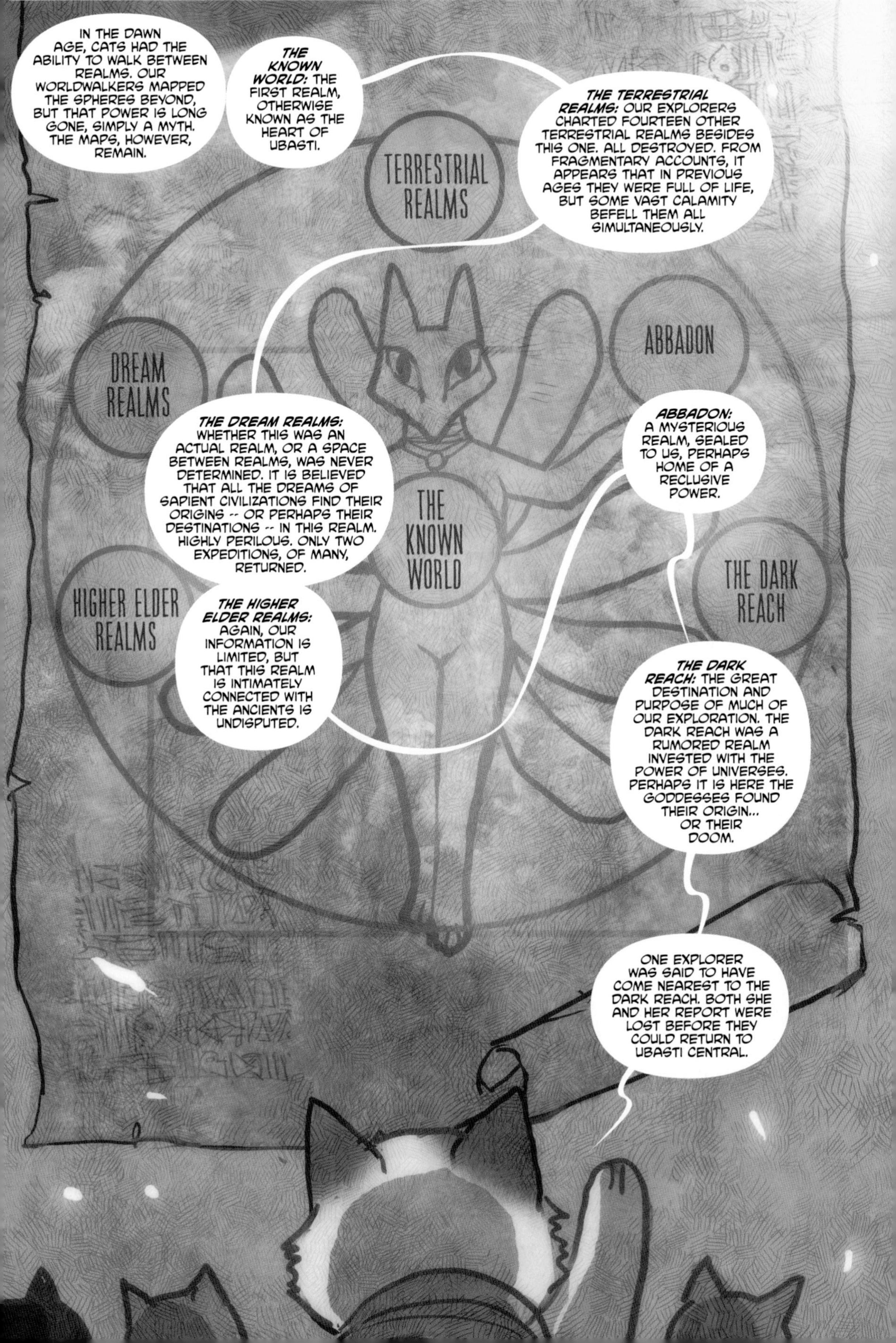

IN THE DAWN AGE, CATS HAD THE ABILITY TO WALK BETWEEN REALMS. OUR WORLDWALKERS MAPPED THE SPHERES BEYOND, BUT THAT POWER IS LONG GONE, SIMPLY A MYTH. THE MAPS, HOWEVER, REMAIN.
THE KNOWN WORLD: THE FIRST REALM, OTHERWISE KNOWN AS THE HEART OF UBASTI.
THE TERRESTRIAL REALMS: OUR EXPLORERS CHARTED FOURTEEN OTHER TERRESTRIAL REALMS BESIDES THIS ONE. ALL DESTROYED. FROM FRAGMENTARY ACCOUNTS, IT APPEARS THAT IN PREVIOUS AGES THEY WERE FULL OF LIFE, BUT SOME VAST CALAMITY BEFELL THEM ALL SIMULTANEOUSLY.
TERRESTRIAL REALMS
DREAM REALMS
ABBADON
THE KNOWN WORLD
HIGHER ELDER REALMS
THE DARK REACH
THE DREAM REALMS: WHETHER THIS WAS AN ACTUAL REALM, OR A SPACE BETWEEN REALMS, WAS NEVER DETERMINED. IT IS BELIEVED THAT ALL THE DREAMS OF SAPIENT CIVILIZATIONS FIND THEIR ORIGINS -- OR PERHAPS THEIR DESTINATIONS -- IN THIS REALM. HIGHLY PERILOUS. ONLY TWO EXPEDITIONS, OF MANY, RETURNED.
THE HIGHER ELDER REALMS: AGAIN, OUR INFORMATION IS LIMITED, BUT THAT THIS REALM IS INTIMATELY CONNECTED WITH THE ANCIENTS IS UNDISPUTED.
ABBADON: A MYSTERIOUS REALM, SEALED TO US, PERHAPS HOME OF A RECLUSIVE POWER.
THE DARK REACH: THE GREAT DESTINATION AND PURPOSE OF MUCH OF OUR EXPLORATION. THE DARK REACH WAS A RUMORED REALM INVESTED WITH THE POWER OF UNIVERSES. PERHAPS IT IS HERE THE GODDESSES FOUND THEIR ORIGIN... OR THEIR DOOM.
ONE EXPLORER WAS SAID TO HAVE COME NEAREST TO THE DARK REACH. BOTH SHE AND HER REPORT WERE LOST BEFORE THEY COULD RETURN TO UBASTI CENTRAL.

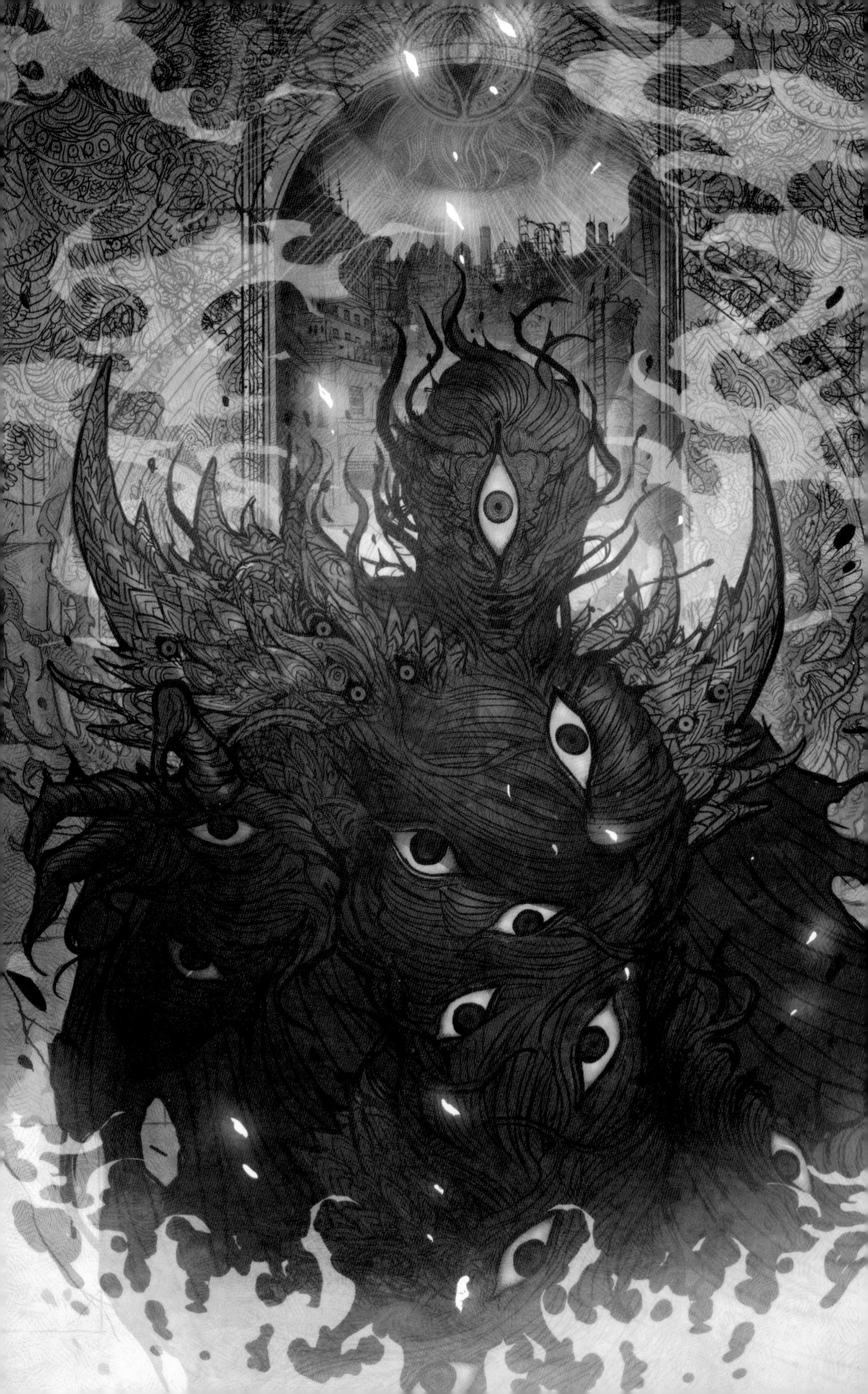

CHAPTER EIGHTEEN

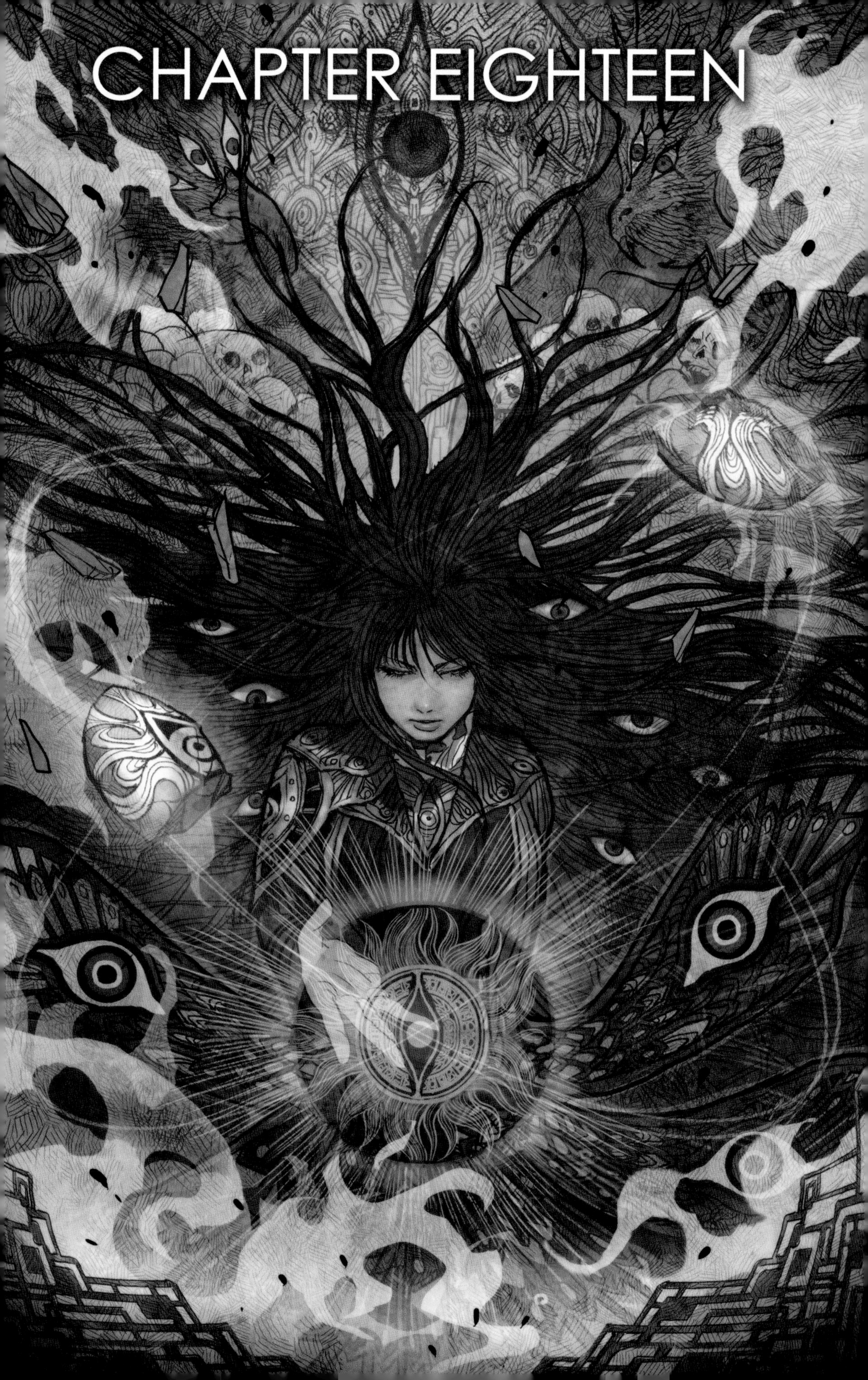

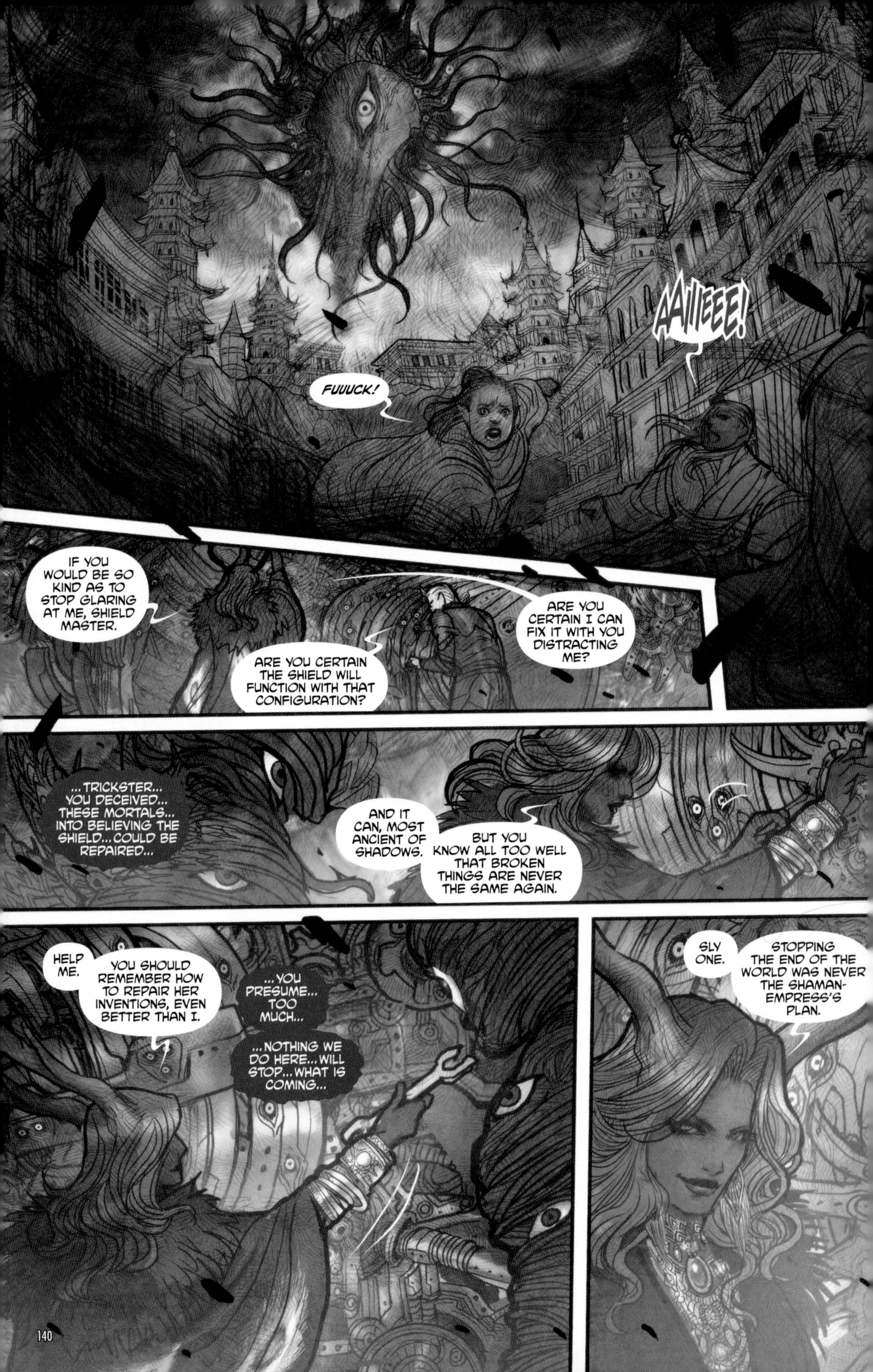
AAIIIEEE!
FUUUCK!
IF YOU WOULD BE SO KIND AS TO STOP GLARING AT ME, SHIELD MASTER.
ARE YOU CERTAIN THE SHIELD WILL FUNCTION WITH THAT CONFIGURATION?
ARE YOU CERTAIN I CAN FIX IT WITH YOU DISTRACTING ME?
...TRICKSTER... YOU DECEIVED... THESE MORTALS... INTO BELIEVING THE SHIELD...COULD BE REPAIRED...
AND IT CAN, MOST ANCIENT OF SHADOWS.
BUT YOU KNOW ALL TOO WELL THAT BROKEN THINGS ARE NEVER THE SAME AGAIN.
HELP ME.
YOU SHOULD REMEMBER HOW TO REPAIR HER INVENTIONS, EVEN BETTER THAN I.
...YOU PRESUME... TOO MUCH...
...NOTHING WE DO HERE...WILL STOP...WHAT IS COMING...
SLY ONE.
STOPPING THE END OF THE WORLD WAS NEVER THE SHAMAN-EMPRESS'S PLAN.

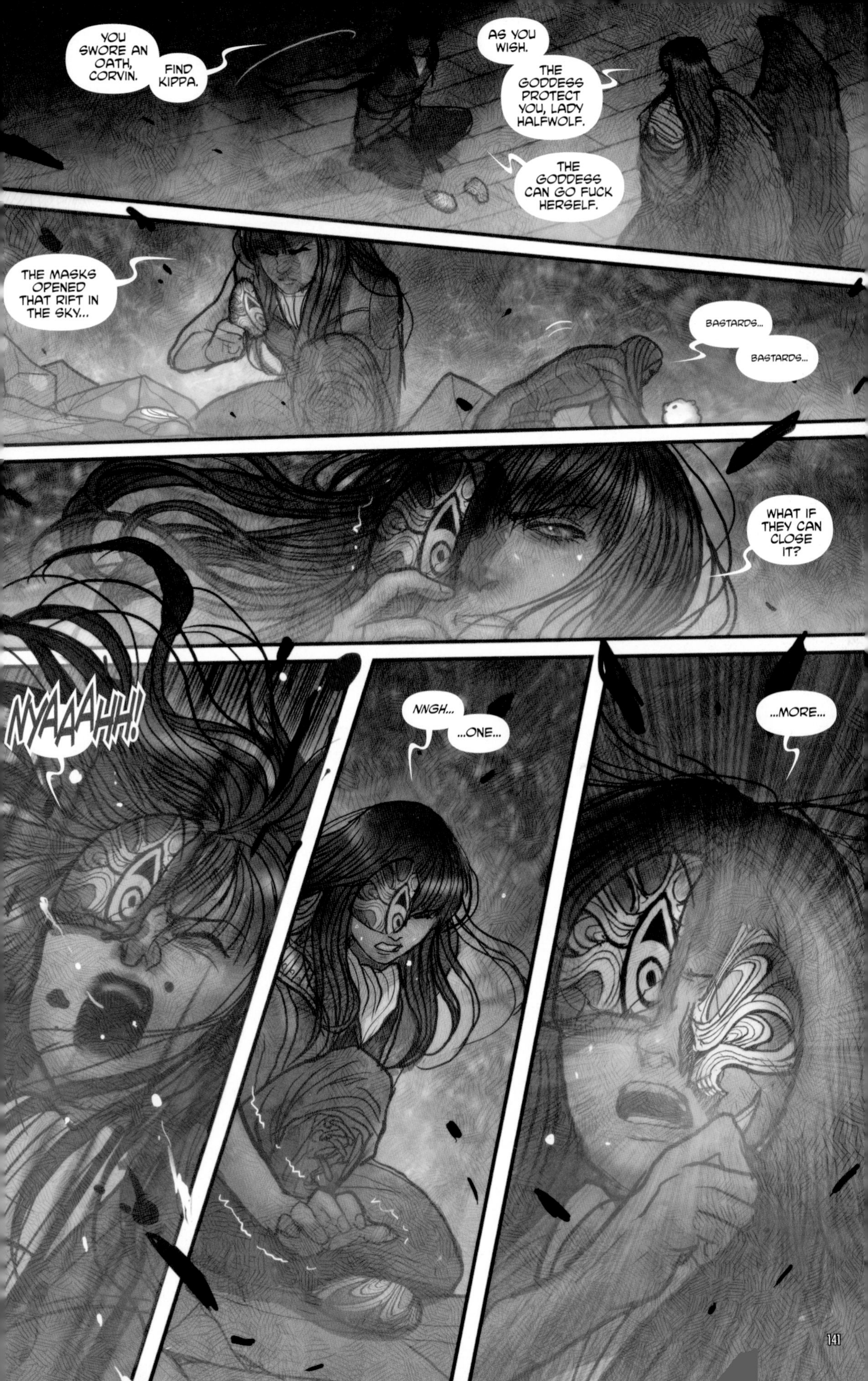
YOU SWORE AN OATH, CORVIN.
FIND KIPPA.
AS YOU WISH.
THE GODDESS PROTECT YOU, LADY HALFWOLF.
THE GODDESS CAN GO FUCK HERSELF.
THE MASKS OPENED THAT RIFT IN THE SKY...
BASTARDS...
BASTARDS...
WHAT IF THEY CAN CLOSE IT?
NYAAAHH!
NNGH...
...ONE...
...MORE...

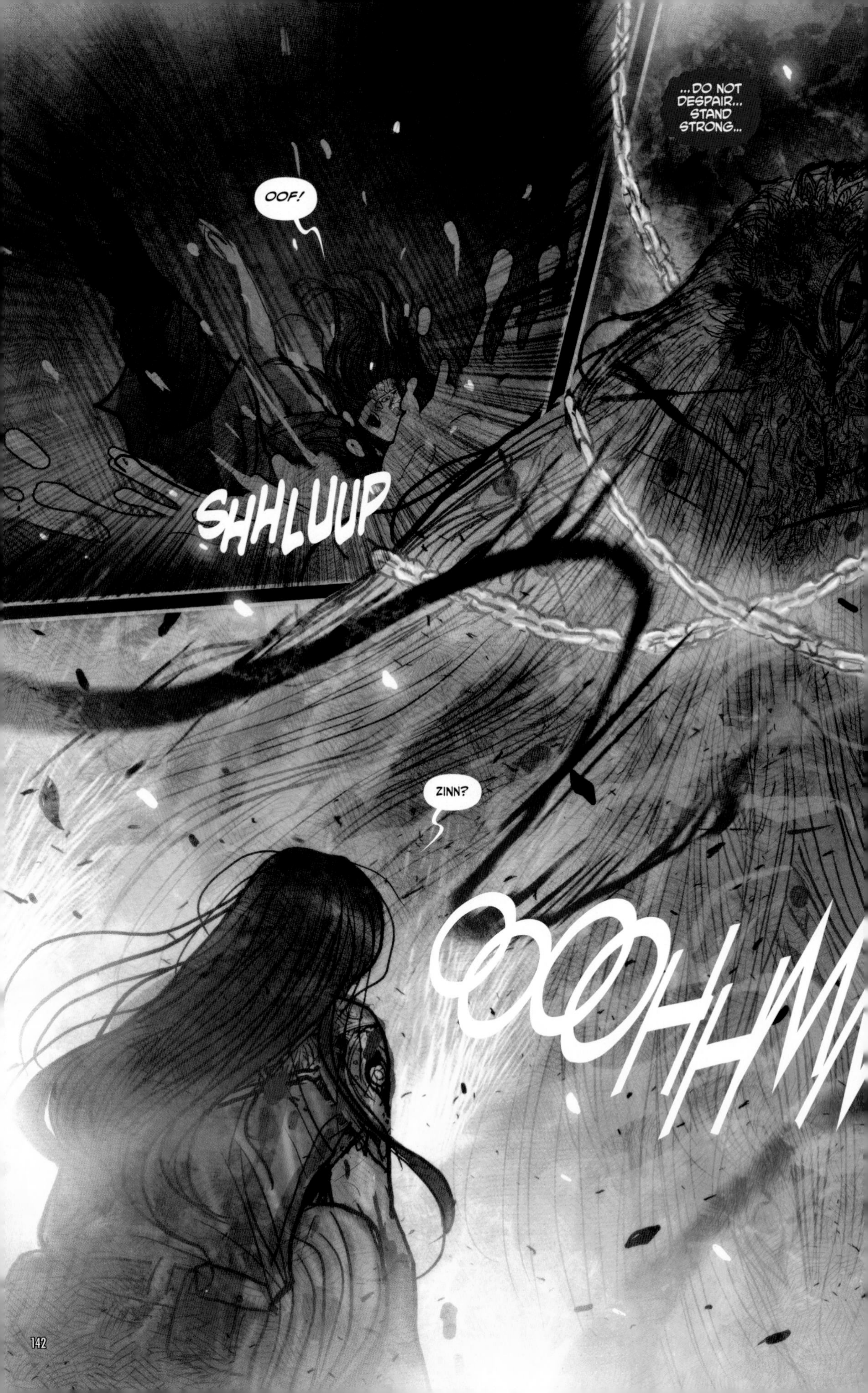
...DO NOT DESPAIR... STAND STRONG...
OOF!
SHHLUUP
ZINN?
OOOHHM

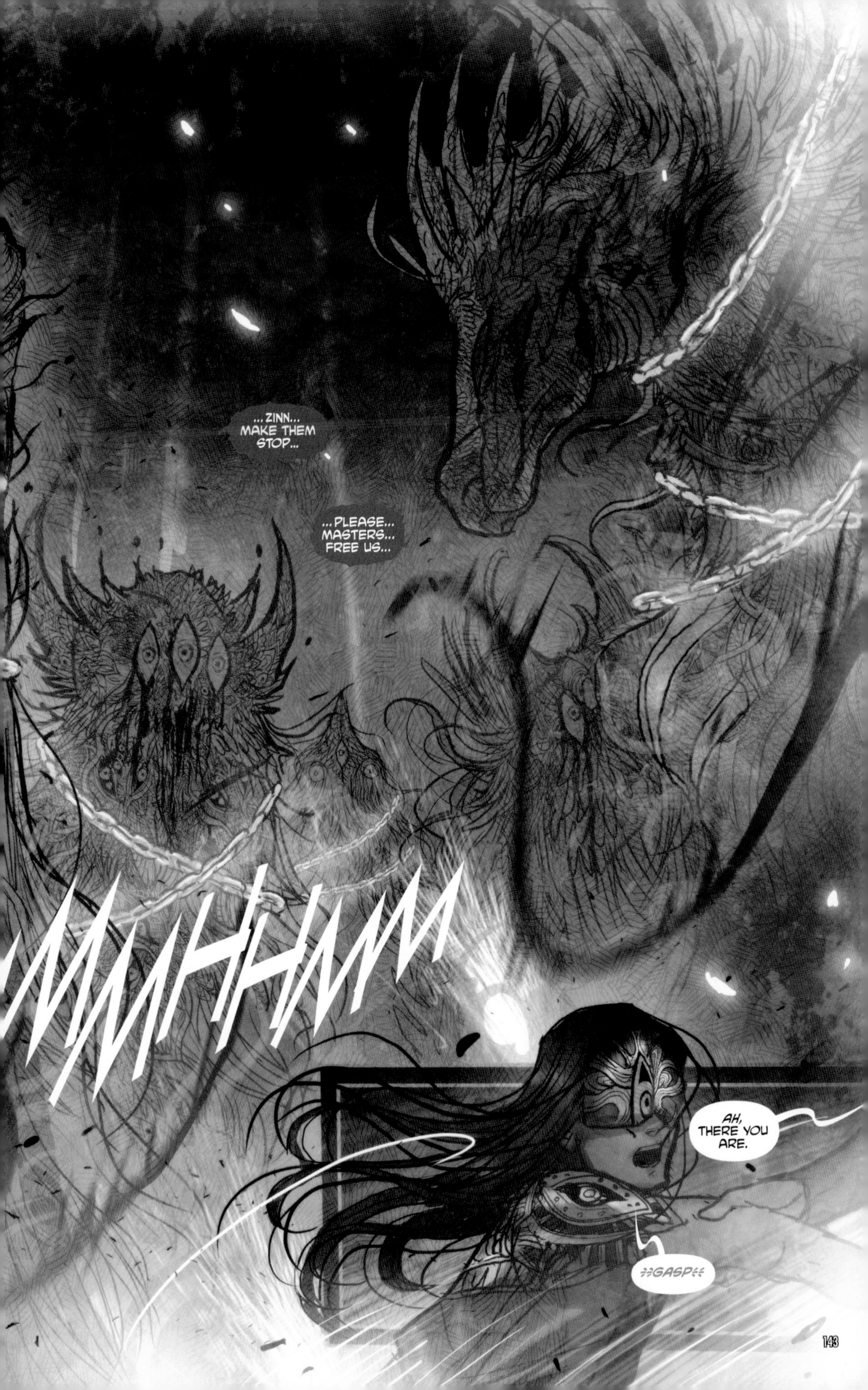
...ZINN... MAKE THEM STOP...
...PLEASE... MASTERS... FREE US...
MMHHMM
AH, THERE YOU ARE.
GASP

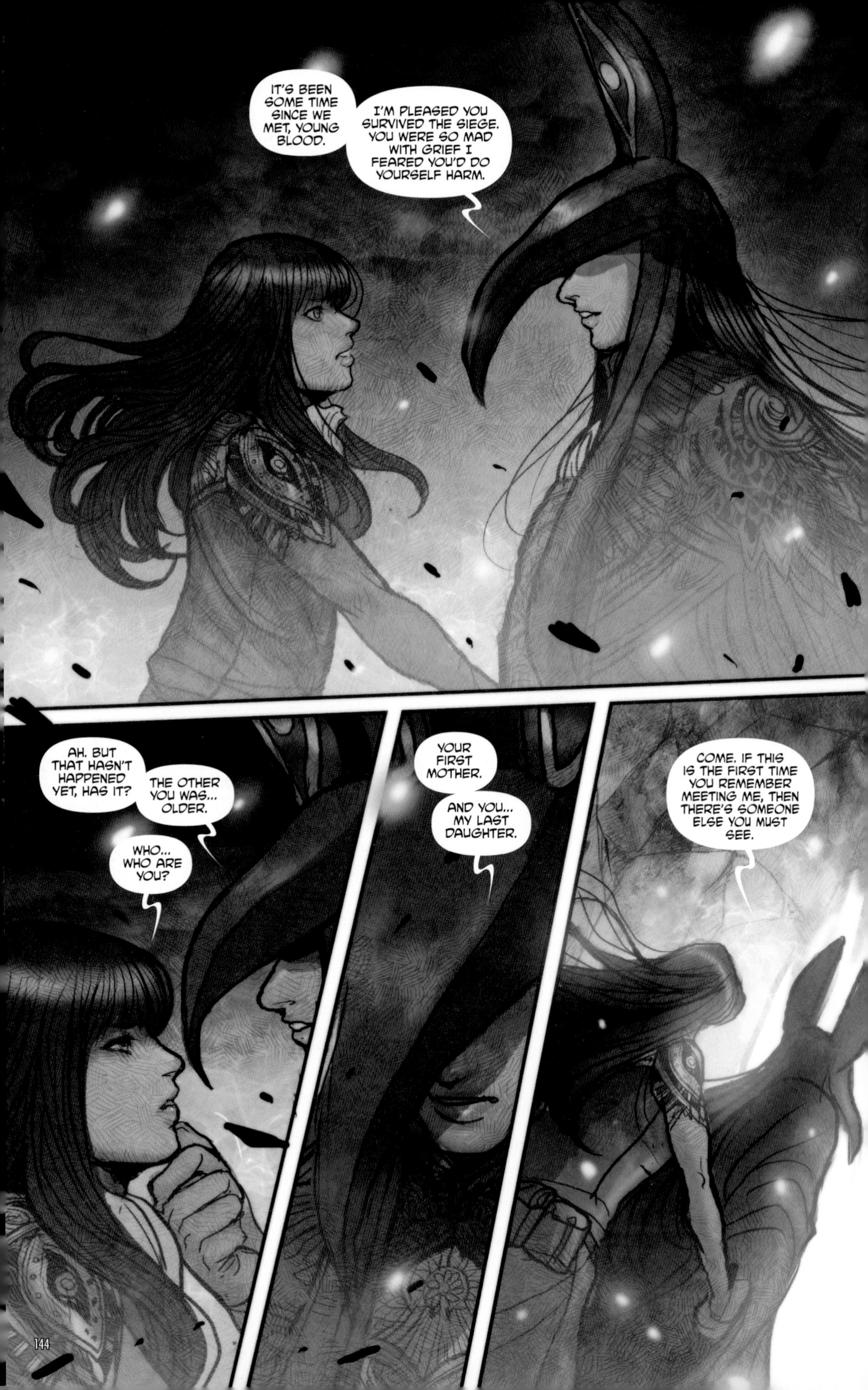
IT'S BEEN SOME TIME SINCE WE MET, YOUNG BLOOD.
I'M PLEASED YOU SURVIVED THE SIEGE. YOU WERE SO MAD WITH GRIEF I FEARED YOU'D DO YOURSELF HARM.
AH. BUT THAT HASN'T HAPPENED YET, HAS IT?
THE OTHER YOU WAS... OLDER.
WHO... WHO ARE YOU?
YOUR FIRST MOTHER.
AND YOU... MY LAST DAUGHTER.
COME. IF THIS IS THE FIRST TIME YOU REMEMBER MEETING ME, THEN THERE'S SOMEONE ELSE YOU MUST SEE.

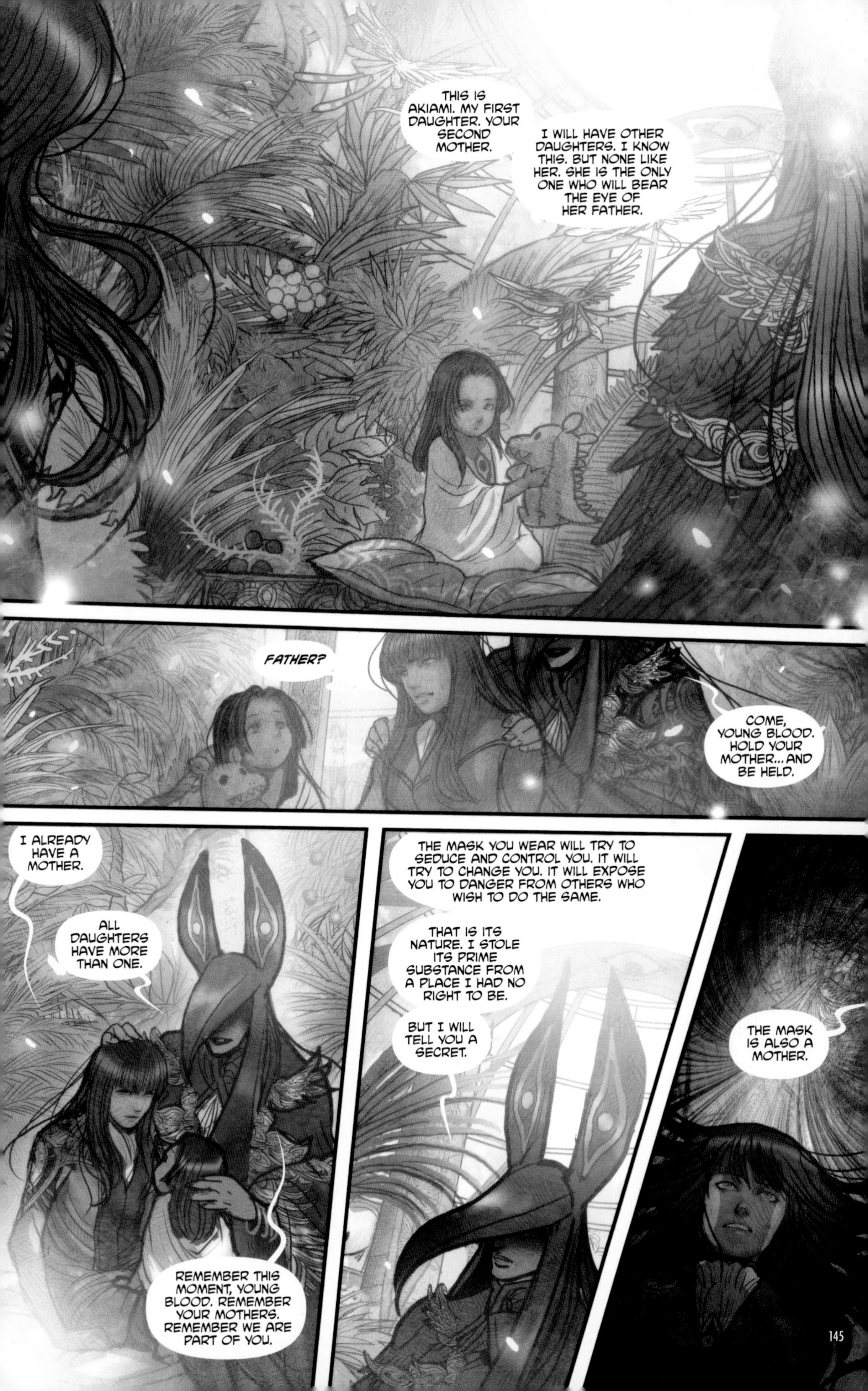

THIS IS AKIAMI. MY FIRST DAUGHTER. YOUR SECOND MOTHER.
I WILL HAVE OTHER DAUGHTERS. I KNOW THIS. BUT NONE LIKE HER. SHE IS THE ONLY ONE WHO WILL BEAR THE EYE OF HER FATHER.
FATHER?
COME, YOUNG BLOOD. HOLD YOUR MOTHER... AND BE HELD.
I ALREADY HAVE A MOTHER.
ALL DAUGHTERS HAVE MORE THAN ONE.
REMEMBER THIS MOMENT, YOUNG BLOOD. REMEMBER YOUR MOTHERS. REMEMBER WE ARE PART OF YOU.
THE MASK YOU WEAR WILL TRY TO SEDUCE AND CONTROL YOU. IT WILL TRY TO CHANGE YOU. IT WILL EXPOSE YOU TO DANGER FROM OTHERS WHO WISH TO DO THE SAME.
THAT IS ITS NATURE. I STOLE ITS PRIME SUBSTANCE FROM A PLACE I HAD NO RIGHT TO BE.
BUT I WILL TELL YOU A SECRET.
THE MASK IS ALSO A MOTHER.

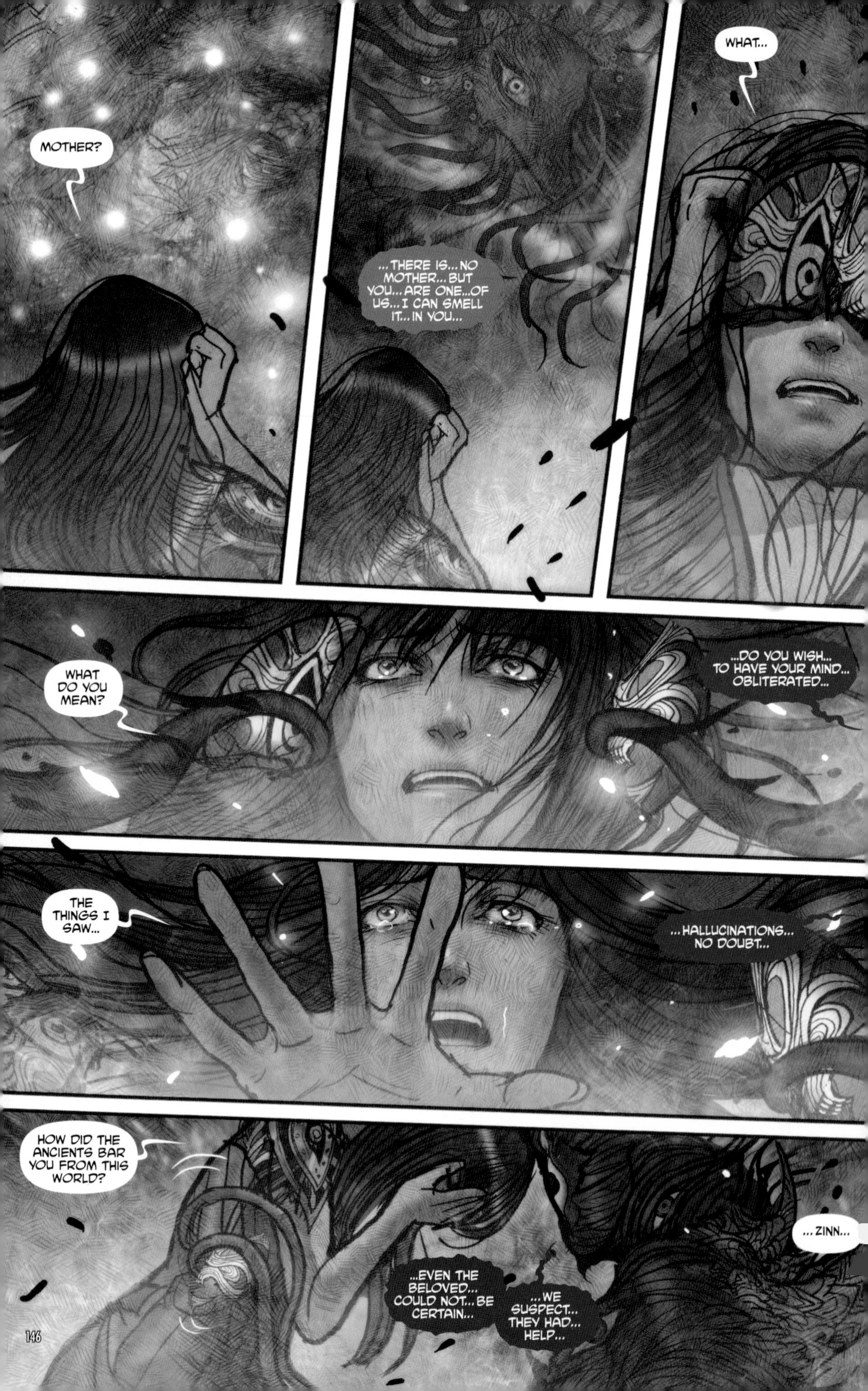
MOTHER?
...THERE IS...NO MOTHER...BUT YOU...ARE ONE...OF US...I CAN SMELL IT...IN YOU...
WHAT...
WHAT DO YOU MEAN?
...DO YOU WISH... TO HAVE YOUR MIND... OBLITERATED...
THE THINGS I SAW...
...HALLUCINATIONS... NO DOUBT...
HOW DID THE ANCIENTS BAR YOU FROM THIS WORLD?
...ZINN...
...EVEN THE BELOVED... COULD NOT... BE CERTAIN...
...WE SUSPECT... THEY HAD... HELP...

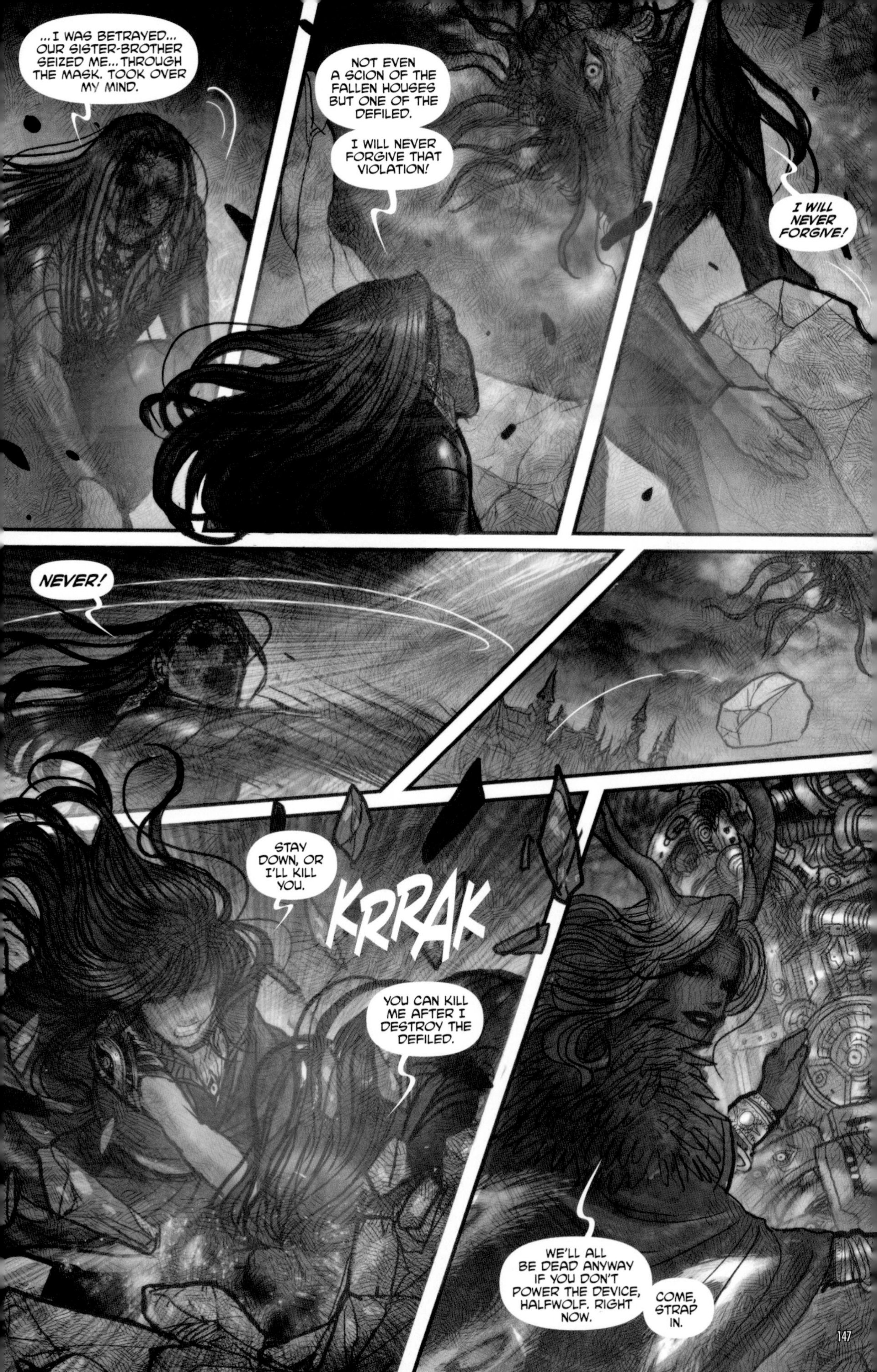
...I WAS BETRAYED... OUR SISTER-BROTHER SEIZED ME...THROUGH THE MASK. TOOK OVER MY MIND.
NOT EVEN A SCION OF THE FALLEN HOUSES BUT ONE OF THE DEFILED.
I WILL NEVER FORGIVE THAT VIOLATION!
I WILL NEVER FORGIVE!
NEVER!
STAY DOWN, OR I'LL KILL YOU.
KRRAK
YOU CAN KILL ME AFTER I DESTROY THE DEFILED.
WE'LL ALL BE DEAD ANYWAY IF YOU DON'T POWER THE DEVICE, HALFWOLF. RIGHT NOW.
COME, STRAP IN.

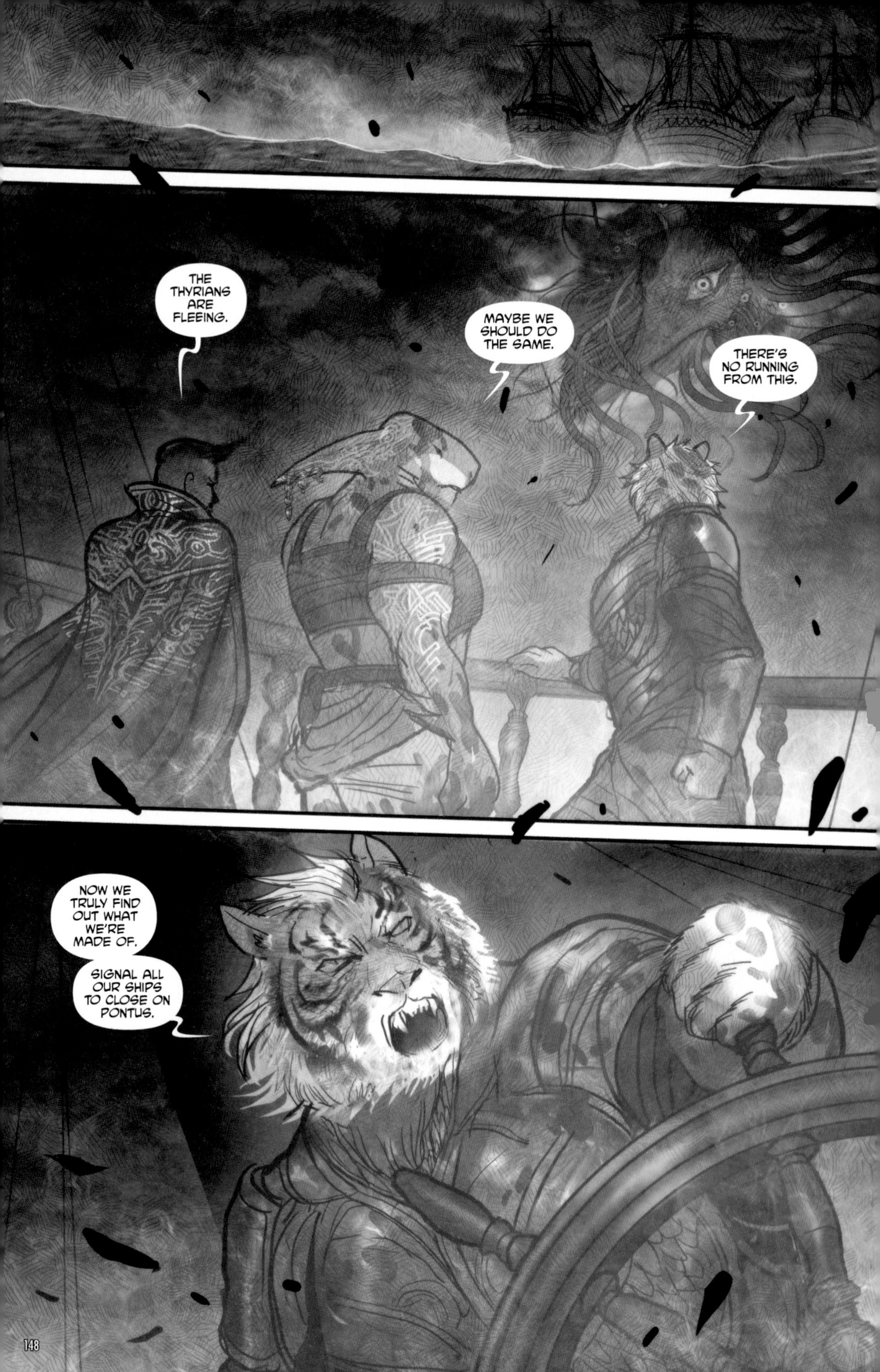
THE THYRIANS ARE FLEEING.
MAYBE WE SHOULD DO THE SAME.
THERE'S NO RUNNING FROM THIS.
NOW WE TRULY FIND OUT WHAT WE'RE MADE OF.
SIGNAL ALL OUR SHIPS TO CLOSE ON PONTUS.

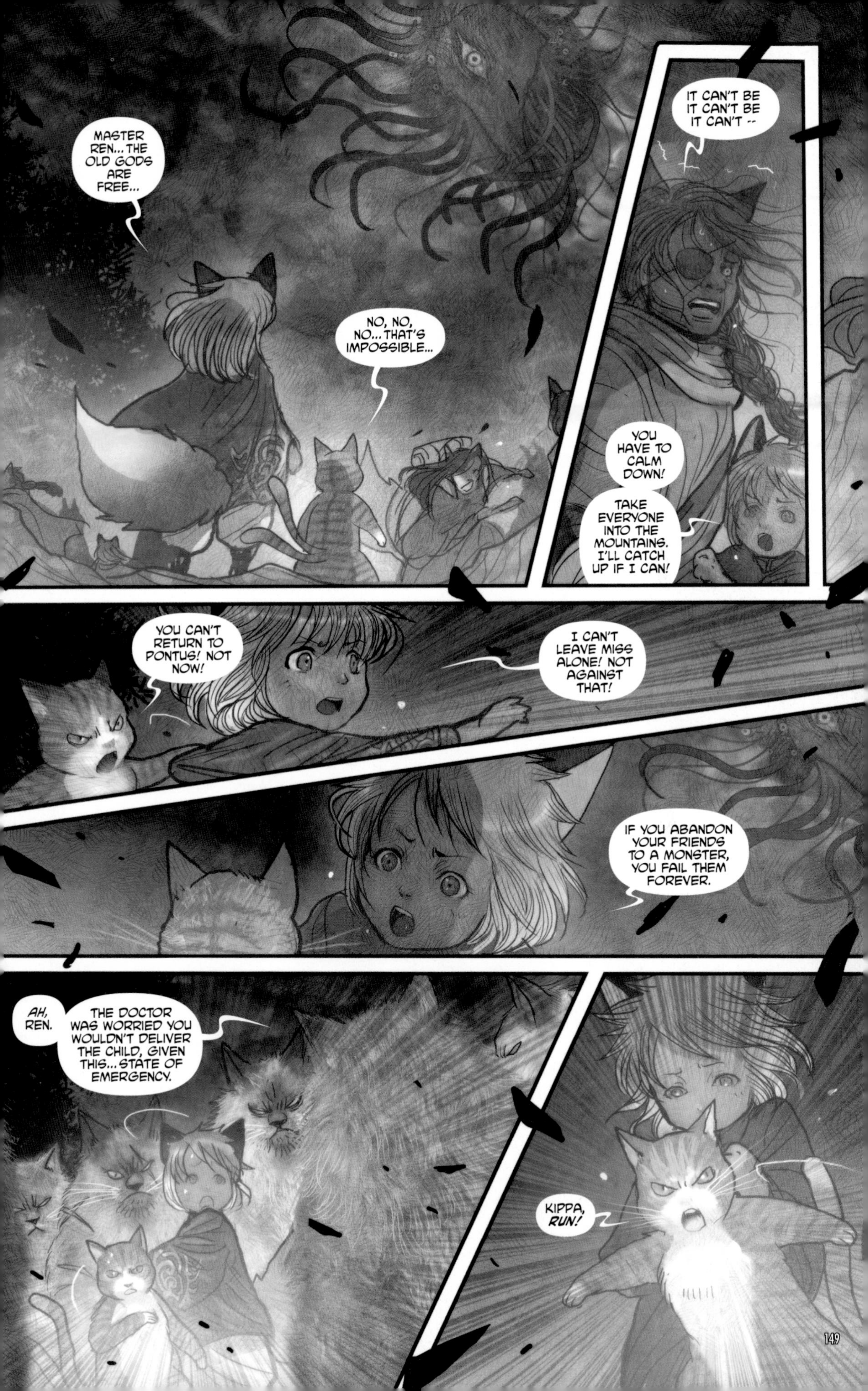
MASTER REN... THE OLD GODS ARE FREE...
NO, NO, NO... THAT'S IMPOSSIBLE...
IT CAN'T BE IT CAN'T BE IT CAN'T --
YOU HAVE TO CALM DOWN!
TAKE EVERYONE INTO THE MOUNTAINS. I'LL CATCH UP IF I CAN!
YOU CAN'T RETURN TO PONTUS! NOT NOW!
I CAN'T LEAVE MISS ALONE! NOT AGAINST THAT!
IF YOU ABANDON YOUR FRIENDS TO A MONSTER, YOU FAIL THEM FOREVER.
AH, REN.
THE DOCTOR WAS WORRIED YOU WOULDN'T DELIVER THE CHILD, GIVEN THIS... STATE OF EMERGENCY.
KIPPA, *RUN!*

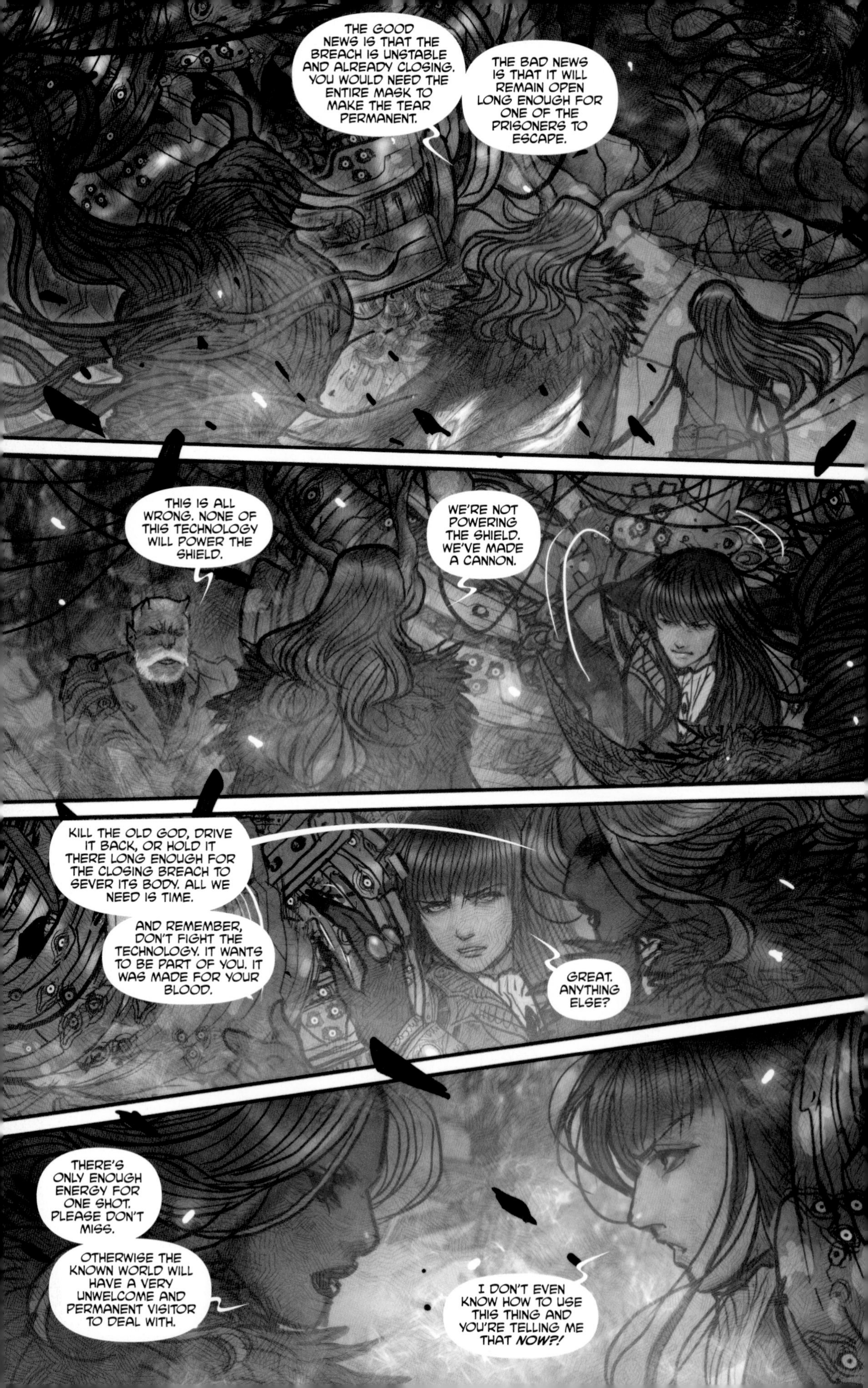
THE GOOD NEWS IS THAT THE BREACH IS UNSTABLE AND ALREADY CLOSING. YOU WOULD NEED THE ENTIRE MASK TO MAKE THE TEAR PERMANENT.
THE BAD NEWS IS THAT IT WILL REMAIN OPEN LONG ENOUGH FOR ONE OF THE PRISONERS TO ESCAPE.
THIS IS ALL WRONG. NONE OF THIS TECHNOLOGY WILL POWER THE SHIELD.
WE'RE NOT POWERING THE SHIELD. WE'VE MADE A CANNON.
KILL THE OLD GOD, DRIVE IT BACK, OR HOLD IT THERE LONG ENOUGH FOR THE CLOSING BREACH TO SEVER ITS BODY. ALL WE NEED IS TIME.
AND REMEMBER, DON'T FIGHT THE TECHNOLOGY. IT WANTS TO BE PART OF YOU. IT WAS MADE FOR YOUR BLOOD.
GREAT. ANYTHING ELSE?
THERE'S ONLY ENOUGH ENERGY FOR ONE SHOT. PLEASE DON'T MISS.
OTHERWISE THE KNOWN WORLD WILL HAVE A VERY UNWELCOME AND PERMANENT VISITOR TO DEAL WITH.
I DON'T EVEN KNOW HOW TO USE THIS THING AND YOU'RE TELLING ME THAT *NOW?!*

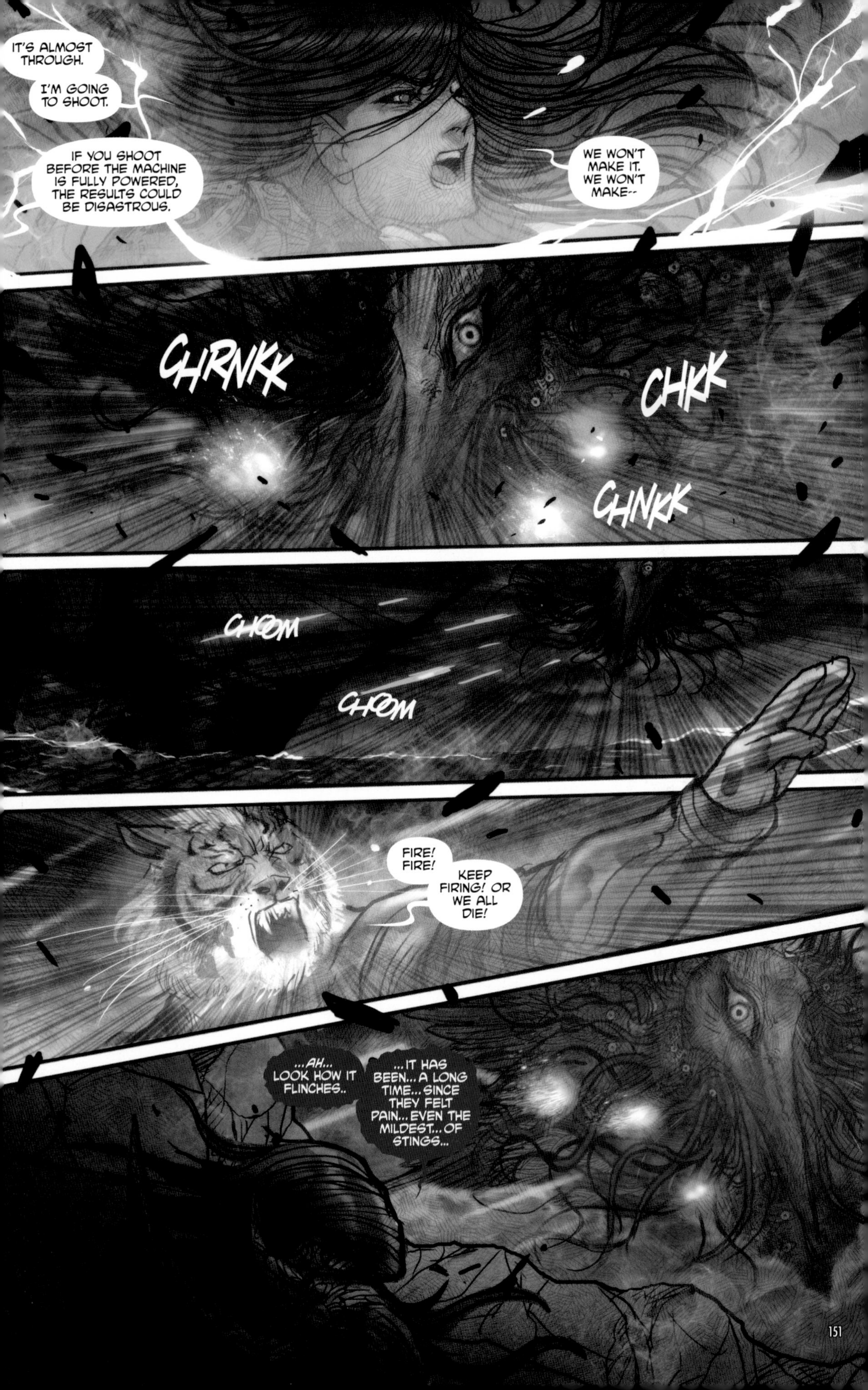
IT'S ALMOST THROUGH.
I'M GOING TO SHOOT.
IF YOU SHOOT BEFORE THE MACHINE IS FULLY POWERED, THE RESULTS COULD BE DISASTROUS.
WE WON'T MAKE IT. WE WON'T MAKE--
CHRNKK
CHKK
CHNKK
CHOOM
CHOOM
FIRE! FIRE!
KEEP FIRING! OR WE ALL DIE!
...AH... LOOK HOW IT FLINCHES..
...IT HAS BEEN... A LONG TIME... SINCE THEY FELT PAIN... EVEN THE MILDEST... OF STINGS...

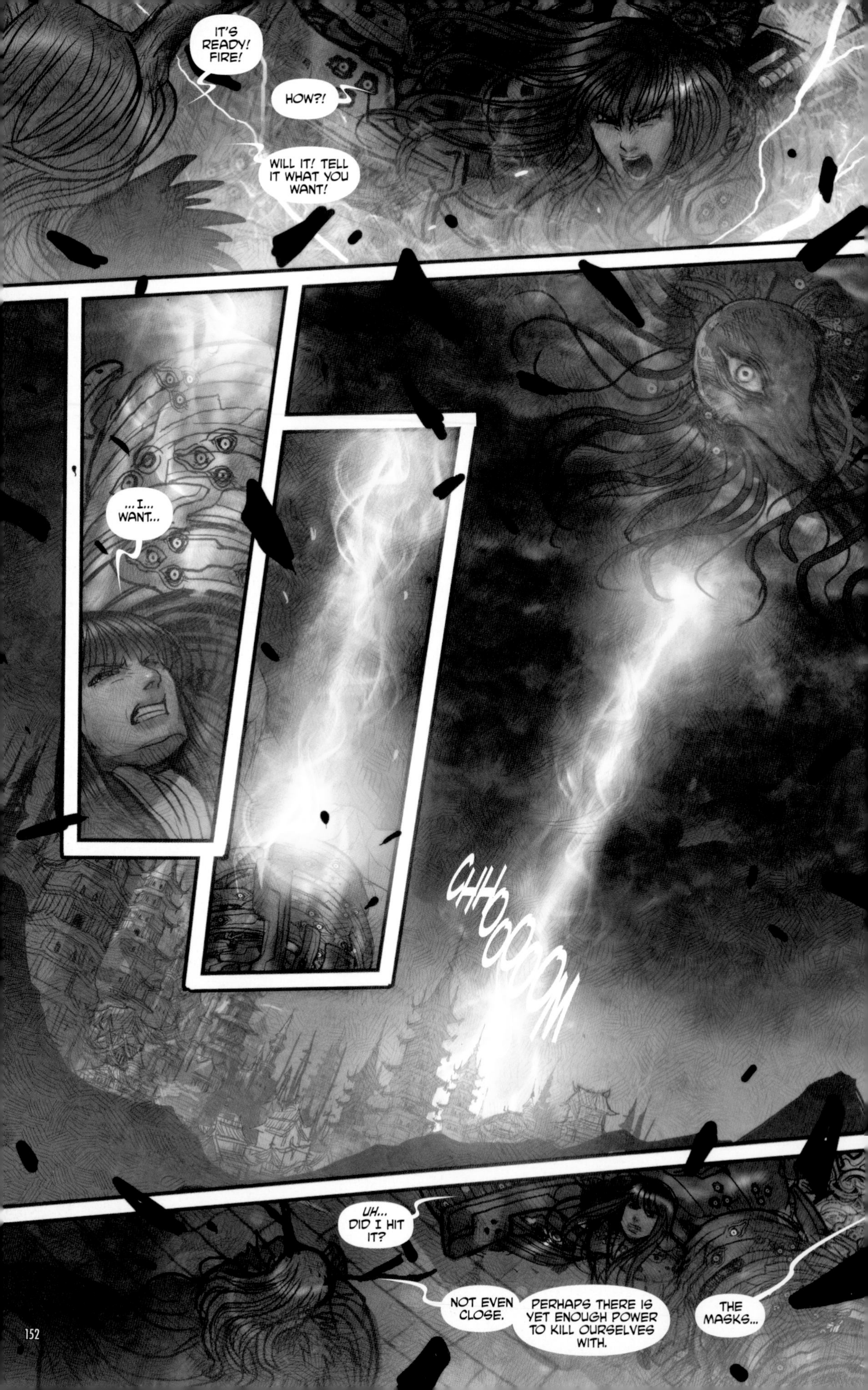
IT'S READY! FIRE!
HOW?!
WILL IT! TELL IT WHAT YOU WANT!
...I... WANT...
CHHOOOOOM
UH... DID I HIT IT?
NOT EVEN CLOSE.
PERHAPS THERE IS YET ENOUGH POWER TO KILL OURSELVES WITH.
THE MASKS...

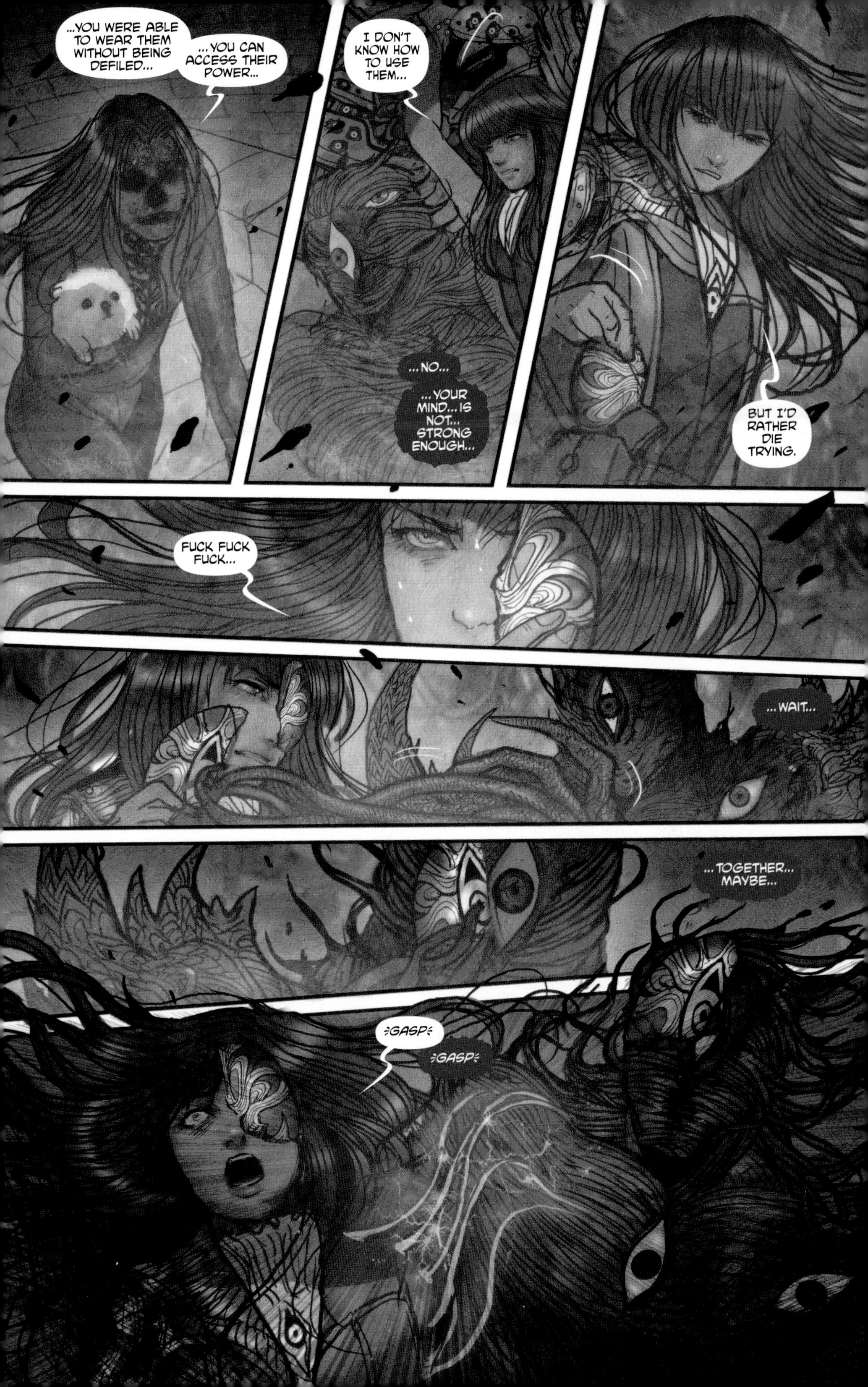
...YOU WERE ABLE TO WEAR THEM WITHOUT BEING DEFILED...
...YOU CAN ACCESS THEIR POWER...
I DON'T KNOW HOW TO USE THEM...
...NO...
...YOUR MIND... IS NOT... STRONG ENOUGH...
BUT I'D RATHER DIE TRYING.
FUCK FUCK FUCK...
...WAIT...
...TOGETHER... MAYBE...
GASP
GASP

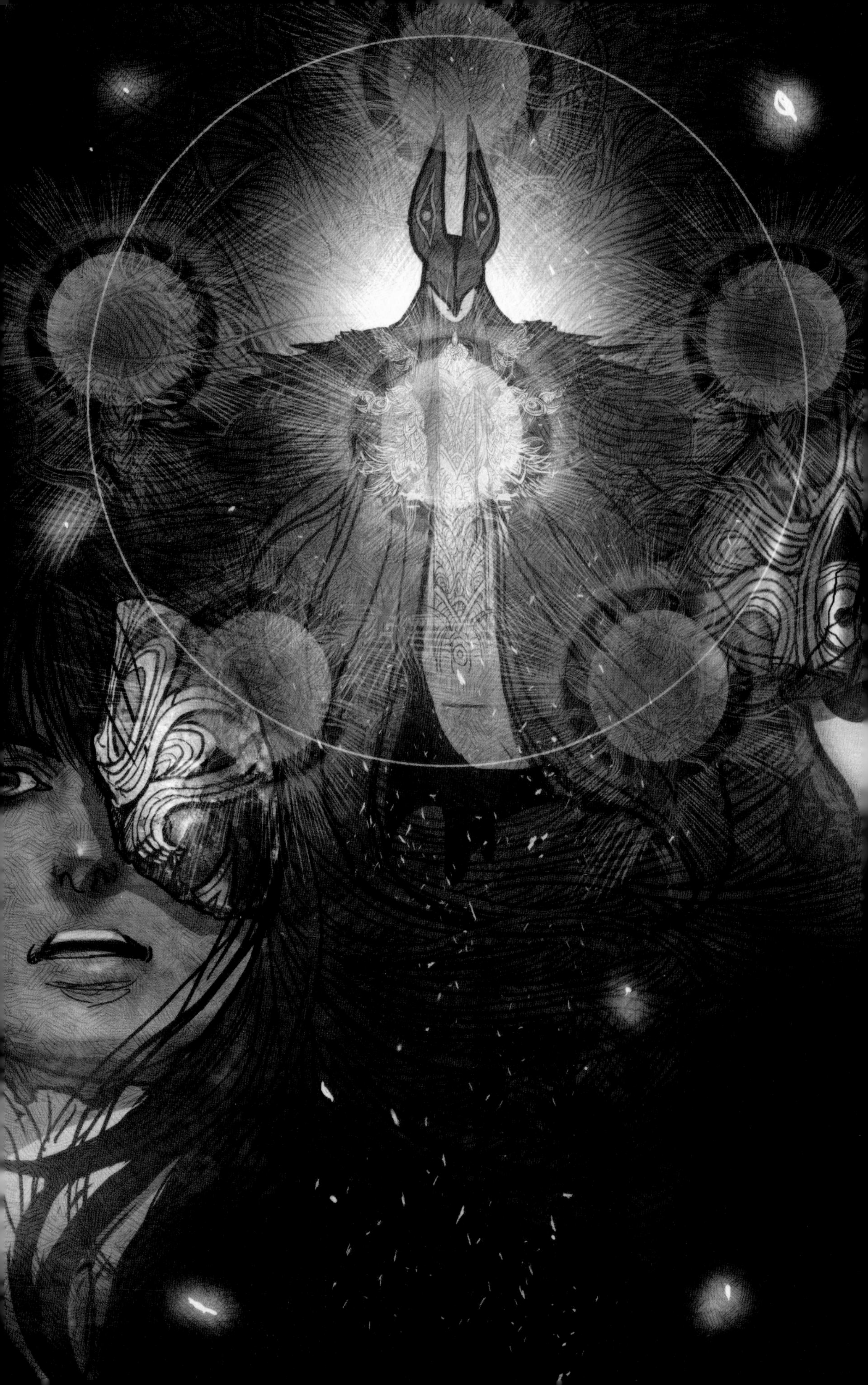

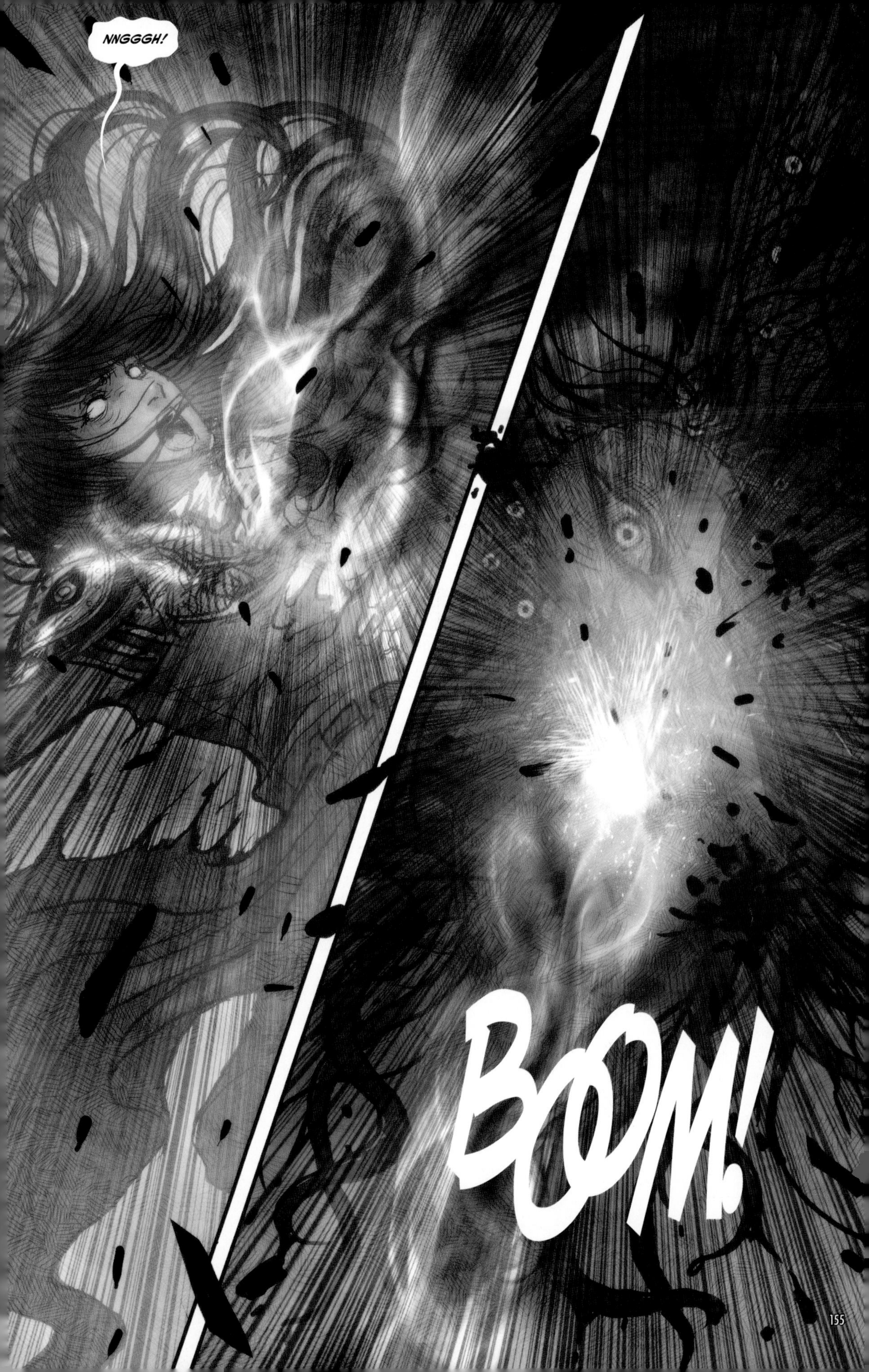
NNGGGH!
BOOM!

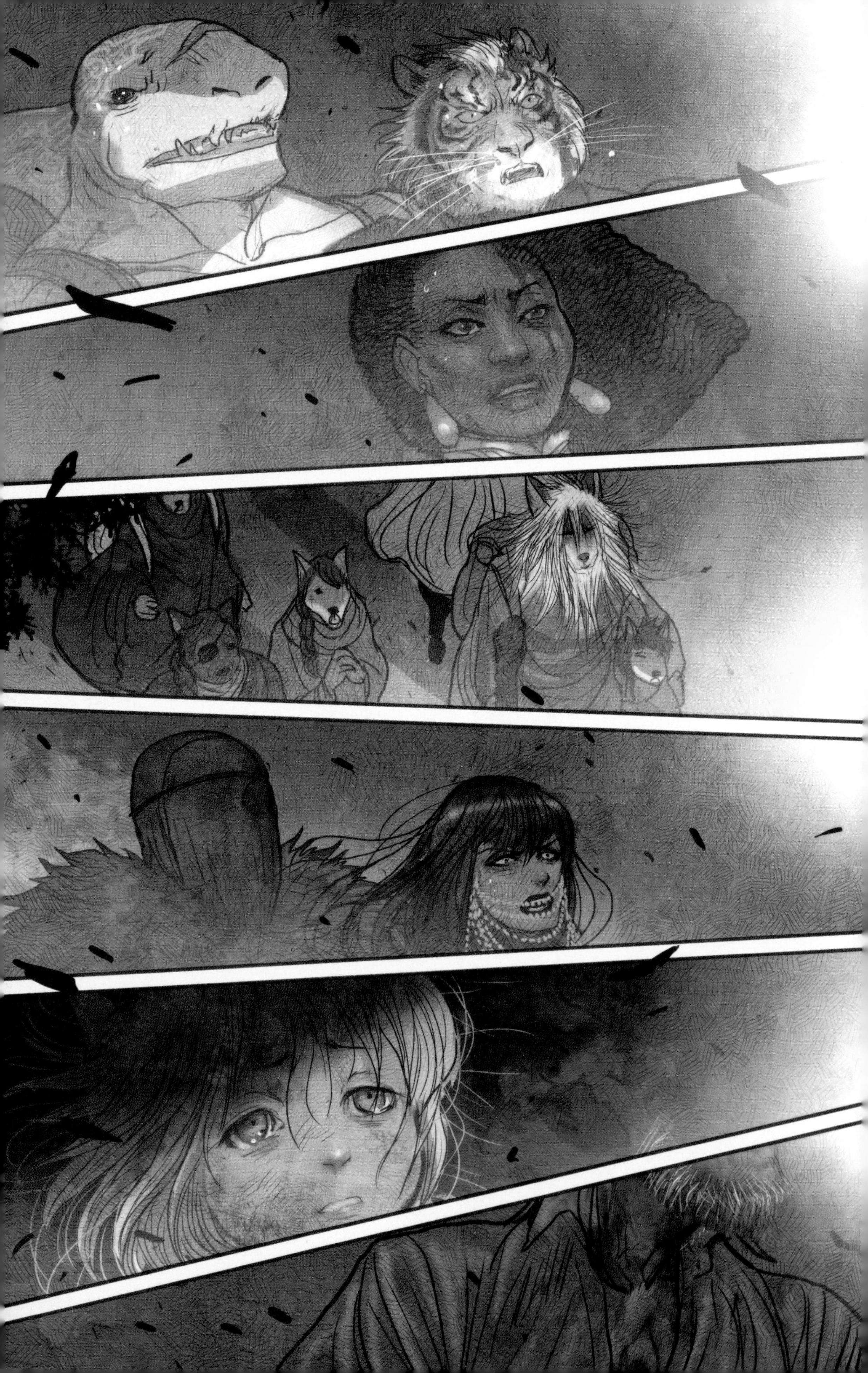

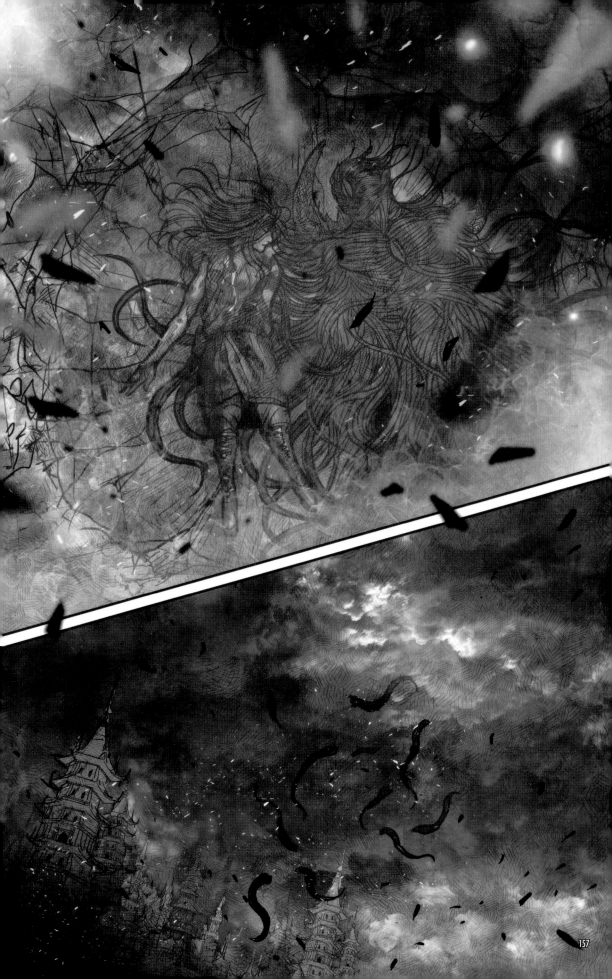

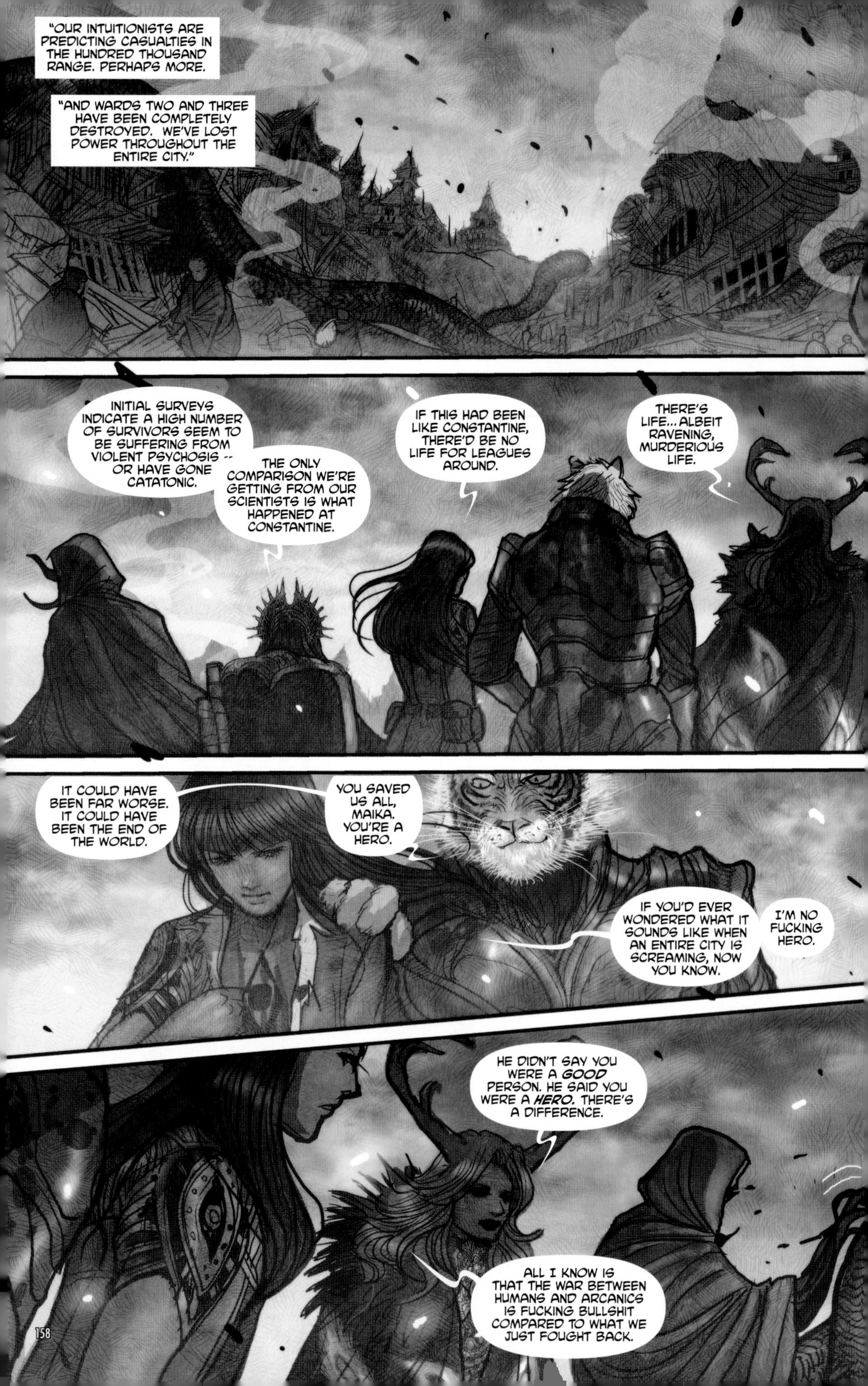
"OUR INTUITIONISTS ARE PREDICTING CASUALTIES IN THE HUNDRED THOUSAND RANGE. PERHAPS MORE.
"AND WARDS TWO AND THREE HAVE BEEN COMPLETELY DESTROYED. WE'VE LOST POWER THROUGHOUT THE ENTIRE CITY."
INITIAL SURVEYS INDICATE A HIGH NUMBER OF SURVIVORS SEEM TO BE SUFFERING FROM VIOLENT PSYCHOSIS -- OR HAVE GONE CATATONIC.
THE ONLY COMPARISON WE'RE GETTING FROM OUR SCIENTISTS IS WHAT HAPPENED AT CONSTANTINE.
IF THIS HAD BEEN LIKE CONSTANTINE, THERE'D BE NO LIFE FOR LEAGUES AROUND.
THERE'S LIFE... ALBEIT RAVENING, MURDERIOUS LIFE.
IT COULD HAVE BEEN FAR WORSE. IT COULD HAVE BEEN THE END OF THE WORLD.
YOU SAVED US ALL, MAIKA. YOU'RE A HERO.
IF YOU'D EVER WONDERED WHAT IT SOUNDS LIKE WHEN AN ENTIRE CITY IS SCREAMING, NOW YOU KNOW.
I'M NO FUCKING HERO.
HE DIDN'T SAY YOU WERE A *GOOD* PERSON. HE SAID YOU WERE A *HERO*. THERE'S A DIFFERENCE.
ALL I KNOW IS THAT THE WAR BETWEEN HUMANS AND ARCANICS IS FUCKING BULLSHIT COMPARED TO WHAT WE JUST FOUGHT BACK.

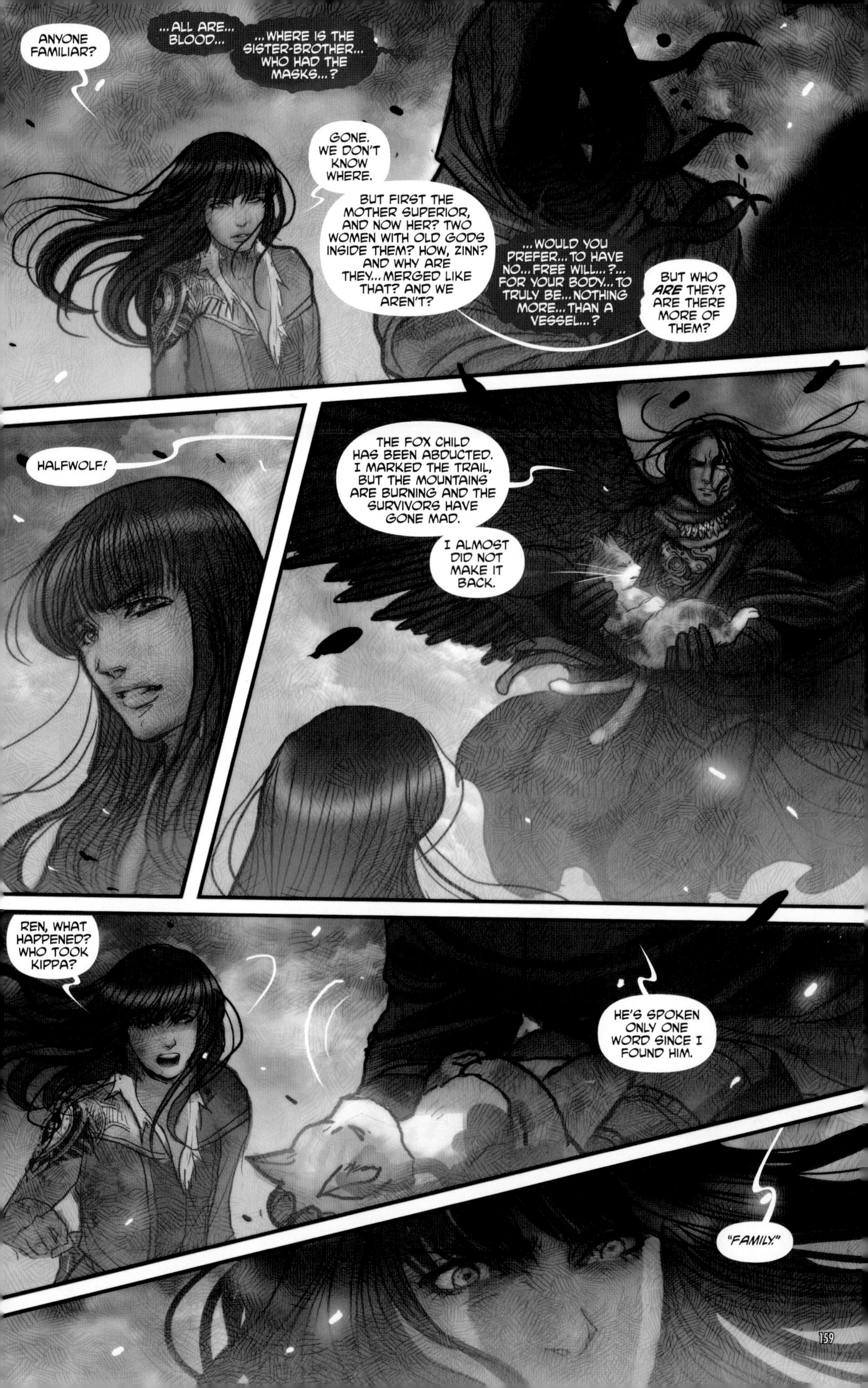
ANYONE FAMILIAR?
...ALL ARE... BLOOD...
...WHERE IS THE SISTER-BROTHER... WHO HAD THE MASKS...?
GONE. WE DON'T KNOW WHERE.
BUT FIRST THE MOTHER SUPERIOR, AND NOW HER? TWO WOMEN WITH OLD GODS INSIDE THEM? HOW, ZINN? AND WHY ARE THEY...MERGED LIKE THAT? AND WE AREN'T?
...WOULD YOU PREFER...TO HAVE NO...FREE WILL...?... FOR YOUR BODY...TO TRULY BE...NOTHING MORE...THAN A VESSEL...?
BUT WHO *ARE* THEY? ARE THERE MORE OF THEM?
HALFWOLF!
THE FOX CHILD HAS BEEN ABDUCTED. I MARKED THE TRAIL, BUT THE MOUNTAINS ARE BURNING AND THE SURVIVORS HAVE GONE MAD.
I ALMOST DID NOT MAKE IT BACK.
REN, WHAT HAPPENED? WHO TOOK KIPPA?
HE'S SPOKEN ONLY ONE WORD SINCE I FOUND HIM.
"FAMILY."

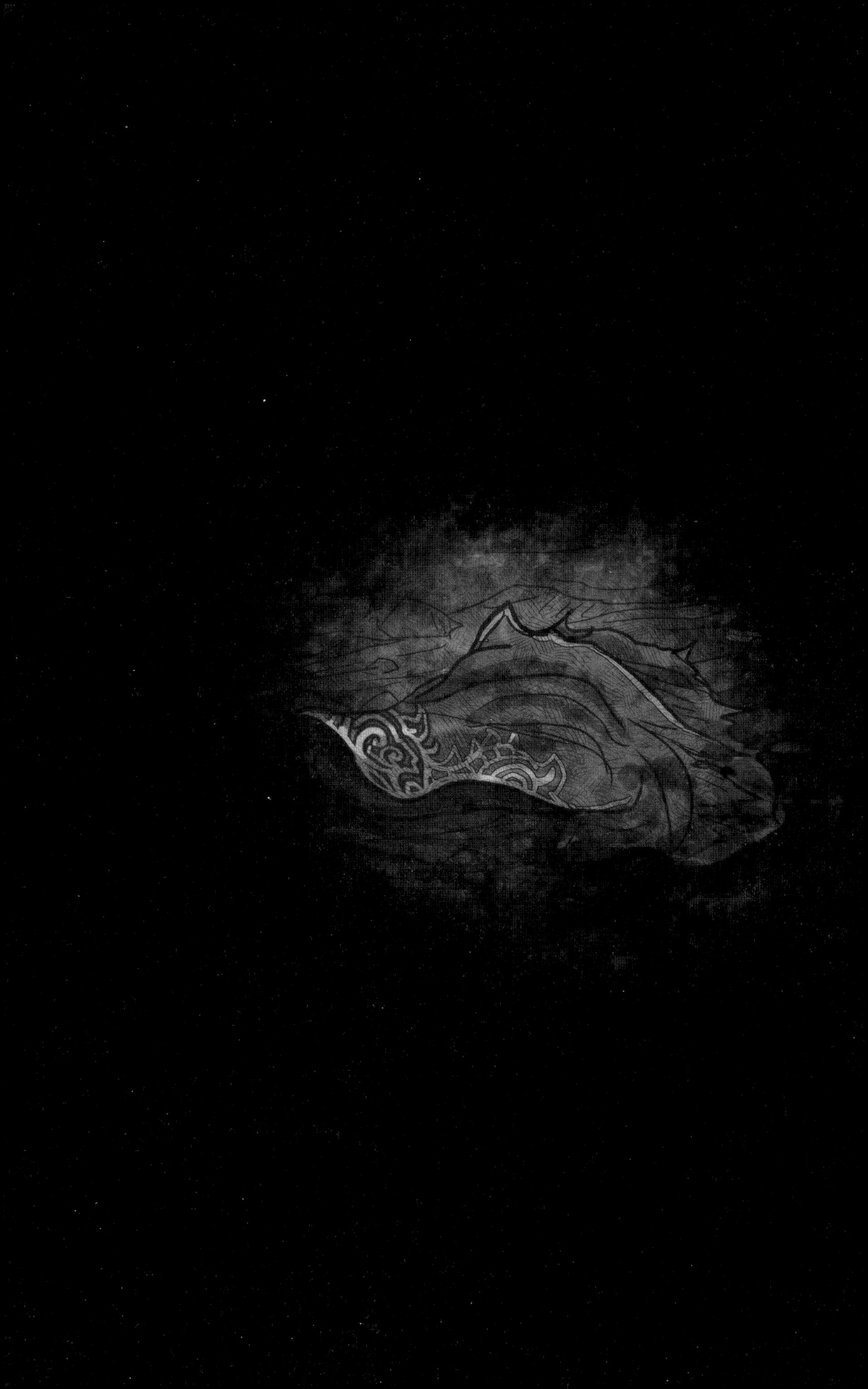

TO BE CONTINUED...

Friends of MONSTRESS...

...lend their talent and vision to some favorite characters...

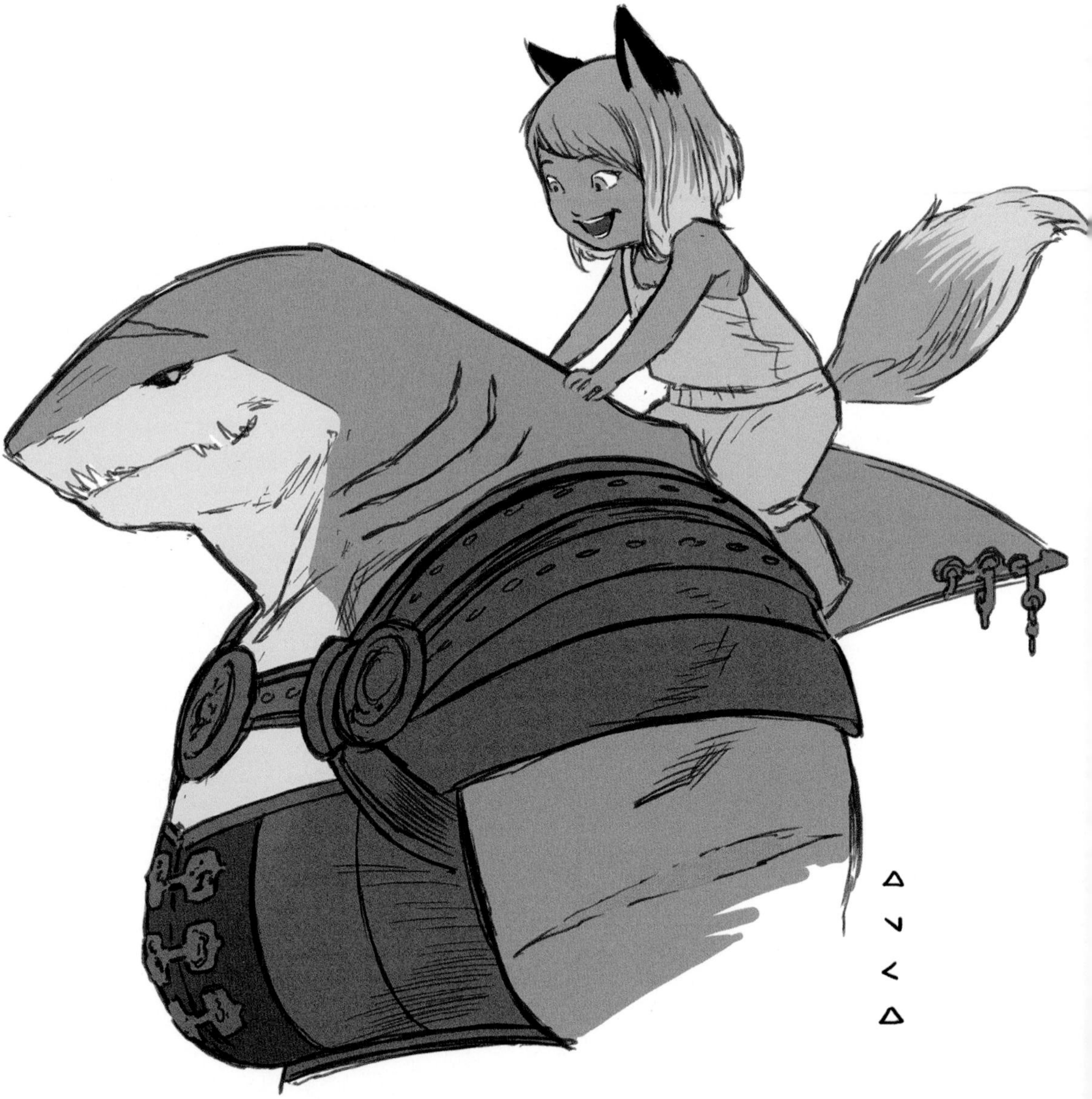

KRIS ANKA
Artist of RUNAWAYS
twitter.com/kristaferanka
kristaferanka.tumblr.com

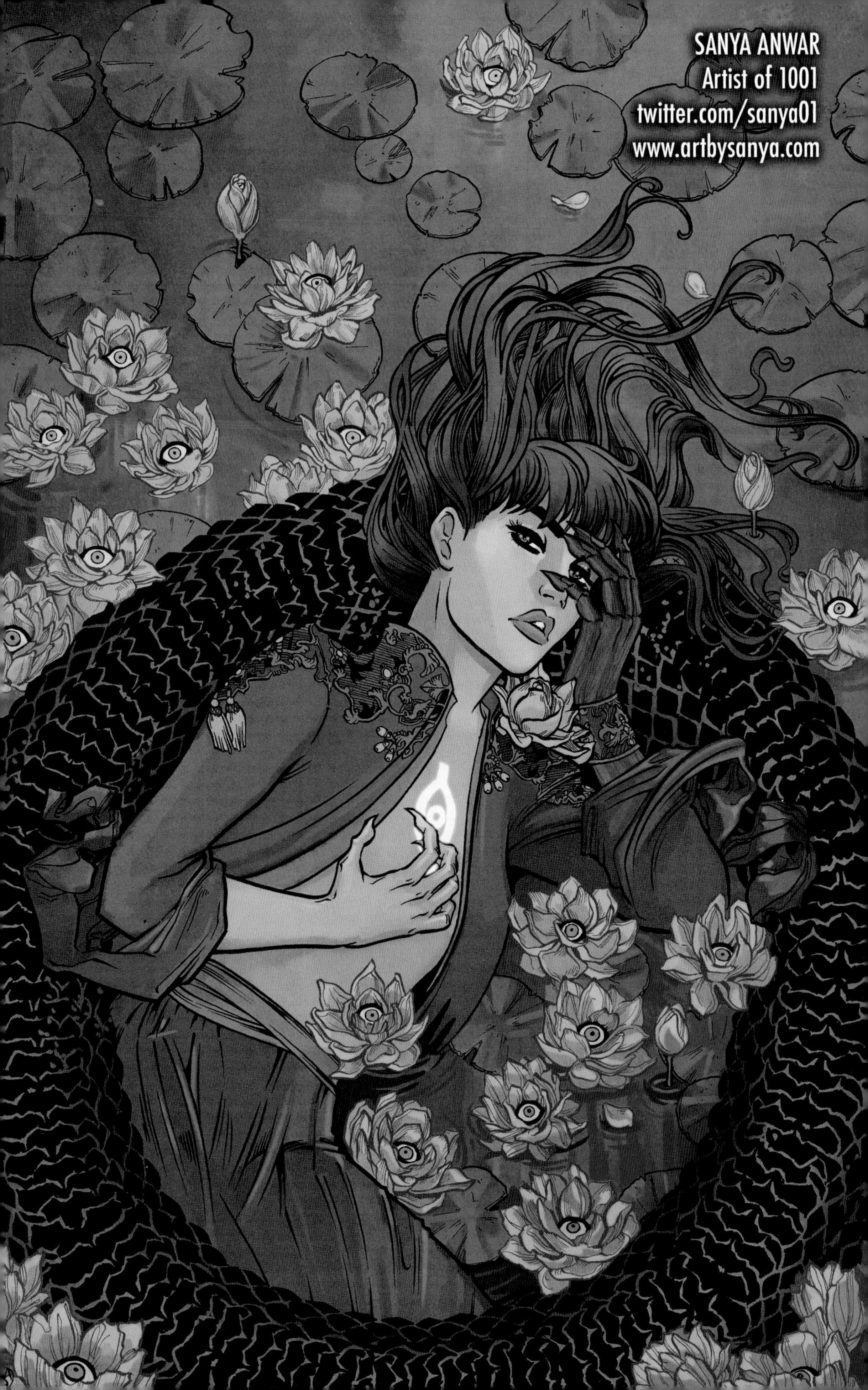
SANYA ANWAR
Artist of 1001
twitter.com/sanya01
www.artbysanya.com

IRENE KOH
Artist of LEGEND OF KORRA
twitter.com/kohquette
prom-knight.tumblr.com

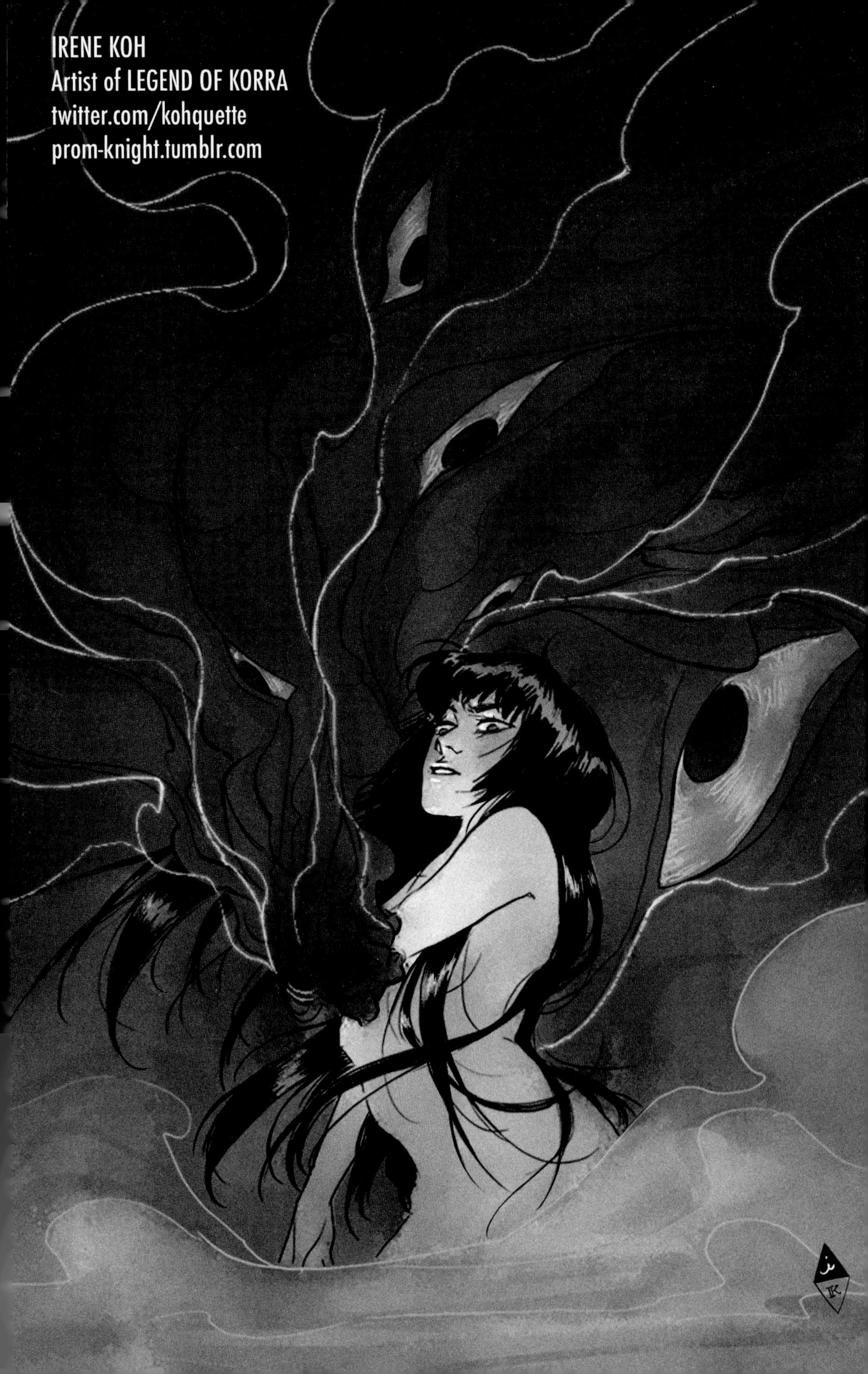

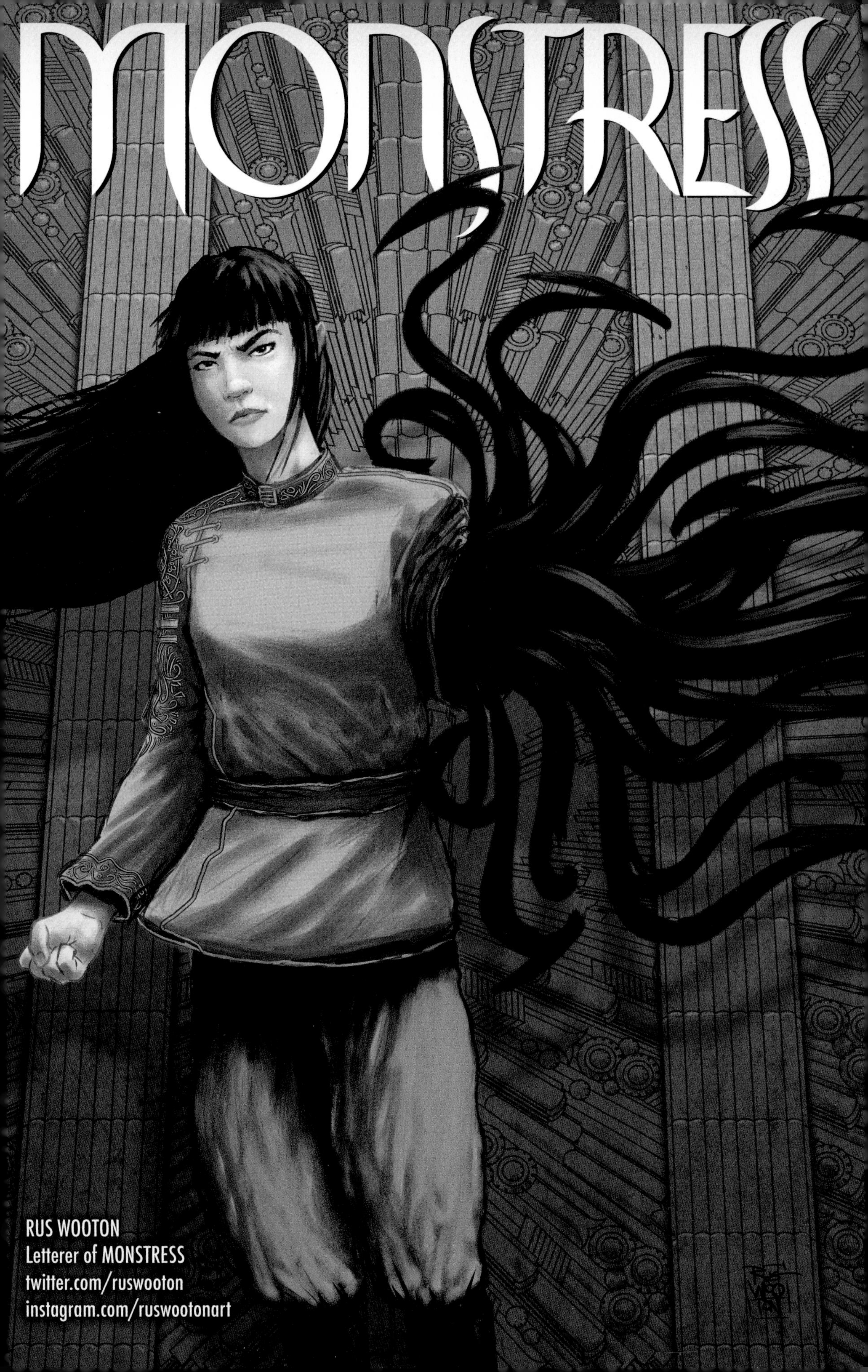
MONSTRESS
RUS WOOTON
Letterer of MONSTRESS
twitter.com/ruswooton
instagram.com/ruswootonart

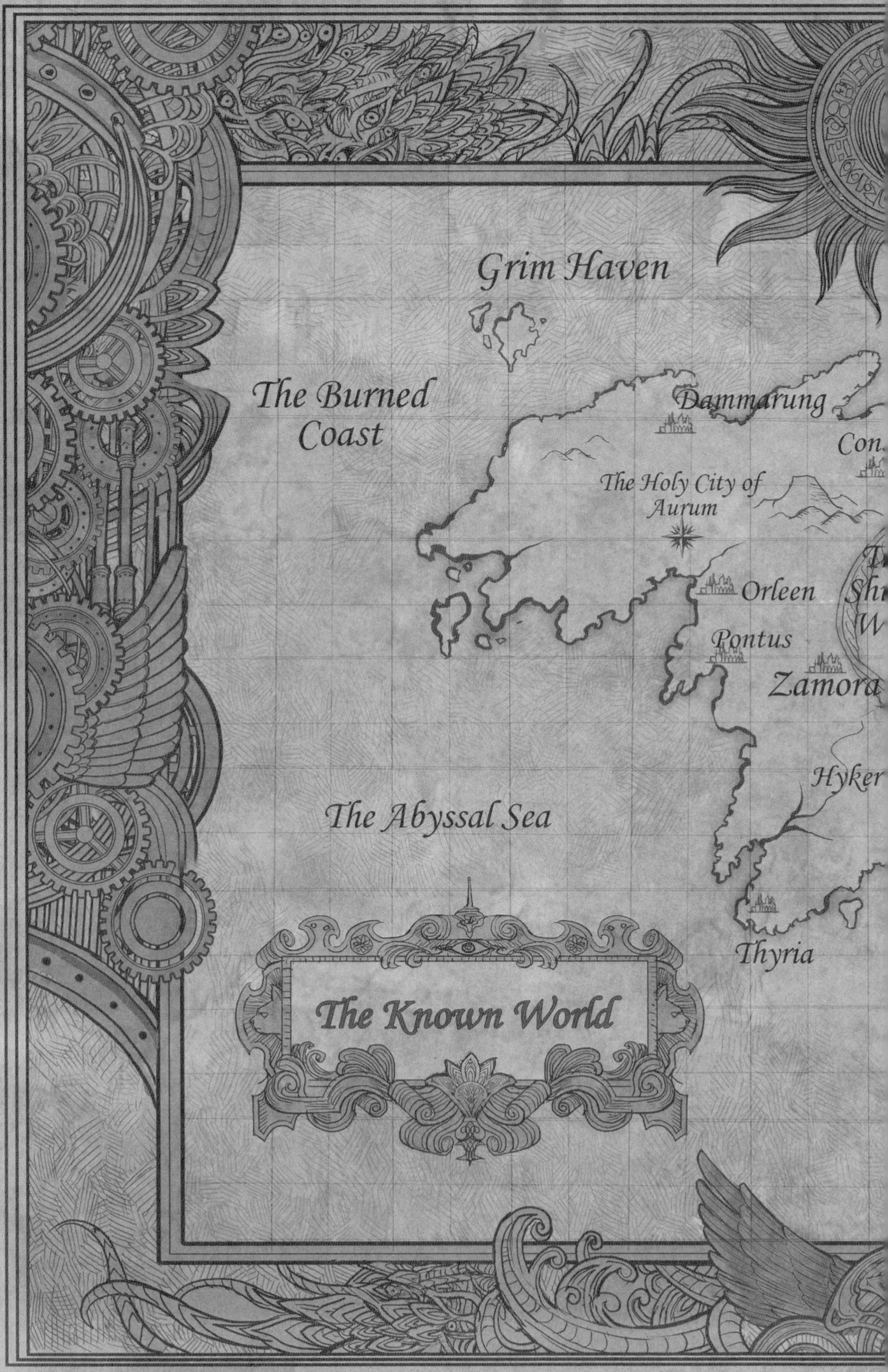
Grim Haven
The Burned Coast
Dammarung
Con
The Holy City of Aurum
Orleen
Pontus
Zamora
Hyker
The Abyssal Sea
Thyria
The Known World

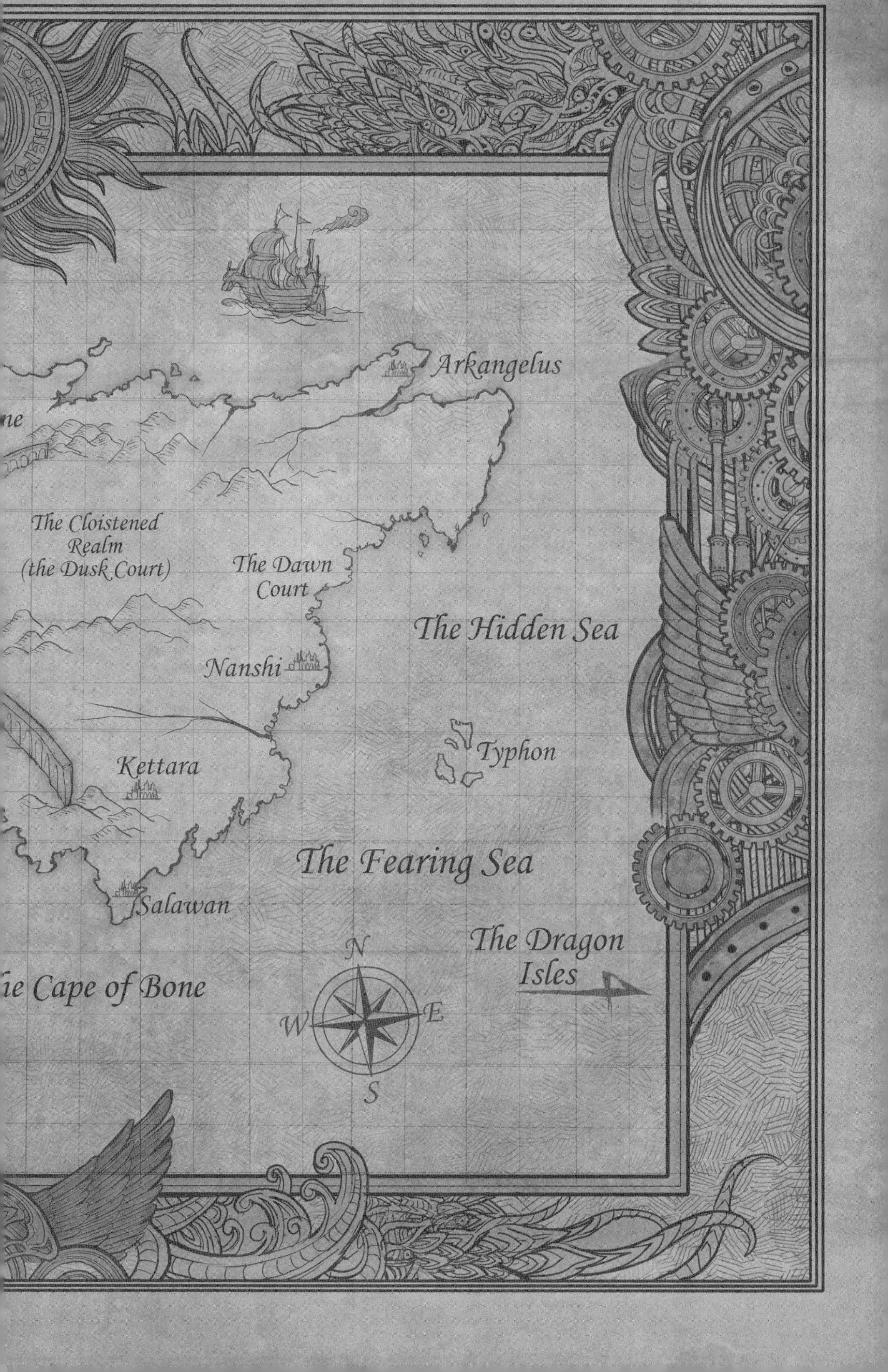
Arkangelus
The Cloistened
Realm
(the Dusk Court)
The Dawn
Court
The Hidden Sea
Nanshi
Typhon
Kettara
The Fearing Sea
Salawan
The Dragon
Isles
ie Cape of Bone
N
E
W
S

CREATORS

MARJORIE LIU is an attorney and *New York Times* bestselling author of over seventeen novels. Her comic book work includes *X-23, Black Widow, Dark Wolverine,* and *Astonishing X-Men,* for which she was nominated for a GLAAD Media Award for outstanding media images of the lesbian, gay, bisexual and transgender community. She teaches a course on comic book writing at MIT, and lives in Cambridge, MA.

SANA TAKEDA is an illustrator and comic book artist who was born in Niigata, and now resides in Tokyo, Japan. At age 20 she started out as a 3D CGI designer for SEGA, a Japanese video game company, and became a freelance artist when she was 25. She is still an artist, and has worked on titles such as *X-23* and *Ms. Marvel* for Marvel Comics, and is an illustrator for trading card games in Japan.